P9-BXY-400

Fortune's Daughter

Other Five Star Titles
by Diana Haviland:

Love's Promised Land
The Passionate Pretenders

Fortune's Daughter

Diana Haviland

Five Star
Unity, Maine

Hav

Five Star Romance.
Published in conjunction with
Kidde, Hoyt & Picard Literary Agency.

February 2000

Cover photograph by Holly Lidstone.

Five Star Standard Print Romance.

The text of this edition is unabridged.

Set in 11 pt. Plantin by Al Chase.

Printed in the United States on permanent paper.

Library of Congress Cataloging-in-Publication Data

Haviland, Diana.
Fortune's daughter / Diana Haviland
p. cm.
ISBN 0-7862-2340-5 (hc : alk. paper)
1. Married people — New York (State) — New York —
I. Title.
PS3558.A784 F6 2000
813′.54—dc21 99-054984

Fortune's Daughter

Chapter 1

It was late afternoon when Vanessa Kenyon found her way, at last, to South Street. The raw cold of the January day and the sharp wind from the East River made her draw her shawl more tightly about her. The dampness from the cobblestone street penetrated the soles of her thin shoes as she moved among the piles of cargo from a hundred foreign ports. She had to dodge the heavy traffic, the carts, drays, and hansom cabs, so she could scarcely spare more than a glance at the jutting bowsprits thrusting into the street high overhead like a line of spears. The web of masts, yards, and rigging of the towering clippers made an intricate pattern against the gray sky, but Vanessa was oblivious to the impressive sight.

The short winter day was drawing to a close, and Vanessa struggled against her own emotions: the depression and loneliness, the painful homesickness for Salem, where she had lived for all of her seventeen years. And as she sidestepped a wagon piled high with wooden crates and tried to avoid the bold stare of a sailor who had come stumbling out of a nearby grog shop, she felt a growing uneasiness.

She dreaded her first meeting with Abel Bradford and wished that she had been able to afford a suitable new costume to wear to New York, but the expenses of the trip from Massachusetts had taken nearly every cent that she had left after the sale of her mother's boardinghouse.

Year after year Vanessa had watched her mother's desperate struggle to keep the boardinghouse going while the small seaport of Salem kept losing more of its trade to the port of New York. Vanessa had known that there was no money for new clothes, and she had worn, without complaint, the prim, high-necked dresses of gray or brown until they were outgrown and shabby.

Those dresses, made by her mother for a small, thin girl of fourteen, would no longer fit the contours of her developing body, with its high, rounded breasts and softly curving hips. She had been fortunate that Mrs. Deverell, who had bought the boardinghouse during the last month of Mama's life, had been generous enough to give her the gaudy clothes she was now wearing.

"No more touring up and down the country for me," said Mrs. Deverell, who had been an actress with a small theatrical company. "I saved my money and now I'm going to settle down and run this boardinghouse at a profit."

The new landlady had lost no time in putting her plans into action. She had not looked for respectable boarders as Mama had, but had rented out rooms to sailors and their women for the night, or even for an hour. While Vanessa's mother lay dying, the boardinghouse was noisy with the heavy footsteps and drunken laughter of the men from the lumber schooners, the shrill voices of their female companions, the raucous songs, and thumping piano music from the parlor.

But by that time Mama, in her small room on the top floor, was already drifting in a delirious stupor, too weak to fight off the pneumonia that had stricken her in this frigid Salem winter of 1847. During one of Mama's lucid moments she had taken Vanessa's hand in her own hot, dry ones.

"Don't stay here," Mama said. "A girl like you . . . young and beautiful . . . so many temptations . . ."

Then, while Vanessa leaned closer to catch the words, Mama had spoken of the Bradfords, of Felicity, who had married Abel Bradford, one of the "merchant princes" of New York. "We were friends, years ago . . . when we were girls. Felicity Bradford will help you, for my sake. She's kind and gentle. . . . She'll find respectable work for you. . . ."

Respectability had always been important to Judith Kenyon, who had been left a widow after a few brief years of marriage, and she had tried to instill her own principles in her daughter. She had been successful up to a point, for when Mrs. Deverell had offered to allow Vanessa to stay on at the boardinghouse after her mother's death, the girl had refused.

"With your looks you won't have any trouble catching a man's eye," the new landlady declared. But Vanessa explained about her mother's plan for her, and when she admitted that Mama had not known where in New York City Felicity might be living, Mrs. Deverell had been helpful.

"If Abel Bradford's a big man in shipping, he'll have offices down by the East River. Pearl Street, or Cherry, or maybe South Street."

And so now, after a long, tedious journey by coach and ferry, Vanessa, having asked directions from several passersby, had finally found her way to South Street, and to the red brick building with its cast iron pillars, and the yellow sign that read: BRADFORD AND COMPANY. Underneath, in smaller letters, the sign said: SHIPPERS. SHIPPING BROKERS. Beside the office building were several huge, cavernous warehouses.

Through the thickening fog that was rolling in from the river, Vanessa saw a towering clipper being unloaded by cursing, sweating stevedores, who carried the cargo through the open doors into the nearest warehouse. As she hesitated, trying to summon up the courage to go into the Bradford office, a small, canvas-covered wagon came rumbling by, and before she could get out of the way, the wheels splashed her sky-blue velvet dress with mud and icy water.

She brushed at the skirt in vain, and she felt her confidence ebbing away, for she realized how bedraggled she must look. Even the shawl, another contribution from Mrs. Deverell, had been spattered, and in any case, it was far too showy, embroidered with flowers and trimmed with tarnished gilt fringe.

Vanessa sighed as she tucked a few stray locks of her red hair under the blue velvet bonnet. Maybe she should have worn her own shabby straw after all, but it was too late now. She straightened her shoulders, took a deep breath, and mounted the scrubbed stone steps leading to the office door.

"And where do you think you're going?"

The thin, hatchet-faced man who had just come out of the office confronted her, his eyes cold and suspicious behind their gold-rimmed spectacles. He had the pallor of one who spends his days indoors. A clerk, perhaps? His manner and bearing were too self-assured for any ordinary clerk, Vanessa decided, and his clothes were too expensive. He wore a fine black broadcloth suit, a dark silk waistcoat, and a tall beaver hat.

"On your way," he said with an impatient wave of his hand. "We want no dockside sluts hanging about here."

Vanessa's face flamed with indignation. How dare he? Just because she wore these clothes, because she had been splashed with mud, how dare he make up his mind about her without even giving her a chance to explain her purpose in coming here?

"I am a friend of the Bradford family," she began.

"Get moving," he interrupted. "And be quick about it or I'll have the law on you." He came forward, thrusting her aside, so that she stumbled. She caught at the railing in time to keep from falling down onto the filthy wet cobblestones. "If I catch you hanging around here, you'll find yourself spending the night in a cell in the Tombs," he told her.

Although she had never heard of the Tombs, his meaning was all too clear. Vanessa picked up her skirts and fled, but she did not go far. Swiftly she moved into the shadow of a pile of crates, not far from the small, canvas-covered wagon that had splashed her with mud. The hatchet-faced man had turned his attention to the stevedore who was loading the wagon.

"You, there. What are you doing? All that cargo from the *Empress of Canton* is to be stored in the warehouse."

"This here's special goods, Mr. Widdicomb," the stevedore said. "Captain McClintock ordered me to load it into this wagon." He turned to the open warehouse doors. "Ain't that so, Captain?"

A tall man in a dark blue coat and visored cap came out of the warehouse. The light from the oil lantern that hung on the side of the wagon caught the glint of gold braid on his cap.

"That's right, Jed," the captain said, and he strode over to the steps where Widdicomb stood. "These articles were ordered by Mrs. Bradford and her daughters, most of them. I added a few small gifts that I thought might take their fancy."

Widdicomb's eyes narrowed behind the gold-rimmed spectacles, and his annoyance was plain when he spoke. "Very well, Captain McClintock. You have my permission to send these—articles—to the Bradfords' home."

"I don't remember asking your permission," McClintock said, pushing his cap back on his head. Vanessa saw that he had dark hair and dark brows. "And I'm not sending these goods," he went on. "I'm driving them over myself."

"Is that necessary?"

"I haven't brought this stuff all the way from China to take a chance on having it stolen here on the docks of New York." There was an easy assurance in his voice, a calm self-confidence in his manner. "Tell me, Widdicomb. Are the Daybreak Boys and the Dead Rabbits as busy as ever?"

"They are. Mr. Bradford has hired extra watchmen for his warehouses, but these gangs of thieves are growing bolder all the time." The pale lips tightened. "Only a few minutes ago a wretched little slut was nosing about these very steps. Looked like any dockside trollop, but now that I think about it, she might be a member of one of those gangs." He gave a short, humorless laugh. "She took to her heels fast enough when I spoke of the Tombs."

Vanessa felt her stomach muscles tighten. She dared not remain around here. But she had to speak with Abel Bradford or, better yet, his wife.

And Captain McClintock was going to drive the wagon to the Bradfords' home.

"Finished loading up?" McClintock asked the stevedore.

"Few more minutes, Captain," the man said, hefting a tall, oddly shaped object heavily wrapped in canvas and tied with ropes.

"And what, may I ask, is that?" Widdicomb demanded.

"A Chinese wisteria, for Mrs. Bradford," the captain told him. "It ought to thrive in the new conservatory."

Now the captain and Widdicomb were talking of ship's business, and Vanessa caught only a few words about manifests, pilot's fees, certificates of registry, and bills of lading. But she no longer listened. The stevedore, having finished his work, went into the warehouse.

For a moment she stood frozen, her muscles tense, fear and determination warring inside her. Then, moving swiftly, covering the short distance between the pile of crates and the wagon, she caught hold of the canvas covering and hauled herself up, slipping underneath its shelter. There, in the darkness, she crouched among the boxes and barrels.

A few minutes later she heard footsteps, then saw Captain McClintock swing himself up on the seat, pick up the reins, and she felt the wagon move forward, its iron-bound wheels adding their clatter to the deafening noise of countless other vehicles.

"Give my regards to the Bradford ladies," Widdicomb called, but McClintock did not answer. Vanessa remained motionless, scarcely daring to draw a deep breath, her body braced against a crate, her eyes fixed on the captain's wide shoulders.

The noisy stream of traffic went on its way, with carts, drays, wagons, and hansom cabs hurrying to and from the wharves. Sailors from clipper ships, coastal freighters, and pilot boats swarmed into the taverns while shivering painted prostitutes in cheap finery offered themselves boldly. Outside one brightly lit grog shop a man played a concertina while a girl who looked about fourteen danced awkwardly, kicking her legs high to reveal her drawers. Runners from the dirty, crowded lodginghouses herded groups of dazed, exhausted immigrants along.

Captain McClintock had just turned the small wagon onto Pearl Street when, from the heavily laden dray ahead, a barrel came crashing down. McClintock jerked at the reins, his powerful muscles straining under his coat as he fought to control his horses. But the terrified animals reared and plunged, and the wagon tilted to one side.

Vanessa, thrown off balance, felt herself being hurled, with sickening force, against the sharp corner of a crate. Pain shot up along her arm and exploded into her shoulder. She cried out.

She pressed her hand over her mouth, but it was too late.

McClintock seized the lantern from the side of the wagon, and, turning, he held it high so that its light glared directly into the back of the wagon.

"Get out of there," he ordered.

For a moment she was too frightened to move.

"Get out or I'll drag you out."

He did not raise his voice, but there was no mistaking the cold determination in his dark-gray eyes. Slowly Vanessa moved forward on her hands and knees. He hauled her onto the seat, forcing her down beside him.

"Let me go."

"Who are you? And what the devil were you doing, hiding back there?"

"I'm Vanessa Kenyon," she managed to say. "I arrived in New York from Salem only a few hours ago."

"It didn't take you long to get into trouble, did it?"

"I have to get to the Bradfords' home, and when I heard you saying that you—"

His eyes moved over her, taking in her mud-spattered dress, the bonnet, which had been knocked off her head and hung by the ribbons around her neck, and her hair, now loosened and falling around her shoulders. "You're not exactly dressed for such a social call," he said with an ironic smile. "And isn't it a little unusual to go visiting in the back of a freight wagon?"

"I tried to explain to Mr. Widdicomb." She replaced her bonnet on her head, her fingers shaking and numb with cold. "He wouldn't listen," she went on. "He called me a—dockside slut and threatened to have me sent to the—the Tombs—but he had no right—"

"You must be the girl who was hanging around with an eye on my cargo," the captain said.

"I don't care about your cargo. I'm not a thief—or a . . . a

. . . If you'll take me to the Bradfords' home and let me speak to Mrs. Bradford—"

He drew his dark brows together. "I don't know what you're up to, but you've wasted enough of my time. Get down."

Vanessa looked around fearfully. If he forced her down on this waterfront street, what would happen to her? She had no money, and she did not know her way around this strange city. But if she did not obey his command, he might turn her over to the law.

Shivering, she got to her feet and took hold of the side of the wagon, but pain caught at her injured arm, and she drew her breath in sharply. The crowded, foggy street swam before her eyes. She swayed and almost fell.

Then McClintock had an arm around her waist. He was drawing her down on the seat. "You're ill," he said.

"No. My arm—I was thrown against a crate."

"Let me see," he said, pushing back the gaudy shawl. He moved his fingers carefully over her arm and shoulder, and she bit her lip. "I don't think any bones are broken," he said slowly. "You'll have some bad bruises, though." He looked at her face. "Feeling faint?"

She nodded, unable to speak. He reached out and took her hands in his, rubbing her icy fingers. Something in his touch sent the warmth and strength flowing back into her body. And she felt her determination returning, so she was able to straighten up and say, "I won't delay you. But please, won't you listen to me while you drive the rest of the way? Won't you at least give me a chance to explain?"

He looked down at her, his eyes thoughtful. Then he started the wagon moving again. "All right. Why is it so important for you to get to Abel Bradford?"

"It's not Abel; it's really Felicity Bradford I want to see,"

Vanessa said. "She and my mother were friends, years ago, in Salem."

"And your mother—"

"She died two weeks ago."

"You have no other relatives?"

"My father was lost at sea when I was three. He was first mate on the *Sally Bonner*, a square rigger on the coastal run between 'Quoddy and Cape Fear. The ship was wrecked off the Cape. A September hurricane."

"Plenty of good ships and good men have been lost there," the captain said. "But isn't there anyone else in Salem who would have helped you?"

They had left the noisy, crowded waterfront streets, and now they were driving through a section of the city where neat brick houses stood in rows, with lamps glowing over the doorways, which were flanked by handsome, fluted Doric columns.

Encouraged by McClintock's willingness to listen, she told him briefly of her circumstances. She spoke, with some hesitation, about Mrs. Deverell. "These clothes are hers," she explained. "She wore them on the stage." Vanessa's lips curved briefly into a smile. "I guess she was a lot slimmer in those days." But then her smile faded. "She wanted me to stay on, but she—rented rooms to sailors and their—their women, and I couldn't . . . Mama wouldn't have wanted me to—"

"And what help do you expect from the Bradfords?"

"I must find respectable work."

The wagon clattered into a square with tall, stately houses on four sides and a park in the center, enclosed by a high iron railing. There was an air of quiet gentility about the square.

"Hudson Square," McClintock said. "Over there, on the

far side, that's the Bradford house."

Vanessa caught a glimpse of columns and steps, gleaming white through the twilight, and she felt her spirits rise. "Mama said that even though she and Felicity Bradford hadn't seen each other for years, I would not be turned away. She said that Felicity is kind and gentle."

"True enough. But it's Abel Bradford you'll be dealing with. He and Horace Widdicomb are cousins—the same sanctimonious breed." The captain gave her a sardonic smile, but his eyes were hard. "Old Abel's a pillar of the community. He gives donations to all those charities his wife works for. But when it comes to taking in a stray like you, that's a different matter."

Ignoring the slur, Vanessa protested. "Surely when his wife explains that she and my mother were friends . . ."

"Mrs. Bradford won't go against her husband's orders. That much I can tell you. Abel won't tolerate the slightest opposition in his office, or in his home either."

"Oh, but if that's true—what am I going to do?"

Vanessa's confidence began to ebb away. She did not have even enough money to return to Salem, and the thought of being stranded here in New York was a frightening one.

McClintock stopped the wagon in front of the imposing Bradford mansion with its fanlight door, its columns in the Greek Revival style, its iron fence. "Why not stay here in the wagon and wait? I won't be long." His eyes moved from her face to her throat and the curve of her breasts.

"And then?" she asked uneasily.

He laughed. "Bradford's a pillar of the community, but I'm not. I'm only a sea captain who has just returned from Canton. A long, lonely voyage it was."

She drew away from him. "Captain McClintock, I—"

"Logan," he said. "Wait for me here, and when I've finished my business with the Bradford ladies, I'll buy you a good hot dinner. We'll go to the Metropolitan Hotel. The bartender there makes a fine punch with rum and spices. It'll warm you up."

Vanessa stiffened. "Please help me down at once," she said. And when he did not move, she went on. "I've told you. I'm looking for respectable work." She gave him a hard, direct look, her eyes darkening with outraged dignity. "If I'd wanted what you're offering, I could have stayed back in Salem, at the boardinghouse."

He gave her an impudent smile, his teeth white against the mahogany tan of his face. "I don't believe I've offered you anything except dinner."

"But you were going to—later," she blurted out.

"And if I was? Vanessa, you're far too pretty to be looking for work as a servant, or a seamstress." He put a hand on her cheek and turned her face toward the lantern light. "No, not pretty. You're more than that. You're a beauty. Your eyes—"

"Are you going to help me down?"

"If that's what you want," he said carelessly.

He got down from the wagon, moving with a swift ease unusual in a man with his tall stature and heavily muscled body. She put her hands on his shoulders and he grasped her around the waist, but after he swung her down he held her against him, and she was shaken by the force in him, the overpowering masculinity. Suppose she had agreed to spend the evening with him. Her ideas of what would have happened were vague, for her mother's modesty had shielded her from any real knowledge of the needs and desires of a man.

But she felt his warmth, the hardness of his body, and she heard herself saying "No!" without a clear idea of what stirred and frightened her.

He set her down. "Very well, then. Come along." He offered his arm, and she took it instinctively. Together they mounted the steps to the Bradfords' home.

Chapter 2

"My dear, I'm so sorry," said Felicity Bradford, a tall, thin woman whose brown eyes now brimmed with tears. "To think of Judith, dead." She put a hand on Vanessa's arm. "We must do all we can to help you."

Vanessa was seated next to Mrs. Bradford on a handsome rosewood sofa upholstered in dark-red velvet. A fire crackled in the parlor fireplace, which was topped by a fine black marble mantelpiece. Against the opposite wall stood a highboy of maple and pine decorated with a Chinese motif.

"An orphan, homeless, in New York," said Kitty Bradford, a pretty girl with a cloud of dark ringlets framing her face. "It's so sad." She sighed. "Why, you are like Araminta Snow, in that charming tale I was reading in—was it *Godey's Lady's Book*, Mama?"

"You know I have no time to read such foolishness," Felicity told her daughter. Felicity had borne her husband two sons, both of whom had died in infancy, and Kitty, her only surviving child, was a disappointment to Abel, who had wanted a male heir to carry on the family's shipping empire. Kitty was also something of a trial to Felicity, for although at eighteen she was pretty and high-spirited, she had a foolishly romantic view of the world that sometimes caused Felicity to be concerned for her future.

But at the moment Felicity was preoccupied by the young girl brought to her by Logan McClintock. "We must find suitable employment for you," she told Vanessa. "What are your qualifications?"

"I helped Mama in the boardinghouse," Vanessa said. "And I nursed her during her last illness. . . ."

Felicity looked doubtful. "I don't suppose you have the training to become a governess," she said.

"I can read and write. And I play the piano . . . a little. Mama taught me."

"Dear Judith was so musical," Felicity said. "I can remember her, singing those sweet ballads. Always so light-hearted, and her laugh . . ."

Vanessa, who remembered her mother as a tired, harassed woman, was surprised by this description. But no doubt her husband's death and the grim struggle to keep the boardinghouse going had robbed Mama of her laughter and her light-hearted ways.

"Do you read French or German?" Felicity was asking.

Vanessa shook her head. "Mama wanted me to have a better education, but we never had enough money to spare."

"Perhaps you could work as a seamstress," Felicity suggested.

"I doubt that I have the skill to earn my living with the needle."

Logan, who had been helping the coachman and the groom to carry in the crates and parcels from the wagon, now came into the parlor and stood, his back against the doorframe.

"We'll find some sort of work for you," Felicity said. "But first—forgive me, Vanessa, but you will have to make a . . . different sort of appearance if you're going to be accepted into a decent household. First impressions are so important."

A corner of Logan's mouth lifted in a sardonic smile.

"Surely you must have something more suitable in your luggage," Felicity went on hopefully.

"I brought only one small trunk," Vanessa said. "And that

was stolen from me at the ferry landing." The memory still filled her with anger. "A woman offered to watch the trunk while I bought my ticket, and when I returned, both she and the trunk were gone." Although there had been only a few shabby garments in the trunk, Vanessa had also packed a miniature of her mother and a few other keepsakes, her only links with the past.

Felicity looked troubled. "There is so much crime in the city these days. New York is growing so quickly. What we need is a proper police force, not this system of watchmen and marshals. A young girl, alone here, faces many dangers, and robbery is, perhaps, the least of them."

Vanessa, glancing at Logan, saw the look of cynical amusement in his dark-gray eyes.

"Come with me," Felicity went on. "I have a pile of used clothing in my room, all clean and pressed. They were donated to the Ladies' Missionary Society, and I'm sure we'll find something suitable among them."

"The Society is one of Mama's pet charities," Kitty said.

Although Vanessa tried to smile politely, the mention of charity was most distasteful to her, as it had been to Mama, who might have written to Felicity years ago to ask for help if her pride had not restrained her. But Vanessa remembered Logan's warning and realized that the formidable Abel Bradford might be returning home at any moment. Horace Widdicomb had thought that she was a trollop, because of her appearance, and she could not allow Abel Bradford to make the same mistake.

"You are most kind," Vanessa said as she rose to follow Felicity upstairs.

Felicity's boudoir, adjacent to the master bedroom, was furnished in tasteful elegance with touches of Oriental origin:

lacquered boxes, bamboo tables, and a tall screen with panels of silk embroidered with cranes and pagodas.

Before changing clothes, Vanessa had tidied herself, grateful for the pitcher of hot water, the scented soap, and soft towel, all provided by her hostess.

"Now, isn't this better?" Felicity asked.

Although the neat gray woolen dress was not flattering, and would have to be taken in a few inches to fit Vanessa's narrow waistline, it was a decided improvement. Now Felicity was helping her to do up her long, heavy red-gold hair, brushing it back from her forehead and braiding it carefully.

"I am beginning to feel more like myself," Vanessa admitted, glancing with distaste at the discarded sky-blue velvet dress and bonnet, the flowered shawl.

"Those garments will not go to waste," Felicity assured her. "Some poor soul down in the Five Points will be thankful for any sort of clothing." She shook her head sadly. "Many of the immigrants arriving here from Ireland are in rags. We at the Ladies Missionary Society do what we can. But there is such a desperate need for charity—"

Vanessa's body went taut at this new mention of charity. "Mama and I made our own way," she said indignantly. "I don't want charity; I want to work."

"Forgive me, Vanessa. I meant no harm. You will spend the night here, and tomorrow I will speak to the other ladies at the Society." She looked troubled. "I must warn you, though—it isn't easy to find employment in New York City. Even so, you were right to come to me. New York is no place for a pretty girl without family or friends."

"Salem has its share of vice," Vanessa said, and then she explained quickly about Mrs. Deverell and the sailors and their women who had filled the boardinghouse.

"No doubt," Felicity said, "but New York is so much

larger. There are whole streets in the Five Points where every house, every cellar, is given over to—to fallen women and their . . . patrons. One day we must open a shelter for such unfortunate women, a place of refuge." She finished braiding Vanessa's hair and now she twisted the long plait into a severe chignon. "But there are so few ladies with time and money who wish to become involved in this kind of work."

"What about Kitty?" Vanessa asked. "Is she—"

"Kitty is far too frivolous to be concerned with such disagreeable matters."

Downstairs, in the parlor, Kitty was exclaiming with delight over a small wicker birdcage in the shape of a pagoda. Her brown eyes glowed as she looked up at Logan. "Oh, it's lovely! I'll ask Mama to buy me a pair of lovebirds. My birthday's only a few weeks away." She clapped her hands together. "And you must come to my party. It's to be a ball, with an orchestra and . . . Do promise to come."

"I'd be honored to, Miss Bradford," Logan said.

Vanessa and Felicity left the boudoir and started down the hall. How splendid it was, Vanessa thought: The walls, which were painted a soft sea green, were lined with gold-framed portraits of somber-looking gentlemen and their ladies, some wearing the powdered wigs of the past century.

But as they were passing a closed door, Vanessa started at the sound of crashing glass. Then she heard the high, thin voice of a woman. "I'm not going to be bundled off to bed, Nell. If Logan McClintock's back from the China run, I'm going to see him!"

"Now, Mrs. Campbell, ma'am, ye mustn't excite yerself." Nell spoke with a thick brogue. "The doctor said ye was t' rest."

"The doctor's a fool. Dosing me with these foul concoctions. You help me finish dressing, Nell, or you'll be back in the kitchen, scrubbing pots!"

Felicity opened the door, and Vanessa saw a thin, frail old lady who must have been in her eighties and a red-faced maid in a starched white cap and apron.

"Mrs. Bradford," Nell pleaded. "Won't ye speak t' yer aunt? Knocked her medicine glass outta my hand, she did. An' now she . . ."

"Please clean up the medicine and the broken glass, Nell," Felicity said calmly. "Aunt Prudence, you must not give way to these fits of temper. Dr. Fairleigh warned you—"

"Bugger that Dr. Fairleigh! Wouldn't trust him to take care of a sick cat!" She came forward, leaning on a gold-headed ebony cane, and peered at Vanessa. "Who're you, girl?" she demanded.

"My name is Vanessa Kenyon, ma'am. I'm from Salem—"

"Kenyon? I know that name." She frowned, trying to remember. "There was a Gifford Kenyon, up in Salem."

"He was my father's uncle," Vanessa said, feeling a warm glow at this recognition.

"Was? What happened to him? Lost at sea, was he?"

Vanessa was startled, for to her Gifford Kenyon was a figure out of the distant past.

"Gifford Kenyon died in 1812, during the war with the British," Vanessa said.

Prudence Campbell blinked rapidly. "Oh, yes, now I remember. Gifford was a fine-looking fellow. Hair as red as yours," she told Vanessa. She lapsed into silence while Nell went about her work of cleaning the medicine stain from the carpet.

"I want to see Logan McClintock now," the old lady said abruptly. "This fool girl"—she jerked her head in Nell's direction—"won't help me to dress properly. Belongs back in the kitchen, she does."

Felicity looked at her aunt with a mixture of impatience and sympathy, but the old lady ignored her.

"You—Vanessa, is it?—give me a hand with these buttons, won't you? I'm not so old that I don't want to look my best when I'm going to see a handsome young man like Logan."

Vanessa hesitated until Felicity gave her a slight nod, then she hurried to obey. "We'll have a long talk later," Aunt Prudence said. "I want to hear all about Salem. But first, I'm going downstairs to visit with Logan McClintock."

"Mrs. Campbell," Logan said with a warm smile as the old lady entered the parlor, followed by Vanessa and Felicity. He took Prudence Campbell's arm and led her to the velvet sofa near the fireplace. Kitty, meanwhile, was going through the packages, taking out ivory-handled fans, embroidered slippers, and a scroll painting of mountains, flowering trees and flying cranes.

"What is in here?" Kitty asked, looking at a large, heavy crate.

"That's the set of porcelain dishes you ordered, Mrs. Bradford," Logan said.

"Dishes, Mama? I'd have thought you had more than enough. Three complete services."

"These are not for me," Felicity said. Vanessa caught a certain uneasiness in her tone. "They are for you. For when you set up housekeeping with Horace."

Kitty whirled around and glared at her mother. "Then they'll never be used. I don't care what Papa's plans are. I'm not going to marry Horace. Why he's—he's a mealy-mouthed little pen-pusher!"

"I don't blame you a bit for feeling the way you do, Kitty," Aunt Prudence said. "All the same, your Pa'll have his way, same as always." She dismissed the matter. "Here, Logan, come sit by me." He obeyed, and Vanessa saw that there was genuine respect and affection in the look he turned on the old lady.

"Don't sulk, Kitty," Aunt Prudence said. "Better to marry anyone, even Horace, than to stay an old maid. You'll be nineteen, your next birthday." She turned to Logan, her faded eyes brightening. "And what about you, young man? Time you found yourself a wife, isn't it?"

"I have no plans to marry," he began.

"Then you should make plans," she said. "Find yourself a fine, healthy girl. A good breeder who'll warm your bed and give you plenty of babies."

Felicity looked away, for Aunt Prudence, with her earthy speech, was something of an embarrassment.

"Really, Aunt Prudence," she said, "I'm sure that Captain McClintock does not wish to discuss such private matters."

But the old lady paid no attention. "Oh, I've no doubt you've left more than one female with a big belly." She cackled with bawdy amusement. "Maybe you've got a bunch of slant-eyed, yellow-skinned bastards running around the gutters of Canton, but I still say . . ."

Kitty gave a little shriek of horror, and her face turned beet-red. "Aunt Prudence," Felicity said quickly, "it's time you were getting back upstairs."

"Not until Logan gives me my present," the old lady said. "What have you brought for me, Logan?" Vanessa was touched, for there was something childlike in Aunt Prudence's expectancy. "Captain Campbell never forgot to bring me a present when he returned from a voyage. Once he brought me a monkey. . . ."

"I haven't brought a monkey," Logan said, rising quickly. He looked among the packages and found a small brassbound wooden chest. "It's jasmine tea," he said. "The finest I could get."

"Tea!" Aunt Prudence sounded outraged.

"I thought you liked it," Logan said.

"I do—if there's a good shot of rum in it. But that fool, Nell, won't even let me have my rum. Feeds me on slops as if I were a baby, and tries to keep me resting in bed all day." She was seized with a spasm of coughing that left her gasping and plainly exhausted.

"Now, Aunt Prudence, do let me ring for Nell, to help you upstairs," Felicity said.

Nell came in answer to the bell, but before Aunt Prudence left the parlor she said, "You'll come back and see me again, won't you, Logan?"

"I'll see you at Miss Bradford's birthday party," he assured her. "And I'll bring you a bottle of rum—the finest Demerara," he added.

When she had gone, Logan remained standing. "I'll have to leave now," he told Felicity. "I still have ship's business down on South Street." He gave Vanessa a long, questioning look. She understood. There was time to go with him if she wanted to. She felt a warm, dizzying tide of feeling at the thought, but she refused to give way to the treacherous emotion.

Even so, she could not let Logan leave without speaking to him once more. "Captain McClintock," she heard herself saying.

"Miss Kenyon?"

"I . . . wanted to thank you for—for helping me—for bringing me here."

"My pleasure, Miss Kenyon," he said. "I hope that you

will find—respectable employment—quickly." There was no mistaking the glint of mockery in his eyes, even though his voice was smooth and polite.

"I'll see you to the door," Kitty said.

Vanessa watched them leaving the parlor, and for the first time in her life she felt a curious pang of jealousy. She tried to console herself with the thought that Kitty was to marry Horace Widdicomb. Both Felicity Bradford and Aunt Prudence had sounded certain of that.

But she heard Kitty's voice from the hall. "Now, you won't forget my party, will you, Captain?"

Then she felt a rush of cold air and heard the door close behind Logan. Kitty returned to the parlor and picked up the birdcage. "Isn't it lovely, Mama?" she said. Logan had brought many other articles from China, but those had been bought and paid for by Abel Bradford; this was a special gift from Logan himself.

"It's charming," Felicity agreed absently.

"Oh, but I hope he wasn't shocked by those dreadful words Aunt Prudence used! I was positively mortified."

"Logan McClintock's a sea captain," Vanessa said with a trace of amusement. "No doubt he's heard worse language."

Kitty gave her a thoughtful look. "Vanessa, do you suppose . . ." She put her head to one side, studying the newcomer. "Aunt Prudence's talk is shocking sometimes, and she can be difficult." Remembering the scene she had witnessed upstairs, Vanessa did not doubt it. But Kitty went on. "Mama, why couldn't Vanessa stay on here as Auntie's companion? She could have that nice little room right next to Aunt Prudence's, so she would not have to share the servants' quarters."

"Vanessa is young to assume such a responsibility," Felicity said slowly. "I'm not at all sure . . ."

"I nursed my mother through her last illness," Vanessa said. Hope stirred again. A room of her own in this fine house, with its warm fires and luxurious furnishings. And, no doubt, three good meals a day. "I'll do my best if you'll give me the chance," she went on.

"I'd like to have you here under my own roof," Felicity said. "And I think that dear Judith would have wanted that too."

"Perhaps she would," Vanessa agreed.

But she found her thoughts going to Logan McClintock, and it took all her resolution to push aside the possibility that there might be another reason for her desire to take on this difficult position in the Bradford household—the realization that she might see Logan again, on the night of Kitty's birthday ball.

Abel Bradford, a portly man with iron-gray hair and thick muttonchops whiskers, fixed his eyes on Vanessa, who was seated beside Aunt Prudence at the massive mahogany dining room table. The maid, having cleared away the dishes from the first course, a thick, hearty fish chowder, left the dining room.

"Vanessa is the daughter of an old and dear friend," Felicity was saying to her husband. "She is quite alone in the world and I thought . . ."

"Let the girl speak for herself," Abel said. "Miss Kenyon, you don't look old enough to take on this position."

"I am not without experience," Vanessa said. "Mrs. Bradford knows that I nursed my mother through her last illness."

"And now she's dead," Abel said coldly. "Maybe if you'd had enough skill and experience . . ."

"Oh, Abel, please!" Felicity protested. "Vanessa is scarcely to blame. It is unkind to even suggest that—"

"I am used to working hard," Vanessa went on. "And Mrs. Bradford has said that her aunt does not need a nurse, only a companion. I'm sure I can do whatever is necessary to—"

"Aunt Prudence never did like Nell," Kitty cut in. "Isn't that true, Auntie?"

"Nell—couldn't stand her. She's better back in the kitchen, scouring pots," Aunt Prudence said. "Vanessa's from Salem; she's promised to give me all the news of the old town."

"That's enough," Abel said. "I'm still master here, and I'll make up my own mind about Miss Kenyon. Who was your mother, girl?"

"Her name was Judith Kenyon. She—"

"Left you without a penny, I suppose," Abel said. "Sent you to beg shelter from strangers."

"Abel, please," Felicity interrupted. "I've told you, Judith and I were friends when we were girls. We lived near Derby's Wharf, and we—"

Abel did not look at his wife, but kept his eyes fixed on Vanessa. "What about the rest of your family?" he demanded.

"My father was lost at sea when I was small. Mama ran a boardinghouse—"

"Sailors' boardinghouse?" He shook his head. "That won't do. Won't do at all. Most of those places are no better than the miserable rookeries that line the East River—"

"Mama ran a respectable boardinghouse," Vanessa said, her anger overcoming her awe of Abel Bradford. "She did take a few sea captains, and their wives. But there were merchants who stayed with us, too, and commercial travelers. Miss Emma Goodhue boarded with us for several years—perhaps you know the name."

"Of course I do," Abel said brusquely. "Goodhue and Company is one of the largest commission houses here in New York."

"There you are, Abel," said Aunt Prudence. "When I first met Captain Campbell he was staying at a boardinghouse in Salem—" She turned to Vanessa. "As fine a man as ever drew breath, my husband was. I was telling Logan McClintock only this afternoon about the time he brought me a monkey, all the way from—"

"We're not talking about Captain Campbell or monkeys, ma'am," Abel said impatiently. He gave Vanessa another searching look, and she was grateful for the prim gray woolen dress, for the unbecoming braided chignon that Felicity had insisted upon. "You may stay for the time being," he told Vanessa.

"Thank you, Mr. Bradford," Vanessa said quietly. "I'll do my best to—"

"I presume you have references to prove that you are what you claim to be."

"Abel, the girl has already told you—" Felicity began.

"I might tell you that I am President Polk's nephew," Abel retorted. "That would not make me so." In the candlelight, his eyes, so light a shade of brown, looked yellow to Vanessa—like the eyes of a cat stalking a mouse. Her jaw tightened. She was no mouse, and she would not allow this hard, domineering man to make her feel like one.

"My trunk was stolen at the ferry landing," she said.

"And your letters of recommendation were in it?"

Vanessa and her mother had been so well known in Salem that it had never occurred to her that such letters would be necessary. But Abel was saying, "I have never hired an office boy without recommendations."

"The letters were in the trunk," Vanessa heard herself say.

"Oh, Abel, please say Vanessa may stay—It is so difficult to find a companion who pleases Aunt Prudence," Felicity implored her husband.

"Very well," he said impatiently. "I've no time to involve myself in these endless domestic difficulties. Certainly not now, with the *Empress of Canton* just arrived in port. Logan McClintock's an arrogant devil, but he knows how to drive ships and men. Ninety-nine days from Canton, off season. I doubt that any of Aspinwall's captains could better that record. Or Low's either."

He turned to his wife. "Felicity, my dear, are you going to ring for the next course, or must we all starve?"

Felicity hastily pressed a button that was set into the wall. But although Vanessa had always had a healthy appetite and the food was delicious, she was not quite as hungry as she might have been.

She had nothing to fear, she told herself. Mama had run a respectable boardinghouse. But now, with Mrs. Deverell in charge, things had changed for the worse. She felt a persistent uneasiness.

But she told herself that surely a man like Abel Bradford, with a shipping empire to control, would hardly bother to investigate the background of a girl who was little more than a servant in his home. So long as she could please Aunt Prudence, she would be allowed to remain here. And in a few weeks she would see Logan again, at Kitty's ball.

Chapter 3

It isn't fair, Vanessa thought. She was seated beside Aunt Prudence on one side of the ballroom, her slippered foot tapping in time to the waltz, unable to suppress her envy as she watched the dancers. She felt a particular pang as Kitty went moving by in Logan McClintock's arms. Kitty's ruffled skirts, trimmed with Brussels lace, swirled about her, and her dark curls made a halo around her face, upturned to her partner.

Vanessa's fingers tightened on her fan, and she forced herself to remember that she was lucky to be here at all. During her first two weeks in the Bradford mansion she had done her best to please Aunt Prudence, and the old lady was satisfied. True, Aunt Prudence, as she had ordered Vanessa to call her, was sometimes difficult, for she was plagued with the aches and discomforts of old age.

But she liked Vanessa, who provided a link with the past back in Salem, the years when Prudence Campbell had been the wife of Captain Benjamin Campbell of the schooner *Ondine.* Vanessa, who had been taught by her mother to treat the elderly with respect, had listened patiently, even when Aunt Prudence had repeated the same story several times. And the old lady was delighted that Vanessa could answer all her questions about the men and women of her generation who still remained alive in her hometown.

Kitty, too, had been kind to Vanessa, insisting that, of course, she must attend the party in a suitable gown. Indeed, Kitty had provided one of her own, a purple silk. "It was a mistake," Kitty explained. "The color does nothing for me.

But it is exactly right for you, Vanessa."

And earlier on the evening of the ball, Vanessa had agreed, for the color made her eyes deepen to violet, and it set off her red-gold hair. She had not taken the liberty of wearing her hair in one of the frivolous styles favored by Kitty and the young ladies who were guests, but at the last moment Vanessa had not been able to resist making a few becoming changes. Although her hair was parted in the center and arranged in a chignon, she had allowed herself a few soft waves at the temples and some small ringlets over her ears.

And much good it does, she thought, moving restlessly on the small velvet and gilt sofa beside Aunt Prudence. On either side were staid matrons in dark gray, brown, or plum, and all of them eyed Vanessa with curiosity. Lows, Grinnells, and Aspinwalls, members of the great shipping dynasties, they were plainly curious about this newcomer in the Bradford household.

Now, as the waltz came to a close, Vanessa saw Horace Widdicomb approaching Logan and Kitty. No doubt he was going to claim the next dance, Vanessa thought, and she felt sorry for Kitty. Then, remembering her own position, she quickly lowered her eyes and hoped that Horace would not notice her.

She had expected Horace to be here tonight, but she had given the matter little thought, for during the past two weeks she had been too absorbed by her new duties. And when before falling asleep she had woven fantasies about the party, it was Logan's face that she had seen. Perhaps he would dance with her. And maybe he would treat her differently now that she had been accepted into the Bradford household.

But so far Logan had seemed unaware of her presence and had danced the first two waltzes with Kitty, a fact noted by the matrons who sat on this side of the room. "A fine seaman," Vanessa had heard one of them whisper. "One of Abel Bradford's best captains, my husband says—but all the same, my dear, hardly suitable for Kitty."

The orchestra, on a platform at the opposite end of the room, struck up another waltz, but Kitty did not allow Horace to take her in his arms for the dance.

Vanessa tensed, for Kitty, with light, swift steps was heading straight in her direction, leaving Horace no choice but to follow. Kitty's dark eyes were sparkling with a touch of mischief as she led Horace up to Vanessa and made the introductions. "You must dance with Vanessa," Kitty said.

"I don't believe I can—" Vanessa began, shielding her face with her fan, a small, painted trifle brought from China and given to her by Aunt Prudence. "My place is here—"

"Nonsense, girl!" the old lady said, her voice shrill above the music. Because Aunt Prudence was hard of hearing, she assumed that others were too. Several of the matrons turned to stare. "You go ahead and dance. Plenty of time for sitting on the sidelines when you're old and stiff like me—and these other crows!" She made a sweeping gesture that took in the rest of the older women and drew an outraged stare from one of the Grinnell ladies.

Horace spoke hastily. "As you wish, ma'am." He bowed to Aunt Prudence. "My pleasure, Miss—" He studied Vanessa, his hatchet face alert, his mouth tightening.

"Jumped-up clerk," Aunt Prudence said, her voice lower, but still audible.

Vanessa rose, and, taking Horace's arm, she let him lead her out onto the ballroom floor. He peered down at her, thrusting his head forward like a turtle, to examine her through his gold-rimmed spectacles. "Have we met before, Miss Kenyon? I do believe—"

"Oh, no!" Vanessa assured him. "I mean I would have remembered you."

Taking the remark for flattery, he gave her a tight, smug smile. "Even so, I could swear I—"

But Vanessa did not give him a chance to finish.

"The polka," she said, forcing a smile. "Such a charming dance, so lively—"

He put his arm around her waist, but although he knew the steps, his movements were stiff and graceless. He must have been in his early thirties, but he had the mannerisms of an older man, and his well-cut suit could not conceal his round-shouldered posture.

She turned her face away and saw Kitty taking Logan's hand, saw the two of them leaving the ballroom together, with Kitty's apple-green taffeta skirt billowing out around her.

"So you are Mrs. Campbell's new companion," Horace was saying. "Not an easy position, I should think. To be confined indoors with an elderly lady—"

"Soon we'll be going out for walks in the park," Vanessa said.

"Ah, yes. The park is charming in spring. It is private, you know."

"Indeed?" Vanessa began to relax, hoping that Horace might be distracted by this new topic of conversation.

"Only residents of the square have keys to open the gates," he assured her. "Abel Bradford favors the arrangement; he would scarcely wish the ladies in his family to be exposed to the advances of strangers. The city is growing so fast that even here, on Hudson Square, one cannot be sure—Respectable ladies must be protected."

Stiff-necked prig, Vanessa thought. No wonder Kitty did not want to be his wife.

"—catalpa trees," he was saying. "Cottonwood and silver

birches. Mrs. Trollope remarked most favorably on the park during her visit here. One of the few things that she found to approve of during her visit to our country. No doubt you've read her book, *Domestic Manners of the Americans.*"

"No, I haven't." The polka came to a spirited close, and Vanessa felt a surge of relief. But then she realized that although Horace's arm had dropped from her waist, he was studying her again.

"I can't get over the notion that we've met before," he said.

The orchestra was tuning up for the next dance and Vanessa, fearing that Horace would ask her to be his partner again, cast about for an excuse.

"Aunt Prudence mislaid her shawl—perhaps she left it in the conservatory."

"I'll go with you," Horace offered, and Vanessa let him take her arm. The library, opposite the ballroom, was filled with gentlemen who preferred to play cards or talk business instead of dancing.

"Steamers!" Abel, who was standing in the library doorway, was talking to one of his guests. "Not for me. Ship tea in a steamer and it'll stink of coal smoke."

"We'll find a way to get around that," the other man said.

"And what about the coal bunkers? They take up half your cargo space—and cost you half your profits. No getting around that, is there?"

"Steamers are faster."

"Unless they blow up. Or break down, like the *Savannah,*" Abel retorted. "You remember her maiden voyage to England? Used her sails a lot more than her paddlewheels. Now, my *Empress of Canton*—she made the voyage in record time and without losing an inch of cargo space." Catching sight of Horace, he said, "There's the man who can tell you about the cargo from the *Empress*—he was down there when she was being unloaded." He gave a triumphant grin. "Horace, come in here," he ordered.

But Horace stood still, looking at Vanessa. "The *Empress of Canton*," he said softly. "The day we were unloading—"

"Horace, what are you waiting for? Come in and tell Grinnell and the rest of them—"

Horace bowed to Vanessa, his eyes narrowed in a look of cold satisfaction. Then he turned and entered the library, and she fled down the hall to the conservatory.

Although the air inside the glass-walled room was warm and heavy with the scent of tropical plants, Vanessa shivered as if she stood, once again, on the dock at South Street. She was scarcely aware of her surroundings: of the gardenias and tuberoses, the trailing vines and tall, thick shrubs in their majolica pots.

Horace Widdicomb had recognized her, and what would prevent him from telling Abel Bradford about the circumstances of their first meeting? True, Felicity, gentle and warmhearted, had accepted Vanessa into the household. But if Abel listened to Horace and believed him, Vanessa might find herself back out on the streets. Or if Abel went so far as to make inquiries about the boardinghouse, how could she hope to convince him that it had been a respectable place when Mama had owned it, that it had been Mrs. Deverell who had changed the house into a—a brothel? Because that was the only name for it now.

Vanessa started when she heard a soft, feminine laugh, and she realized that she was not alone here in the conservatory. Peering into the dimness through a tangle of flowering vines and potted palms, she caught a glimpse of a girl in an apple-green skirt trimmed with Brussels lace, and a man, standing close to her.

Logan and Kitty. Even as Vanessa watched, she saw Kitty stand on tiptoe and tilt her head back, saw her arms go around Logan's shoulders, her body molding itself against his.

Vanessa felt a constriction in her throat, and she tried to take a deep breath, but she was impeded by her tightly laced stays. The fragrance of gardenias and tuberoses was sickening to her, and she felt a little dizzy. She had never fainted, and she must not do so now, she told herself sternly. Moving lightly, she backed out of the conservatory and returned to the ballroom.

Supper was served at midnight, and although Aunt Prudence was obviously tiring, she refused to go up to bed. "I like parties," she told Vanessa with a grin. "And I don't know how many more I'll be going to."

The old lady spoke with a complete lack of self-pity, a calm acceptance of her age and frailty. "Now, go get me something to eat," she ordered, seating herself on a love seat in one of the dining room alcoves. Vanessa obeyed, although she herself had little appetite for the magnificent spread: the baked hams, turkey simmered in wine, the ices and cakes.

When Aunt Prudence had finished, Vanessa asked if she wanted a cup of punch, but the old lady shook her head. "That bilge water? I've got a bottle of Demerara rum up in my room. Logan smuggled it up for me, and I'll have some in my tea later. Good lad, Logan is. Reminds me of my husband—"

The orchestra had struck up a reel in the ballroom and some of the younger guests were returning to dance. "A good lad," Aunt Prudence repeated. "Tough and smart. Ah—speak of the devil!"

Logan had come up to them, but Kitty was not with him. "Will you dance with me, Vanessa?" he asked.

"I can't. Aunt Prudence needs me."

"I do not! You go and dance," the old lady ordered. And as Vanessa still hesitated, she snapped, "Don't be coy about it, girl. Your dancing days won't last forever."

In the ballroom Logan took Vanessa's hands and they joined the line of dancers. "I wanted to dance with you before I left tonight," he told her. "We probably won't be seeing each other again, not for a long time."

"Are you going to sea again so soon?"

"No, but I won't be coming here again."

She looked up at him in bewilderment. "You work for Mr. Bradford," she began. "You're one of his captains."

"Not any longer. The next time I put to sea it'll be as master of my own ship. I haven't told Bradford yet, but I'm going to, before I leave."

"Your own ship—"

She saw his dark-gray eyes shine with triumph. "A clipper. The *Athena*. She'll be completed soon. A real beauty she is."

He might have been speaking of a woman, Vanessa thought. Under other circumstances she might have shared his enthusiasm, but now she could not.

"I'll be sailing for China around the end of May," he said.

"With Kitty, I suppose."

"Kitty?" He gave her a look of genuine surprise. "Whatever put that into your head?"

She tried to keep her voice light and indifferent.

"I thought perhaps—a honeymoon voyage—"

"When Kitty goes on her honeymoon, it'll be with Horace Widdicomb aboard one of the Bradford ships," he said.

"Oh, but she can't—she mustn't—"

"I don't blame you for disliking the man, after the cool reception he gave you that afternoon down at South Street. But you must admit, he had some excuse. You did look like a dockside drab."

She glared at him, but he was not disturbed. He went on calmly. "Tonight, though, you look every inch a lady, and a lovely one."

"Much good that may do me," she said bitterly.

"What's wrong? You've found a comfortable home here and the kind of respectable work you said you wanted. Or have you changed your mind?" His eyes were sardonic.

"No, I haven't. But I'm not likely to be here much longer now that Horace has recognized me. He'll talk to Abel, I know he will, and then—"

"You're really afraid, aren't you?" Logan's voice was no longer mocking, and she saw that he looked genuinely concerned. The first figure of the reel came to a close, and he took her arm and led her off the floor to a nearby corner sofa. "What makes you so sure that Horace recognized you?"

"Oh, I know he did. And the way he looked at me, I—"

"I don't doubt that he looked at you with interest," Logan said. "He's a man, for all his stuffy holier-than-thou talk. But I wouldn't worry about Horace. He might want to get into your bed—" Vanessa's cheeks burned and she looked away as Logan went on. "Can't say I blame him for that. But it's Kitty he's after, and I suspect that his greed's a lot more powerful than his—animal impulses."

"Are you saying that Horace is marrying Kitty for her money?"

"Why not? She's Abel's only daughter, and Horace's branch of the family doesn't have much money. When Abel dies, Horace will inherit one of the greatest shipping fortunes in New York—as Kitty's husband."

He spoke with cold cynicism. Vanessa's voice was unsteady. "I wondered why you—you don't marry Kitty yourself, since you want a shipping empire too."

"Marry Kitty!" He laughed. "Not a chance."

"She's pretty," Vanessa challenged him. "And you were obviously enjoying yourself when you . . ." She broke off.

"Go on."

"When you were dancing with her," Vanessa finished lamely.

"My dear girl, I wouldn't care if Kitty had the face of a flounder if I could get what I want by marrying her." He shook his head. "But it's out of the question. Too many obstacles." Vanessa looked at him in bewilderment, and he explained. "Abel Bradford would never consent to our marriage. He'd disinherit Kitty." He spoke with brutal directness. "I have no use for a penniless wife."

Vanessa was shocked and repelled by Logan's words.

"Maybe you're underestimating yourself. I'm sure Abel respects your skill as a captain."

"No doubt. But he's got his family pride to think about. He'd scarcely welcome a son-in-law who is the product of the Five Points. Or haven't you been in New York long enough to know what that means?"

"Felicity Bradford told me about the Five Points," Vanessa said slowly. "I know that the people who live there are poor. But surely it's to your credit that you rose from such beginnings and became a ship's captain."

"Vanessa, my sweet innocent," Logan said, "I doubt that Abel would see it as you do. In any case, there's another problem. I want ships. A fleet of them. The best and the fastest. But they have to be mine. Abel built his own shipping empire, but he's got it right in the palm of his hand, and he'll never let go. I'll build my own, and when I do, I'll answer to no man."

In spite of herself, Vanessa felt a stirring of excitement at his words, for his drive was a palpable thing. But she would not allow herself to be carried away. This man was hard and calculating, and he did not take the trouble to hide it.

"Horace will probably be satisfied to marry Kitty and then to wait for Abel to die so that he can take over. But Abel's a tough old bird. And while he lives, there'll be no doubt as to who's in control of Bradford Shipping. I want my own ships—and I want them as fast as I can get them built."

"A fine dream," Vanessa said, "for a man with one clipper, and that one not yet finished."

"She will be. The *Athena* will set sail in May, and I'll be in command." He gave her a smile. "You'll come to see me off, won't you? And bring Prudence Campbell along, if the old girl's up to it."

"It's not likely I'll be here with her. If Horace—"

"Still worrying about Horace? Look, if he makes trouble for you, come to me and tell me. I'll be at Silas Pringle's shipyard at Corlear's Hook, on the East River."

"And what could you possibly do to help me?"

She rose, and Logan, too, got to his feet. He looked her up and down, his eyes moving over her white shoulders, the soft swell of her breasts. "I could take you off to China with me," he said.

"You have an odd sense of humor," she told him.

"I wasn't being humorous. The *Athena* will have a fine master's cabin, large enough for two."

"You said you had no use for a penniless wife, and I am not an heiress like Kitty."

He threw back his head and laughed. "Wife? Who said anything about a wife? If I ever do marry—and that's most unlikely—it will be years from now."

She took a step away from him. "You—why, you're worse than Horace! What have I done to make you think that I would—and after you—"

"After I what?" he asked with amusement.

"You were kissing Kitty!"

"Why, Vanessa! I had no idea you were watching."

"I didn't mean to. I went into the conservatory and—"

"No need to apologize," he said lightly. "Or do you expect an apology from me? Have I offended your rock-ribbed New England morality?"

"That's not what I—"

"Or can it be that you're jealous?"

She stared at him with indignation. "You are the most arrogant, the most—"

"I believe you are jealous." She turned away, but he caught her arm and swung her back to face him. "You must allow me to make amends." Before she realized what was about to happen, he drew her against him and held her so tightly that she could feel the pressure of his hard thighs against her, and the warmth of his breath on her cheek.

The words came unbidden. "Not here, please, not with everyone looking on."

He laughed and released her. "As you wish," he said. "I'll restrain my ardor until we're alone, and the surroundings are more . . . suitable. But I'm not a patient man, Vanessa. Don't keep me waiting too long."

She fought back the urge to tell him what she thought of him. Her fingers tingled with the need to strike out at him. Instead, she walked away quickly, back to the dining room, where Aunt Prudence was waiting.

But as she made her way through the crowd of guests, she could not help wondering what it would have felt like to be kissed by Logan.

Chapter 4

Kitty's dark eyes narrowed, and her voice was sharp.

"Nell," she said, trying to control her irritation, "you've got to help me this one time more."

The maid looked away and began to polish the small, rose-wood table beside Kitty's bed with unusual vigor.

"Oh, do stop that and listen!" Kitty demanded. "You won't get into trouble. There's no risk."

"There is, for me," Nell said, but she stopped her polishing and twisted the cloth in her plump, work-reddened hands. "I never wanted t' deceive the master, nor yer mother neither. You talked me into it."

"And I gave you my tortoise-shell bracelet and my coral combs," Kitty reminded her.

"I know, miss. Real fine, they are. But ye've been forbidden t' see Captain McClintock. Ye told me so."

Kitty clenched her hands and tried to keep her temper. "If you'll go to the shipyard with me once more, I'll give you my pink bonnet. Think what your young man will say when he sees you in it."

Nell wavered, then said: "It's a lovely bonnet, miss." She shook her head. "But I can't be takin' no more chances. If the master found out I'd been helpin' ye t' meet Captain McClintock on the sly, I'd lose my job here for sure."

"Papa won't find out. I'll say we're taking baskets to the seamen's wives, and we will."

"Ye mean I will, like those other times. After I drive ye down t' Pringle's shipyard. An' then I'll have to come back for ye. Oh, no, miss! Not after last time, when I saw Mr. Widdicomb comin' outta that tavern, right across from the shipyard. He stared straight at the gig."

"There must be a dozen gigs like it in the city. I'm sure he did not make any connection; you were scared and you are exaggerating the whole thing." Kitty tossed her head. "Besides, once I'm married to Captain McClintock, there'll be nothing Horace can do to make trouble for me. And you'll be safe, because I'll have you come and work for me as my personal maid."

"Will that be before or after ye run off with the captain on that new clipper of his?" There was no mistaking the sarcasm in the maid's voice.

"Captain McClintock's going to marry me!" Kitty insisted. "He will!" But he had not yet spoken of marriage; he had not even kissed her since that evening of the ball.

Oh, but he would. When they were properly married and together in the cabin aboard the *Athena*, Logan would kiss her over and over again; his lips would claim her mouth, her throat, her breasts, and then he would . . . Her ignorance of such matters kept her imagination from going beyond this. But whatever they did in that bed in the cabin would be wonderful, she was sure.

First, though, she would have to get him to propose. Tomorrow, at the shipyard, she would get him away from Silas Pringle and those everlasting plans and blueprints. Away from the workmen with their interruptions. And then she would find a way to make him ask her to be his wife.

Surely he would have proposed weeks ago, had it not been for his pride. He didn't have a fortune, or even a suitable family background. Maybe he was afraid that Papa would refuse permission, or that she would turn from him in scorn or laugh at him for daring to think that she might become his wife.

He did not know she loved him, for, even that night in the conservatory, she had not told him so. She had been taught that a young lady must wait for a gentleman to propose before admitting that she shared his feelings. But she would have to forget the rules taught her by Mama. She would have to assure Logan that she did not care that he had come from the Five Points, that he had no fortune.

And she would have to act quickly, for there was little time left. As soon as the *Athena* was ready to sail, Logan would be off to China.

But he won't sail without me. Kitty's full, soft lips tightened.

"I'd be takin' the chance, miss," Nell was saying. "Except for seein' Mr. Widdicomb down there—"

"If he'd suspected what was going on, he'd have told Papa right away," Kitty said. "And Papa would have been furious with me. You know what a temper he has."

"That he has, miss. The master won't stand for nobody under his roof disobeyin' him." Her eyes grew sly. "If I was t' do my duty an' tell him what ye've been up to with Captain McClintock . . ."

"You wouldn't dare," Kitty said uneasily. "He'd blame you for helping me."

"Not if I put it t' him right. I didn't want t' go with ye, miss, but I'm used t' takin' orders. Now that yer talkin' about runnin' off with the captain, though—why I see my duty plain. I got t' tell the master."

Kitty was trapped and she knew it. She must not lose her head. "All right," she told Nell. "I won't ask you to help me. And maybe—maybe you're right. If Papa wants me to marry Horace Widdicomb, then perhaps it is my duty to obey him. No matter what my feelings may be."

"Now yer talkin' sense, miss," Nell said. But she looked at

Kitty uncertainly, startled and confused by this abrupt change of attitude.

"You can still have the pink bonnet," Kitty said, thrusting the round striped box into Nell's hands. "Here, take it."

The gift should ensure Nell's silence about those previous visits to the shipyard. But after Nell had left the bedroom, clutching her loot, Kitty realized that she would have to find someone else to go with her so that she could meet Logan tomorrow.

The March wind blew briskly the next day, and large white clouds sailed across the sky. Vanessa, seated beside Kitty in the small blue, yellow-wheeled gig, handled the reins expertly. Abel had gone down to South Street early that morning in the large, imposing, family carriage, while Aunt Prudence and Felicity had set off in the landau to pay a few calls.

Although Vanessa had been happy to get out of the house and to see something of the city, she was puzzled and uneasy now. Why had Kitty chosen this particular day to make her charity visits for the Ladies' Society for the Relief of the Wives of Seamen? Surely she might have waited until tomorrow and used the landau, which was much larger and better suited to delivering baskets. And when Timothy, the stablehand, had offered to drive the gig, Kitty had told him firmly that she would not need him.

"How lucky that you're an experienced driver," Kitty said as the gig rolled along Hudson Square with the mare stepping out at a brisk trot.

Luck had nothing to do with it, Vanessa thought wryly. During the last few years, as her mother grew more frail, more easily tired, Vanessa had taken over the task of driving out to the farms around Salem to buy fresh milk and eggs for the boardinghouse. But Vanessa, grateful for her present good fortune in finding work in the Bradford house, had resolved to try to put her unhappy memories behind her.

During these past weeks Vanessa had come to enjoy her position, for although Aunt Prudence was occasionally difficult, the old lady had taken a real liking to her new companion. Vanessa listened patiently when Aunt Prudence told her stories of Salem and of the happy years with Captain Campbell, of the voyages that she and her late husband had made on the *Ondine*, the captain's coastwise schooner.

"Turn here," Kitty said, and Vanessa obeyed. She gave Kitty a puzzled look. Why on earth, Vanessa wondered, had Kitty worn her new rose-colored velvet dress and her sealskin pelisse? And why had she kept Vanessa waiting nearly an hour while she arranged her hair in a new way, with a mass of jet-black ringlets over each ear, and small, flirtatious curls at the temples?

Now, as Vanessa turned the gig into the heavy traffic that streamed along Broadway, she tried to keep all her attention on her driving, but it was not easy, for Kitty, in obvious high spirits, chattered incessantly.

"Look Vanessa, over there. That's the Astor House, the finest hotel in New York. Hot water in all the rooms. They pump it up from the basement by steam. And every room has gaslight. But Papa says that's a mixed blessing, because some of the guests do not understand how it works and keep blowing out the flames. Isn't that dreadful?"

Vanessa nodded, and Kitty went on. "A business acquaintance of Papa's who was staying at the hotel said that the door of his room was full of holes."

"But why—"

"The locks had to be wrenched off so many times," Kitty explained. "To get to the guests who'd been overcome by gas."

"Shocking," Vanessa said as she pulled sharply on the reins and managed to maneuver the gig between a splendid black carriage drawn by a team of high-stepping horses with silver-plated harness and a shabby hansom cab whose equally shabby driver cursed hoarsely. Vanessa had never been faced with such difficult driving conditions on the familiar roads around Salem, and she sighed with relief when she had managed to get the gig across Broadway, and into a less congested section.

On Barclay Street, which was lined with shabby wooden roominghouses, Kitty said, "Here's where you'll deliver the baskets. I've written a list for you."

"But you'll be coming with me," Vanessa began.

Kitty shook her head. "I've an errand of my own," she said, speaking quickly and keeping her eyes fixed on her sealskin muff. "Drive me to Corlear's Hook—I'll tell you how to get there—and then come back and deliver the baskets. And call for me afterward."

"Where shall I call for you?" Vanessa was confused now, and uneasy. What was Kitty up to?

"Silas Pringle's shipyard," Kitty said.

"But that's where . . . Kitty, how could you involve me in such a scheme?" Vanessa demanded.

"Scheme? I don't know what you mean. Mama wants me to make inquiries about a workman in Pringle's yard. He had an accident, and if he is unable to work, Mama's organization will see to it that his family is provided with—"

"Stop it!" Vanessa's hands tightened on the reins, and she felt a surge of anger. "Logan will be at Silas Pringle's shipyard overseeing the construction work on the *Athena*." Vanessa had not forgotten her talk with Logan at the ball. Now she understood the reason for Kitty's finery. "It's Logan you're going to see," she said.

"No one must know," Kitty said, her voice placating. "Mama's pleased that I'm helping with one of her charities."

"She wouldn't be pleased if she knew the truth, and your father . . ." Vanessa shuddered as she thought of what Abel's response would be if he learned that his orders were being flouted. "Your parents trust me. They took me into their home when I had nowhere else to go."

"I helped talk Papa into letting you stay," Kitty reminded her. "And I've treated you like a—a guest—never like a servant."

"You've been most kind," Vanessa admitted but then she went on, speaking urgently. "But surely you know that I can't help you to deceive your parents."

"Do you want to see me married to Horace?"

"Your father's made that decision," Vanessa said.

"Then he'll have to change his plans. Logan and I will be married and we'll sail to China. We'll be gone for months." She gave Vanessa a sly little smile. "When we return, Papa will have to give us his blessing. Especially if I'm in—a certain condition."

Vanessa understood, and she felt a swift thrust of unhappiness at the thought of Kitty married to Logan and bearing his child. But why? She herself was not in love with him. She must not be in love with him, for he had told her that he had no desire to marry her. She tried not to remember the current of warm longing that had swept through her when he had danced with her on the night of the ball.

"Papa'll have to give Logan an important position in the company," Kitty was saying.

"Logan doesn't want to work for your father."

"Don't be silly. It will be a wonderful opportunity for Logan. And when Papa sees how happy we are . . . It'll be like that play I saw about an English heiress and a Gypsy. Only it turned out he wasn't really a Gypsy; he was of noble birth. But the Gypsies stole him away when he was a baby, and then . . ."

Vanessa jerked at the reins and brought the gig to a halt in front of a chandler's shop. "Kitty, this isn't a play, and Logan isn't a Gypsy of noble birth. You're talking nonsense." She paused, then looked squarely at Kitty. "Has Logan asked you to marry him?"

"He's going to. I know he is."

"How do you know?"

Kitty's round face went pink, and her dark eyes sparkled. "When he kissed me—on the night of the ball . . . Oh, Vanessa, I've been kissed before—but never like that."

Vanessa fought down an impulse to seize Kitty by her plump little shoulders and shake her until her teeth rattled. Silly, romantic Kitty, pampered all her life, sought after by young men from New York's wealthiest families. Kitty, complacent and vain, because she had a pretty face and a shapely figure. And the Bradford fortune behind her. How could Kitty be made to believe that Logan did not want to marry her?

"Logan's a sailor," Vanessa said, not bothering to speak with delicacy. "A sailor back from a long voyage is hot for any female he can get his hands on. If Logan kissed you in a different way from what you're used to, it was only because he'd been at sea so long."

Kitty's eyes flashed with anger. "You don't know anything about him."

"And you do?"

"I love him, and when a girl's in love, she knows." She shot Vanessa a sharp, probing look. "You're not jealous, are you? Because you don't have an admirer of your own?"

"Certainly not. I'm only trying to make you see that Logan's not in love, even if you are. He's a hard, ambitious man. He told me at the ball that he doesn't want to marry anyone, not until he's built his own fleet. He wants money and power."

"I know all that," Kitty said impatiently. "He's had to fight his way up from the Five Points. He's not like those other young men I've known, whose fathers handed them their fortunes." She gave a shiver of excitement. "Logan's different. He's strong and masterful and he's . . . Don't you think he's handsome, Vanessa?"

Once more Vanessa felt the swift, hot current of excitement that she had known in his arms as he had led her through the dance at Kitty's ball.

"I suppose he's good-looking enough," she said. "And different from the other young men you've met. But that's no reason to want to marry him."

"Oh, Vanessa, you're so strait-laced and sensible. I'm not like that at all; I don't want to be. You don't know what it's like to be in love. If Logan leaves for China without me, I'll waste away and die. I will." She clutched at Vanessa's arm. "Oh, drive on, please."

Vanessa did not obey at once.

"I'll walk to the shipyard if I have to," Kitty threatened, rising in her seat.

Vanessa was tempted to say, Go ahead and walk, then. But she knew that an elegantly dressed young lady would not be safe on foot in these narrow streets around the waterfront. Down here, there were many respectable if shabby eating houses and ships' chandlers' shops, but there were also rowdy grog shops and concert saloons, and, no doubt, more than a few sporting houses catering to sailors.

Vanessa brought the reins down on the mare's sleek back, and the startled animal sprang forward, almost upsetting the gig. The damp March wind was stronger now, moving in from the docks, carrying the smells of tar and rope, tea and cinnamon. Vanessa sighed. Kitty would have to hear the truth from Logan himself, she thought, and she guessed, with a twinge of pity, that Logan would not be one to spare Kitty's feelings.

The pale March sunlight was fading now. Long shadows stretched over the paving stones. Vanessa, having delivered the baskets of food and clothing, had returned to pick up Kitty in front of Silas Pringle's shipyard. But there was no sign of Kitty here at the gates.

Then Vanessa's gaze shifted, and she looked across the low wooden fence into the yard. She saw the long, sleek hull of a clipper resting on its bed of keelblocks, while men working with adze, auger, and mallet swarmed over the scaffolding of the vessel under construction. Was it the *Athena*? It must be, for the only other vessels that she could see in the yard were a small schooner, the kind used for coastwise trading, and a stubby little tug. Vanessa guessed that Pringle's yard was not one of the larger sort, those owned by the more prosperous and long-established East River shipbuilders, like William H. Webb and Jacob Westervelt.

Vanessa leaned forward on the seat to get a closer look, but she could not see either Logan or Kitty. Maybe they had gone into that long wooden building in the corner of the yard, where they could speak more privately.

Had Logan already told Kitty that he was not going to marry her? Or—Vanessa's lips tightened—or had Logan had second thoughts about Kitty since the night of the ball? Had he been tempted by the Bradford fortune, and had he decided that even having Abel for a father-in-law was not too high a price to pay for satisfying his ambitions?

She forced her thoughts away and made herself remember how eagerly she had been welcomed into those shabby cottages on Barclay Street. In those cottages, a loaf of fresh bread, a piece of bacon, a warm shawl, meant so much to a seaman's wife waiting eagerly for her man's return and trying to stretch out the last few cents of his meager allotment.

And because Vanessa was not a fine lady, because she had explained that she knew, from her own experience, the difficulties faced by these women, they had warmed to her quickly.

One sailor's wife had insisted on making a cup of tea for her, while another had shown her a new baby, born since its father had sailed.

But Vanessa's satisfaction in making these errands had been dampened by the knowledge that Kitty had only used the occasion to cover up her visit to Pringle's shipyard. Kitty would not involve her in such a deception again, she told herself.

"Why, Miss Kenyon, what an unexpected pleasure."

Vanessa turned to see Horace Widdicomb looking up at her, his eyes glinting behind his gold-rimmed spectacles. "I've been dining at that tavern across the way for several days now."

Why would Horace think she cared where he took his meals?

"The last time Miss Bradford came down to the shipyard, I recognized the gig, quite by chance. But the two of you drove off before I could speak."

"I haven't been down here with Kitty before," Vanessa began.

"Oh, come now, why try to deceive me?"

"I'm not—"

"You're a poor liar," Horace went on smoothly. "I knew you for what you were the first time I saw you. I never dreamed you'd be able to establish yourself in the Bradford household, though. Tell me; did you manage it alone, or did Captain McClintock help you, in exchange for your cooperation?"

"I don't know what you're talking about. Why would Logan—"

"So that you could influence the mind of an innocent young girl, so that you could make it possible for Kitty and Logan to meet secretly—as they're doing right now."

"You have no right—"

"I have every right," Horace said, "since Kitty's going to marry me."

"She doesn't want to be your wife," Vanessa blurted out. "It's Logan she wants."

"And she's been visiting him down here, with your help. At Logan's suggestion, no doubt."

Vanessa flared into anger. "Why would I help them to meet secretly? Why would I conspire with a man I scarcely know?"

"An interesting point. Can it be that you know him better than you pretend? That you met him in some dockside tavern after I turned you away from the shipping office?"

"Logan found me hiding in the wagon that day, and he took me to the Bradford home because he felt sorry for me."

"McClintock's not the sort to be moved by charitable impulses, as we both know. But ambition—the desire to control the Bradford money by marrying Kitty—that's quite another matter. That would have a powerful appeal for a dockside slut and a gutter rat out of the Five Points."

Vanessa's eyes tightened on the whip in the holder beside her. Her eyes darkened to violet, and her voice shook with anger when she challenged him. "Why not go into the shipyard right now and confront Logan with your suspicions?"

Horace did not answer, and Vanessa, her temper rising, went on. "You'd better be careful what you call him, though. Unless you want to risk a broken jaw."

"Brawling in public is not my way," Horace said calmly. "But I'm grateful for your concern." He took a step closer to the gig and Vanessa instinctively drew back as his eyes moved over the curves of her breasts and her slender waist.

"You have a good position at the Bradford home," he said. "Better than you might have hoped for. But it's dull, isn't it, for a girl who is used to more stimulating surroundings. A girl who was raised in a sailors' brothel. Oh, yes, I know more about you than you think."

"You know nothing! You're evil-minded, hateful—"

Horace ignored her protest and continued speaking, his eyes still flicking over her body. She pulled up the woolen carriage robe. "Taking care of an old woman, reading aloud to her and helping her to wind her knitting yarn. Oh, no, that's not enough for a girl of your experience. But I can change all that."

Horace rested an arm against the side of the gig.

"First, you'll stop helping Kitty to meet Logan against her father's orders."

"She tricked me into driving her down here," Vanessa said hotly. "And you needn't worry, because it won't happen again."

"I'm not worried," Horace said. "But you are—or you ought to be."

Vanessa felt a stirring of fear. Horace had the power to get her dismissed from the Bradford home, and if he did, what could she do in New York without friends or money? Those women she had brought the charity baskets to only an hour ago were respectable, at least. There were organizations to help them. And their men would return—most of them—with wages from their voyages. But for a girl, alone and unmarried, the prospect was bleak indeed.

Although she hated having to plead with Horace, she could not stop herself from saying, "You won't tell Mr. Bradford, will you? I give you my word, I didn't know what Kitty was up to, and now that I do, I'll never—"

"Why don't we talk it over on your afternoon off?" Horace put a hand on her arm and she shrank from his touch.

"You do have an afternoon off, don't you?" His eyes, so hostile only a few minutes before, now held quite a different look, one that frightened her far more.

"Every other Saturday."

Horace passed his tongue over his lips and spoke quickly. "We'll have a private talk in that tavern over there. One of the rooms upstairs . . . no one will interrupt us."

Vanessa jerked her arm away.

"Kitty's kept me waiting a long time. A man has his needs. You should know all about that."

Although Vanessa controlled the urge to strike out at him with the whip, she could not hold back her words.

"Even if I were . . . even if I'd lain with a dozen men, I wouldn't let you have me. You—you disgust me!"

Horace went white, and his sharp nose looked pinched. He opened his mouth, closed it, his lips folded in against each other. Then he walked away with quick, jerky steps.

"Logan didn't have a chance to tell me he loves me," Kitty said as the two girls drove back to Hudson Square. "It was Mr. Pringle's fault, coming over, interrupting us to talk of blueprints and cost estimates. The *Athena* will be far more expensive than Logan had planned. But he wants everything to be the best in quality."

Vanessa wondered if she should tell Kitty about the encounter with Horace, then decided against it, for Kitty was completely absorbed in her own worries. "Oh, Vanessa, I know Logan loves me," Kitty said. "And next time we're together . . ."

Vanessa scarcely listened to Kitty, for, disturbed as she was by her encounter with Horace and her fear of the possible consequences, she still felt relief, even a curious reassurance, in the knowledge that Logan had not proposed to this pretty, infatuated girl.

The lamps had been lit on Hudson Square by the time they got back. The Bradford house stood, a bastion of respectability. Vanessa wondered, uneasily, whether Horace would rob her of her secure position here, whether he would take his revenge on her for the blow she had dealt his male pride.

Chapter 5

"It's going to be a small dinner party," Felicity said. "Mr. Bradford's brother and his wife, Mr. and Mrs. Grinnell, and the Lows."

But Felicity wore a worried frown as she went about preparing for the party, and once, when a maid chipped the edge of a platter, she was unusually sharp with the girl.

Vanessa, however, was preoccupied by her own worries, her nerves tensed for the blow she was sure would fall. Horace was not a kindly or forgiving man, and those words, spoken in anger at the shipyard, had wounded his self-esteem.

Not that she was sorry for having refused to meet him in a private room at the tavern, for she knew well enough what he had expected from her.

I should have appealed to his chivalry, I should have been tactful, she thought as she walked along the paths inside the tall iron fence of the park with Aunt Prudence leaning on her arm. They selected a bench, and Vanessa tried to listen attentively as the old lady told her now-familiar stories about her early years in Salem.

"You're a good girl, Vanessa," Aunt Prudence was saying. "Your ma raised you right, even if she was poor as a churchmouse. And you're pretty too. You'll find yourself a fine husband one day. And then I hope you'll be as happy as I was with Captain Campbell." Then she said abruptly, "Haven't seen Logan McClintock lately. Where's he keeping himself?"

"You remember"—Vanessa was used to the old lady's forgetfulness, her moments of confusion—"Logan's building a clipper of his own. It takes all his time."

"A clipper. Yes, certainly I remember. Logan'll make his mark in the world. And he'll do it on his own, not like that smarmy boot-licker Horace Widdicomb."

Vanessa flinched at the mention of Horace. During the two weeks that had passed since their meeting at the shipyard, Vanessa had caught a glimpse of Horace only once. He had come to the Bradford home after dinner and had closeted himself in the library with Abel. Vanessa had kept out of sight until he had taken his leave.

On the evening of the small dinner party, however, Vanessa could not avoid Horace, who was one of the invited guests, for Felicity had said that she must sit beside Aunt Prudence at the table, to create a diversion should the old lady make one of her unfortunate remarks. Felicity was obviously under a strain, and Vanessa wanted to do what she could to make things easier. But she was puzzled, for she remembered how calm Felicity had been on the night of Kitty's ball, a much larger, more elaborate entertainment.

No matter what Felicity's state of mind, her preparations did her credit on this April evening. The long table was bright with candles. The crystal epergne with its hanging baskets held an impressive arrangement of pink and white hothouse roses and maidenhair ferns; the chandeliers overhead had been polished, under Felicity's supervision, so now they glittered like icicles.

Vanessa wore the same lilac silk that she had worn to the birthday ball, and since she received no salary, only room and board, Felicity had given her money for a pair of new shoes, for the old ones were beyond repair. Kitty wore willow-green taffeta trimmed with yards of creamy lace. Like Felicity, she, too, looked drawn and nervous, and she showed little appetite for the elaborate dishes before her.

With Horace seated at the opposite end of the table, Vanessa was uneasy. Horace had given her a long, searching stare as they all took their seats. Since then, he had ignored her.

After dessert, a jellied wine compote laced with Tokay and spiced with cloves and cinnamon, the ladies prepared to depart for the drawing room, leaving the gentlemen to discuss business or politics, but Abel signaled Felicity to remain seated. He ordered the maid to fill everyone's glass, then rose and spoke.

"I have an announcement to make. I propose that we drink to the health of my daughter, Kitty, and the health of her future husband, Horace Widdicomb."

Kitty stifled a cry, pressing her knuckles against her lips, and her face turned a sickly white.

"A toast to the happy couple," Abel went on, raising his glass, and the guests, although somewhat bewildered by the unusual reaction of the bride-to-be, followed suit, sipping Abel's best Madeira.

Vanessa drank mechanically while the guests offered congratulations. Several of the gentlemen called for a speech from Horace, who stood and raised his glass to Kitty.

"I am aware of my great good fortune in winning such a charming bride," Horace said. In spite of his rounded shoulders and sallow complexion, he looked almost imposing in a new suit of fine, pearl-gray broadcloth, with a high, white silk cravat and a black and gray striped waistcoat. "I trust that I may make Miss Bradford as happy as . . . she deserves to be."

Vanessa thought she heard a certain menace in his tone, although his words were quite conventional. No matter how insensitive Horace might be, surely he would have wanted a bride who liked and respected him, even if she could not love him.

Kitty's face was paler than ever, but there were now splotches of red on her cheeks and temples, and she looked about, like a trapped animal seeking escape.

"Papa, I—" But before she could go on, Edith Bradford, Abel's sister-in-law, a stout woman in plum-colored velvet, cut her off, announcing that Kitty was a most fortunate girl, for she would be going to Paris to buy her trousseau.

This caused a stir among the ladies, for although all of them were wealthy, they had always thought that a trousseau made right here in New York was fashionable enough. And a few exchanged glances when Edith explained that she and her husband would accompany Kitty abroad, that they were to leave within the week and return early in September.

This information was plainly a surprise to Kitty, and once more she tried to protest. "Papa, I can't. . . ." she began, but Felicity rose and led the ladies from the dining room to the drawing room across the hall. Kitty glanced at the stairway, as if hoping to run upstairs to her room, but Felicity took her arm and firmly guided her through the sliding doors of the drawing room to a small velvet sofa near the window.

Then Felicity was besieged by questions from the ladies, and she made suitable answers. Yes, the marriage would take place in mid-September, and the young couple would make their home here in this house. And yes, dear Kitty was certainly lucky, traveling to Paris for her trousseau. Kitty and her aunt and uncle would have the finest accommodations on the newest of the Bradford ships. No, Horace would not be joining her in Europe . . . certain pressing business matters . . . perhaps later, a honeymoon . . . Saratoga Springs. . . .

The conversation turned to Parisian fashions. Vanessa,

seated beside Aunt Prudence, remained silent. Abel had planned carefully, Vanessa thought. He was putting the width of an ocean between Kitty and Logan, and when she returned from Paris, the marriage to Horace would take place at once.

"Our voyage should take no more than three weeks," Edith Bradford was saying. "Dear Abel has made every possible arrangement for our comfort."

"What did I tell you?" Aunt Prudence shrilled at Vanessa. "Abel always has his way."

Several ladies turned to stare, but Aunt Prudence went on. "Will you look at poor little Kitty, nearly as green as that dress she's wearing. Looks like she's seasick already."

"Aunt Prudence, please, everyone is—" Vanessa began.

"I don't blame the girl," Aunt Prudence went on. "The thought of marrying that smarmy little clerk is enough to make any female sick, especially when she's had her heart set on a real man like Logan."

Vanessa caught Felicity's desperate look and said, "Wouldn't you like to go upstairs now?"

But Aunt Prudence ignored her and went on. "I knew all along that Abel'd marry Kitty off to that weasel-faced . . ."

The gentlemen, having finished their cigars and conversation, were coming into the drawing room, and Aunt Prudence subsided. Mrs. Grinnell agreed to favor the guests with a few songs, and although her voice was not particularly good, it was loud enough to cover whatever other remarks Aunt Prudence might have made.

Horace sat beside Kitty in the alcove near the window, and once, when Mrs. Grinnell paused between songs, Vanessa noticed that he was saying something to his betrothed, who stared at him in horrified silence. Only once did Vanessa hear Kitty speak, and then it was to cry out. "Oh, no! You can't!

You mustn't—" Then Mrs. Grinnell launched into the opening bars of *The Wounded Hussar*, drowning out whatever Kitty was saying.

After the guests had departed, Vanessa awakened Aunt Prudence, who had fallen into a light doze, and she was about to lead the old lady upstairs when Abel stopped her.

"After you have completed your duties, Miss Kenyon, come into the library." His voice was hard, his eyes icy. "I want a word with you."

When she had settled Aunt Prudence for the night, Vanessa went out into the upstairs hall, her mind churning with uneasiness. Before she could reach the stairway, Kitty slipped out of her own room. "Vanessa, wait. I must speak with you."

"Your father wants to see me in the library."

But Kitty put a hand on Vanessa's arm. "You've got to help me."

"Oh, Kitty, what can I do? I know how you feel about Horace but your father . . ."

"Papa will have me watched until it's time to sail. But you can get this note to Logan before then." She pressed a folded square of paper into Vanessa's hand, along with an embroidered silk reticule. "Here's all my pocket money," she went on. "Take a hansom cab to the shipyard; give my note to Logan."

"Kitty, for heaven's sake, it's nearly midnight. Logan won't be at the shipyard."

For a moment Kitty looked bewildered. Then she said, "Ask the night watchman at the yard where Logan's lodgings are. He's got to be warned."

"Warned about what?"

Kitty's voice shook with anger. "Horace told me . . . down

in the drawing room. He and Papa plan to ruin Logan. To prevent him from getting a cargo and—and cutting off Silas Pringle's credit at Prime, King, and Ward. They're private bankers and . . . Oh, I don't understand anything about business, but Logan will know. He'll have to get the *Athena* finished and under sail before Papa can send me off to Paris. Tell him that, Vanessa." Tears spilled over her cheeks. "I'll die if I have to marry Horace." She turned and fled back to her room, and Vanessa, with an automatic gesture, slipped the note and the reticule into her dress pocket and went down to the library.

Horace was in the library with Abel and Felicity. Abel, his feet set wide apart, stood on one side of the fireplace, and Felicity sat on the other side, her slender body crumpled in a chair, her face chalk-white.

"Miss Kenyon," Abel said without preamble, "I took you into this house against my better judgment, and without references. At that time I knew nothing about you. Now that I have learned what sort of female you are, I want you to pack your belongings and leave. At once."

"Surely you'll give the child a chance to tell us her side of the matter," Felicity protested.

"Those lies about a stolen trunk and lost references!" Abel wheeled on Vanessa. "There never were any references, were there, girl?"

"No, Mr. Bradford. But I didn't think—"

"You didn't think I'd take time to investigate. You were mistaken. I gave the task to Horace. And I've learned all I need to know. You have no place in a respectable home."

"You can't turn her out into the streets," Felicity said.

"There are plenty of grog shops down around South Street," Abel told his wife. "And other establishments. I hope

I need not name them in your presence, ma'am."

Vanessa understood and she flinched at his brutal words, but she fought down her panic. "If you'll let me explain—"

"Explain? You knew that I'd forbidden Kitty to see Captain McClintock. Yet you accompanied her to the waterfront, where she met him secretly. You encouraged her—"

"That's not true," Vanessa interrupted indignantly. "It was Kitty who—"

"Horace saw you waiting for Kitty at Pringle's shipyard." Abel's face was red with anger.

"I didn't know that she planned to go there. I give you my word."

"The word of a trollop."

Felicity cried out in reproach, but Abel would not be silenced.

"A trollop whose mother kept a disreputable house for sailors," he went on.

"Mama never—" Vanessa began.

Felicity, although cowed by her husband, said in a shaky voice, "I'm sure that dear Judith would never have . . . You did not know her, Abel, or you could not imagine that she—"

"Be still, or leave the room," Abel ordered. "You have always been a trusting fool, ma'am. Forever being taken in by any hard-luck story. Horace, you will tell my wife exactly what you learned about this so called boardinghouse in Salem."

Horace gave his future father-in-law an ingratiating smile. "I really don't think that I should speak of such matters before Mrs. Bradford."

"Tell her," Abel said.

"As you wish, sir. On your orders I sought out and questioned a mate from the *Maisie Trowbridge.* A lumber schooner. She made port in Salem regularly and—"

"Get on with it!" Abel said.

"The woman who runs the—the house in question, a Mrs. Deverell, has a bad reputation. She has twice been fined by the local authorities, once when a seaman was robbed by one of her . . . girls . . . and once when a man was stabbed in a brawl."

"That has nothing to do with me—or my mother," Vanessa said, her anger rising. "After Mama died and Mrs. Deverell took over the boardinghouse, I left as quickly as I could." She turned on Horace, her eyes hot with rage. "As for you, you've got your own reasons for trying to destroy my reputation. You'd have been willing enough to forget what you learned about Mrs. Deverell if I'd agreed to—"

"You do admit that what he says about the boardinghouse is true," Abel interrupted. "And you also admit that you lied about having references. You don't deny that you went with Kitty down to Pringle's shipyard so that she could meet Logan McClintock—against my express orders."

"If you'll let me explain—"

"I see no need to go on with this sordid discussion." Abel turned to Felicity. "And you have much to answer for, ma'am. You've given me one living child, a daughter. And you could not even guard her properly. You left her to fall under the influence of this—this dockside drab!"

Vanessa wondered how many times during the course of their marriage Abel had reminded Felicity of her failure to give him sons to carry on his shipping business. She felt a stab of pity for the older woman, who even now was trying to defend her.

"I cannot believe that Vanessa is . . . what you say. There must be some mistake." Felicity fumbled for her handkerchief.

But Abel went on, hard and inexorable. "Whatever mistakes have been made," he told his wife, "you have made them. You encouraged Kitty to put off her marriage to Horace. You allowed her to go chasing after that unprincipled upstart out of the Five Points."

"Logan was one of your best captains," Felicity reminded her husband.

"I raised him to that position of trust. And he repaid me by leaving my service when it suited him. Thinks he'll set himself up in the China trade." Abel gave a harsh bark of laughter. "When I've finished with McClintock, he'll be lucky to get work as a deckhand on a Mississippi pigboat."

Vanessa's thoughts shot back to Kitty's words about Logan. Abel *was* planning to prevent him from starting his own shipping company.

Abel turned back to Vanessa. "McClintock brought you to my home," he said. "Maybe he'll offer you a bed for the night—if you make it worth his while."

Vanessa realized that it would be useless to defend herself any longer against Abel's charges, and she might only make Felicity's position more difficult. Then, stronger than her concern for her own future or her pity for Felicity, came the memory of Logan's face, his eyes shining with the force of his ambition when he had told her about his plans for the *Athena*, the first of the fleet he planned to build. He must not lose the *Athena*. Abel and Horace must not be allowed to break him, not without a fight.

Vanessa's hand slid into her dress pocket and her fingers closed around the reticule. She knew what she had to do.

It was nearly two in the morning when Vanessa, her possessions wrapped in her black shawl, climbed the stairs to Logan's third-floor lodgings in a narrow wooden building on Tompkins Street. She had dismissed Kitty's suggestion that she should take a hansom to the shipyard, for she was painfully aware that the few coins Kitty had given her were all that stood between her and complete destitution.

Instead, she had walked swiftly, doggedly, while her gray woolen dress had grown damp from the chill fog that blanketed the city and her feet started to hurt in their thin-soled shoes. After she had crossed Broadway and plunged into the maze of narrow streets leading to the East River, she had forgotten her physical discomfort, for she was frightened at the realization that a girl out alone at this hour might be picked up by the police, who sometimes rounded up streetwalkers and had them sent to the Tombs.

Worse still, after she had reached the shipyard and had gotten Logan's address from the startled night watchman, she had been forced to dodge the advances of passing sailors. Once, when she was only a few streets away from Logan's lodginghouse, a man, more determined than the others, had reached out for her, muttering drunken obscenities as he tried to drag her into a nearby grog shop. But she had broken away and had darted into the fog, finding refuge in an alley that was foul-smelling and littered with garbage. She had crouched there until she was sure her pursuer had gone.

Now, shaken and tired, she hesitated before Logan's door. No girl with the slightest claim to respectability would visit a man in his lodgings at any hour. Certainly not after midnight.

But she had to warn Logan of Abel's plans, although, like Kitty, she was not sure of exactly how Abel meant to gain his ends. She asked herself why it should matter to her if Abel Bradford ruined Logan's chance to build a fleet of his own.

All these weeks since the ball she had told herself to forget Logan. He had meant it when he had said that he had no need of a penniless bride. She cherished no romantic illusions about him as Kitty did. Logan McClintock was possessed by ambition, hungry for power. His ship and those other ships that would come after were all that mattered to him.

Even now her common sense told her that she should turn from his door, but she could not, for she had been drawn here by forces beyond her control, by a need of her own, only half-recognized, but already as deep and consuming as Logan's passion for a shipping empire.

She knocked and waited until he came to open the door. He was in his shirt-sleeves, his dark hair rumpled, his gray eyes widening in surprise at the sight of her.

"Vanessa!" He drew her inside and closed the door, and she found herself in the larger of two rooms, with an oil lamp burning on the table where charts and blueprints were spread out. Even at this hour Logan had been working. The coal stove in the corner held a battered coffeepot, and the room was filled with the harsh, acrid smell of overbrewed coffee.

"What are you doing here?"

"I came to tell you . . . that is, I thought you should know . . ."

"Sit down." He pulled out a chair close to the stove and she obeyed, grateful for the warmth of the fire.

Logan glanced at the shawl-wrapped bundle that held her clothes, and his lips curved in a smile. "Have you decided to accept my offer? Are you going to sail with me on the *Athena*?"

"No, I'm not. I came to tell you that your precious *Athena* may not sail at all if Abel has his way."

"What's Abel got to do with it?"

"He means to stop you, Logan. To ruin you, if he can."

"Tell me." His hand closed on her shoulder.

"Abel and Horace were talking tonight at the Bradford house. Abel said that when he was finished with you, you'd be lucky to get a berth on a—a Mississippi pigboat."

Logan's fingers tightened in a punishing grip.

"Go on."

"Abel's going to keep you from getting cargo. And he's going to use his influence to keep Silas Pringle from getting an extension of credit from Prime, King, and Ward." She winced under the pressure of his hand. "Turn me loose," she said. "You're hurting me."

His grip slackened. He was looking past her, his gray eyes bleak. "I've got to get a cargo. I can't afford to make the voyage out to China under ballast and pay for the tea crop in cash, like Bradford. I plan to sail west, around Cape Horn, instead of east, around Africa, with the other ships in the tea fleet. I'll deliver a cargo at Valparaiso, in Chile, and then I'll head out across the Pacific and anchor in the harbor at Hong Kong in time to get the best of the new tea crop, early in January." His face darkened. "That was my plan, at any rate. I've got to have a cargo, though. Tobacco, New England rum—"

"But Abel Bradford can't stop you from buying a cargo."

"Don't be so sure, Vanessa. He and that tight little circle of ship owners—they control the trade here in New York. If Abel uses his influence, he'll get them to close ranks, all of them. The Lows, the Grinnells . . . And as for Prime, King, and Ward, that bank holds the mortgage on Pringle's shipyard. Silas Pringle's got to have an extension, and soon, because we need more time to finish the *Athena.*"

"I didn't realize," Vanessa said. "But Abel is furious with you—I know that much—and when I heard him talk of ruining you, I had to come, because I know how much the ship means to you, and I . . ."

She broke off under Logan's probing gaze. "How did you find me?" he asked.

"The night watchman at the shipyard told me where you live."

"And you drove here at this time of night?"

"I walked."

"Good God, Vanessa! Have you any idea of the risk you took? Have you no common sense at all?"

Vanessa shuddered, remembering the flushed faces, the outstretched hands of the sailors, the stench of rotting garbage in the alley where she had hidden from her pursuer.

"Why did you come to warn me?" Logan asked more quietly.

She looked away.

"Answer me, Vanessa."

Her pride would not allow her to speak the truth. Instead, she took Kitty's letter from the reticule and handed it to him. "Abel announced Kitty's engagement to Horace tonight at dinner," she said.

Logan scanned the letter quickly. "The empty-headed little fool." He tossed the paper into the coal stove. "I never gave her cause to think I wanted to marry her."

"She thought that you were afraid to tell her you loved her because you felt you weren't good enough."

"Did she indeed?" Logan shook his head. "She has a remarkable gift for self-deception. If I wanted to marry her . . ." He broke off. "Horace found out about her visits to the shipyard, didn't he?" Vanessa nodded and he went on. "I'm beginning to understand. Horace told Abel that I was after Kitty. That's why Abel's out to ruin me."

"That's only part of it," Vanessa said. "Abel resents your leaving his service."

"Maybe, but he has other captains, good ones. I doubt he'd set out to break me simply because I'd walked out on his company. But his daughter—that's a different matter." He spoke with cold anger now. "You can go back and tell that silly, vaporing female that for all I care, she can marry Horace tomorrow. I won't lift a finger to stop the wedding."

"I can't go back and tell her anything," Vanessa said. "I've been dismissed. I'm no longer working at the Bradford house."

"But why?"

"Abel believes that I helped to arrange those meetings between you and Kitty at the shipyard. Horace has convinced him that I'm a common trollop. That Mama's boardinghouse was no more than a—a brothel." She began to tremble with the memory of the humiliation she had suffered in the Bradfords' library only a few hours ago.

"Tell me what happened," Logan said quietly.

Vanessa obeyed, beginning with her meeting with Horace outside the shipyard, but when she came to the part about Horace's advances and her refusal, she looked away, her eyes fixed on the iron coal stove. "Horace hates me because I refused him. Tonight he struck back at me."

"I see. And what will you do now?"

"I don't know."

"Do you have any money?"

She opened the reticule and poured the coins into her other hand.

"That won't even get you a night's lodging in this place. It will buy a week in one of those dens in the Five Points and enough food to keep you from starving, no more."

Fighting off her weariness, Vanessa stood up, and, putting the coins back into the reticule, she lifted her bundle.

"Where are you going?"

"You said . . . the Five Points."

She started for the door, but Logan blocked her way.

"I'll have to go there and—" she began.

"The hell you will," he told her. "You're sleeping here tonight."

She looked up at him, at his tall, wide-shouldered body, the heavily muscled chest and powerful arms. For the first time since she had entered his rooms she felt a stirring of fear. He did not love her, but he had told her on the night of the ball that he desired her.

"Logan, I've done what I could to help you. Now please let me leave."

He shook his head. "Not a chance," he said.

Chapter 6

Vanessa tried to move past Logan, to get to the door, but he caught her arm and held her.

"You can't force me to stay."

"Try me," he said. He pushed her against the wall, then put an arm on either side of her. She lunged forward, only to feel herself completely immobilized by his body. Now she was aware of his long, hard thighs pressing against her, his chest crushing her breasts, and, for a moment, her thoughts began to whirl confusedly. She knew that she had not only Logan to fear, but herself, for his closeness stirred those same feelings she had experienced when he had danced with her at the ball.

Fighting for control, she said, "Logan, I came here only to help you. To warn you about Abel's scheme to stop you from completing the *Athena.* Now that I have, you must let me go."

His gray eyes held her so that she could not look away. "You came to warn me. Was that your only reason?" When she did not answer he persisted. "Why is it so important to you that I finish the ship?"

"Because it—it isn't fair that a man with Abel's influence and power should keep other men from making their way in the world. From succeeding as he has. I'd have tried to help anyone in your position who stood to lose everything."

"A generous impulse," Logan said with a smile. "I can be no less generous. Vanessa, my bed is yours."

He lifted her into his arms, and while she still clutched at her bundle with one hand and tried to fight him off with the other, he carried her into the bedroom and dropped her onto the bed. She landed on her back, her petticoats billowing around her. Her heart began to hammer against her ribs, and she found it hard to take a deep breath. Her bonnet fell from her head, so now only the ribbons held it around her neck.

He gestured toward her bundle. "You have a nightgown in there?"

When she did not answer he reached for the bundle. She made a grab for it, but he was too fast for her. He undid the knot and went through her belongings. "Here we are," he said, picking up her nightgown, a prim garment with a high neck and long sleeves. She had made it during her stay at Hudson Square.

He grinned with amusement. "This looks like something Prudence Campbell might wear," he said.

"Give me that! You have no right to—"

"Are you going to put it on?"

"I'll do no such thing. I'm going to the Five Points and seek lodgings."

"No, you're not. You're going to get ready for bed right now. Or must I help you?"

He leaned over and his hand reached for the top button of her snugly fitted bodice, his fingers brushing the swell of her breasts. She could let him take his pleasure with her, she thought, but it would mean no more to him than tumbling a slut on a bed in some sportinghouse on the waterfront. She felt a surge of warm desire welling up inside her, but warring against that feeling was her inbred pride. She looked up into his face, her gaze lingering on his high, jutting cheekbones, the strong line of his jaw, his wide, sensual mouth. Her pride won out.

She got to her feet, and her fingers shook as she straightened her bonnet, tucking the loose strands of hair underneath the brim. Logan pulled her hands away.

"You're not going to the Five Points. It's a foul hole not fit for any decent human being to spend even a single night in."

"You came from there," she challenged him.

"I was a child when my mother brought me to that cellar in the Old Brewery."

When Felicity had spoken to Vanessa about the Five Points, she had never mentioned any details. Indeed, Felicity had never set foot in the area herself but, like the other ladies, had only collected and sorted used clothing for others to distribute there.

"The Old Brewery?" Vanessa repeated.

"It really was a brewery, until it became too dilapidated for that. Then it became a lodginghouse for over a thousand people. The cellars are rented out by the night. A few pennies buy a mattress, crammed in among dozens of others, with only a few inches of space between. Those mattresses are crawling with vermin. And always damp. The cellars get the run-off from the sewers and the privies of Paradise Square."

Vanessa gagged at his words. "Don't, I don't want to hear about—"

"You should, though, if you plan to move in there," he said. "The police are afraid to go into the Old Brewery or even into the alleys around it. That's why the place has become a refuge for murderers and thieves. And a place of business for streetwalkers who bring their customers there—only the most miserable females—those who've become too old or too badly diseased to find a more particular sort of man."

Vanessa stared at him. "And yet your parents lived there," she began.

"My father had died the year before. My mother was a gentle, helpless creature without friends or family. She . . ." He turned his back on Vanessa, and she felt a stab of pity for

Logan. What must his life have been like during those early years?

"My mother died of typhoid soon after we moved to the Five Points," he said, his voice expressionless now.

"How old were you when she—"

"I was nine."

"But who took care of you after she died?"

"I took care of myself. Like hundreds of other children down there. Some of us managed to survive."

Vanessa remembered her own childhood. She and her mother had not had an easy time of it, but they had been together. Mama had loved her and cared for her, had taught her to be respectable and proud.

"The younger girls in the Five Points pick rags, or whatever else they can sell," Logan said. He turned back to face Vanessa. "When they're a little older they sell themselves."

And what of the boys, Vanessa wondered, but she did not want to hear anything more, for she was too badly shaken, too disgusted by what he had already told her. Dear God, how could she go to the Five Points?

She sank down on the edge of the bed, her hands lying in her lap. She made no move to fix her bonnet or to pack up her belongings. Instead, she let her head droop forward, her eyes fixed on her hands.

"I have work to do," Logan told her. "Schedules to change. If I can get Silas Pringle to drive his men hard enough, we may have a chance to finish the *Athena* before Abel can stop us."

He turned and walked into the other room and sat down at the table. Vanessa waited until he had begun working over the papers spread out before him; then she got up, closed the door that separated the two rooms, and got undressed. She pulled the nightgown over her head, then buttoned it carefully, even while she mocked herself for doing so.

She turned down the oil lamp and climbed into the wide bed. At least it was clean and dry, she thought, remembering what Logan had told her about the lodgings at the Old Brewery, and with the coarse woolen blanket and the thick comforter over her, she was warm enough. The warmth made her taut muscles relax, and her lids began to grow heavy. Fragmented memories went through her mind. Abel's face flushed with anger. Kitty's unhappy eyes.

I didn't have a chance to say good-bye to Aunt Prudence, Vanessa thought. She was kind to me, and I had to leave without a word. . . . I hope she won't be too upset when she wakes and finds me gone. . . .

Then Vanessa forgot all about Aunt Prudence, for she heard the door that separated the two rooms creak open. Logan stood for a moment on the threshold of the small bedroom; he was striding toward her. Her body tensed, and her jaw muscles tightened as she tried to still the shiver that swept through her. In the weeks after Mrs. Deverell had taken over the boardinghouse, Vanessa had tried to avoid the flamboyant woman and her "girls," but she had overheard enough to have some notion of what might await her. What would it be like with Logan? Would he hurt her? What would he expect of her?

She crouched under the coverings, and now he was standing over the bed, his features shadowed by the dim light. He reached out and with one quick movement he pulled away the thick comforter. She clutched at the coarse woolen blanket with icy fingers. In spite of herself she gave a cry of protest. "Logan, no . . . please wait. . . ."

Then, to her surprise, she heard him laugh softly. As she watched he rolled up the comforter under his arm and started back toward the outer room. "I'll leave the door open," he said, pausing for a moment. "That way you'll have some of the heat from the stove."

Still holding the blanket around her, she watched in stunned silence as he threw the comforter down in front of the stove. Then he turned off the oil lamp on his desk, and in the faint, reddish glow of the fire she saw him lie down and wrap the comforter around his body.

Her lips parted in surprise. A man like Logan, raised in the Five Points. How could she have guessed that he would not be at least as demanding as Horace had been? She realized that there were many things she did not know about Logan McClintock.

During the next couple of weeks he kept to the same arrangement as the first night. She wondered whether he was perhaps too driven by his desperate attempts to complete his ship to have time to think of anything else. Certainly he rose early, and he was often gone before she woke up. Sometimes he stayed away from the lodginghouse until late at night.

She did what she could during this time to find work, but her searches were fruitless. There were, she discovered, few respectable positions for young girls without references here in New York, and she refused to seek employment in a waterfront grog shop or in a concert saloon where she would be expected to go upstairs with the customers. One evening she returned to the lodgings she shared with Logan to tell him that she had been offered work as a chambermaid at the Pearsall and Fox Hotel in Dover Street off Water. "I told the landlady I'd had experience running the boardinghouse back in Salem and she said she might give me a try."

To her surprise and annoyance Logan threw back his head and laughed.

"I don't relish the idea of scrubbing floors," she began, "but if I must—"

"Vanessa, that Pearsall and Fox dive has a dance hall in the basement and a brothel on the second and third floors. The upper floors are rented out for assignations."

"But it was quiet enough this morning."

"The girls were probably resting up for the evening." His eyes moved over her. "With your looks, you would surely be in demand there—but not as a chambermaid."

By the end of the third week with Logan, she had still found no work. Because she knew that he was short of money, she had taken over the cooking, and she shopped for inexpensive food in the outdoor stalls on Front Street. Her experience in marketing for her mother had given her a sharp eye for a bargain. She mended Logan's clothes and scrubbed them, too, in a huge iron pot, heating the water on the stove. It was all she could do in return for the shelter he had provided.

On a rain-swept night late in April he failed to come home for dinner, and as the hours dragged by she felt a growing uneasiness. He had been late before, but he had never stayed out past midnight. Tonight, however, she had heard a nearby clock strike twelve, and still he had not come.

Logan could take care of himself, but the New York waterfront was a rough place, and a first mate short of a crew would go out with a couple of seamen armed with clubs or lead pipes to shanghai any able-bodied man in sight. The thought of Logan, battered and unconscious, lying in the hold of a ship bound for the African slave coast, or perhaps around Cape Horn to the barren sealing islands, filled Vanessa with fear.

She picked up one of Logan's shirts and tried to keep occupied in the tedious work of turning the frayed collar. The rain was coming down harder now, and the wind from the river rattled the windowpanes.

When at last she heard Logan's now-familiar step on the stairs, she felt a surge of relief so overpowering that she let the shirt drop from her fingers, and once again she was forced to admit to herself how much this man meant to her. Foolish, she told herself. Stupid and senseless to care so much for a man who did not return her feelings.

She folded the shirt, then hastened to get down a tin mug from the shelf. He would be soaked to the skin on such a night, and a cup of hot coffee would revive him.

But when he opened the door and she saw his face, she stopped halfway to the stove, the cup in her hand.

"Logan, what's happened?"

He did not answer. He walked past her as if he had never seen her before and went into the bedroom. He sat down on the edge of the bed. Quickly she poured the coffee and added a generous shot of rum, then brought the drink in to him. His dark blue coat was soaked through; his hair was plastered against his forehead. His face was drawn, the tanned skin stretched tightly across the jutting cheekbones.

"Drink this," she said, handing him the cup. "Then get out of those clothes." When he made no move she closed his hands around the cup. He lifted it and drained it.

Timidly she touched his shoulder. "Logan, you're ill."

He shook his head.

"Then what—"

"I've lost the *Athena.* Pringle was forced to sell his shares, and I sold mine too."

"You sold your ship?"

"I had no choice. Horace made the terms—with Abel's backing. The bank wouldn't extend the loan on the mortgage for the shipyard. Silas doesn't own the yard anymore. Horace has that, too. He has everything." The anger in his face frightened her.

"It's so unfair," she said. "Abel Bradford doesn't need the *Athena*."

"Don't you think I know that? You were right, Vanessa. He's out to break me any way he can."

"But couldn't you have refused to sell him your shares?"

"I don't have the money to finish the ship, and Abel knows that." His jaw hardened. "Horace enjoyed running Abel's errand this time. You should have seen him strutting around the yard. I wanted to break his neck and set fire to the *Athena* to keep her out of Abel's hands."

"Why didn't you?"

"Because I'm not the only one involved. Horace said that if I sold my shares to Abel, along with the shipyard, Silas would be able to stay on in full charge there."

Logan pulled off his sodden coat and gold-braided cap and tossed them down, but Vanessa hung them carefully on the pegs next to the bed. She would not have thought that Logan was a man who would consider another man's problems when faced with personal disaster.

"Pringle is a good friend," Logan said. "He helped me once when I needed help. At least he won't have to start over, looking for work as a mallet man. I owe him that much." Logan bent and tugged at his rain-soaked boots and dropped them beside the bed. "I wanted the *Athena*."

He spoke with a quiet intensity that sent a shiver through her body. "I wanted to be her master and to stand on her deck when she sailed into the harbor at Wampoa."

"Logan, I know what the ship meant to you, and I'm so sorry."

He looked at her, his gray eyes burning. "Don't waste your pity on me. I don't need it."

"But with the *Athena* gone, what can you do?"

"I'll get another ship and I'll have my fleet one day, no matter what I have to do to get it."

His confidence, his calm certainty, was communicated to her, so in spite of the odds she believed him.

"You will," she said. "I know you will. Why, a man like you who has already come so far, done so much—you'll find a way."

For the first time since he had come home to her she sensed that he was really seeing her, and there was a look of discovery in his eyes. "Come here," he said, and when she obeyed he caught her in his arms and held her so tightly that it was hard for her to breathe. She felt the warmth of him and smelled his rain-wet skin.

She reached out and clung to him, her hands moving over the hard muscles of his back, her body bending backward in his embrace as he buried his face in the red-gold masses of her hair. She felt the hunger, the driving need in him, and the answering desire in her own body. Although she knew nothing of lovemaking, she sensed that she had the power to give him what he needed. This man, hard and ruthless in so many ways, driven by ambition, had possessed her thoughts since their first meeting.

She feared what was to come, and she told herself that it was wrong to give herself to a man like Logan, that she risked everything. He made her no promises, said nothing about their future. "I want you, Vanessa," she heard him say, his voice muffled against her hair.

Then he drew her down onto the bed, and his fingers moved quickly, unbuttoning her bodice, sliding under the thin camisole, to cup her breast. She drew her breath in sharply as she felt the nipple rise and harden under his touch, felt the hot tremors that spread outward, downward, until every nerve of her body was stirred to a vibrant response she had never known before. She gave a soft, wordless cry.

He took his fingers away and she tried to withdraw, but a moment later his mouth claimed her breast, his tongue flicking at the sensitive flesh. He drew away and she struggled to control the treacherous current that was sweeping her toward an unknown place. "Logan, I don't know. I've never—"

"You know what you want . . . and so do I."

He was stripping away her dress, her underclothes. She wanted to cry out, to protest against the calm certainty, the arrogance with which he had spoken, but she could not deny his words. He undressed himself quickly and then she felt his skin, warm and damp, against hers. "Don't be frightened," he said softly. "I won't force you."

She drew reassurance from his words and from the understanding she heard in his voice. His hands were gentle, caressing, as they moved over her shoulders, her breasts, and downward. He parted her thighs, and she cried out in protest at the shocking intimacy of his exploring fingers. But even at that moment her arms went around him, held him, as if she sensed with a part of herself too primitive for reason that her fear, her shame, did not matter. That only he could lead her, guide her, teach her what she must know.

Now he took her hand. "Touch me," he said. "There's nothing to be afraid of."

"I don't know how. . . ."

He laughed softly. "Like this," he said, guiding her fingers over his hard chest, the lean, muscled abdomen, and then . . .

Now it was Logan who responded, making a sound in his throat of half-pleasure, half-pain as her fingers curved around his hardness. "Vanessa . . ." His breathing had quickened, and she saw his eyes, dark in the glow from the oil lamp.

"Logan, not yet . . . I . . ."

But he was kneeling between her thighs, his hands closing on her wrists, holding them down at her sides. She feared what was to come, but she knew that there was no turning back, not now.

At the first thrust she cried out against the sharp, searing pain. He did not move, but gave her time to accept their joining. She heard his voice, low and deep, the whispered endearments. "Vanessa, my love."

His voice, calming her, reassuring her. Then he was moving within her, slowly at first, pausing to kiss her lips, her throat, her breasts. The pain was receding now, lost in a new sensation, and she realized that she, too, had begun to move, driven by the compelling need that stirred into life, a need that he could satisfy. Her legs closed around him, drawing him deeper. Her body arched upward, demanding release in a language older than time. He answered her with quickening thrusts, and the pulsing in her loins spread to every nerve, every fiber of her body. Her hands clung to him, her fingers pressing into his back. "Now, love," she heard him say. And then came the shattering soaring moment that went on and on. . . .

He fell asleep afterward, his face resting against her breast, his arms still holding her close. She lay awake for a few moments, savoring the sensation of fulfillment, of utter contentment. Tenderly she stroked his face. He stirred and drew her closer, and his hand moved, tangled itself in the waves of her red-gold hair. Then he lay still again, and she felt the slow, even rhythm of his breathing. She smiled and closed her eyes. Tomorrow there would be time enough to speak of the future. Their future, together.

The rain had stopped at dawn and now the pale spring

sunlight came slanting through the single bedroom window. Vanessa sat up in bed, the blanket around her, and tried to make sense of Logan's words. He spoke crisply as he moved about the small room.

"I'll have to get work as a stevedore for the time being," he said, his face set. "It doesn't pay much, but it will have to do until I find a berth on a ship. I'll have to sail as mate, or even as ordinary seaman. I won't get another master's place for a long time. Abel will see to that."

"Logan, I . . ." Vanessa's voice was unsteady. Surely after what had happened between them last night, Logan would speak of his love for her. He would ask her to marry him. "How can you—"

"I'll probably have to ship out on a whaler—they're always short of seamen." He reached for his coat, still damp from last night's rain. "I hope I won't have to settle for a slaver," he went on. "Slaving's a dirty business."

How could he dismiss what they had shared only a few hours before as if it were a casual matter?

No more than tumbling a slut on a bed in some sportinghouse. That was what she had thought that first night she had come here. She had feared that if she gave herself to him, he would think her no different from all the other girls he must have had.

Oh, but it hadn't been like that last night. Logan had been loving, considerate of her fears, patient with her inexperience. Now she longed to plead with him for reassurance. If only he would say he loved her and wanted to marry her. To marry a seaman was, she knew, to accept a life of loneliness, of long separations; to live as her mother had, with the constant fear that his ship might go down, that he might be washed overboard in a storm or fall from an ice-sheathed mast and be smashed on the deck below. She knew what it meant to be a seaman's wife.

But Logan was not asking her to be his wife. He had not even kissed her this morning or said that he loved her. She longed to go to him now, to embrace him, to speak of marriage, but her pride would not permit it.

Instead, she spoke evenly, her voice controlled. "You must not sail on a slaver if you can help it. It is a wicked trade."

"It pays well enough for the owners," he said dryly. "All the same, I'll try for a whaler first. But I'll do whatever I must to work my way up to a captaincy again. And when I have a ship of my own, no one—not Abel Bradford or the devil himself—will take her from me."

His own ship. She stifled a cry of protest. Any ship, however beautiful, was only a thing of wood and canvas. She wanted to cry, but she held back her tears. Nothing had changed for him. How could she have been foolish enough to think that an hour or two of passion had made him love her? He had needed her to blot out the pain of his defeat, the memory of his loss. She wanted to lash out at him for having used her, but she could not, for now, remembering the way it had happened between them, her own honesty made her admit that he had not forced her. She had given herself willingly.

"You must have breakfast," she said, getting out of bed and starting to dress. "I'll make a pot of coffee, and there's a little bread and cheese left."

He shook his head. "I want to get down to the docks as soon as I can," he told her. "There are plenty of men fighting for a day's work, loading cargo."

He looked at her, and she thought that she saw a brief flicker of tenderness in his eyes, but she would not let herself respond. "I'll be home for dinner though," he said. He reached into his pocket and handed her a few coins. "Here," he said. "Not much, but you'll have to do the best you can."

Her first impulse was to push the money back at him, to rail at him for his calm certainty that she would be waiting when he came back, eager to cook for him, to wash his clothes, and share his bed. But how could she, when she knew that she would not leave him?

He came to her and kissed her, his mouth claiming hers. She would stay, she told herself, but she would not deceive herself with senseless hopes about their future together. So long as she could be with him until he sailed . . .

Chapter 7

The brilliant September sunlight was deceptive, Felicity Bradford thought, for it was accompanied by a gusty wind blowing in from the river. She leaned back against the soft black leather upholstery of the seat in the landau and drew her cloak, with its rich trimming of beaver, more closely about her. The wind held a foretaste of winter, which would be a cruel time, as always, for the wives and children of the seamen served by her charity organization. She would speak to the other ladies about increasing their offerings, she told herself.

Then her thoughts moved to more personal concerns, and she stared, unseeing, at the broad back of Liam O'Connell, the coachman, while she fretted about Kitty, now off on her honeymoon with Horace. Ever since that dreadful week last April when Kitty had been told that she must marry Horace, the girl had been miserable. For the first few days after the dinner at which Abel had announced the engagement Kitty's mood had fluctuated from moment to moment, so that sometimes she lapsed into desolate silence, while at other times she appeared possessed by a kind of strange excitement. Then, as the time came to board the ship for Europe, Kitty was overcome by a depression so deep that Felicity feared for her. She scarcely ate, and her eyes were always red and swollen.

All during the transatlantic crossing, and then, through the weeks in Paris, Kitty had not shown the slightest interest in her elegant and expensive trousseau: the ball gowns, the traveling costumes, the delicate, handmade silk and lace underwear, the cape and muff of Russian sable. Even the wedding gown, a marvelous creation of creamy white satin and Brussels lace, had left her indifferent. The French dressmaker who had presided over the fittings had been puzzled and offended by Kitty's lack of enthusiasm. Aunt Edith Bradford had remarked several times on Kitty's ingratitude.

"A trousseau fit for Queen Victoria herself—and that spoiled girl might as well be going to the altar in a calico smock."

Felicity had not replied, but she had understood Kitty's attitude well enough, even though she had been powerless to comfort her daughter. Abel had decreed that Kitty must marry Horace, and Abel's word was law.

Now, as the landau turned into Front Street, which was lined with outdoor marketstalls and crowded with women haggling over fish, potatoes, candles, and cheap yardgoods, Felicity tried to comfort herself. Kitty would have to learn to accept her marriage, and if she could never love Horace, she could give all her love to her children. Men, Felicity knew, took some inexplicable pleasure in the act of begetting children, but for a woman, married happiness lay in rearing her family.

Her own marriage had been arranged by her parents, and she had fulfilled her marital obligations to Abel in a dutiful way and had prayed for sons. Even how she felt pain, remembering the two little boys who had died within a few weeks after they had been born.

Abel's bitter disappointment had scarcely been eased when Felicity had presented him with Kitty, although the infant was sturdy and beautiful, and he had been shocked, then furious when the doctor had insisted that Felicity must have no more children, for each of her labors had been agonizing and dangerous, and Kitty's birth had nearly cost Felicity her life.

Although Abel had accepted the doctor's verdict, he had made no secret of his disappointment, and Felicity had lived all these years with the knowledge that she had failed him.

Now, as the landau made its way down Front Street, Felicity glanced at her list: two more charity calls to be made, two more seamen's wives to be given assistance. Had it not been for her charity work, she would have been miserable indeed, but she had managed to find an outlet, helping women less fortunate than she in a material way.

She thought wistfully of the woman she had visited only an hour ago, the wife of a mate on a coastwise schooner, mother of three strong sons, and pregnant again. Felicity told herself that she must not question the will of Providence, but if only she could have given Abel even one healthy boy . . .

Then she forgot her sadness. Her eyes widened and she called out, "Stop here, Liam!" The huge, burly Irishman pulled the horses to a halt, and Felicity peered over the side of the landau. That girl leaving one of the market stalls, her bright hair gleaming red-gold from under her bonnet. The delicate features, the erect carriage.

"Vanessa, over here," Felicity called.

"I don't have far to go," Vanessa said. "I live on Tompkins Street."

"No matter," Felicity said firmly, tucking the thick, soft carriage robe around Vanessa. "It's chilly, and you've so much to carry," she said. She helped Vanessa to arrange her parcels, then ordered Liam to drive to Tompkins Street. "Besides," she went on, "I do want to know everything that has happened since you . . . since we . . ."

Felicity broke off, and Vanessa, sensing the older woman's embarrassment at the memory of that last meeting in the library of the house on Hudson Square, spoke quickly.

"How is Aunt Prudence?" she asked. "Is she well?"

Felicity sighed and shook her head. "I wish she were better, my dear. It rained on the day of the wedding, and she took a chill."

"I am sorry," Vanessa said, remembering Aunt Prudence with affection. Then as the full impact of Felicity's words came through, she said, "The wedding? Kitty and Horace?"

"They were married last week at Trinity Church. Kitty looked beautiful. She and Horace are away on their honeymoon now, in Saratoga Springs."

"I hope she'll be . . ." But Vanessa lapsed into silence, for she could not bring herself to make even a pretense of believing that Kitty would be happy as the wife of Horace Widdicomb.

Now it was Felicity who turned the direction of the conversation. "I've thought of you so often, my dear, while I was away in Paris with Kitty. Have you found employment?"

Vanessa shook her head. "It was not possible to find respectable work without references."

"But how have you lived all these months?" Felicity's cheeks went pink. "Oh, my poor child. Have you been forced to—to . . ."

Vanessa looked away and felt a sense of relief as they reached the lodginghouse. "I live here," she told Felicity. "Thank you for the ride. Please give Aunt Prudence my love."

Without waiting for the coachman to spring down from his high seat, Vanessa gathered up her parcels and got out. But Felicity obviously had no intention of allowing her to escape so easily. "I can't leave you like this," she said. "O'Connell, you will wait for us here."

Vanessa hurried on ahead, but in a moment Felicity was beside her. "I live on the third floor. It is a steep climb."

"No matter," Felicity said firmly.

Vanessa hurried up the stairs, Felicity close behind her. What on earth was she to tell Felicity? she wondered, wishing that she had not met the older woman. Her breath came in uneven little gasps, and at the third landing she saw tiny black spots begin to dance before her eyes. She clutched at the railing, her hands icy. Then Felicity's arm was around her, supporting her. "Give me your key."

Dizzy, and a little nauseated, Vanessa obeyed, too shaken to resist. Felicity led her inside, took her parcels, and helped her to a chair. But as Vanessa sat down, her shawl slipped from her shoulders, and she saw the look Felicity was giving her, saw how the woman's brown eyes moved over her body. But surely it was still too soon for even a woman of Felicity's experience and maturity to guess . . .

"Oh, Vanessa! Are you—have you . . ." And when Vanessa nodded, she went on. "I should have stood firm that night. I should not have allowed Abel to have his way for once. I knew that he was wrong about you then, but now—now you have become what he thought you'd been all along."

"No, I haven't," Vanessa said firmly. "I'm not a streetwalker. I give you my word I'm not."

"But then, who—"

"Logan McClintock," Vanessa said, surprised by the control in her voice. She was not ashamed of having given herself to Logan. "These are his lodgings," she went on. "I have lived with him since that night I left your home."

"You are carrying Logan's child?"

"Yes, and he's been the only one."

Felicity studied Vanessa's face. "You're in love with him, aren't you?" she asked.

"Yes," Vanessa said quietly.

Felicity looked somewhat relieved. "And he loves you?

You are to be married?"

Now Vanessa looked away, unable to answer.

"You've told him about the baby."

"No! And he mustn't be told!"

"But I don't understand. Surely he has the right to know." Then she added with brisk practicality, "He'll know soon enough, in any case."

"Maybe not," Vanessa said. "He's leaving soon. He has found a berth on a whaling ship as first mate."

"But that means he'll be gone for two years, perhaps longer," Felicity protested. "What will become of you and the child?"

This question had tormented Vanessa more and more during the past month as she had lain awake beside Logan, staring into the darkness. "I'll manage somehow," she said. "Maybe if you'd be willing to give me a reference now, I could find some sort of work. As a kitchen maid or—"

"And how long would that last? Perhaps you'll be able to hide your secret from Logan until he sails, but how long will it be before an employer finds out? No woman will keep you on in such a condition. And certainly none will want a housemaid who is encumbered with a baby."

"But there must be a way," Vanessa persisted.

"Oh, yes, there are ways." There was a hard edge to Felicity's voice as she went on. "A baby farm—that's what they call such places. I've heard what goes on there. Infants abused and neglected, drugged with laudanum to keep them quiet. So many die in their first year. Is that what you want for your baby? Surely you must see that—"

Neither of them had heard the footsteps on the stairs, and both started when the door swung open and Logan came in. Vanessa clutched briefly at Felicity's hand and whispered "Please, you must not—"

But there was no time for any more as Logan spoke.

"Mrs. Bradford, I hadn't expected to find you here."

Whatever his feelings toward Abel, he spoke to Felicity with quiet courtesy.

"I met Vanessa on Front Street quite by chance," Felicity told him. "And a most fortunate chance, under the circumstances."

Logan looked puzzled, and Vanessa tried to signal Felicity with her eyes, to warn her, plead with her to say nothing about the baby.

Never once had he told her that he loved her, that he wanted to marry her. He wanted only his freedom, the chance to work his way up to a captaincy again, and go on to get his own ship. And Vanessa loved him too much to use her pregnancy to force him into marriage—if indeed Logan could be forced to do anything against his will. With painful honesty Vanessa had reminded herself over and over that Logan had not seduced her, that she had slept with him willingly.

"I saw the landau down in the street," Logan said. "No doubt you were bound on charitable errands in this part of the city when you met Vanessa."

"Why yes," Felicity said, and Vanessa wondered if the older woman was aware of the faintly sardonic note in Logan's voice. "The Ladies' Society for the Relief of the Wives of Seamen—so many sailors are unemployed, while others have not returned when expected, and their wives and children are suffering great hardships."

"But they are all decent and respectable, no doubt," Logan said, and Vanessa saw something in his eyes that she did not understand. "The deserving poor."

"Why yes, certainly—"

"I'm sure Mrs. Bradford has more errands to do," Vanessa said, seeing an opportunity for cutting short the conversation. "We must not detain her."

Felicity had to be gotten out of there before she told Logan what she had discovered. But Felicity, usually gentle and pliable, now showed unexpected determination.

"Those stairs are so steep," she said. "I was hoping—perhaps a cup of tea?"

"I—I'll put the kettle on," Vanessa said.

"We can't offer you the best Souchong, I'm afraid," Logan said. "The kind carried on your husband's ships."

"I'm sorry for what happened—your losing the *Athena.*"

Felicity spoke with sincerity, not flinching under Logan's steady look, and at last it was he who gave way. "You were not to blame for that, ma'am," he said. "And at least I am in a rather better situation than Abel predicted. I've not been forced to become a deckhand on a Mississippi pigboat."

"But you are going to sail off soon," Felicity said.

Logan turned a hard look on Vanessa. "I—I told her. I did not think it would matter. . . ." Vanessa confessed. In her agitation over Felicity's discovery of her pregnancy, Vanessa had not considered the possible need for secrecy about Logan's new berth.

"You need not worry about that," Felicity told Logan. "I doubt Abel would interfere, and in any case, I will not tell him. But before you sail—"

"The water's boiling," Vanessa said in desperation. "There's no milk, but we do have a little sugar if you—"

"I'll take it plain," Felicity said. But when she held the steaming mug she went on as if she had not been interrupted. "Before you sail there are certain arrangements you must make, Logan."

"Oh, please, you must not—" Vanessa interrupted, but Felicity was not deterred. She took a sip of tea and set down her cup, and although her cheeks were scarlet with embarrassment, her dark brown eyes did not waver.

"You must marry Vanessa. She will need the protection of marriage. You must make the proper arrangements at once."

Logan looked startled, and then annoyed. "That's a matter for the two of us to decide, and with all due respect, ma'am—"

"She will need your name," Felicity said with uncharacteristic directness. "And so will your child."

He drew a deep breath, and for a moment Vanessa thought he would speak, but instead, he gave her a long, searching look in which she saw nothing of tenderness or pleasure. She had been right, then. He did not want the responsibility of a wife and a child.

"I will make all the arrangements," Felicity said, and although her embarrassment was plain, her sense of duty was obviously stronger. "A simple ceremony, and a marriage certificate so that she will be able to collect your allotment. It won't be much, but even so . . ."

"I'd have given her the allotment in any case," Logan told Felicity, "but as for marriage—"

"As your wife, she and the child will be eligible for help from the organizations I work with. In case you should not return—a whaling voyage is dangerous, as I hardly have to tell you—I and several other ladies are working to establish a shelter for the wives and children of seamen who—"

"A charity shelter." Never had Vanessa seen such anger in Logan's face, not even on the night when he had come home to tell her that he had lost the *Athena*.

"No doubt you limit your charity to what you call the 'deserving poor,' respectable married women who come with a wedding license to show you."

"I do not make the rules." Felicity was frightened by Logan's cold anger, but she stood up to him. "I have never believed that a young girl should be denied help because she has made a mistake. But many of the other ladies—"

"Vanessa doesn't need their charity, or yours." His voice was tight with controlled fury. "I'll take care of my wife and child."

What did he mean? Had she understood him? A moment later he came to her and took her hands in his. "We'll be married at once, Vanessa," he told her. "Before I sail."

Joy leaped inside her as she realized that she was to be Logan's wife. Then, looking up at him, searching his face, she could find no tenderness. Logan had the determined expression of a man performing a necessary duty.

She could refuse, she told herself, but she knew that she would not, for there was the baby to be considered. The child had a right to his father's name. She tried to tell herself that she would agree for the child's sake only, but she could not deceive herself. She loved Logan, and although she was sure that he did not love her, not yet, he was willing to marry her. He must feel some concern for her, she mused. And one day perhaps he might come to love her. It was a slender hope, but it was all she had, and she held on to it.

They were married the next day at the Seamen's Bethel Mission on Water Street with Felicity and Silas Pringle as witnesses. Silas, a tall, lean man in his late thirties, with a weather-beaten face, handed Logan the plain gold band, which had come from a waterfront pawnshop. Logan slid the ring onto Vanessa's finger and his hand pressed hers briefly.

Later, Felicity explained that Aunt Prudence had wanted to attend but that she was confined to bed with an inflammation of the lungs; but, she added, the news of Vanessa's marriage had cheered the old lady. "She's always liked you, Logan."

For the first time that day, Logan smiled with genuine

warmth, and Vanessa's heart lifted. She would not let herself think about why he had married her, or remember that in a few weeks he would be gone on a long and perhaps dangerous voyage. Today he was hers, and tonight she would lie in his arms, cherishing the warm strength of his body. This was all the honeymoon she would have, and she would make the most of it.

Chapter 8

In the suite she shared with Horace at Saratoga's United States Hotel, Kitty gave a shiver of distaste as she glanced at the wide, rumpled bed. The maid had not yet come in to make up the room, and Kitty tried, without success, not to remember what had taken place there last night.

I should be used to it by now, she told herself, for she and Horace had been on their honeymoon nearly two weeks. Now Horace was out, driving to the Congress Spring to drink the water with other early risers; Kitty had refused to accompany him, as she had refused every morning.

"You really should try it, my dear," he had told her. "Most beneficial to the digestion. Besides, since we are here at Saratoga, we ought to get our money's worth."

But Kitty had remained and now she sat before the dressing table, awaiting Horace's return. Once more they would go through the daily activities offered by the resort, and she would try not to think of the night to come, when Horace would strip her silk nightdress from her body with clumsy, impatient hands and force himself on her, indifferent to her complete lack of response.

She thought of that first night, when she had cried until she was sure she had no more tears left, until her eyes burned and her whole being felt drained, until Horace had told her coldly that since she was now his wife, it was his right to possess her body as often as he pleased. Physical release, he had informed her, was necessary to a man's health. After delivering himself of this information, he had turned over on his side, away from her, and had fallen asleep almost at once.

Since then she had learned to accept his invasion of her body with silent revulsion, to lie perfectly still and endure until he had reached his climax and lifted his weight from her.

She had always known that she would loathe being married to Horace, but at least she might have been prepared for the physical side of marriage; she might have had some idea of what to expect if only Mama had been more explicit. "You must do whatever your husband asks of you," Mama had said, not meeting her eyes. "You will get used to . . . fulfilling the duties of a wife, in time."

Now Kitty thought of the flowery descriptions of married bliss she had read in her ladies' annuals and her mouth tightened as she remembered those charming gift books, bound in embossed leather or watered silk, bearing titles such as *The Casket of Love*, *The Flower Vase*, or *The Hare-Bell*, filled with stories containing coy references to "Cupid's sweet bower" and "the hallowed joys of the long-awaited bridal night." They had not prepared her for her first experience with Horace.

She shuddered, remembering how she had been crushed into submission by the weight of his body, frightened by his hoarse breathing, sickened by his wet mouth and the acrid smell of his sweating flesh. He had prodded her impatiently, had squeezed her breasts until she had cried out in pain. Then he had forced her legs apart and had rammed himself into her so that she had thought she was being torn apart.

After the first night the pain lessened, but her disgust had not. Because she sensed that her fear, her struggling, stimulated Horace in some incomprehensible way, she quickly learned to pretend indifference.

Were all men like Horace? Surely not, she told herself. Marriage would have been different with Logan. She had loved Logan. But Logan had never loved her, for he had not come to take her away.

She knew that Papa and Horace had managed to get possession of the *Athena* so that Logan could not have eloped with her to China aboard his beautiful clipper. But if he had loved her, he could have taken her off on another ship. She would have gone anywhere with Logan and would have endured any hardship gladly, she told herself. She would have washed his clothes and polished his boots, if only . . .

The sound of the carriages returning from the Congress Spring brought her back to reality. She smoothed the flounces on her full-skirted dress of dark-green damask over violet silk. She had discovered that by keeping occupied with the endless round of activities provided by the management of the United States Hotel and by changing, every few hours, from one splendid costume to another, she could shut out thoughts of the night to come.

She and Horace would breakfast together in the hotel dining room, where an enormous meal was served between eight and ten. Then perhaps they might go driving to the Hamilton and Flat Rock Springs, and she would wear her new leghorn bonnet with the pale blue ribbons, to match her gown of sky-blue tarlatan; and she would hold her small shot-silk parasol over her head to protect her pink and white complexion. Then, after changing again, perhaps into her wine-colored taffeta, she would sit beside Horace on the piazza, watching the endless parade of coaches, broughams, and landaus drawn by fine, high-stepping horses and carrying ladies and their escorts back and forth to the springs.

And tonight, at the ball—there was a ball almost every night at the hotel—she would wear the white gros de Naples with its tightly fitting bodice and daringly low-cut neckline.

Papa had spared no expense in providing her with an elaborate trousseau, she thought, sighing. If only she might have worn these lovely garments for Logan to see.

The doorknob turned and Horace came in, his hatchet face solemn. He handed her a letter, which he had already opened. "From your father," he said. "Prudence Campbell died yesterday. We will have to return to New York immediately, of course."

Poor Aunt Prudence, Kitty thought. But almost at once she felt a sense of relief, tinged with guilt, for she realized that she would not have to spend another night in the hotel bed with Horace. And maybe—if she made a point of her grief and the proprieties demanded by the death of a close relative—perhaps she might be able to avoid Horace's unwelcome embraces for at least a few nights to come.

Enoch Halliwell's law office on Warren Street was large and handsomely furnished, so for a few moments Vanessa, in her worn dress and shawl, felt ill at ease. Then the soft-spoken middle-aged lawyer gave her an encouraging smile as he offered her a glass of sherry wine.

"Mrs. Campbell thought highly of you," he told her. "All the same, this is an unusual bequest, my dear." He glanced at the document before him on the wide golden-oak desk. "But then, Prudence Campbell was an unusual woman in many ways. She gave her jewelry, what there was of it, to Felicity Bradford, shortly before her death. As for her will, you are the sole beneficiary mentioned."

Vanessa, still shaken at having learned of Aunt Prudence's death, stared at the lawyer, scarcely able to take in his words. Sole beneficiary. With Logan to sail in a few weeks, with her waistline thickening slightly and her breasts growing fuller with her advancing pregnancy, she had felt anxious, more than once, over her future and that of her child. Logan had been working every day on docks, loading and unloading ships, taking on the heaviest jobs to add whatever he could to the small allotment he would leave with her when he set out on the whaling voyage. But now this news of a bequest from Aunt Prudence opened new vistas.

"She has left you the *Ondine*," Enoch Halliwell was saying. "An odd legacy to leave a young woman, but she was determined that you should have it."

"The *Ondine*?"

"The schooner that belonged to her husband, Captain Benjamin Campbell. It must be in sad disrepair by now. It's been sitting in Salem harbor for I don't know how many years."

The lawyer's eyes moved over Vanessa. It was plain from the way she dressed that she was short of money.

"It would take a great deal of cash to put the *Ondine* into seaworthy condition," he told her. "And even then, it would be of little use to you, Mrs. McClintock. My advice is to put it up for auction and take whatever is offered by the highest bidder. You must not expect a large sum," he added gently.

His advice was sensible, Vanessa told herself, but she put it aside almost at once. Her breathing quickened and her cheeks flushed slightly with excitement. A ship, she thought. She was the owner of a ship. She began, now, to remember Aunt Prudence's talk of the *Ondine*. It was small but swift and well built.

"The ship is mine," she said quietly. "Aunt Prudence wanted me to have it. And I'm going to keep it."

"But my dear young lady," Halliwell asked, "what use have you for a ship?"

"Aunt Prudence had her reasons for making the bequest." She felt a swift surge of affection for the old lady. "She understood."

"Prudence Campbell drew up this new will only a few days before her death. I don't mean that she was not of sound mind right up until the end. But she had a sentimental attachment to the *Ondine.*" He gave her a faint smile. "You may be sure that if the ship had any real monetary value, Abel Bradford would already be contesting the will. No, I fear that Mrs. Campbell only valued the *Ondine* because it was Captain Campbell's ship, and so she—"

"My husband is a sea captain too," Vanessa interrupted. "Aunt Prudence knew that Logan and I were married."

"A sea captain? Ah, I begin to understand. What owner does he sail for?"

"He . . . used to work for Abel Bradford."

"And now?"

"He resigned his command. He planned to have a ship of his own—a China clipper. But there were certain business difficulties."

"He is unemployed, then," the lawyer probed.

"He's been offered a berth as first mate on a whaler."

And soon he would sail, unless . . . "My husband and I will go to Salem to look over the *Ondine,*" Vanessa said.

"That's your right," Halliwell conceded. But he shook his head doubtfully. A man who had been master of a China clipper and who was now forced to take a berth as a mate on a whaler was not likely to have the money to repair the *Ondine.* "It takes time to make a ship seaworthy when she's been left to rot in the harbor for so many years. Expert workmen would be needed, and expensive materials. Why, a new set of sails alone would cost—"

"We have the ship. We'll find a way to raise the money for repairs."

"Even if you do," Halliwell said, trying to keep the impatience out of his voice, "your husband, with a single schooner, would have hell's own time—begging your pardon—trying to compete with the big fish like Bradford and Grinnell, and the others. Shipping's a cutthroat business—"

"I've already learned that," Vanessa said, her eyes darkening with anger as she remembered how Abel had taken over Pringle's shipyard and the *Athena.*

"If your husband decides to sell," Halliwell told her, "I may be able to help. My son Jeremy has a law practice in Salem."

"Jeremy Halliwell? And have you another son—Ross?"

"How did you know that?"

"I was born and raised in Salem. My mother was Judith Kenyon."

Halliwell stared at her in surprise, and then, for a moment, his eyes looked young and somehow wistful. "A beauty, she was," he said softly. "Judith Kenyon. She could've had her pick of a dozen young men in Salem." Then he added quickly, "Your father was a fine man, my dear, but I've heard he was lost at sea only a few years after they were married. And your mother—"

"She died last winter."

Halliwell was silent for a moment, and his eyes no longer looked young. "And now you've married a sailor too."

"A captain," she corrected him. "Logan will command his own ship again. I'll make that possible for him." She stood up and smoothed her worn skirt.

"Your husband is most fortunate to have such a devoted wife. But it will take more than devotion to—"

"Whatever it takes, Logan will be master of the *Ondine.*"

She smiled, and Halliwell found himself dazzled by the warmth, the radiant beauty, of her face. He had seen plenty of beauties in his time, but she had something more than the fine-boned features, the violet eyes, fringed with thick, dark lashes, the red-gold hair that was so like Judith's. She had an inner glow and a strength and sense of purpose surprising in a girl of her years.

Now she spoke again, half to herself. "Perhaps Logan has married a woman of fortune after all."

"A ship that's been sitting in the harbor for years, neglected." Logan stood before the small iron stove in their lodgings. "A hulk, left to rot."

"You can't be sure what condition she's in until you've seen her," Vanessa said stubbornly.

"Even if we could afford to have her overhauled, she'd probably be fit for nothing better than hauling timber down from Maine."

"Captain Campbell sailed her down the coast to Charleston and Savannah for cargoes of cotton and indigo," Vanessa said, remembering the stories Aunt Prudence had told her. "She was built of live oak from Georgia. And red cedar from Chesapeake Bay." Vanessa, born and raised in Salem, knew that live oak was the finest wood for those parts of the ship's frame that would have to bear the greatest strain. It was costly, but the tensile strength and durability made it worth the price. And the cedar was needed to offset the weight of the live oak, so she had heard sailors say.

Logan's eyes were thoughtful now, and he began to pace up and down the small room. "I ought to be working on the docks right up until I sail," he reminded her. "Even with the money I'll make in that time, along with the allotment, you won't have it easy after I'm gone. If Halliwell's son will take care of the auction, that'll give you something more to get by on until I come back."

Vanessa felt the tense, charged silence that followed his

words. He knew, as she did, how many men did not come back at all. And there would be the child to think about. For the first time since she had discovered that she was pregnant, Vanessa thought of the child not as a burden, another mouth to feed, but as a living thing—Logan's son, with his crisply curling dark hair, his wide mouth and gray eyes. Or perhaps a girl, small, graceful . . . A helpless infant to be cared for as her own mother had looked after her and managed to keep her fed and clothed after Papa's ship had been wrecked off the Carolinas.

No seaman's wife could count on her husband's safe return, and a nest egg, however small, could be precious. But Vanessa would not allow herself to be held back by her fears for her own future or that of her child. Her fingers tightened on Logan's arm.

"You told me once that you had no use for a penniless wife," she reminded him, her voice level. "The *Ondine* is the only dowry I have to offer you."

"I didn't expect a dowry when I married you," he told her. She tensed, waiting, hoping for him to add that he loved her and that his love made all thought of a dowry unimportant. A foolish, senseless hope, she knew even before he went on. "Aunt Prudence left the *Ondine* to you, Vanessa."

"A wife's property belongs to her husband. The *Ondine* is yours. If you're man enough to claim her."

His dark brows drew together.

"Have you forgotten the night you came home and told me you'd lost the *Athena*? You said that Abel hadn't broken you, that you'd have command of your own ship. Maybe that was only talk. Maybe you'd rather play it safe, sail under another man's command."

For a moment his face was grim, and his hands closed hard on her shoulders. "I was thinking of your security and the child's."

"Security? Then you don't know me, Logan. I'm an ambitious woman. I want to be married to a ship owner, and a man who'll have a fleet one day."

He looked down at her and then he was smiling. "A calculating female—and a shrew to the bargain," he said. His smile deepened, and he drew her to him. "All right, Vanessa. I'll go and take a look at this . . . dowry of yours."

"We'll go," she told him. "Together."

Chapter 9

Standing on the dock in Salem with the wind tossing the ribbons of her bonnet, Vanessa shaded her eyes against the glare of the sunlight on the choppy waters of the bay. She watched as the rowboat pulled away from the shore, carrying Logan and Jeremy Halliwell out to the *Ondine.*

If only her mother could have been here today to see her to know that she was happily married and pregnant with Logan's child. She tried to push the sadness away, and fixed her eyes on Logan, who was rowing with rhythmic, easy strokes.

She had not been surprised when Jeremy Halliwell, a stocky, dignified man in his early thirties, had offered to go out with Logan to inspect the *Ondine*, for she knew that here in Salem the sea and the ships dominated the imagination of every male. Even now, when Salem's shipyard workers were feeling the grip of the severe trade recession, when experienced seamen were desperate to find a berth, still their thoughts turned to the sea.

Prominent Salem families like the Lows had moved their shipping companies to the port of New York and now made their homes on Brooklyn Heights. Salem, because of her shallow harbor, was losing trade not only to New York but to Boston, Philadelphia, and Baltimore as well. Many of the Salem wharves were deserted, and only a few fishing schooners or lumber boats were in port.

"Do you think that Captain McClintock will want to have the *Ondine* overhauled and take her out to sea?"

Vanessa looked up at Ross Halliwell, Jeremy's younger

brother, who had offered to keep her company there on the dock.

"I hope the schooner can be made seaworthy again," Vanessa said, "because Logan will never be satisfied until he is master of his own ship."

Ross smiled, his brown eyes warm. "I went to sea myself when I was fourteen," he told her.

She was surprised, for Ross did not have the look of a seaman. He was a handsome young man in his early twenties and more fashionably dressed than most Salem men. His tall beaver hat was set at a smart angle on his thick light-brown hair; he wore a high-collared waistcoat of fine cashmere, tightly fitting fawn-colored trousers, and a handsome black silk cravat. But he was more than a dandy, Vanessa decided, seeing the lines of the strong, wiry body beneath his fine clothes. Although Ross was not as tall as Logan, he carried himself with confidence and an air of purpose.

"You made only one voyage?" she asked politely, her thoughts still with Logan. What would he find when he reached the *Ondine*? A worthless hulk, or a schooner that would capture his imagination as the *Athena* had?

"Only one voyage," Ross was saying, and she made herself listen. "To Barbados. That was enough to show me what my future was to be." He smiled, and now she saw the glinting amber lights in his brown eyes and heard the excitement in his voice. "We went ashore at Bridgetown. It was a new world to me. A world of light and color and . . . I'd never imagined anything like it." He laughed. "The rest of the crew made straight for the taverns and the—the . . ." He broke off as he remembered that he was talking to a respectably married lady. Then he went on. "I can still see it all—the black shadows of the palms cutting across the white coral road. The wide-winged, coral houses where the sugar planters lived, and the fields of sugar cane, blazing green in the sunlight. And the trees . . . I'd never seen such trees. Pomegranate and orange and lime. And the pale green of the sea, where it washed the shore, and then, farther out, the water was lilac and turquoise."

He shook his head regretfully. "Of course, I had no paints with me. All I could do was to try to remember those colors."

"And then you came back to Salem," Vanessa prompted.

"I did, and Pa and I had some great battles, I can tell you. He wanted me to go into a sensible career—if not as a sea captain, then surely as a lawyer, like him and Jeremy. Oh, I studied law at Harvard College for a year or so, but then I started skipping lectures to go for lessons at the studio of an Italian painter in Boston. When Pa found out . . ." He shook his head at the memory. "I don't know if I've convinced him even now. But it doesn't matter, because I have to paint. I have to."

He spoke quietly, but with the same conviction she had heard so often in Logan's voice when he had talked about owning his own fleet.

"What do you paint?" she asked.

"Seascapes mostly. The bay out there. And the islands. Sometimes the wharves and the ships."

"No portraits?"

She was remembering the Bradford family portraits in their ornate gold frames that had lined the upstairs hall back in the house on Hudson Square.

Ross's eyes lingered on her red-gold hair. A few soft strands had escaped from her bonnet to brush against her cheeks. He looked at her skin, touched with a rosy glow from the force of the brisk wind. "I wonder if I'll ever have the skill to capture beauty like yours."

Her eyes widened in surprise, for she recognized that here

was no formal compliment; he spoke with absolute sincerity.

"Forgive me," he said quickly. "I must not presume upon a childhood friendship. Although I've not forgotten those days at Mistress Harker's grammar school."

Vanessa refrained from reminding him that they had scarcely been friends, that they had been separated, even then, by the lines of class and fortune, for the Halliwells had always had money. Ross had left Mistress Harker's school at twelve to study with a private tutor in the Halliwells' fine house, built in the new style, with a front door arched and embellished with a fanlight and flanked by Ionic columns. Vanessa, when she had left school, had gone to help her mother scrub floors and cook meals at the boardinghouse. After that, she and Ross had only had brief glimpses of each other, when she had been out doing the marketing.

His eyes were still on her, and she knew how much she had changed from the thin, long-legged child he must be remembering. Her woolen cape, bought from a second-hand shop on Pearl Street at Logan's insistence, was long, and full enough to conceal the thickening of her waist. Now that the bouts of nausea that had marked the early weeks of her pregnancy had passed, she felt strong and possessed of a sense of fulfillment. But her quiet contentment was shaken by the thought of Logan's departure. If only he would take command of the *Ondine* instead of accepting the berth aboard the whaler.

How many nights she had lain awake listening to Logan's even breathing, feeling the warmth of his body beside her, and thinking of the future. She had grown up, like all Salem children, hearing stories of the dangers of a whaling voyage, the long months of hunting whales around the Horn and up the coast of South America; of young Asa Hicks, who had become tangled in a harpoon line and dragged overboard; of the longboat of the *Isabella Barr*, smashed to pieces by the threshing flukes of a wounded whale, and every man lost. She knew that months, even years, went by while wives waited for word of a man who might never return.

She thought of herself with only Logan's child for company—a child he might not live to see. The thought, returning now, sent a shudder through her, and she drew her cloak around her more tightly. Ross, noticing the gesture, suggested that they should go back to the Pepper Tree Inn, where she and Logan were staying and where they were to join the Halliwell brothers for dinner.

"The hull's still sound enough," Logan was saying over dinner. "The *Ondine*'s got fine lines. She'll handle well even in a heavy sea."

The four were seated around a table in the dining room of the Pepper Tree near the huge stone fireplace, where the warmth of the leaping flames was most welcome. Even now, in late September, Salem was touched by the first chill that heralded the approaching winter.

"Live oak and red cedar," Logan went on. "And built by men who knew their trade. She must have been a beauty in her day."

"Not a large vessel, though," Jeremy pointed out. "No more than one hundred feet long, and about twenty-eight feet in the beam. And her shallow draft—"

"All Salem-built ships were designed with a shallow draft," Logan interrupted.

"Ah, yes, but that was because they were built to pick their way through the reefs of the Malay archipelago, Captain, as you know." He shook his head and took a sip of wine. "Such ships did well at the height of the pepper trade. Salem had a monopoly then on pepper from Sumatra, and fortunes were made." He shrugged. "That monopoly's been broken. Cargoes of pepper from the Dutch East Indies are delivered straight to New York." His resentment of New York was plain in the way he spoke the name. "Tea's the thing now, and New York's taken over the tea trade too. We've been feeling the pinch here in Salem, let me tell you. Why, I can remember my father talking about a time when ships from the East Indies trade were tiered three deep in the wharves here, and—"

"There are other lucrative cargoes," Logan cut in impatiently. "Cotton from Mobile. Indigo and rice from Charleston." He stopped, his mouth tightened, and Vanessa saw the frustration in his face. "It would take cash, though, to put the *Ondine* back into seaworthy condition. And I don't have it. I don't want to see her put up for auction, but it looks as though—"

"Logan! No!" Vanessa knew well enough that it was the men who made the decisions in business matters. Certainly when the business was shipping. But she also knew how much Logan wanted his ship. More than he wanted anything else in the world, she thought with painful honesty.

"You can't sell the *Ondine*," she cried. "I won't let you."

All three men were staring at her, and she was aware that her words were unseemly, unfeminine. But she could not restrain herself. "There must be a way to get the money for repairs."

Hearing her, looking at her, Ross was stirred in a way that no woman had ever moved him before. Down on the wharf a little while ago, he had been drawn by her loveliness, but now he saw something more than the beauty of the strong yet delicate bone structure, the warm glow of her cheeks, the red-gold hair, for now the intensity of her feelings had made her eyes glow with violet lights. Her high, rounded breasts under the modestly cut woolen bodice rose and fell more quickly, and her voice held a rich, low resonance. If only he could be the one to stir such emotions in her, he thought. If only she were looking at him this way. But her eyes were fixed on her husband's face.

Ross spoke without planning, without weighing the practicality of his words. "You could sell shares in the *Ondine* and use the money to get her refitted."

"As your brother has said, Salem's been feeling the pinch. Who has spare cash for such an investment?"

But Logan had not ruled out the possibility, Vanessa realized.

"I have," Ross said quietly. "Not a great deal, but perhaps, if others would come in with us, we might—"

"What money are you talking about?" Jeremy demanded.

"Grandfather Copley's trust fund." Ross turned back to Logan, ignoring his brother's startled expression. "Our maternal grandfather left a modest trust fund for Jeremy and me. If you're willing to sell shares in the schooner Jeremy and I—"

"Slow down a bit, Ross," Jeremy said. "I'll do my own investing of my own funds. As for yours, you've hardly been able to wait until you turned twenty-one to get your hands on your share. To go to Europe, that's what you've said. To study painting in Paris, or Rome." He gave Logan a wry grin. "My brother has the notion he can make a living painting pictures."

"I can go to Europe in a year or so," Ross said. He had learned to ignore Jeremy's barely concealed misgivings about his choice of a career. But he could not deny that Jeremy was right about the proposed trip to Europe. He refused to admit to himself why he was willing, all at once, to put off that journey.

"Europe'll still be there in a year or so," Ross said. "And

with the profits from my shares in the *Ondine*, I'll have that much more for traveling expenses. What do you say, Captain McClintock? Wouldn't it be better to own the vessel jointly with shareholders than to give her up entirely?"

Logan was silent for a moment, and Vanessa saw the hunger in his eyes. But when he spoke his tone was even, almost casual. "Perhaps a man of your . . . artistic leanings does not understand the risks of business. The shipping business in particular."

"I'm not a fool, Captain. I'm a Salem man and I believe I know the uncertainty in any voyage. I know I might lose every cent, but I also know that I could make a handsome profit. And I think there may be a few other Salem men who would be willing to take the same risks . . . even if my brother won't."

"I haven't said I won't," Jeremy said. "If we might meet at my office tomorrow to discuss the details, and if Captain McClintock can convince me that he has at least a reasonable chance to turn a profit—coastwise trade with the South and later, perhaps, a voyage to the sugar islands—Cuba, Jamaica . . ."

"That sort of voyage would scarcely offer any great risk for a man like my husband, who has sailed to China for Abel Bradford, who made one of the fastest passages on record. Surely when Mr. Bradford made Logan master of—"

"You've not been employed by Abel Bradford for some time," Jeremy said to Logan, his tone polite but cautious. "Forgive me, ma'am, but in matters like these, it is necessary to have the facts."

"I left Bradford of my own free will to build my own clipper," Logan said. "I wanted to be master and owner—to answer to no man."

"You have an independent spirit then," Jeremy began.

Vanessa stiffened, for she thought she heard a touch of

condescension in Jeremy's voice, and although she knew that he had money and an established social position here in Salem, that did not give him the right to speak to Logan as he had spoken to his own brother, moments before—with good-natured mockery. But Logan, if he caught the overtones in Jeremy's speech, was plainly unperturbed as he said, "I want to make a fortune in shipping, Mr. Halliwell. And it's the owner, not the hired captain, who gets the lion's share of the profits."

In the silence that followed, Vanessa could hear the crackling of the fire and the wind that rattled the windows of the inn.

Logan fixed his eyes on Jeremy and drained his glass before he went on in the same calm way. "As for selling shares, I don't remember agreeing to that—it was your brother's idea."

"But you'd consider it?" Jeremy asked.

"Maybe. On my terms."

"And your terms are—"

"You'll find them clearly stated in any contract I may choose to put my name to. Ross chooses to go in with me, and if I can find enough other businessmen who aren't afraid to risk a reasonable sum, to make a far larger one—"

Vanessa held her breath, her hands pressed together tightly. Logan gave Jeremy a frosty smile. "Maybe I won't be able to get the financial backing I need here. As you yourself said, Salem's past her prime as a shipping center. Maybe the men here are content to live on their memories of glory. If that's so, I'd better try Boston—or New York."

"Look here, Captain McClintock," Jeremy began, his face reddening, "we've had our reverses here but we—"

"Reverses? What shipping do you have here now? How many deep-water ships are in port at this moment? Why, the docks are so quiet I could hear the gulls dropping clam shells on their pavement."

Vanessa spoke quickly. "I was born and raised in Salem, Mr. Halliwell," she reminded Jeremy. "I know there are plenty of expert carpenters and caulkers and sailmakers who would jump at the chance to get work right now—and they could do the job as well as any of the shipyard workers in New York. And if the shipyards are standing idle, surely we could lease one. . . ."

She faltered into silence, fearing that Logan might resent her interference. But he picked up where she had left off. "Those men will work for a lot less too. They're desperate by now. That means lower investments for the same profits."

She was taken aback, but only for a moment, knowing as she did how ruthless Logan could be in his driving ambition. It was not right to talk of profiting from the desperation of unemployed workers.

"A man with a wife and children to feed and no money coming in will work for whatever he's offered," Logan said.

Vanessa wondered if Logan might have gone too far in his desire to persuade Jeremy, who was, after all, a Salem man and might take offense at the suggestion that other Salem men were in such desperate straits that they could be had at the lowest wages. But Jeremy nodded, and after a long pause he raised his hand to catch the attention of the landlord's wife. "Another bottle of port over here, if you please."

By the time dinner was over and the second bottle stood empty, Jeremy and Logan had approached an understanding. "You'll need other investors," Jeremy said. "But I know of a few men here who might be interested. I'll speak to them, and if they are willing, we'll have a meeting at my office in a few days. You'll find that there is still some capital here in Salem if one knows where to look for it, Captain McClintock."

* * * * *

Later that night, when Logan and Vanessa had retired to their small, slightly shabby room overlooking the stableyard of the Pepper Tree, he stared at her for a moment with great intensity, and she feared he might be angry with her for forgetting herself and becoming involved in his business negotiations. Such behavior was not proper in a wife.

"Logan," she began, but a moment later her fears were swept away as he caught her in his arms and drew her against him.

"We've done it," he said triumphantly. "The *Ondine* is as good as mine right now." He held her away and his eyes searched her face. "You're a clever woman, Vanessa. You knew the bait that Jeremy would swallow and you tossed it to him at exactly the right time. We'll get all the workmen we need, and they'll be willing to break their backs for whatever we can pay them."

Vanessa was pleased by Logan's approval, but she was taken aback by his cool appraisal of the advantages to be taken from Salem's unemployment conditions.

"Is it right to pay these men low wages because they have no choice but to accept them?" she asked slowly.

"It's sound business practice," he told her. "The kind of business practice that Jeremy Halliwell and those other prospective investors can understand. Don't look so troubled, Vanessa. Isn't it better for the shipyard workers up here to bring some money home than none at all?"

"Maybe so, but I still don't think—"

"I can't afford to pay high wages, not now, when I'm starting out in business," he told her firmly. "Besides, you know these people here. Would they prefer charity to steady wages, no matter how small?"

"Mama hated the idea of charity," Vanessa said. Logan's

reasoning confused her, and she did not wish to spoil his triumph.

"You've done your part today," he told her, drawing her to him once more. "Now leave the rest to me."

He lifted her and held her against the hardness of his chest, but she could not yield at once, for she sensed that he was not really concerned with her scruples, that perhaps such scruples were a matter of indifference to him. For a man like Logan, who had fought his way up from the New York slums, who had come close to his goal of owning his own clipper only to see it snatched away from him, a certain ruthlessness might be inevitable.

She wanted to resist, but she could not, for since that first night when she had given herself to him her desire for him had grown stronger, deeper. Often he had only to look at her and she felt herself go weak with her need for him. Was it right to feel this way? Should a woman have such urgent hunger, even for her own husband?

Still cradling her against him, he bent his head and kissed her, and her arms tightened around him.

Now he was carrying her across the room and putting her down on the bed. He bent over her and his mouth claimed hers, his kisses driving all thought from her mind, shutting out everything except her need for him. He did not put out the candle, and by its faint light she looked up at him. He stripped off her clothes, then his own, and without giving her time to put on a nightgown, he drew her against him.

She knew that he needed her in his triumph as much as he had needed her on that first night, when he had been filled with unhappiness over the loss of the *Athena.* He had not yet told her that he loved her, but she sensed with a certainty far more elemental than any words could have been that he came to her now, as then, to satisfy a deep hunger only partly physical.

His hands were sure, commanding, as they moved over her warm, smooth skin. During all those other nights she had lost her first shyness little by little and had learned to draw strength and reassurance from him, to glory in each caress.

His lips moved down along the curves of her body, the swell of her breasts, and still downward. But when he parted her thighs she gave a short, swift gasp. This was unfamiliar, and for a moment her body tensed. "It's all right, love," he said softly, his breath warm against the flesh of her thigh. Another pathway to be explored, and she could not hold back, could not deny him. His mouth found her, claimed her, and now she cried out, not in modesty but in pleasure, and her hands stroked his hair, the strong neck and wide, heavily muscled shoulders.

She was shocked at her own boldness, her willingness to give pleasure as well as to take it. Was it decent for a wife to respond so fiercely? Once more he moved and now he was above her, thrusting into her, and she could think no more, for she was conscious only of the complete merging, the joining that made her a part of him. She wanted what he wanted, and hungered for the surging upward spiral that carried them both to a timeless interval of fulfillment.

He rested his head against the curve of her breast, and she thought he was asleep. Then all at once she felt him tense and lift himself away from her. Supporting himself on his arms, he looked down at her; his eyes, in the candlelight, held an expression she had never seen there before. "Vanessa . . . I didn't stop to think. The baby . . . is it . . . all right?"

She understood, and, reaching out, she drew him against her. "There's nothing to worry about. We'll be able to—to go on as we have been until the last few months."

"How do you know?" he demanded, and she was touched

by the concern in his voice.

Should she tell him that an hour before their wedding, when Felicity was helping her to prepare, she had asked the older woman, seeking reassurance? Felicity had been embarrassed, but her sense of obligation to Vanessa's mother had been stronger than her modesty, and she had told Vanessa what she knew of pregnancy and childbirth, omitting only the description of the ordeal she herself had experienced each time she had given birth. She had also comforted Vanessa, saying, "If Logan is away at sea when your time comes, you must get word to me. Not at the house. Send a message to the headquarters of the Ladies' Society for the Relief of the Wives of Seamen." She had given Vanessa the address, and Vanessa had tucked it away carefully.

"How can you be sure?" Logan was asking. "This is your first baby. How can you—"

"I'm sure," she told him with so much conviction that he was satisfied. He asked no more questions but put his arms around her, carefully this time, and in a few moments he was asleep. She lay beside him, feeling secure in the knowledge that she would have a few more precious months with him during the time the *Ondine* was being refitted for her first voyage under the command of her new master.

She wondered how long it would be before Logan set sail. Would he be with her when she gave birth to their child?

Logan, having gotten financial backing, took a lease on Crookshanks' yard, on the creek near Norman Street, a district where there had once been so many yards that the area had been given the name Knockers' Hole, because of the noise of the mallets and hammers. Now that noise was heard once more, for Logan was eager to complete refitting on the *Ondine* as quickly as possible. Ross and Jeremy had both invested in the schooner, and the remaining shares had been bought by two other Salem men: Thomas Drysdale and Samuel Oliphant, both of whom had inherited wealth from their hard-driving ancestors. The Drysdale fortune had been made in the East Indies spice trade, while the Oliphants had prospered in bringing tea and silks from China.

Now, on a chilly, overcast day in early November, Vanessa had accompanied Logan to Crookshanks' yard to see the progress being made in the refitting of the *Ondine*.

She watched while carpenters, dubbers, joiners, and caulkers swarmed over the schooner, each doing his task with speed and efficiency. A team of caulkers were hard at work sealing the deck with oakum and tar. Silas Pringle, who was in charge of the work, appeared to be everywhere at once, shouting orders, driving the men.

"It was good of you to send for Silas," Vanessa told Logan. "I know he's happier up here working for you than he was back in New York taking orders from Horace."

"I sent for Silas because he's the best man for the job," Logan said. "He'll see to it that there's no waste of time or materials. With Silas in charge, these Salem men will toe the mark—if they want to go on working."

"And will the work go on right through the winter?" Vanessa asked.

"It will. I agreed to sell shares in the vessel because I had no other way to raise cash, but after a few successful voyages, I'll pay off the shareholders with a handsome profit. And then she'll be mine."

"Then you'll want to—to put to sea as quickly as you can," Vanessa said, trying to sound calm and unemotional. But Logan turned away from the ship and put his arm around her, and she knew that she had not been able to conceal her feelings from him.

"I don't want to leave you with the baby coming," he said. "If you had a mother or a sister to be with you . . ." He hesitated. She wondered whether she could sway him, keep him with her at least until the child would be born. Then she thought better of it, reminding herself sternly that he had not married her for love. She must not stand in the way of his ambition. Having provided him with a ship, she must let him feel free to take command as soon as the work of refitting would be completed.

"I'll stay here in Salem with you until you sail," she told him. "Then I'll go back to our lodgings in New York. Perhaps Silas can take me there."

For a moment Logan looked profoundly relieved, and she realized that he was grateful to her because she had not clung to him and pleaded with him to stay until after the baby's birth.

"You'll need someone—some woman—when the baby comes, though," he said. "A midwife."

"Felicity Bradford promised to find me a reliable midwife. She—"

His dark brows drew together, and his gray eyes turned cold. "Felicity again. Why the hell is she always meddling in our affairs? You're not one of her charity cases, not now."

Vanessa felt her own temper rising. "Felicity was my mother's friend. She feels a responsibility toward me."

"No need to tell me that," Logan shot back. "If she hadn't been there that day, back in our rooms on Tompkins Street . . .

He broke off. Vanessa was trembling now, and not with the chill breeze from the harbor. "If she hadn't been there, you wouldn't have been pushed into marrying me."

"I didn't mean that." But he was looking away, his eyes fixed on the *Ondine.*

"You didn't want a wife, certainly not one without

money," she said. She waited for him to deny it, to tell her that he loved her, but he did not speak, and she felt the familiar doubts rising again. She needed reassurance and he offered none. "I think you married me out of pride," she went on, "because you didn't want me or your child to have to take charity."

"That was part of it," he said. "It was enough that Abel Bradford got hold of my ship. Do you think I'd have wanted you to take food baskets and cast-off clothes from his wife?"

Vanessa tried to be honest with herself. Even that first night when Logan had taken her, he had said nothing about love. Taken her? No, there had been no need for force; she had given herself willingly. Once more she felt ashamed that she had yielded to him, putting her whole future into his keeping without asking for the promise of love in return.

Even now she sensed his eagerness to be back at sea so that he could start building a coastwise trade. "Our marriage isn't such a bad bargain," she said. "You have the *Ondine*."

He gripped her shoulders. "How was I to know when I married you that Prudence Campbell would leave you the ship?"

It was a reasonable question, but Vanessa was in no mood for reason. She wanted tenderness and affection, loving words that she could remember during the months when Logan would be far away. Recalling what Logan had told her about his childhood, she wondered if he would ever have any such emotions to share. She pulled away from him, and, turning, she ran toward the gate of the shipyard. Because she was blinded by tears, she failed to see a coil of rope in her path. Her foot struck it and she lurched forward, but at that moment Logan was beside her, steadying her. He held her against him. "This is no place for a woman in your condition," he said.

She turned to look at him.

"What are you crying for?" he demanded.

"A woman in my condition cries easily," she said.

He looked so shamefaced and helpless that Vanessa was moved in spite of herself. They stood in silence and now she became aware of the din of the yard: a mallet man struck the head of a hawsing iron to drive the oakum into the cracks on the ship's deck, while other workers pounded on the hull's copper sheathing. A caulker shouted to an apprentice, calling for more tar.

"Don't upset yourself; it can't be good for the baby." His arm tightened around her. "I want a son, Vanessa, and if you'll feel better having Felicity around when your time comes, then have her there. But if she finds you a midwife, you tell her to get the best one in New York. I'll see to it that money's put aside to pay the fee. My wife's no charity case, and you can tell her so."

Vanessa felt somewhat comforted by his words, but there was no time for further talk between them, for the wagon carrying the ropes had pulled to a stop, and now Silas was here, his face reddened by the wind, his eyes bright with enthusiasm for this new work. He touched his cap to Vanessa, and then he and Logan were walking over to the wagon.

She stood aside, not wanting to get in Logan's way, knowing his eagerness to complete the refitting and put to sea. They had made up their quarrel, and he was concerned for her. She tried to draw reassurance from his words, from the tone in which he had called her "my wife."

That night when she was lying beside him in bed, she felt a fluttering inside her, then a sharp kick. The baby was strong and healthy and was making his presence known. Logan was asleep, and after a moment's hesitation she decided not to wake him. He had been down at the shipyard all day and would rise at dawn tomorrow to go to the sailmakers' lofts, to hurry them along in the work of cutting, fastening, and binding of the huge sheets of cotton duck. She would let him sleep.

She put a hand lightly on her belly and sighed with satisfaction. If only she could present Logan with a fine, strong son when he came home from his first voyage as master of the *Ondine*, perhaps then he would come to love her.

Chapter 10

Vanessa turned into Schermerhorn Row, her face set, her teeth biting hard into her lower lip. She should not have given in to impulse and walked all the way over to Broadway on this March morning to try to find exactly the kind of fine lawn and lace she wanted—and at a bargain price. But she had been restless after being cooped up in those two small rooms, and she had been feeling perfectly well.

Now, as she clutched at her small parcel, she knew with certainty that there would be no time for her to make the baby's christening dress. Not until after he had been born, surely.

The first pain had struck a few moments ago, and she had wavered in her mind between returning to her lodgings at once or going to seek Felicity Bradford at the headquarters of the Ladies' Society for the Relief of Seamen's Wives. She had come to the society offices only because they were much closer than the lodginghouse. She glanced once more at the crumpled piece of paper she had been carrying around with her all these months. Yes, this was the right place. A small, rather shabby bakeshop stood on the ground floor, and over it were windows with painted lettering that proclaimed the offices of the society.

How she longed to see Felicity's calm face, to hear the gentle reassurance in the older woman's voice. Felicity would take charge. She would know what to do.

Another pain struck, and Vanessa had to wait for a moment, bracing herself against a lamppost. She felt the perspiration break out on her face and turn icy in the March wind. The pain eased off, and then Vanessa saw the gleam of polished brass on the fine landau across the street, the Bradfords' landau, all shining and freshly painted, and there was the Bradfords' coachman, Liam O'Connell, seated up on the box in his smart dark-blue uniform. Felicity must be here at the society's headquarters, then, Vanessa thought with relief; she would know of a suitable midwife, and she would accompany her back to the lodgings on Tompkins Street.

Since Logan had sailed a month before, Vanessa, once she was settled back in their New York lodgings, had made no attempt to see Felicity but had let the days drift by, wrapped in that peculiar, drowsy peace so common in the last stage of pregnancy. Often she had abandoned herself to daydreams, remembering Logan's good-bye on the wharf back in Salem, feeling once more in her imagination the strength of his arms around her and the warmth of his mouth on hers. Perhaps he did love her in his way, and perhaps after the baby came Logan would give her the affection she wanted so much; there night even be a new closeness in their marriage.

She could not be sure, she told herself sadly, for a man like Logan, who was driven by ambition, might still regret his ties with any woman; he might even have second thoughts about fatherhood and might see the child as another burden.

Vanessa's teeth closed on her lower lip as she felt the start of another pain, and she knew that whatever Logan's feelings might be she wanted this baby so much that even the ordeal of childbirth did not frighten her. Other women had gone through it, and now it was her time. If only her mother could have been with her, she thought, her hands closing more tightly on the parcel she carried.

The pain reached its height and then began to pass, so she was able to go into the small red-brick building and up the long, steep flight of stairs to the headquarters of Felicity's society.

Kitty Widdicomb tapped her foot impatiently and tried to ignore the other people in the outer office: the seamen's wives in their worn clothes, surrounded by their crying, squabbling children. These women waited stolidly to have a chance to speak to Miss Hatcher, the thin-lipped spinster who was the society's only paid employee. Miss Hatcher sat behind a scarred wooden desk dispensing coins from a metal box and writing down names; she asked sharp, often painfully personal questions of the women who had come here seeking help.

They had to show their marriage certificates and their children's birth or baptism papers and then to convince Miss Hatcher that their needs were really desperate. Even so, they received little sympathy from her.

"Why on earth do they keep on having children if they cannot provide for them?" Miss Hatcher had said to Mama only a few days ago, in Kitty's hearing. "These people are lacking in self-restraint, even the women."

As if a woman could help getting pregnant, Kitty thought bitterly. She had managed to keep Horace at a distance as much as possible since they had returned from their honeymoon but he was her husband, and when he was really determined to exercise his rights she could not stop him. She shuddered and thought of how awful it would be to have Horace's baby even in the comfort of the house on Hudson Square and attended by Dr. Fairleigh.

Naturally a spinster like Miss Hatcher could not be expected to understand that a wife might be forced to have children whether she wanted them or not. Kitty consoled herself with the thought that perhaps she would be one of the fortunate women who could not conceive a child. Even Horace could do nothing about that.

She pushed the thought to the back of her mind and glanced at the door, hoping Mama would arrive soon. Kitty had come here in the landau to try to get Mama to come out with her, to do a little shopping and then have lunch at one of those delightful new ice cream saloons where it was perfectly respectable for ladies to dine without male escorts. Now that she was married, Kitty no longer had any need to pretend to have a delicate appetite, to pick at her food in a way that was proper for young ladies. She would have an omelette, ice cream, and pastries, she thought, and perhaps a cup of chocolate, thick with cream.

Mama had taken the large carriage this morning, leaving Kitty the landau, for Mama had a great number of charitable errands. Papa grumbled, saying that he had bought the carriage for his own use, to take him down to his offices on South Street. "Isn't it enough that you've set up a society to take care of these people?" he demanded.

"Some of the women are too ill or too far away to come to the office. Some are not even the wives of seamen."

"But they are in need," Felicity had explained to Kitty after Abel's departure. "All these Irish who are coming over are half-starved, poor creatures. The Five Points can't hold them all any longer, and they are forced to set up new shanty settlements on the bluffs overlooking the East River. They cannot be left to die of disease and starvation."

Kitty gave a fastidious little shudder as she remembered her mother's words. She saw the women on the bench, and their children, staring at her, examining her in her velvet and furs, and she got up and went to stand at the window, her back to the room. But even though she no longer had to look at them, she could smell them—unwashed bodies and clothing. Oh, if only Mama would hurry back.

Vanessa was weak and dizzy when she reached the head of the stairs, pushed open the office door, and stumbled into the room. She went directly to the oak desk, where a thin-lipped woman was seated, making notes in a ledger.

"I must see Felicity Bradford—at once. . . ." she managed to say.

The woman looked up from the ledger, her voice icy. "Indeed? You'll take a seat and wait your turn. We have rules here, and there are questions you will have to answer before we can—"

"Wait 'er turn, is it? And questions t' answer?" A heavyset woman with an untidy mop of black hair and a loud voice broke in. "Ain't ye got eyes in yer head, miss? If this girl don't get help quick, she'll be havin' 'er baby right here."

The thin-lipped woman stood up, her eyes uncertain, her whole manner flustered. Another pain was starting to take hold, and Vanessa braced her swollen body against the desk.

"Vanessa!"

A moment later Vanessa caught the scent of a delicate verbena perfume that was somehow familiar and felt an arm supporting her. Through the dizziness that was blurring her vision, she squinted and gasped, "Kitty?"

The two girls had not seen each other since that night when Vanessa had been turned out of the Bradford mansion. Under ordinary conditions Vanessa would have been embarrassed, wondering how Kitty felt about her having married Logan. Now such considerations were swept aside as the pain gripped her, grasping at her like a vise.

"Your mother promised to help me . . . when my time came—"

"Mama's out on an errand," Kitty said. "I'll take you home." Turning briefly to the woman behind the desk, Kitty said, "Tell my mother where I've gone."

Then she paused. "Where are you and . . . Logan living now?"

"Tompkins Street," Vanessa said. "Your mother will know. She's been there before."

"Ye'll be needin' a midwife," the black-haired woman broke in. "Mrs. Dacey's good, and she don't charge much. Tell 'er that Lottie Gunn sent ye."

In the bedroom of the lodgings on Tompkins Street, Kitty was helping Vanessa out of her clothing and into a nightgown. Liam O'Connell had been dispatched to find Mrs. Dacey and drive her back as quickly as possible. Meanwhile, Kitty tried to make Vanessa comfortable. "You don't think the baby will come . . . right away?" Kitty asked uneasily. "I've never . . . I wouldn't know what to do."

The pains had abated for the time being, and Vanessa realized that she would have to comfort and reassure Kitty. She managed a smile. "Don't worry," she said. "I've heard that first babies take a long time."

"Oh, thank heaven for that," Kitty said. Then she added quickly, "I didn't mean—I wasn't thinking. All that dreadful pain. Oh, poor Vanessa—and it's all my fault."

"Your fault?" Vanessa stared at her in bewilderment.

"If I hadn't sent you to Logan that night . . . I was so foolish, so innocent then. I didn't know what men are like, how awful they can be when their—their animal needs are aroused."

Vanessa wanted to explain to Kitty that it had not been that way for her and Logan. But Kitty was babbling on.

"At least Mama forced him to marry you when she found out about your . . . unfortunate condition."

It wasn't like that, Vanessa thought, but she knew that this was not the time to try to make Kitty understand the truth: that she had given herself to Logan willingly, and that his lovemaking had been passionate, yes, but considerate and tender too. That she wanted his baby so much that even the ordeal ahead of her was not important.

"And where is Logan now?" Kitty demanded.

"At sea."

Kitty's soft mouth tightened. "He got you into this terrible predicament and now he's gone off without a thought for you. He's deserted you."

Vanessa tried to find the words to explain, but she felt another pain coming on and she lay back against the pillows, pressing her fist against her mouth to stifle a cry. Logan had not deserted her. He would come back, and he would be pleased with her for having given him a child. Of course he would.

In the long hours that followed, she held on to that hope. As the day wore on, the pains started coming closer together, and Kitty, pale and shaken, remained by her side, bathing her forehead with cologne from a small vial she carried in her reticule.

The sunlight was fading, and it was nearly evening when Felicity arrived at last; and then, minutes later, Mrs. Dacey, the midwife, came, panting, up the steep flights of stairs.

Mrs. Dacey, a stout, efficient-looking woman, explained briefly as she put on a clean, starched white apron that she had been off on another case. She examined Vanessa quickly and nodded with satisfaction. "Everything's going fine, dearie," she assured Vanessa. "Won't be long now." She glanced curiously at Kitty and Felicity, evidently surprised to find two such elegantly dressed ladies in a sailors' lodginghouse down on the waterfront. Then she shrugged and turned her attention back to her patient.

"You got to help, dearie. Bear down—that's it. Lord, this is a big baby."

Vanessa, no longer able to hold back a scream of pure agony, cried out. Felicity gripped her hand, and she saw the sympathy in the familiar, gentle face. Kitty, shaking now, clapped her hands over her ears. "I can't stand it," Kitty choked out, and fled into the next room.

Mrs. Dacey looked after her briefly, shrugged, and turned her attention back to Vanessa. "Again, dearie. There's the head, now. Again—"

"I can't!" Vanessa gasped. Her body was drenched with sweat and she felt as if she were being torn apart.

"Think of Logan, how proud he'll be." Felicity's voice came from a long way off.

"Will he?" Vanessa could not be sure if she had spoken the words aloud or if they had only echoed through her pain-dazed mind. Then her instincts took over. She no longer cared about the pain or anything else except the need to bring her child into the world. She bore down again with every bit of strength she could muster. . . .

From somewhere she heard a soft, whimpering sound, like the mewing of a kitten. And then, moments later, a louder, lustier cry, strong and indignant.

"The baby?" she whispered.

"A fine big boy, dearie." Then, "You ever seen a handsomer little one, ma'am?"

And Felicity's voice, through the soft fog that was enveloping Vanessa now, "Never. He's perfect." Vanessa thought that she caught a kind of wistfulness in Felicity's tone, but she could not think about that now, for she was drifting into an exhausted sleep.

The baby, Christopher, was nearly two months old and

Logan had not yet returned from his first voyage as captain of the *Ondine*.

She had long since regained her strength and vitality, and the new, fuller curves of her breasts served only to accentuate the slenderness of her waist.

Now, on this afternoon early in June, the weather had turned unseasonably warm, and she had brought the baby's cradle out of the bedroom into the front room, which was a little larger. She had opened the window so that the baby might have a little air, but the street noises assaulted her: the iron-clad wheels of carts and drays rattling over the cobblestones; the raucous cursing of the teamsters as they maneuvered their heavily laden vehicles down to the docks; the shouts of the sailors who, even at this hour, were already stumbling out of the taverns; the shrill laughter of the street women who preyed upon them. And the air was not particularly refreshing, Vanessa told herself sadly, for the heat of the day had stirred up the noxious stench that was a combination of decaying garbage, stagnant puddles of water, and rotting carcasses of dead cats.

Vanessa sighed as she rocked the cradle, a gift from Felicity, and wished that she could raise her baby in Salem, where the air was clean and bracing. So far, Christopher was healthy, but Vanessa dreaded the coming summer. Everyone knew that for a baby, the first summer was the most dangerous, particularly down here in the teeming waterfront district, where cholera, diphtheria, and typhoid ran rampant.

She sighed and bent to adjust the baby's blanket, then stopped, her hand outstretched, for she heard familiar footsteps on the stairs. Her heart started hammering in her chest, and she was on her feet in one swift motion even as Logan came striding through the door. He carried his heavy canvas seabag slung over one shoulder.

Then he stopped short, staring at the cradle, and the seabag dropped from his hand. He stood motionless. Vanessa was torn between her leaping joy at his return and a stir of uneasiness. Surely he had realized that the baby would be born before his return.

"It's a boy," she stammered. "A son, Christopher. Felicity thought he should be baptized as soon as possible. I didn't know how long it would be before you returned and—and so I . . ."

He came to stand beside her, and put an arm around her shoulders, but his eyes were still fixed on the cradle. "Christopher." He nodded. "Yes, I like that. Chris."

The baby was awake now, his blue eyes wide, his small fists moving aimlessly. "He looks healthy enough," Logan said.

"Oh, he is. He has an enormous appetite, and he's been gaining weight so quickly."

Logan hesitated, then reached down and took one of Chris's fists between two of his fingers.

His touch was careful, and Vanessa smiled. "A son," Logan said again. "I'll need sons to help me carry on my shipping line."

Although she had hoped for a somewhat warmer response, she found a little of the tension was easing out of her.

"You had a good voyage, then?"

"Good? It was far better than I ever expected." He released the baby's hand, took off his heavy dark-blue coat and his cap, and tossed them onto a convenient chair. Then he started pacing back and forth the length of the room. "The big shippers, like Bradford and Grinnell—all that lot—they've got the cotton ports of the South tied up. They have their own employees down there, running the commission houses. But I did find a good cargo of naval stores in North Carolina—in

Wilmington." He stopped and turned to face her, and now he was smiling in triumph. "The *Ondine*—she's small, but she handles like a Thoroughbred. She was built for shallow waters, and she proved herself—took those tricky inlets off the Carolina coast and never once touched bottom on a sandbar."

Although Vanessa shared his satisfaction at the success of the voyage, she still longed to hear something quite different. She wanted him to ask about Chris's birth, to exclaim over him not because he was a healthy boy who would one day help to run the shipping line—a line that had not yet been established—but because he was their firstborn son. And Logan might at least have asked if she had had a difficult time during the baby's birth.

She put a hand on his arm, half-afraid that he would shake it off, but instead, he drew her against him. Now she felt her heart lift with joy, for this was the moment she had dreamed of, longed for, during the months of their separation. She breathed in deeply, inhaling the familiar scent of shaving soap and rough, damp wool. Her body molded itself against his, and his arms tightened around her. He kissed her, a long, searching kiss, his tongue parting her lips, exploring the softness of her mouth. When he raised his lips from hers, she stayed pressed to him, feeling the hardness of his chest against her cheek.

Then, too soon, he released her. "You were right to insist that I should see the *Ondine* instead of having her auctioned off without taking a look at her. She'll make our fortune—see if she doesn't. It'll take time, though. I'm going to buy out the stockholders up there in Salem, the Halliwells and the others, if business goes on as it did this first voyage out."

"Suppose they don't want to sell?"

"They'll sell if the price is high enough; don't worry about that."

She longed to have him hold her again, but she saw that his thoughts were with the ship now and the voyage he had completed. "We went on from the Carolinas down to the West Indies," he told her. "First to Cuba. That's where the real profit is. Sugar—muscovado sugar. Those Cuban planters are making a fortune on the stuff, but they're short of refining equipment, and a lot of them would as soon ship the stuff as muscovado, raw brown sugar, and have it processed up here. Some of the big ship owners are starting to set up their commission houses in Havana, too, but there are small ports along the coast that are still wide open." He laughed. "I learned a lot about trading when I was on the China run. I made some good deals, and I'm going to make more next time out."

Next time out. Already Logan's thoughts were on the next voyage, and the one after that.

"They're in the market for all kinds of goods from up here too," Logan went on. "We picked up a deck cargo of horses in the Carolinas and sold them in Cuba. Those planters and their women want fine horses and carriages to go riding around the streets of Havana. They leave the plantations to the overseers, many of them. Next time I go down there, I'm going to have a cargo of the showiest carriages I can find." He strode to the window and pushed it open as far as it would go, then shook his head. "Getting hot here already," he said. He was silent, his eyes thoughtful. Then he said abruptly, "I'm getting you and the baby out of here before I sail again."

"But where—"

"There are better neighborhoods in New York, the whole city's moving north." He nodded. "I'll find a decent place for the two of you."

"We managed here last summer—"

"That was the two of us," he interrupted impatiently. "My

son's going to have something better. Clean air and quiet streets."

"But you're saving to pay off the shareholders. You said so—"

"And I meant it. But in a few weeks that street out there'll stink like an open sewer. And there'll be epidemics—always are. No matter, I'll have a house for both of you before then."

He took her by the shoulders, his eyes somber.

"I've told you about the Five Points, Vanessa. I survived, but there were plenty who didn't. I owe Chris something better than that. And you too. I'm not forgetting that without you, I wouldn't have the *Ondine.*"

She knew that he had no understanding of the impact of his words, but they hurt all the same. She tried to tell herself that she should be grateful, if only for the baby's sake. Logan was willing to delay the fulfillment of his ambition, sole ownership of the *Ondine*, to assure that his wife and child would have a decent place to live. He had a strong sense of responsibility. But she could not forget that he had not once said he loved her, only that he was grateful to her for bringing him the ship he wanted so much.

That night, when they were together in bed, she was still unable to forget his words, and she remained stiff and unyielding in his embrace. Sensing her reluctance without understanding the reason for it, he released her, and, raising himself on one arm, he looked down into her face. "Is it too soon?" he asked her with uncharacteristic gentleness. He sounded like an awkward boy, and there was a lack of his usual assurance. "Too soon after the baby, I mean? You look so well. I don't know about such things."

Her hurt gave way to the urgency of her need, and her eagerness to satisfy his hunger for her. She was his wife, and she wanted him. She reached up and stroked his dark hair. "It's not too soon—not at all. I'm fine and I've . . ." She threw pride to the winds now. "I've missed you so much."

He pulled back the thin blanket and looked at her body, the swell of her breasts, the thrust of her nipples against the thin cambric of her nightgown. Then, with a swift motion, he drew the gown away from her shoulders and her breasts. He buried his face in her softness.

"You're sure it's all right?" he said, his voice muffled against her body.

She felt the hard urgency of him, and she could no longer hold back. She finished stripping off the gown, her fingers shaking with her need, and then she opened her arms to receive him. Her husband—her love.

Her body responded swiftly to his, and when his hands began to trace the curves of her breasts, hips, and buttocks, she cried out shamelessly in pleasure. He could not doubt her willingness, her eagerness, and he positioned himself between her thighs and entered her. Her legs tightened around him, for she wanted to draw him deeper and still deeper inside her, to be one with him. She had no pride now, no time for doubts or fears. She gloried in his power, his strength, in the driving force with which he claimed her.

She fell asleep in his arms, her body pressed against his, feeling the weight of his arm across her breasts and the warmth of his breath against her face. Only now could she admit to herself the full measure of her loneliness during his absence. . . .

It was when she awoke at dawn and looked down at Logan's sleeping face that she was assailed by the familiar doubts. She knew more than ever now how deeply she loved him, and surely, after last night, she could not question his physical passion for her. But she needed more than this joining of their bodies, this fierce yet tender act of possession. She loved him with all her being, and she wondered if he would ever understand, or come to love her in the same way.

Then Logan stirred, his eyes opened, and he smiled up at her as he drew her closer. And she told herself that he did care, he must, that once they were settled in the new home he had spoken about, they would be a real family, she and Logan and little Chris.

But her doubts, though they were lulled, did not wholly disappear. Could a man like Logan, whose whole childhood had been a fierce struggle to survive over brutal odds, ever come to understand what it was she had to offer him?

Chapter 11

Even during those first few weeks, when Vanessa was getting settled in the new house, she was not always able to close her mind to doubts, for it was plain that although Logan wanted her and little Chris to have a safe, comfortable home, he was businesslike, not at all sentimental about the upward move. He chose the house on Gramercy Park with the same speed and efficiency, the same eye for a sharp deal, that he showed in getting together a cargo for the next voyage of the *Ondine.*

Nevertheless, Vanessa loved the house from the first time she walked through the clean, high-ceilinged, freshly painted rooms. "I've never had a real home," she told Logan.

"That place up in Salem—what about that?" he asked.

"Mama was there, and she tried to make it a home, but there were always boarders to be served, strangers coming and going." She smiled with warm satisfaction. "This house is mine," she said.

Logan looked down at her and spoke quietly. "Ours," was all he said, but she caught the warmth, the unaccustomed half-teasing affection in the word and in the look that accompanied it. She waited for him to reach out and draw her into his arms, but instead, he began pacing the room that was to be the parlor, his footsteps echoing in the empty space.

"I've signed a year's lease, with an option to buy the house," he said. "Right now we're a long way from the center of the city, but property values will be going up here, you'll see. This house will prove a good investment."

Before she could reply, he went on. "I've ordered the furniture," he told her.

She stared at him. "But Logan, I could have—"

"We're getting it at wholesale," he told her, "from Oliver Nash. He's the furnituremaker whose cargo I'll be taking down to Cuba on this next voyage. I've chosen only a few pieces, but good ones. When I return I'll buy the rest."

Vanessa wanted to protest. Wasn't it the wife's business to select the furniture? But Logan was going on, still pacing the polished floor. "We'll need servants."

"I trust you haven't hired them too," she said with a touch of asperity.

He shook his head. "I'll leave that to you," he told her. "You'll have to train them, after all. A cook and a housemaid to begin with."

"I can cook," Vanessa protested.

"I know that," Logan told her impatiently, "but before long you'll have other claims on your time. We'll be doing a good deal of entertaining, and we'll need a suitable, well-trained staff."

"Entertaining?"

"For business reasons. Ship brokers, commission merchants, and their wives. You'll take your place in the parlor, where you belong. I won't have you down in the kitchen polishing grates."

And so, for the next few weeks, while Logan was away in Connecticut bargaining for a deck cargo of horses and breeding cattle destined for the Cuban planters, Vanessa was busy interviewing a procession of servants. Felicity gave her the name of a reputable agency on Duane Street, and from among the applicants who came to the house, Vanessa chose Bessie Skene, a plump, round-faced woman with an even disposition, who proved to have a light hand with pastry dough and an expert skill with sauces; and a small, sturdy housemaid, Alice, a farm girl from up the Hudson, who went to work with a will, delighted to find herself in this wonderful, bustling city.

"I'll expect to find this house running like a well-organized business when I come home from my next voyage," he told Vanessa. He was seated with her at the table, and he nodded approvingly as he sampled Mrs. Skene's beef and kidney pie. "You've chosen well," he said with a smile. "Later, of course, we'll have more of a staff here. I expect to make an excellent profit out of this voyage."

The thought of Logan's next voyage was the only cloud on Vanessa's horizon as summer sped away and the trees in Gramercy Park began to change from dusty green to gold. A few days before Logan sailed she tried to share her feelings with her husband. "Back in Salem, there were captains' wives who went along with their men."

"I want you safe, here at home," Logan told her. "And the baby too."

But the prospect of the long separation drove her to plead with him. "We could take Chris along. Oh, Logan, please . . ."

His face hardened and his dark brows drew together.

"I thought you had better sense, Vanessa," he said with an edge to his voice. "You know I'm only getting started. Sailing from port to port, scrounging for cargo wherever I can get it. The last thing I need is to be burdened by a woman and an infant."

His words stung, and she retorted, "Not a woman—your wife! And Chris is your son!"

She turned away quickly to hide the tears that were even

now stinging her eyelids. A burden. Was that all she meant to him, and Chris too?

A moment later she felt his hands on her shoulders, the fingers strong and warm through the material of her bodice. He turned her around to face him. "I've provided you and Chris with a home so you'd have security and comfort while I'm away. Life aboard ship is hard, even for a man. And we'll be going into the autumn hurricane season. That can be dangerous."

"Then if you'll be going into danger . . ." she began, feeling sick at the pit of her stomach, remembering her own father, lost off Cape Fear during an autumn hurricane.

"I want to know you're safe," he told her. "And my son too."

She knew that there was nothing more she could say to change his mind. His lips brushed hers lightly, but when her mouth clung, she felt his kiss deepen, felt the rising passion in him. At least he hungered for her, even if he did not love her. She pressed the length of her body against his, feeling the steel buttons of his coat cutting into her breasts and welcoming the hard pressure of his thighs through the fullness of her skirt and petticoats. And she knew that tonight, when he would reach out for her in bed, she would give herself freely, eagerly, that he would at least take to sea with him the memory of a loving, ardent wife.

But after he had sailed once more, the first week in September, Vanessa's spirits sank. Chris was a joy, lively and healthy, gaining weight and strength, and when she held him, sang to him, talked to him, she felt contented, fulfilled. But when he was asleep upstairs in the nursery and she sat alone in the parlor, she could not fight off the growing pangs of loneliness. She told herself sternly that a Salem woman, a captain's wife, should be able to cope with these frequent periods of isolation, that although some captains' wives did sail with their men, many more did not.

Only it had been different back home in Salem, for there, the wives of absent seamen gathered together often for tea and gossip. They exchanged recipes and quilt patterns and advice on the best ways to comfort a baby who was suffering the pains of teething or colic. They would go to church services together when their men were away at sea; and in groups, they would attend lectures or borrow books at the Salem Athenaeum.

But here in New York, Vanessa's only female friends were Felicity and Kitty, and she could hardly call upon either of them at the Bradford mansion on Hudson Square.

A few weeks after Logan had sailed, Vanessa sent Alice with a note to the headquarters of the Society for the Relief of Seamen's Wives, only to learn that Felicity was away visiting Abel's brother, Jasper, and his wife, Edith, at their home in Peekskill; but Alice left the note, and several days later Felicity appeared on the doorstep of the small, trim new house on Gramercy Park.

Felicity admired the house, and later she held little Chris in her arms, pressing her cheek against his dark curls. "How fortunate you are, my dear, to have such a beautiful son. And how pleased Logan must be," she added wistfully.

She explained that Kitty would have come, too, but that she could not. "Kitty is in the family way," she said delicately, "and she is often incapacitated. The doctor assures us that she is perfectly healthy, but she has morning sickness nearly every day, and then she has to spend the rest of the day in bed, she's so exhausted," Felicity said. "Horace does what he can to comfort her, but he is dreadfully distressed."

Horace Widdicomb was less distressed than angered by

his wife's condition. He wanted a son, and, more important, he was eager that Kitty should present Abel with grandsons so that the old man might be satisfied in this ambition; it pleased Horace to think of the Bradford fortune passing first from Abel to him, and then on to a line of his stalwart sons.

As for Kitty's ailments, uncomfortable though they might be, they were not serious; it was perfectly natural, Dr. Fairleigh had assured him, that a sensitive, high-strung young woman like Kitty would have certain "unpleasant weaknesses" during the early weeks of her pregnancy. Even though these weaknesses kept Horace from sharing Kitty's bed, he did not find this deprivation unduly burdensome, since, after all, there were any number of obliging young girls in the better parlor houses of the city whose services could be bought, girls who were expert and willing to submit to any variations of the sexual act that Horace might fancy and who could suggest a few of their own. Kitty, in spite of her rounded, promising body and pink and white prettiness, had been anything but ardent in bed.

What was far more irritating than the temporary curtailment of his marital rights, Horace thought as he walked briskly up Broadway in the direction of the Astor House, was Kitty's explosive temper. No matter how fatigued she claimed to be, she was never too exhausted to turn on him like an angry cat, her eyes slitted with rage. This morning's quarrel, however, had been different, more bitter than any of the others.

"It's all well enough for you to want sons," she told him, her voice shrill and venomous. "You don't have to go through this horrible—this—this disgusting—"

"The morning sickness will soon pass," Horace told her in what he hoped was a comforting tone. "Dr. Fairleigh has explained that in a month or so you'll feel much better, and after that—"

Kitty got to her feet, clutching her crumpled wrapper of rose-colored silk and Brussels lace around her. "After that I'll have to go through the torture of labor!" Horace saw the panic, the terror, in her eyes.

"Really, my dear, it is all perfectly natural. Every woman must—"

"I can't! I won't! I'd rather die right now than to have to go through—"

Horace, fast losing patience, snapped out, "Kitty, control yourself. Think of the child. These outbursts are surely harmful to—"

"The child!" He put out his hand to touch her, but she drew away in revulsion. "Your child! I don't want any child of yours. I never have—and you know it! If Papa had not forced me to marry you—"

"You'd have run off with Logan McClintock," Horace said. "You'd have thrown yourself at that—that gutter rat—even without a wedding ring, if that was what he wanted." He did not raise his voice, but he saw her flinch at his words and had the cold satisfaction of knowing that he had hit home. "Too bad that McClintock preferred that trashy little red-haired slut, isn't it?"

Now, as Horace made his way through the crowds on Broadway in the direction of Vesey and Barclay Streets, where he was to dine with Abel in the Astor House, he tried to dismiss the memory of Kitty's face, the bitterness with which she had told him that she had not wanted to marry him, that she had been forced into it. Not that Horace had ever deceived himself into believing that he would have been her choice as a husband, but he had hoped that since women were, after all, adaptable creatures, she would learn to accept him and to look forward to the birth of their children. She would forget her girlish daydreams about Logan McClintock, who was, surely, a totally unsuitable match for the heiress to the Bradford shipping fortune.

He stopped short, realizing that he had almost walked past the Astor House. Now he turned and mounted the steps and walked briskly through the handsome inner court and into the dining room, where Abel was already waiting for him in a secluded alcove; the older man was studying the impressive menu, which bore an engraving of the hotel along with a screaming eagle with the national shield, a temple of Liberty, and a rising sun above an imposing list of choices for each course.

"Sit down, Horace," Abel said briskly. Then, when the waiter hurried over in answer to his gesture, he ordered for both of them. Although Horace was now his son-in-law instead of only his chief clerk, Abel's manner had not changed.

"Have you found a suitable shipyard yet?" Abel demanded, unfolding his heavily starched white napkin. A few weeks before, Abel had given Horace the responsibility of finding a shipyard that could be bought or leased at a reasonable sum. "I want to start building those new clippers as quickly as possible."

"There are several possibilities, sir," Horace began carefully.

"Possibilities? I want to begin right away. I thought I'd made that clear."

"I don't quite understand," Horace said. "The yards we already have—"

"Our yards are working to capacity right now," Abel said. "I want to lay the keels for at least two new clippers—probably more—and I want them completed and ready to sail by spring." He tossed down a half glass of port and wiped his lips.

"But our tea clippers will be sailing in two weeks," Horace said.

"I'm aware of the sailing date of the tea fleet," Abel retorted with undisguised sarcasm. "I gave you an order—to find another yard, and be quick about it. Obviously you've not been able to do even that much."

Horace smarted under Abel's words and his look, but he had learned long ago to conceal his feelings when it was to his interest to do so. "I'll have the list of possible properties on your desk tomorrow," he said quickly. "The fact is, I've been pursuing other matters—important matters—in the interests of the company."

The waiter put down a tureen of oxtail soup laced with claret, served the two men, and left.

Abel savored the soup and smacked his lips. "And what are these important matters?"

"It's about Logan McClintock's ship, the *Ondine.* I cannot imagine what possessed Mrs. Campbell to leave the ship to such a man."

"She left the ship to Vanessa. A broken-down old trading schooner," Abel said. "What the devil do you find so important about that?"

"McClintock's married Vanessa, and the ship's his. He made one voyage, a most successful one from what I've heard, and now he's off again. He's established connections in the Carolinas, trading for naval stores, and he brought back a cargo of muscovado sugar from Cuba. He's made a deal with a couple of commission merchants in Havana and Matanzas." Horace leaned across the table, ignoring the tureen of soup there. "I also have reason to believe that he got backing from a few businessmen up in Salem. I'm sure I could get their names for you, sir."

"Good Lord, man, don't you think I've got more to concern me than the doings of Logan McClintock?" Abel shook his head. "If you hope to rise in the shipping business, you'd best learn what's important and what is not. No man makes his way to the top if he thinks like a pettifogging little clerk."

Horace looked away for a moment, fearing that his eyes would betray him. He forced down the anger aroused in him by Abel's words, and the reminder that he had risen from the post of clerk only a short time ago. "I did not think you would regard the matter as trivial, sir," he said. "Perhaps you have forgotten how that gutter rat, McClintock, had the arrogance to make advances to Kitty. And she was infatuated with the man. Why, if you hadn't stepped in and—"

"But I did, and Kitty's your wife now, and carrying my first grandson."

Horace tried not to think how furious Abel would be if the child turned out to be a girl.

"As for McClintock, he's married to that red-haired wench now—two of a kind, they are." He tapped Horace on the arm. "You take my advice and see that Kitty knows who is master. A woman needs a firm hand. It's all they understand." He gave Horace a shrewd, searching look, and added, "If she's still got any flighty notions, it's high time she got rid of them. That's your job, Horace."

He broke off long enough for the waiter to remove the soup plates and tureen and put down the next course, a filet of beef with roasted potatoes.

"Now," he resumed, "if we've got these domestic matters out of the way, Horace, perhaps you'll be able to turn your mind to business. Urgent business, and profitable."

But Horace was angry and resentful at Abel's treatment. "Perhaps, sir, if you would do me the honor of confiding these important business matters to me, I might be more helpful. You've not yet seen fit to tell me what need you have for the new shipyard and the clippers you want to build there. I can scarcely be expected to—"

"All right, then," Abel cut in. "You've heard the talk of those gold nuggets that were discovered out in California. Back in January, it was."

"Rumors," Horace said. "I read something about it in the *New York Herald*, I believe—"

"More than rumors," Abel retorted. "A Colonel Mason, military governor of California, dispatched a messenger straight to Washington with a report on those gold mines. The man was carrying three thousand dollars' worth of nuggets. There are swarms of men from San Francisco heading for the diggings, and more coming every day. Won't be long before there'll be men from the East heading out there too."

"But we're in the tea trade—" Horace began slowly.

"We're in whatever trade brings in the cash," Abel said. "It will take time for the news about gold to sink in, but when it does . . . Some men will go overland. We're not concerned with them. But there'll be plenty who'll pay whatever we ask for a fast passage around the Horn and on to San Francisco."

Horace's eyes began to glitter behind his spectacles.

"And they'll need supplies too. California's a wilderness."

Abel nodded. "Now you begin to understand. We'll carry passengers and supplies. As for our tea clippers, they've been sailing to China under ballast, so only the return voyage is profitable. Now we'll make a profit both ways."

Horace felt a rising excitement as he reminded himself that the profits from these voyages, along with all the other assets of the Bradford Line, would one day be his. He would be treated with respect then, and men would make way for him when he walked through the Merchants' Exchange.

His father-in-law's next words put a damper on his elation, however. "We'll need more good captains, seasoned men who know how to get speed out of a ship, run her to her limits without tearing the canvas out of her. 'Bully' Waterman—he's the kind I need. But he's signed with Howland and Aspinwall." Abel shook his head. "Or McClintock. Why, if he hadn't left my service . . . Arrogant bastard, but he can drive a crew, and his seamanship's as good as Waterman's." He gave a short, hard laugh. "A strong hand at the wheel—that's what's wanted."

Horace's heart sank. Maybe Abel was beginning to regret having given Kitty to him in marriage. He looked at his father-in-law from behind his spectacles, watching as Abel put away a huge serving of beef and potatoes. A strong man, even now in his fifties, Abel was—tough and shrewd. Why, a man like that could keep going for another thirty-five years, and while he lived he would keep a firm grip on the business. Horace tried to force down a mouthful of the savory beef, but he could take no pleasure in its fine flavor.

What kind of bargain had he made? All well and good for Abel to tell him that he must show Kitty who was master of the house. He did not even have a house of his own as yet, but continued to live in the mansion on Hudson Square. And if these first months of marriage were any kind of a sample, his plump, pink-checked little wife was capable of making his life one long misery. He winced, remembering the words she had flung at him that morning.

I don't want any child of yours.

A married woman, who carried his child in her body, and she was still daydreaming about Logan McClintock. It was indecent, unnatural. She had come to his bed a virgin, but that had been only because McClintock for some inexplicable reason had not reached out for her. If he had, no doubt she would have given herself shamelessly in some hidden corner of the shipyard like any dockside drab. McClintock was to blame for this unwillingness in Kitty to behave like a decent woman, a proper wife. Horace felt his dislike of the tall, black-browed captain rise up in him, choking him, making him long for revenge.

But when he spoke, Horace was careful to keep his voice dry and businesslike. "Naturally I now see the importance of this new California route," Horace told Abel.

He took a sip of wine. "We'll need all our clippers for that, including those yet to be built. But there's the schooner *Ellen Grey*. She's in port right now. She's fast. She could make the voyage to Cuba while McClintock's going from port to port seeking cargo in the South. We could send a representative with orders to use his influence to persuade these Cuban commission merchants not to deal with McClintock. We could undercut him on freight rates."

"And to what end? Where's the profit in that?"

"McClintock would be driven off the seas," Horace persisted. "Once that was accomplished, we could raise our rates again, naturally."

Abel's eyes narrowed but he did not answer.

Horace hurried on. "Logan McClintock's no real competition to us yet. But he's ambitious. As we both have cause to know. And disloyal. Didn't he walk out on the Bradford Line when you needed him? After you'd raised him to captain. He said he'd set up his own shipping line, and he will if he isn't stopped."

Abel gave a sour laugh. "Maybe you'd like to go to Cuba as our representative, Horace," he said. "Maybe you'd like to set up a commission house for the company in Havana."

Taken aback, Horace said hastily, "I—I don't think that's necessary, sir. And my place is here with my wife now." Horace was not about to allow Abel to exile him to Cuba when the important affairs of the Bradford Line were being transacted right here in New York. "But we can surely find someone in the company who will be competent to represent us down in Havana," he added quickly.

Abel nodded. "We can spare the *Ellen Grey.*" His eyes were thoughtful now. "There's no harm getting a foot in the door with those Cuban sugar planters," he went on. "Cuba's coffee exports do not amount to much since the hurricane back in forty-four. All those coffee trees uprooted. But their sugar production's been increasing steadily." He slapped his hand down on the table. "All right, Horace," he said. "You make the arrangements. Find a suitable man to send, and see that the *Ellen Grey* sails for Havana as quickly as possible."

"I've come to ask a favor, Vanessa, my dear."

Vanessa, seated beside Felicity on the parlor sofa, looked with some surprise at the older woman.

It was late afternoon, and the October twilight was falling. Only a few moments ago Alice had drawn the heavy red velvet drapes across the window that looked out on Gramercy Park, and had set down the tray with its steaming teapot and its plates of small sandwiches and cakes.

"A favor?" Vanessa was puzzled. "You know I'll do whatever I can. What is it?"

"I'm trying to find work for a woman who is in desperate need," Felicity said. "Her name is Delia." Seeing the question in Vanessa's eyes, she went on. "It isn't customary for a slave woman to have more than a first name. Delia was a slave on a Louisiana plantation. She has only recently come north."

"A runaway slave?"

Felicity nodded. "She's a quadroon—one quarter black, you see—and she has had considerable experience in caring for children. She raised all of her former master's children.

And three of her own as well."

"Why did she run away?"

Felicity sighed, her dark eyes sad. "Her master's children were all grown—too old for a nursemaid. And as for her own children . . . When her master died, his widow inherited the plantation along with the rest of his property."

It was a moment before Vanessa understood. Once, a few years before, she had attended an antislavery lecture at the Salem Athenaeum. She knew that the slave woman, Delia, and her children were property in Louisiana, like cattle or horses. Vanessa found the thought sickening.

"Delia's mistress was short of cash. So she sold Delia and her three children to a slave trader who disposed of all of them, each to a different bidder. It was after the auction that Delia made her break for freedom."

Vanessa's fingers tightened on the handle of her teacup. She tried to take in the full meaning, and as she did, she was shaken by a feeling of outrage. What would it be like if someone were to take Chris away from her, to sell him to a passing stranger?

"These things happen every day in the South," Felicity was saying. "Sooner or later this evil traffic in human beings must be stopped, as it was in England. But until then, those of us who can help, in whatever small way, are going to. I have been attending the services at the Plymouth Church over in Brooklyn. There is a young preacher there, Mr. Henry Ward Beecher, who is speaking out most strongly against slavery. Indeed, his church is becoming a center of the abolitionist movement. He is convinced that slavery can be abolished through constitutional means. But for the time being we must all do what we can to aid those who have escaped and come up north."

Vanessa realized with a surge of guilt that she had been so

absorbed in her concern for Logan and in caring for her baby that she had given little thought to outside matters. "I want to help," she assured Felicity. "But how can I?"

"Surely you might hire Delia to care for Chris. I am convinced, from talking to her, that she is trustworthy. If she had been allowed to keep her own children, even one of them, she would have served her new master faithfully, she said."

"But another servant. Logan's shipping line is not yet established. I am trying to keep our household expenses as modest as possible."

"Oh, but Delia wouldn't want a salary. She'd be willing to work for a roof over her head and her food—and she'd be so grateful."

Vanessa hesitated. "Surely there are many wealthy ladies here in New York who would hire her."

"A few years ago perhaps. But the city is changing. In many households, nursemaids are chosen according to the current fashion. And right now an English nanny, or a Scotswoman, is in demand."

"I don't know much about fashionable circles," Vanessa said with a smile. "If your Delia's good with babies, and if Chris takes to her, that's all that matters to me."

"Then you'll give her a chance to prove herself?"

"Bring her to the house whenever you like," Vanessa said.

When Felicity had finished her tea and was preparing to leave she said, "I know how isolated you must feel, with Logan away at sea again. But now that you'll have Delia, perhaps you'll be able to get about more. It would do you good, my dear."

Then, seeing Vanessa's doubtful look, she went on.

"I don't mean shopping for gowns or attending musicales. There are many charities to which you might give your time."

"That afternoon, when I delivered baskets to the seamen's

wives," Vanessa said, "I felt useful then—and I think they liked me. If I could do that again, I'd be more than willing."

Felicity rose and smoothed her full skirts around her. "I'll find something for you to do." She paused and gave Vanessa a long, appraising look. "Some of the charity work is not particularly pleasant. Oh, I wouldn't think of asking you to go to the Five Points. Indeed, Abel would not permit me to go there. But with this influx of immigrants, there are shantytowns springing up on the edges of the city. The people there need help—even the barest necessities."

"I'll go wherever I'm needed," Vanessa assured her. If she kept busy and active, the time would pass quickly and then Logan would be home again.

Chapter 12

Logan blotted the ship's log and closed it. Then he addressed an envelope and, taking out a sheet of paper, he began his letter to Vanessa. He had never written her a letter before, and he was not sure how to phrase it.

"My dear wife . . ."

He stared out the porthole of the master's cabin, squinting into the glare of the sunswept waters of Havana harbor. The *Ondine* rode at anchor, but in a few hours he would catch the outgoing tide and head for Rio de Janeiro. He had not anticipated this turn of events when he had left Vanessa back in New York. It was only fair to inform her that his return would be delayed by a matter of weeks, or, more likely, months.

His mouth set into a tight line. Even under the best of circumstances, he knew, West Indian trade was an uncertain business. Small schooners, like the *Ondine*, were at the mercy of countless unpredictable conditions, both natural and man-made. He shook his head. The British and European markets were far better organized, for there were always the transatlantic packets to bring fresh information. Even Canton's tea trade was reasonably well coordinated. But the trade down here in the Caribbean—that was quite a different matter. A captain of a single schooner, like the *Ondine*, had no way of knowing whether he would find an empty market clamoring for his goods, or whether a particular port had been so glutted by other vessels that he would scarcely be able to give his cargo away. That was why many ships like his own recorded clearances for the "West Indies" or the "Spanish Main," and then were forced to go from port to port, trying to dispose of their cargoes. He remembered how Vanessa had asked to go along on this voyage and to take their son, and he had shaken his head. So far, matters had gone badly enough, even without the encumbrance of a woman and an infant.

It had started when he had run into that hurricane off Cape Fear. His face went bleak as he remembered the terrified screaming noises made by the horses, part of his prized deck cargo; those sounds had blended with the shrieking of the wind as the ship had been driven toward the reefs off the Carolina coast. Afterward, he and his first mate, a tough, bearded New Englander, Dermot Rankin, had shot nearly half the horses, and some of the breeding cattle, too, for the beasts had been hopelessly injured. Several of the animals had been struck by falling spars and rigging.

Had it not been for his own expert seamanship in getting the *Ondine* into Wilmington, and Pringle's skill in repairing the damage, the schooner itself might have been a total loss. As it was, he had lost another precious commodity: time.

For on his arrival in Cuba he found the commission agents with whom he had done business on the first voyage embarrassed, strangely reticent about explaining why they had no sugar for him. Only one, a Señor Gutiérrez, had been communicative. "Two weeks before your arrival, Capitán, our firm was approached by a representative of the Bradford Line. He offered us rates that were so—so ridiculously low, we could not refuse." The short, stout Cuban looked regretful, and Logan understood. Business was business, and in the same situation Logan would have behaved as the Cuban merchant had.

Abel Bradford, again. First the matter of the *Athena*, and now this. Bradford was not a particularly generous man, but this sort of action was uncharacteristic. Kitty was safely married to that conniving clerk, Widdicomb. Horace Widdicomb—no doubt he was at the bottom of this.

Logan had restrained his anger and had invited Señor Gutiérrez out to a nearby café to share a bottle of wine. It was the sort of gesture the Cuban understood and admired. He insisted on reciprocating, and halfway through the second bottle, he asked, "And where will you go now, Capitán McClintock?"

"I haven't decided," Logan said. "Jamaica, perhaps, or—"

"I have a brother-in-law in Brazil. He owns a large coffee plantation there. Our own coffee crop here in Cuba has been wiped out, as you know, but in Brazil—that's another matter. If a letter of introduction would be of help to you . . ."

And now, with the letter from Gutiérrez in his desk, Logan was preparing to sail for Rio. His message to Vanessa would be carried back to New York by the captain of a brig with whom he had struck up an acquaintance during his brief stay here in Havana.

He was hesitating over the letter. He did not see the point of frightening Vanessa with a detailed account of the hurricane. And there was no need to worry her by telling her that Abel Bradford, armed with his far greater financial resources, was still intent on carrying on their feud.

He would find a way to make a profit on this voyage yet. Meanwhile, she and Chris were secure and comfortable in the house on Gramercy Park. Nothing could harm them there. His son would never know the stench, the filth, the dangers, of the Five Points. He would see to that.

Quickly he wrote a few lines, telling Vanessa only of the vagaries of the West Indian trade, saying that he had decided to venture farther south in search of a profitable cargo. He did not tell her he was bound for Brazil. She might entertain

Felicity Bradford, and women did have a tendency to gossip. Instead, he mentioned a number of Caribbean ports and added that she should not expect him home until late winter or even early spring.

He hesitated over the closing. He had never in his life written a love letter. What were his feelings for Vanessa? He thought of her now, and he remembered her beautiful, softly curved body, the glowing cascade of red-gold hair. He felt a sudden hunger. Then he thought of her dignity, her composure, when he had refused to take her with him on the *Ondine.* Another woman might have gone on about it, but she had accepted his decision. She had pride and self-control, admirable qualities in a wife. But she was passionate, too, abandoning herself to him during their nights together, giving herself completely. Once she had gotten over her first fears she had been all any man could ask for.

He dipped his pen into the inkstand. *Yr. Devoted Husband,* he wrote, feeling somewhat embarrassed even by so commonplace a phrase. Quickly he thrust the letter into an envelope and addressed it to the house on Gramercy Park.

He knew the harbor at Rio de Janeiro well, for he had often made port there on his voyages to Canton. But on this particular morning he was instantly aware of something different, disturbing.

He stood on the poopdeck, raised his glass to his eye, and examined the shipping. True, the harbor here was always crowded with shipping from all over the world, but now it was far busier than usual; a forest of masts and riggings were etched against the brilliant blue of the sky. His first mate, Dermot Rankin, had the same opinion. The big, bearded New Englander came to join him, shaking his head. "What do you make of it, sir?"

"I'm not sure yet." Some of the clippers, brigs, and schooners that rode at anchor were handsome, well-rigged, and freshly painted, but many more were in shockingly bad condition.

He passed the glass to Rankin, who said, "Half those vessels are ready for the breaker's yard. Coffin ships, no doubt of it." He was about to hand back the glass when something caught in his eye. "Look there, sir. That little fishing boat's making straight for us."

It was not the only small boat to do so. Several rowboats and even a few native canoes were slicing through the green tropical waters. And far beyond, Logan saw that the beach was crammed with people and with makeshift shelters and huts.

"Some kind of a revolution," Rankin suggested. "Have plenty of those down here. Do you want me to open the arms locker, sir?"

Logan shook his head. "Not yet," he said, and he turned his glass on the long curving stretch of sparkling white beach. He was puzzled by what he saw: crowds of people, most of them looking bedraggled but none of them armed, milling about among a collection of makeshift wood and canvas shelters or cooking over open fires.

"They're not blacks," Logan said. "This isn't a slave uprising. It doesn't look like any revolution either. Señor Gutiérrez said that conditions are fairly stable here, because the emperor Dom Pedro's always been popular with these people. He's done a lot to improve their living conditions."

Logan gave Rankin the order to drop anchor. The fishing boat drew alongside, followed by a motley flotilla of rowboats, and native canoes.

A tall, thin man stood up and waved from the bow of the fishing boat. "Captain, where are you bound for?" Although there was urgency in his voice, he did not sound threatening. He wore a well-tailored, though somewhat rumpled suit of black broadcloth, and his tall beaver hat was set at a jaunty angle.

Before Logan had a chance to answer, the rest of the passengers were standing up and shoving their way forward so that he thought the small craft might overturn.

"California?" one of them shouted, and the rest took up the question. "Are you bound for California?" Logan noticed that a few of the passengers were women, whose gowns, although the worse for wear, had once been fashionable.

"Are you going to California? California!"

"No, I am not," Logan called back.

"I'll make it worth your while," the tall, thin man shouted. "Name your price."

The small fishing boat careened dangerously, but the passengers were oblivious to the danger. Plainly they were driven only by the need to get to California, and nothing else was important.

"Allerton's my name," said the tall thin man in black broadcloth, and he drew out his wallet. He was seated with Logan and Silas Pringle in a small private room in a waterfront hotel called La Perla. He slapped a sheaf of bills down on the table. "I've got to get to California, and I'll pay whatever you ask." His dark eyes burned with desperate urgency.

"I've already explained that I'm here to pick up a cargo of schooner," Logan said.

"That means she wasn't built to go around the Horn," Silas explained patiently. "She's a good ship, but even when she was new, it's not likely she could have taken that kind of punishment."

"It's worth the risk," Allerton insisted. "There are hundreds of people here in Rio stranded and wanting to get to the gold diggings in California. That ship of yours looks a lot better than the rotten tub I took from Savannah. She barely made it here before she fell apart." He pushed the pile of bills toward Logan.

"I've already explained that I'm here to pick up a cargo of coffee," Logan began, but he was looking at the money thoughtfully.

"Coffee!" Allerton made a contemptuous gesture with a pale, manicured hand. "I'm talking about gold! A river of gold out there for the taking!"

"You don't look like a miner to me," Logan said with a thin smile.

"I haven't said I was," Allerton replied. "There are other ways of making a fortune in California right now. I want passage around the Horn to San Francisco. The men who strike it rich will want a place where they can find pleasure, and refreshments. I have nearly one hundred cases of good whiskey—"

"And those who don't find gold will need consolation," Silas Pringle put in.

Allerton nodded. "Exactly so," he said. Then turning back to Logan, he urged, "Will you take me—and my cargo, sir?"

"If I were to undertake the voyage—and I'm not saying I would—I'd need more than one passenger. Even with a cargo of good whiskey."

"You will find more," the man said eagerly. "You could pick and choose. There are plenty of men here in Rio who'd pay handsomely for deck space to sleep on."

Logan had heard, months ago, of the discovery of gold in California, but this was his first encounter with the gold fever that was sweeping the continent and spreading even to Europe. But he hesitated to commit himself and the *Ondine*.

The vessel made a good appearance, with her freshly painted hull and her trim rigging; Silas had done his repair work well. Nevertheless, Logan had taken clippers around the Horn, and he was well aware that the small schooner had not been designed for such a passage.

Silas, too, saw the hazards, for he spoke again to Allerton. "You lost part of your cargo of whiskey coming this far, mister," he pointed out quietly. "What makes you think you won't lose the rest on the passage to California? You're no seaman, but maybe you've heard of the dangers going around the Horn."

"I've heard." Allerton gave Silas Pringle a long, steady look. "But I'm going to get to San Francisco one way or another."

A shrill female voice from the other side of the closed door cut off anything more he might have wished to say.

"I demand to see the captain."

There were a few protestations from the waiter, but a moment later a stout, hard-faced female flung open the door and came bustling inside. Her tightly corseted body was encased in wine-colored satin, and a plumed bonnet of the same color was set atop her unnaturally bright yellow hair. Behind her, clustered in a group, like a small flock of bedraggled chickens, were a half dozen buxom young girls in brightly colored finery.

The hard-faced woman said, "I want passage, Captain. For myself and my young ladies. Passage to San Francisco. I am prepared to pay six hundred dollars for a stateroom, no matter how small."

"I am not bound for San Francisco," Logan told her. "I don't carry passengers—and certainly not female passengers—"

"Eight hundred dollars," the woman said. Her pale blue eyes were as hard as steel. "My young ladies will make no difficulties. I will see to that."

One corner of Logan's mouth rose in the trace of a smile. He knew her kind, for he had met others like her in many seaports—harridans with dyed hair and rouged cheeks who commanded their girls as ruthlessly as the most hardened captain drove his crew.

"I've already told you, I'm not bound for San Francisco," Logan repeated. But he was reckoning rapidly. He had a letter of introduction to the brother-in-law of the obliging Señor Gutiérrez, but in order to do business with the man he would have to journey to the interior of the country, and then, perhaps, wait weeks or months if the coffee beans had not yet been harvested, and he had no way of knowing how much this plantation owner was prepared to pay for the shipment of his cargo.

Here, in Rio, on the other hand, was a desperate horde of people who would bid against one another for any sort of accommodations aboard the *Ondine.* A man like him, with a single schooner, might spend years carrying cargo from the West Indies and the ports of South America before he could make enough to buy more ships, to start a fleet of his own. And if Abel Bradford and Horace Widdicomb were prepared to carry on their vendetta in these waters, there was no telling how many ports he might find closed to him.

"You are your own master," Allerton was saying. "You are free to change your destination, aren't you?"

"I'm not provisioned for a voyage around the Horn," Logan said slowly. "It would mean a wait of at least three days. I'd need oranges and lemons. I want no scurvy aboard my ship. I can provide one cabin for you and your girls, ma'am, and you'll see that they stay in it. Any trouble among the men and I'll put you and those girls ashore, whatever the nearest port may be."

The woman reached into the bodice of her dress and pulled out a small leather bag. She opened it and put several bills down on the table. Allerton tapped his own sheaf of bills.

"Six hundred," he said.

"That won't get you a stateroom," Logan told him. "Deck space—that's all. And you'll provide your own bedding or sleep on bare planks."

Allerton hesitated, but he did not take his money back.

"And you'll pay me another three hundred to ship that whiskey of yours. Unless I miss my guess, it'll be worth ten times that much in San Francisco."

"Two hundred," Allerton bargained.

Then, as if a dam had broken, there was a rush of people into the back room. Husky, red-faced men in work clothes, with picks and shovels and tin pans. Pale, soberly dressed men who looked as if they belonged behind a desk in a Boston countinghouse or a ladies' drapery shop. One proclaimed himself to be a doctor, and Logan decided that he should come along, even if he could not offer as much passage money as some of the others. They would be needing a doctor before they finished this voyage, he suspected. As for the rest, he would sell deck space to the highest bidders.

It was not until the following morning that Logan and Silas returned to the ship. Although Logan had always thought Rio one of the most beautiful ports he had ever seen, he had no eye for its charms now. The two men walked quickly past shimmering white houses, breathing the mingled scents from the flowering jacaranda and the splendid "golden rain" trees, with their vivid yellow blossoms, and the heady fragrances of cinnamon and orange trees. Brilliant hummingbirds hovered about the trees, and iridescent blue butterflies drifted on the soft air, but neither man took notice of the surroundings.

Logan was aware, however, of a different tempo in these narrow streets where, on former voyages, the natives had moved with tropical languor, where church pageants and processions offered the only excitement. Now these streets were swarming with men who spoke in nasal New England accents, others with the soft drawl of Georgia in their voices. And there were women, too, like those to whom he had sold cabin space; most traveled in groups, but a few were alone, expensively dressed, and, no doubt, adventurous enough, or perhaps greedy enough, to take their chances.

As they came to the beach Silas spoke at last.

"You're asking for trouble," he said, shaking his head. "The *Ondine*'s a good ship, but she wasn't built for a passage around the Horn. She's going to be overloaded too."

"There's risk," Logan admitted. He stopped and turned to face Silas. "You didn't sign on for San Francisco. If you want to turn back, I'll see you get passage on a ship for New York."

Silas glared at him. "You're going, aren't you? You'll need a good ship's carpenter along."

They said no more as they walked across the beach among the makeshift shelters and the shabby, stranded men who were preparing their scanty food over small fires. There was no need for further talk, for Logan understood.

Slitting his eyes against the glare of the blazing tropical sunlight, the sparkling water ringed by mountains, Logan was seeing himself, a dirty, half-starved savage of twelve who had been keeping alive by running with a gang of boys who survived by stealing, down on the New York waterfront. He had hated the life, not because he had any scruples about stealing, but because, unlike most of his companions, he had enough imagination to see where such a life would lead him: to a jail cell and, later perhaps, to a gallows.

Silas had saved him from that. He had caught Logan stealing, and it would have been easy for him to beat the boy senseless and turn him over to the police, for Silas was ten years older, big, and muscular from swinging a mallet in a shipyard. But instead, he had pinned Logan to the ground, forced him to return the sextant he had stolen, then found work for him in the shipyard where he was employed as an apprentice.

Now, as Logan and Silas strode along the white beach and then rowed back out to the *Ondine*, which was anchored in the bay, her white sails furled, the captain put aside his memories of the past. He had to concentrate all his energies on the hours ahead: on provisioning the ship for this crowd of passengers and rearranging the accommodations to make room for them all. It would be a difficult passage at best, and Logan suspected that some of the passengers would regret their impulsiveness when they experienced, for the first time, the passage around the Horn, which was an ordeal even for experienced seamen.

"Lucky I didn't sell those barrels of flour in Cuba," he told Silas. "I'll get ten times more than I paid for them when we reach San Francisco."

Silas nodded. "Men have to eat if they're going to dig for gold," he agreed. "But the rest of the cargo—gilt-framed mirrors and them fancy satin chairs—"

"I have a feeling that yellow-haired madam will have a use for them when she sets up in business," Logan said with a grin. "I'll talk to her about it once we're on our way."

He fell silent again, calculating rapidly. The crew would have to be moved together into even more cramped quarters than usual, for he would have to set up pigpens, chicken coops, and take on additional water casks as well. And he must talk to that doctor from Baltimore about medical supplies to augment those in his own small medicine chest. They would need more Peruvian bark, alum, and blue vitriol. Logan was far too experienced a shipmaster not to understand the risks of an outbreak of cholera, typhus, or a host of other contagious diseases that could sweep a ship where so many people were crowded together for five or six months.

It was a gamble he was taking, yes, but his mind was fixed on the possible reward: money enough to buy more ships, to establish a fleet of his own.

Not until three days later, when the *Ondine*, jammed with passengers, had left Rio harbor and was heading south, did he remember the letter he had sent to Vanessa. She would be expecting him home this winter, but it would be many more months before she would see him again.

A moment later all thought of Vanessa was banished when Dermot Rankin came up on deck to report a knife fight between two passengers. "Had to knock one of 'em senseless," he told Logan calmly. "Could be his jaw's broken. The other one's only bruised a bit. What do I do with them now, sir?"

"Put them in irons and toss them into the wheelhouse," Logan said. "And do the same with any of the others who get out of hand."

The last day of December brought a snowstorm to New York City, and Vanessa, who had been making charity visits to the shantytown settlement on the bluff overlooking the East River, had returned home barely in time to escape the storm's full fury. When she awoke, on the first morning of 1849, she saw that the wind had abated, that the sun was brilliant in a cloudless, bright blue sky, and that the leafless trees below her window were tipped with glittering icicles.

By ten o'clock the smooth snow was marked by the wheels of carriages and the runners of sleighs as fashionably dressed ladies and gentlemen took to the streets, bound on their New Year's calls. This convivial custom, brought over by the Dutch settlers, had grown far more widespread and elaborate with the years. For the past week, prosperous households from Hudson Square to Murray Hill were bustling with activity; dressmakers were busy putting the finishing touches on elaborate gowns, and the best china and glassware were polished by busy maids while cooks gathered the ingredients for their most impressive recipes.

In Vanessa's home, however, the day was no different from any other, for she was expecting no visitors, not even Felicity, who would be entertaining in the Bradford mansion. All through the holiday season Vanessa had been hoping for Logan's return. She had reread his letter, sent from Havana, so often that the paper was nearly falling apart, but she wanted Logan with her; she longed for the sight of him, the warmth of his arms around her. Having learned what it was to give herself to the man she loved, her young, eager body ached for his touch, and she lay awake at night in their big double bed, taut with unsatisfied hunger.

She tried to keep busy on New Year's morning, playing with Chris, taking joy in this beautiful little son of hers. In the afternoon, when he was ready for his nap, she carried him upstairs to the nursery, where Delia, the quadroon nursemaid, was busy folding clean clothes. The woman, tall, sturdy, and tireless, had quickly become a part of the small household, and Chris had taken to her at once.

Vanessa had no experience with babies, and no female relatives to advise her, and she had been grateful for Delia's presence in the nursery—for her expert advice and her skill in brewing mixtures for colic and teething pains.

"Ain't enough to do, takin' care of one little baby, Miz McClintock, ma'am," Delia had told Vanessa, and had quietly assumed a host of other chores—washing Vanessa's clothing and the baby's, sewing and ironing, even brushing Vanessa's hair and laying out her nightdress. Vanessa promised herself that when Logan returned, if he had made a good profit from the voyage, she would give Delia a salary.

Now Vanessa sat down in the rocking chair near the nursery window and cradled Chris in her arms. Delia, having finished putting away the fresh laundry, left the room.

Vanessa cherished these times with Chris. How like Logan the baby looked. He was nearly a year old, and his blue eyes had darkened to gray, like his father's; his thick, curly hair was dark, too, like Logan's.

She sighed and asked herself when Logan would be home. She tried to console herself, thinking how lucky she was to be living in this spacious house in one of the most respectable sections of New York, to have a warm fire when she wanted one and good, nourishing food on the table.

She was well aware how different her situation was from that of the women of Dutch Hill, the immigrant squatter settlement she had visited so often these past months. Those women, with their broods of children, were crowded into stinking, windowless hovels that clung to the bluff and were buffeted by the freezing winds from the East River. They stood by helplessly while they saw their children turning to petty thievery, and they themselves were often driven to selling their bodies to earn enough to stay alive. Vanessa knew well enough that the donations of food and clothing she brought to them were not nearly enough, and there were more immigrants pouring into the shanty settlement every day.

This morning, while hostesses presided over tables heaped with hams, turkeys, and pastries, there were mothers in the Dutch Hill shacks who were too undernourished to nurse their babies and there were children growing up with rickets and consumption. She shuddered, remembering how only a few days ago she had seen an infant who had been bitten by rats.

She drew Chris closer and realized that if Logan had deserted her, she might have found herself and her baby in that same shantytown. She pushed the thought away, for it was too terrible to contemplate. She sang softly until the baby's eyes closed and his small, sturdy body relaxed in her arms. Then she rose and carried him to his cradle and tucked the blankets around him.

She sighed, thinking of the long, empty afternoon that stretched before her. Then, turning, she went downstairs. She would read the new novel she had taken from the lending library: *Jane Eyre,* it was called, the work of an English writer with the odd name Currer Bell.

But before she reached the downstairs hall, the doorbell rang and for a moment she stood, her heart rising with the hope that Logan had come home at last, and on New Year's Day. Then she saw that the visitor was not Logan. He was Ross Halliwell, as fashionably dressed as he had been when she had seen him last, on the dock in Salem. His eyes were fixed on her face, and she was aware of the warmth of his gaze.

He took off his tall beaver hat. "Vanessa, I hope I'm not intruding," he said. "I saw no basket on your door, so I thought you might be holding open house and I . . ." Then seeing the lack of comprehension in her face, he explained quickly. "Here in New York, a family that doesn't want to receive callers on New Year's Day hangs a basket on the front doorknob. The caller deposits his card and goes on his way. Are you going to send me on my way?"

She smiled then and led him into the parlor.

"I haven't made any preparations for open house," she said. "I know no one here except Felicity and Kitty, and because of Abel Bradford's quarrel with Logan—"

"I see," he said. "But you must not spend this fine day indoors, alone. Since Logan's still away . . . Oh, yes, I visited my father last night, and he told me that the *Ondine* has not yet returned. Perhaps you will come driving with me. I've a fine sleigh waiting right outside. Say you'll come."

"Why, I—"

"You must, really," he went on quickly, as if fearing a refusal. "You have to help me to celebrate. The fact is, I've sold my first painting. A small watercolor of Salem harbor."

"That's wonderful, but I . . . There's the baby, you see. . . ."

But before she could go on, Delia, who had brought in a tea tray, smiled warmly. "You go along, Miz McClintock, ma'am. The fresh air'll do you good. I'll take my mending up to the nursery, and if the baby wakes up, I'll look after him."

Ross gave Delia a grateful nod. "There, now," he said. "That settles the matter. Put on a warm cloak and come along. I'll get you back before sundown, I promise."

The sleigh, a trim, freshly painted cutter, sped along through the snowy streets, and Vanessa found that she was caught up in the holiday mood of the city. "It *is* a beautiful day," she told Ross. They moved uptown with the crowd. Oh, it was good to be part of the bustling life of the city. She had not fully realized how drab her days had been since Logan had sailed. Her spirits soared as she looked at the other sleighs moving through the streets and heard their bells chiming out in the clear, icy air.

"Look at that one," Ross said, gesturing with his whip, and she stared at the elaborate sleigh carved in the shape of a sea-green shell and lined with glowing crimson velvet. The driver, a big, well-dressed gentleman, tipped his hat, and the lady with him, who was swathed in a sable-trimmed cloak, gave them a smile. Ross and Vanessa returned their greetings, for it was that kind of day.

"And see, over there," Vanessa said. Ross nodded as a large, roomy family sleigh holding a middle-aged couple and five pretty young daughters covered with gray lynx lap robes passed them by. There were omnibus sleighs, too, lumbering along, drawn by their six horses and crammed with passengers.

Ross headed out of the city and into the steep hills on the outskirts. "We'll stop at Wintergreen's tavern for hot cider," he said.

"I'd like that," Vanessa said.

He turned and looked at her closely. "How long have you been cooped up in your home?" he asked.

"I don't stay indoors all the time," she assured him. "It is true I'm not in New York's society, but I'm not a recluse either." She pointed to her left. "I go there, to Dutch Hill, at least twice a week, and sometimes oftener."

Ross stared at her. "But those dreadful shacks—what on earth do you find to do there?"

"I work for Felicity Bradford's new committee, the Society for Aid to Destitute Immigrants."

And later, as they sat in the dining room of the comfortable tavern filled with others who sought the warmth of the fire and the mugs of hot, spicy cider, she told him more about her activities. "Since Delia has become part of the household, I am able to get about."

"Delia, that's the quadroon woman who cares for your child. A freed woman, is she?"

"Not . . . exactly." Vanessa had wanted to talk over the

matter of Delia with Logan, but that had been impossible, and now she was relieved to be able to speak of her misgivings to an old friend. "She's a runaway slave. She has had a most unhappy history, and . . . I know it's wrong to harbor a fugitive. Someone's property. But Ross, I can't think of her or of any human being as property."

"And neither can I," Ross assured her. "Jeremy says that slavery's necessary to the economy of the South, and of New England, too, but I can't see it that way." Then, seeing her bewilderment, he explained. "New England needs southern-grown cotton. The textile mills of Lowell depend on the work of the slaves as surely as do the plantations of Georgia."

"I've never thought—"

"Few New Englanders do, but it's true. And I find it hypocritical to talk about the evils of slavery while New England factory owners build fortunes on cotton textiles and . . ." He broke off. "I'm sorry," he said. "I promised you a holiday outing and here I am, sounding like a lecturer at the Salem Lyceum."

"Do you attend lectures there often?"

"Indeed, I do," Ross said. "Mr. Nathaniel Hawthorne's manager and corresponding secretary for the Lyceum now, and he's found several excellent speakers this winter."

Vanessa tried to imagine Logan attending lectures at the Lyceum and being occupied with social questions like the movement for abolition, but she could not, for her husband was bent on building a fortune, driven by his ambition.

Ross was speaking, and she tried to push away the thought of Logan to concentrate on what the young man across the table was saying. "Back in November a Mr. Henry Thoreau gave a talk—he's a naturalist and writer from Concord. His ideas are quite unconventional, but I like him the better for that. I've never followed a conventional path myself."

"If you had, no doubt you'd be practicing law with your brother," Vanessa said with a smile.

The warmth from the huge open fireplace near their table had given a soft, pink glow to her cheeks. Her hair, falling in loose waves from beneath her bonnet, was a dazzling shade of copper in the firelight.

"I wish I could paint you as you look right now," Ross said, and Vanessa saw something in his eyes that made her faintly uneasy. For the first time she was aware of him not as an old friend who had gone to school with her back in Salem, but as a young man, handsome and virile.

She turned her face away, fearing that he would somehow be able to read her thoughts. Then, drawing her cloak around her, she said quickly, "I'm sure Logan would like to have a portrait of me and Chris, one day—when we can afford it. You haven't seen Chris yet. He's the image of Logan. Such a beautiful child. Perhaps when we get back to the house he'll be awake."

"Yes, indeed," Ross said, but all at once he was remote, and Vanessa sensed a change in his mood. On the drive back he was subdued, speaking little, and when they reached the house on Gramercy Park, he refused her invitation to come in and see little Chris. "I've promised to dine with my father," he told her almost brusquely. "Another time, perhaps."

Although she was taken aback by his abrupt manner, she was relieved too, that he was leaving, for her own confused feelings toward him had made her uneasy. "Thank you for a most pleasant afternoon," she said as they stood together at the top of the steps. "Please give your father and Jeremy my best wishes for a happy new year."

She could not go on, for in the light of the lantern that hung from the portico, she saw that all remoteness had fallen away from him, that his brown eyes were warm and ardent.

He took her hand. Then, with a swift movement, he drew her to him. "Vanessa," he said. His lips brushed hers lightly. She felt a brief, treacherous response before she pulled away. But he was already hurrying down the steps, and she stood watching as he drove off.

Shaken, she tried to understand her confused emotions. Logan had stirred her, had made her know what passion between a man and woman could be, then he had sailed off and left her alone. She stared into the violet shadows that mantled the small park and her lips moved. "Oh, Logan, Logan my love, I need you. Come back to me—soon. . . ."

Chapter 13

The heavy fog rolling in across San Francisco Bay enveloped the *Ondine.* The passengers, exhausted, dirty, and bedraggled, stumbled to the deck for their first glimpse of the city. Many of those who had pleaded or demanded to be taken aboard in Rio had had cause to question their decision, for the voyage had been a rough one.

During the passage around the Horn most of them had been convinced that they would not survive to reach their destination. The bitter cold and the fierce winds that had battered the small schooner as she had clawed her way about the tip of South America had shaken the nerves of even the most determined of them. And in spite of the ministrations of the doctor, a few had succumbed to dysentery and one to malaria. Almost all had been taken ill when a storm had smashed up the galley and they had been forced to live on raw salt pork and biscuits until repairs had been made. At one point, the *Ondine* had been so badly damaged that Logan had feared she was on the point of breaking up, and he had ordered a part of the deck cargo jettisoned.

Now, standing on the poopdeck, he picked up his telescope and peered into the fog. At first, he could see nothing, then, as the morning sun burned through the fog, he could make out the sand dunes and bare hills of Yerba Buena cove.

He heard a murmur of dismay from the passengers. The view was so desolate that they began asking one another if the gold mines had been played out—if they had come all this way on a fool's errand.

Allerton, determined to open a gambling and drinking establishment, was speaking to Mamie Doyle, the stout blond madam, who was surrounded by her "young ladies." Logan heard her shrill voice, although he could not make out her words.

Now, as the *Ondine* came around Yerba Buena cove, Logan and his passengers had their first look at the settlement, but although it was crowded, it was far from inviting, for it consisted only of clustered shacks and tents and a few rickety two-story buildings. No matter, Logan thought, there were men here who would be eager to buy his cargo.

Getting the passengers and cargo ashore was no easy matter, for there was only one wharf, and small boats had to make countless trips back and forth. But as the sun rose higher, he felt his spirits soar. There was a sense of feverish activity here, and the potential for making a fortune. Men had to eat, and he had casks of flour. They needed tools—pans, shovels, nails—and he had a good supply of those, too; they had been intended for the plantations of Cuba, but they would fetch far more here in San Francisco.

A few days of trading brought Logan higher profits than even he, in his most optimistic moments, had anticipated. The flour had gone for forty dollars a barrel. A shovel for twenty-five dollars. A tin pan for five dollars. Mamie Doyle, who had set herself up in business, had bought the gilt-framed mirrors and the rosewood and satin furniture. She had no use for them yet, she told him. Right now she had set up her business in a dismal building with only muslin sheets to divide the premises into cubicles for her "young ladies." One day soon, however, she would have a parlor house as fine as any in New York, or in New Orleans, she assured him. He looked at her doubtfully, for her "young ladies," seen up close, were no beauties, and the voyage had not improved their looks. But then, Logan told himself, with the shortage of females out here, the gold seekers were in no position to be critical.

After two weeks of trading, Logan was ready to start the voyage back to New York. Silas Pringle had done what he could to repair the *Ondine.* "Though I doubt there's another voyage left in her," he told Logan as the two sat in the captain's cabin. Logan shrugged.

"With the profits from this voyage, I'll not only be able to buy back the shares from the Halliwell brothers and the other investors; I'll be able to buy a new ship." His eyes looked past Silas. "A steamer, perhaps."

"A steamer! A floating stinkpot that'll need enough coal to burn up your profits as fast as you make 'em. You're not serious, are you?"

Before Logan could reply, there was a discreet knock at the cabin door, and Dermot Rankin came inside. He looked ill at ease.

"We sail at dawn," Logan told him. "Are all the hands back aboard and reasonably sober?"

The first mate was silent.

"What's wrong?" Logan demanded.

"Fact is, sir, they've gone and jumped ship. Off in search of gold, they are. Mad for gold, like all those others here in San Francisco—"

Logan cut him off. "We'll have to get a new crew, and fast." He had seen other ships deserted, rotting in the bay. That must not be allowed to happen to the *Ondine.*

Rankin remained unmoving, his broad, bearded face troubled.

"How many men do we still have aboard?" Logan asked.

"Three, not counting myself and Mr. Pringle here. Five men, sir. We'll need at least ten more—fifteen, if we can get 'em."

"Then get them," Logan ordered. "Go to the crimps and round up a crew. And be quick about it."

"Beggin' your pardon, sir, this ain't Liverpool, nor South Street, neither. Got no crimps, properly speaking."

Logan thought with longing of the established system for procuring seamen in both those ports, and in a dozen others, of tavern owners and lodginghouse keepers who could be relied upon to get together a crew of sailors, drunk, drugged, but able seamen all the same. San Francisco was too raw, too new.

"You'll stay on board for the rest of the night," Logan ordered. "Make sure we don't lose what's left of our crew." Then, turning to Silas, he ordered, "You come with me."

"I'm sorry, McClintock," Allerton said. "It isn't a matter of scruples. I've only set up in business here. If my place gets the wrong kind of reputation—men being shanghaied and taken off to sea—I'll lose my trade." He shook his head. "Ten men disappearing in one night—"

"Five, then. Get me five." He gave Allerton a long, steady look.

Allerton said, "I'll try." He jerked his head toward several men gathered around a faro table, which was presided over by a dealer in an expensively tailored black suit, a tall, lean man with hard, watchful eyes. "I can't promise to deliver experienced seamen."

"So long as they're able-bodied, Dermot Rankin will make seamen of them before we reach the Horn," Logan said. "Five won't be enough, though."

"Try Mamie Doyle's place," Allerton suggested. "She has

plenty of customers. A few shots of rum laced with laudanum . . ."

Logan nodded. He disliked the idea of drugging men and forcing them to sail the ship, but he would not leave the *Ondine* here to rot in the harbor along with so many other vessels.

He pushed back his chair. "I'll go and speak to the lady now," he said. "I'd hoped to be under sail at dawn, but if I have to wait a few days longer, then I'll wait." He broke off abruptly and stared over at one of the tables, where four men were playing poker. Although poker was not a popular game here in San Francisco, where men preferred the faster action of faro or blackjack, they would take a hand if the stakes were high enough. One of the poker players, a handsome, hard-faced man, was approached by a young girl.

Logan looked her over with interest. He had seen few enough females here, and they had been a shopworn lot of harpies, their haggard faces plastered with rice powder and smeared with rouge, their eyes weary.

This girl was different. She was young, no more than nineteen, with a delicate complexion and a soft, vulnerable mouth. Her blond hair framing her face in loose ringlets looked silvery-gilt in the light of the oil lamp over the table. Her dove-gray dress, with its high neck and long sleeves, was well worn, but it fitted her slender, softly rounded body to perfection.

She spoke to the hard-faced man—a professional gambler, Logan judged. The man was angered by the interruption and spoke to her sharply. She put a hand on his arm, but he shook it off. "Get back to the tent and wait for me there," he told her before turning his attention on his cards.

The girl moved away, her shoulders drooping. She was close to tears. Logan gave Allerton an inquiring look.

"She doesn't belong here," Allerton said. "From the way she looks, I'd guess she comes from a good family somewhere back east. She should have stayed there—but you know these gamblers have a way with the ladies."

"Is she his wife?"

Allerton shrugged. "She claims to be, but who knows? Talks like a real, high-toned lady—southern, I think. He treats her badly. Better for her if she'd never hooked up with him."

Logan nodded, and then dismissed the matter, for he had pressing concerns of his own. He said good night to Allerton and left the gambling shack, heading for Mamie Doyle's cribhouse.

Mamie did not disappoint him, and Allerton, too, came through, so within a few days he had a motley collection of unwilling crewmen trussed up and locked belowdecks. Before he made ready to sail he went ashore one last time, to pay off Mamie first, then Allerton. The gamblinghouse proprietor was in a bad mood. "That gambler—the one with the pretty young blonde—he nearly ruined my business for me," Allerton explained. "Good thing I spotted him cheating before there was a riot here. Took a bag of nuggets from one man and fleeced a couple of others. I told him not to show his face here again." He shook his head. "Those miners have a fair idea of what was going on, though, and they're out for blood."

"He'll probably head for one of the mining camps in the hills," Logan said.

It was after midnight when Logan, accompanied by Silas Pringle, headed for the wharf to find a boat to carry them back to the *Ondine.* Logan's mind was working quickly, looking ahead to the return voyage and then New York, where he would start looking for a second ship. "I know what you think of steamers, Silas," he said, "but speed's what I want."

"Speed, is it?" Silas sounded outraged. "Are you saying you can't get speed out of a clipper?"

"Given favorable winds, certainly. But a steamer's not at the mercy of the winds. She can—"

Silas interrupted him. "What was that?" he asked.

Logan had heard it too, a sound like the whimpering of a tortured animal. "A dog?" he began.

They were at the edge of a straggling cluster of tents and shacks. It was difficult to see through the fog. "It's coming from over there," Silas said.

The two men looked at each other, and Logan shook his head. "That's no dog."

They headed for a small tent set somewhat apart from the others. Pulling the flap aside, Logan started to go in, then froze. A man's body was sprawled, facedown, on the dirt floor, and it was plain even before Logan knelt to get a better look that the sounds had not come from the man. He was dead, his body already stiffening. There was something vaguely familiar about him. The few crude furnishings of the tent had been smashed.

The sound came again, from under a threadbare blanket in one corner. Then it was stifled in a sharp gasp of fright. Logan strode over and pulled aside the blanket. A girl looked up at him, her face bruised, one eye half-closed and swelling. Her body was covered by the torn remains of a thin shift. Her silver-blond ringlets fell in a tangled mass around her face and over her shoulders and barely concealed her rounded breasts, with their pink nipples. Logan's mouth tightened, for he saw the ugly, livid bruises on her breasts and on her thighs. There were streaks of blood on her torn shift.

The gambler's girl, the one he had seen a few nights before, at Allerton's place. He reached out to help her to her feet, but she gave a strangled cry of panic, and when he took her by the arms she fought with the strength of a cornered, abused animal. Her sea-green eyes were filled with mindless panic.

"We won't hurt you," Logan told her. "You're safe now, you're all right." He released her only long enough to strip off his coat and wrap it around her shaking body.

Silas, meanwhile, had managed to find a half bottle of whiskey that had fallen from the shelf but had remained unbroken. While Logan supported the girl, Silas forced the bottle between her lips. "Swallow it," Logan ordered.

She obeyed, then choked and coughed as the burning liquid went down her throat. Logan felt a little of the tension go out of her body. "They killed him," she whispered. "He's dead—Keith's dead. They said he'd been cheating, and they—they beat him to death . . . and I tried to run—to get help . . . but they grabbed me and two of them held me down . . . and the other . . ."

She was weeping now, but Logan decided that it was better than her half-crazed panic of a few moments ago. He had little sympathy for the man she had called Keith—a dishonest gambler knew what he was letting himself in for if his cheating was discovered by his victims. But there had been no reason to punish the girl.

"Do you have a woman friend you can stay with?" Logan asked. He pitied the girl, but he had not forgotten that he had business to attend to. He had to get back to the *Ondine* to make sure that his shanghaied crew was under control, that his passengers had been settled aboard. Besides, he was ill at ease in a situation like this one, particularly with the girl giving him and Silas fearful looks. They were strangers, men—and she had been brutalized by other men. "If you have some woman who'll help you, we'll take you to her," Logan said, trying to control his impatience.

"No one—there's no one." She rubbed at her swollen eyes with the back of her hand. Logan thought briefly of taking her over to Mamie Doyle's place, but decided against it. Mamie would have only one use for a girl so young and attractive. And Logan sensed, as Allerton had, that this girl, no matter how foolishly she had behaved in getting involved with the gambler, was no whore. Her speech, even now, was the speech of a lady, and there was the soft drawl in it that Logan had often heard in the seaports of the South.

She had managed to regain some control now, and she said, "Keith must have a decent burial."

Damn it, Logan thought, *what had he gotten himself into?*

"Was he your husband?" Silas asked, jerking his head in the direction of the body.

The girl hesitated. "He was going to marry me. He promised me he would."

She turned away. Logan put a hand on her shoulder, and shook her gently. "Look, miss—"

"Spencer," she said softly. "Garnet Spencer."

"Miss Spencer," he went on. "Mr. Pringle and I have to get back to my ship. We sail at dawn. I'd like to help you, but I have no time to—"

"Your ship?"

"The *Ondine*—a schooner, out of New York."

"You are master of the ship?" she asked.

"Captain Logan McClintock," he told her.

She clutched at his arm. "Oh, please, you can take me away from this horrible place." She raised her head, and in spite of her bruised face there was a certain strength in her. "I can't stay here. I've no one to protect me . . . and these men are like—like animals. They—"

"I don't take passengers unless they can pay," Logan told her. But he was in a quandary, for he knew what would happen to Garnet Spencer if he left her here now: she would soon be on her back in one of the bunks at Mamie's place, or a similar establishment, where each small cubicle was separated from those on either side by thin sheets of muslin, where girls were forced to entertain any man with a few coins in his pocket.

"I don't have passage money," Garnet said. Then, as panic welled up in her again, she begged, "Don't leave me here . . . please."

Logan hesitated. He had done far better on this voyage than he could ever have imagined. He didn't need Garnet's passage money, and on this return voyage there would be extra space, for there were not that many men hurrying back to the East Coast. "Get your things together," he ordered her, "and be quick about it. Silas, see if you can borrow a shovel." He gestured in the direction of the body, still sprawled on the floor of the tent.

Garnet, with Logan's heavy coat still draped over her shoulders, began to move about a little shakily as she gathered up her few possessions. "I'll never forget your kindness," she began.

Logan gave her a half smile. "Don't start thanking me until we dock on South Street," he told her. "The *Ondine*'s already taken a battering coming out here. The return voyage will be no pleasure trip."

Although it was already September, the heat of summer lingered in New York, and Vanessa, returning home from the shantytown settlement on Dutch Hill, felt hot and exhausted. She climbed the front steps and went into the hall, wincing as the headache that had started a few hours ago clamped down on her temples like an iron vise. Her legs ached too, and there was a dull throbbing in the small of her back.

No wonder, she told herself. Last week she had found a family of Irish immigrants jammed together in a one-room shack—a mother and four children—and all stricken with fever. It had been useless to try to get a doctor to come out to the squalid cluster of shanties, and the neighbors were of little help, for many of them had also been ill. "Ship fever," some called it, and others spoke of the ailment as "jail fever" or "spotted fever."

Vanessa had done what she could, carrying water, changing bedding, cleaning the shack. The mother and three of the children had come through. The fourth had died in Vanessa's arms only yesterday.

Now, standing in the hallway, she gritted her teeth against the pain in her head. Alice came to take her cape and bonnet, and Vanessa realized that she no longer felt hot. Instead, a chill swept through her. She shook as if she stood in an icy wind.

"Cook's got a lovely dinner all ready for you, and—What's wrong, ma'am?"

"Not hungry." Vanessa heard her voice, thin and distant. "I want to lie down. My head hurts."

Alice supported her with a thin, wiry arm and called for Delia. The polished black and white tiles on the hall floor were shifting, blurring.

Delia and Alice, between them, got her up to her room and into bed. Her teeth were chattering, and Delia pulled the blankets up over her.

"We got t' get somebody t' help," Delia was saying.

Vanessa tried to think, but her head throbbed mercilessly. Logan. No, he was far away . . . months since she'd had word of him. . . . Felicity. But Felicity was away at Saratoga Springs with Kitty and the new baby. . . .

"Dr. Fairleigh," she heard herself saying. "Hudson Square." He had attended Aunt Prudence.

"You heard Miz McClintock," Delia told Alice. "Go get that doctor. Hurry, girl!"

Chapter 14

"Look here, Garnet, you still have time to change your mind and return to Charleston," Logan said. The *Ondine* had survived the long, dangerous voyage around the Horn and now lay at anchor in Jamaica's Kingston harbor. "I can find a small coastal freighter and arrange passage if you—"

"I can never go home to Charleston," Garnet said. "Even if Papa took me back, he'd never let me forget how I've disgraced him. None of my friends would speak to me, and I wouldn't be received in any respectable home."

He and Garnet stood side by side at the rail, looking out across the harbor at the Blue Mountains, now hazy in the mists of late afternoon. "Charleston is closed to me," she went on, her voice calm with acceptance. "I must go on to New York and find work there. Respectable work."

Garnet had changed from the terrified creature who had awakened, sobbing, from nightmares of rape and murder. Whatever terrors still lingered, she had regained a façade of self-control, an air of dignity.

"There must be many fine dressmaking establishments in New York," she was saying. "My embroidery is excellent, and I can do plain sewing too. I'll work hard, and I'll pay you back for the passage."

No need for that, Logan thought, for luck had been with him all the way; even here in Jamaica, where, although sugar production had fallen off after England had passed her abolition laws, he had managed to buy a cargo of muscovado sugar outright from a planter in desperate financial straits.

"Give me your address before we disembark," Garnet went on. "It may take time, but I'll pay back every cent." She looked away, her cheeks flushing softly. "You have been so generous and—and you have made no demands. You are a gentleman."

Later, when Garnet had returned to her cabin, Logan thought of her words. A gentleman. No one had ever called him that before. Then, as the *Ondine* spread her canvas and moved into the humid tropical night, Logan's thoughts sped forward, making plans for the future. Vanessa was waiting for him, and he would see his son again. Chris was no longer an infant, he reminded himself; he might be walking now, saying a few words. Logan smiled with satisfaction. He was a man with a family and a home to return to. And there would be more sons. Fine, strong boys who would grow to manhood, safe and carefully reared, to carry on the business. More ships and more sons. And a beautiful, passionate wife.

He stared into the blackness, and pictures formed in his mind. Vanessa, lying in his arms, her face upturned to his, her warm, pliant body rising to draw him closer, the soft white breasts and long beautiful legs.

He smiled, wondering at the change in himself. Once, on a return voyage, he had felt a hunger for any one of the multitude of nameless women who haunted the waterfront. Women taken casually and then forgotten.

Now he wanted only one woman. Vanessa.

Someone was drowning her in a fiery pit, and flames licked at her body. Hellfire. But what had she done? How had she sinned? She had given herself to Logan before marriage. But that had not been sinful. . . . It had not been wrong . . . because she had loved Logan so much. . . .

Vanessa's lips, cracked with fever, moved, but she could

make no sound. She wanted to cry out for Logan. He had to come and help her, save her from this torture, from the crushing pain in her head, from the devils who were stabbing at her arms and legs with hot knives, making her writhe in a hopeless effort to escape.

But Logan was far away. He might never come back. Her father had sailed away and had never come back. . . .

Someone was bathing her forehead, and she heard a woman saying, "She's mighty sick, ain't she, Doctuh?"

Delia's voice, soft and husky. And then another voice, a man speaking with calm authority. "Unless the fever breaks within the next few days . . ."

"If only her man would come home—been gone so long now. An' she got no kin I know about, nobody at all."

"Mrs. Bradford wanted to come, but Mr. Bradford would not permit it. And quite rightly so. Their daughter's baby . . ."

Kitty's baby? Did Kitty have a baby? Vanessa tried to remember, but the pain drove out all coherent thought.

"I'll call tomorrow morning," the man was saying. "Sponge baths and quinine." And then: "You are an excellent nurse, Delia. . . ."

Then demon claws were pushing Vanessa back into the pit of hellfire again.

The lamp on the bedside table glowed softly, and Vanessa knew it was evening. She was drained, exhausted, but the fever was gone, and the pain too.

"Water . . . please," she whispered. Someone held a glass to her lips and she drank thirstily.

"Slowly, my dear. That's it." She knew that voice and the delicate scent of Felicity's orange flower cologne.

"I thought you could not come. Someone said . . ."

Who had said it? Her memory of the days since her collapse were blurred, confused.

"Abel does not know I am here," Felicity said, and Vanessa saw that her soft brown eyes were filled with tears. "I could not stay away. I could not bear to think of you here, alone. Not now."

"Because Logan's still away at sea?" Vanessa felt afraid for him, all at once. "Has there been word of the *Ondine*?"

Felicity shook her head. "I've heard nothing about the ship. But Chris—"

Then a new terror surged up within Vanessa, a terror too great to think about. But it had to be faced.

"Chris?"

"Oh, my dear—"

"Chris has the fever too?"

"Yes—Delia is with him now."

"He is going to get well." Felicity did not answer. Vanessa clutched at her hand. "He is—he's got to . . ." She tried to raise herself, but even that small effort caused the perspiration to pour from her, soaking through her nightdress. She fell back against the pillows.

"You must not think of getting up," Felicity said.

"But Chris, he is going to be all right?"

Her eyes met Felicity's, and she cried out, for she read the truth in her friend's stricken face.

The *Ondine* docked on South Street on a clear, cold morning in November. Logan said good-bye to Garnet, and at her insistence he gave her his address; then he directed her to Broadway, where she would be likely to find work in a dressmaking shop.

For the next few hours he was busy making out the necessary customs documents, hiring stevedores to begin unloading the cargo, arranging for warehouse space. It was afternoon before he was free to go striding up South Street, heading for home.

He paused briefly to glance at the offices of the Bradford Line. Before long, he told himself, he would set up an office nearby and hire a clerk or two.

A hansom cab drew to a stop at his signal.

"Gramercy Park," Logan told the driver.

Alice stared at him as if she were seeing an apparition. He brushed aside her stammered greetings and asked for Vanessa.

"The mistress is upstairs. . . ."

Logan raced up the steps and flung open the door of the master bedroom. Vanessa stood frozen for a moment, then, with a strangled cry, she ran and flung herself into his arms. "You came back! You're here." Her words were muffled, her face pressed against his chest, her arms clinging to him.

When he drew away it was only to cup her face in his hands and kiss her. Then he looked at her more closely. Surely she was thinner, and so pale.

"I was so afraid I'd never see you again."

"I'm sorry," he said. "That letter from Havana—I know you were expecting me months ago. But after that I went on to Rio to try to pick up a cargo of coffee and then . . . so much happened, and so fast." He smiled down at her in triumph. "There's such a lot to tell," he went on. "I never would have believed the *Ondine*—"

"Logan," Vanessa began, but he went on.

"All the way around the Horn to San Francisco and back again. That last storm off the Argentines damn near tore the masts out of her. But she's berthed at South Street. And I've made a fortune on this one voyage."

She looked up at him, her eyes uncomprehending.

"But how could you understand?" he said. "All those people stranded in Rio and fighting for passage to San Francisco at any price. And I got them there. It was a gamble, but it paid off. I have enough to buy another ship—a steamer, this time. And you and Chris . . . Where is Chris? I'll bet he's walking now."

"Logan, listen to me."

Something in her voice stopped him, and then she was speaking, her eyes tormented. "I've been ill. Typhus. Chris caught it. Dr. Fairleigh did all he could. But Chris's fever kept going up. And then . . . he had convulsions. And he . . . he died. More than two months ago."

Grief for the son he had scarcely known mingled with pity for Vanessa. She had been left alone, had gone through the ordeal without him. Unable to find the words with which to comfort her, he drew her against him and stroked her hair.

"Typhus," he said. "But here . . . how did you get it? I was so sure that you'd be safe here."

"There was an epidemic on Dutch Hill," she said.

"Dutch Hill? Where the devil is that?" What was she talking about?

"It's a kind of shantytown. Irish and German immigrants live there. On a bluff overhanging the East River."

She drew away, out of the protective circle of his arm. "I went there to bring food and clothing and to care for some of the women and children who were taken ill."

Anger flared up inside him. It had not been blind chance then, that had killed his son. "A hellhole like that, full of disease-ridden immigrants, infested with rats, no doubt and—"

"Yes, there were rats. It is a dreadful place. That's why I felt I must do something to help. I brought food and clothing, and when I found a woman and her children stricken with fever, untended, I felt it was my duty—"

"Your duty! You had a baby to care for. My son."

"Chris was mine too," she said. "Logan, please, if you'll only listen, try to understand."

"I don't understand," he said. Then his lips clamped together and the hard line of his jaw stood out as he made an effort to control himself. He turned and started for the door. She hurried after him and caught his arm, but he jerked away from her touch.

"Where are you going?" Her voice was unsteady.

"I have business down on South Street," he told her. "They're unloading the *Ondine.*"

"Logan, you'll come back. . . ."

For a moment he was touched by the unhappiness and the fear he heard in her question. She was pleading for reassurance, for comfort, but he had none to give.

Logan did not return until long after midnight, and Vanessa, who had been lying awake, sat up in bed, but she heard his footsteps going past their bedroom door and on down the hall. He was going to spend the night in one of the guest rooms.

Staring into the darkness, she fought down her misery and drew on a reserve of strength deep inside her. She told herself that Logan was back safely from his voyage, that he was here, under the same roof with her.

It was unfair, cruel of him to blame her for Chris's death, but she made excuses for him: perhaps a man, particularly a man like Logan, could not give way to unrestrained grief. Perhaps anger was his only outlet. But given time, he would understand that she was not to blame for the child's death.

Oh, surely, having grown up in the poverty of the Five Points, he could be made to see that she had had to help those who still lived in such horrible conditions. She sighed and turned over, burying her face in her pillow.

Tomorrow they would talk. She would make him understand. Then they would comfort each other, sharing the pain of their loss.

But the following day at breakfast, Logan announced that he was going up to Salem to settle accounts with the Halliwell brothers and the other shareholders of the *Ondine.* She wanted to ask Logan if she could come with him, but she did not dare, and she tried to console herself with the hope that maybe while he was away he would have time to recover from the first overwhelming shock of Chris's death.

She would not let herself sink back into apathy, she resolved, and after he had left she began to take walks in Gramercy Park, where the brisk autumn wind brought a touch of color to her cheeks. She forced herself to eat the nourishing beef soups and puddings and the fresh eggs beaten into cream and sherry prepared for her by Mrs. Skene. Delia washed her hair and brushed it until it had recovered its red-gold sheen once more.

On the evening when Logan came home from Salem, a letter was waiting for him, brought to the house by a messenger, and addressed in a delicate, unmistakably feminine hand. At dinner he read it and said, "It is from Garnet Spencer." Seeing Vanessa's puzzled look, he explained. "She is one of the passengers I brought back from San Francisco. Her . . . husband died there."

He nodded approvingly. "She's lost no time in finding work as she said she would."

"What is she working at?" Vanessa asked.

"She says she's apprenticed to a dressmaker on Chambers Street."

Vanessa remembered how Felicity had often spoken of the drudgery endured by such women. Some sewed for eighteen hours a day, and even so, they were unable to make a decent living. Many, according to Felicity, were eventually driven to a life of prostitution. Logan put the letter aside and dismissed the matter, speaking instead of his visit to Salem. His manner was polite but businesslike, and it disquieted Vanessa, for she knew that sooner or later they must talk about Chris, no matter how painful it might be for both of them. "Trade is still slow in Salem," he told her. "Her harbor is too shallow."

If only he would look at her, really look at her. She wanted to get through the barrier he had raised between them, but she did not know how.

"The Lows knew what they were about when they moved to New York," he went on. "And those who aren't here in the city are off in China, running the factory in Hong Kong." Vanessa knew that factories, in China, meant the stone buildings that held showrooms, vaults, and living quarters for American businessmen and their clerks stationed in Canton. "The Halliwells and the other shareholders were more than satisfied with their profits. They don't want to sell their shares, though, and who can blame them?" He shrugged. "I explained the risks, but they insisted that they want to send her around the Horn again with another cargo."

At least he was speaking to her, Vanessa thought, but in such an impersonal way that she felt a barrier still between them.

"As soon as the *Ondine*'s seaworthy again," he went on, "she'll be off for San Francisco with a cargo of shovels, pans, canvas, and flour."

Logan would be leaving for San Francisco again, and she told herself that she should have expected it. She was a captain's wife and she would have to get used to these separations. But before he went she would have to make him understand about her reasons for going to Dutch Hill. How could she stand by and let him sail away still blaming her for the death of their son?

"The *Ondine* is a far better ship than even I had hoped," he went on in the same impersonal way. "But I'm not going to build more sailing ships; I've made up my mind about that. My next ship will be a steamer for the China trade. I've met a young Scottish engineer who has had solid experience designing steamers for David Napier's company, over there on the Clyde. The Scots are far ahead of us in their knowledge of steamers. But that'll change in the next few years—wait and see."

His gray eyes were hard as he looked past her. "I'll give Bradford a run for his money and I'll cut myself a piece of the China trade."

She wanted to ask him how long it would be before he sailed, but the words would not come, and she felt as if he were already far from her.

"The Halliwells are willing to put money into the construction of the new steamer, and so are several Salem businessmen. Once I have the designs for the engine, I may be able to find more backers right here in New York."

Later when they went upstairs together she wondered if he would go to sleep in the guest room, and she was relieved when he followed her into their bedroom instead. She seated herself on a small velvet chair beside the fireplace while he paced the floor, still speaking of his plans.

"A steamer won't be stopped by a hurricane or a typhoon," he said. "She won't drift becalmed if the wind falls off. I may have to do some persuading to get Silas to take charge of building the steamer. He's still convinced that the clipper is the only vessel for the China trade. Think of it, Vanessa, my first steamer."

"I'm thinking of all those months I'll have to spend alone here," she began, unable to keep the bitterness from her voice.

"Maybe you won't be alone," he said. "Maybe by the time I sail, you'll be looking ahead to raising our next son." She stared at him in disbelief as he went on. "Kitty and Horace have a fine, healthy son, and Abel's been boasting about his new grandson up and down South Street. He's even named his new California clipper after the boy. The *Thomas Widdicomb.*"

"And you want me to bear sons to carry on your feud with Abel Bradford . . . and Horace. You don't understand that a woman does not bear children to satisfy a man's ambition. She does not go through the agony of childbirth and of—Oh, Logan, when Chris died you were not here. When Chris was buried you were away at sea and I—"

"We won't speak of Chris again."

"But we will!" She rose and went to him. "We must, so that you will know—"

"I know all I want to know," he told her.

"You don't! You can't, or you would not look at me that way." She put a hand on his arm. "I know you blame me for Chris's death. But surely—Oh, Logan, you grew up in poverty; you've told me about the hunger and filth of the Five Points. You, of all people, should realize the desperate need here in the city for—"

He jerked his arm away. "I also told you that I managed to fight my way out of all that. I stole to stay alive when I had to. I shipped out for the first time on a rotten tub, and I worked like a dog. Stinking food, and not enough of that, and a rope's end across my back when I didn't move fast enough." He drew in his breath, and she saw that he was making an effort to control himself. In the silence that stretched between them she heard a log split on the hearth and the sound of the autumn wind rattling the branches of the trees in the square.

"You will give me another son, Vanessa. And you will take proper care of him. No more expeditions to that shantytown or anyplace like it."

She flinched as though he had struck her, but she stood her ground. "You're not aboard your ship now," she told him. "You can't—"

He took her by the shoulders. "I'm your husband. And your first duty is to me." She watched in stunned silence as he began to undress. How many nights during the length of his voyage she had ached for the warmth of his body beside her in their bed. But this was not the man she remembered. He was a cold-eyed stranger, and she was afraid of him.

When he tried to embrace her she pushed him away.

"Not now. Not until we've talked."

"I've had enough of talk for tonight," he said. His arms tightened around her, and then he was carrying her to the bed, stripping her clothes away. She felt the driving hunger inside him and the weight of his body on hers.

Since that first night when she had given herself to him she had welcomed his lovemaking and had gloried in the strength of his body. She had been moved by his tenderness, and had shared the fierce passion that followed.

Even that first time, when she had recoiled from her fear of the unknown, she had sensed his wish that she should receive pleasure as well as give it. She had been touched by his consideration.

But tonight was different—he was different, and as she lay beneath his crushing weight she felt that he was using her not only to satisfy his pent-up physical need—she might have been able to accept that—but as the instrument he had chosen to fulfill his driving ambition. Because it would be futile to go on struggling, she lay motionless now, her face turned away from him.

She felt his hands moving over her flesh, seeking to arouse a response. For an instant, her treacherous body almost betrayed her, for this was Logan, and the touch of him, the heat of his breath against her skin, stirred her own long-unsatisfied hunger.

But she remembered his cold arrogance, and her sense of outrage made the muscles of her body stiffen. Even when he was poised above her, when he thrust into her, she remained rigid, unyielding. She tasted the salt of her own tears as he came to climax, then turned away from her and fell asleep.

It was nearly dawn when she awoke, to find him already gone. He was probably down on South Street or maybe Corlear's Hook, looking for a shipyard, discussing repairs on the *Ondine* with Silas Pringle, or perhaps he was already meeting with the young Scottish engineer to discuss the steamer for the China run.

The long day dragged by and still he did not return. She picked at her dinner alone, and she was already upstairs and getting into bed when she heard him coming home at last. She sprang to her feet as he mounted the stairs. She did not plan her next move, but acted out of instinct alone.

When he stopped outside the bedroom door she pushed the heavy bolt into the lock. In the quiet of the hallway it sounded like a pistol shot.

"Vanessa!"

She did not answer.

"Vanessa, open this door!"

She made no move to comply.

Would he smash the door in? He could do so easily, she knew. And he was not the sort of man to care what the servants might think.

He said her name once more, quietly this time, and still she did not answer. Then she heard his steps heading down the hall, heard the door of one of the other bedrooms open, then close.

Trembling, confused, miserable, she went back to bed. He would not humble himself to her or to any woman. That much she knew of him. If he had not smashed down the door, it was because he wanted her to make the first move, to come to him. He was her husband, and the only man she would ever want; even after last night, she knew that. But her own pride kept her from going to him, and she lay, dry-eyed, her throat aching, as she stared up at the canopy overhead.

Chapter 15

As Garnet hurried along Broadway past the handsome Italianate façade of the A. T. Stewart Department Store, she heard the bells of a nearby church strike nine and she felt her heart sink. Dinner would be over by now in the basement dining room of Madame Arlette's dressmaking establishment, and she knew that she would have to make a hasty meal of rolls and watery coffee before going to bed. She did not pause, as she had in the past, to stare longingly into Stewart's windows, to admire the display of warm, fur-trimmed cloaks and fine velvet dresses. These fashionable garments were far beyond her reach.

She had not earned a dollar so far. She had been working for her board and lodgings, and, as the other seamstresses had told her, she was fortunate to have food and a place to sleep. Usually a dressmaker's apprentice paid a premium in exchange for her training.

In the few weeks since she had started working in the small shop, she had come to loathe the place. The sewing room was badly ventilated, and the lighting was insufficient for the close work the girls were required to do. A few of them were consumptive; all were pale and haggard and looked older than their years. Garnet wondered how long it would be before she came to look like the rest.

She flinched as the wind tore at her cloak, and she brushed the snow from her eyes with an impatient hand. Back home in Charleston she had never even seen snow, never felt the bone-chilling cold of a New York winter.

Now a tall, dark shape loomed up in front of her, and

before she could step aside, a man took her arm. She felt a moment of terror, then heard him speak. "Garnet!" A moment later she was looking up at Logan McClintock, an impressive figure in a fine heavy coat and a tall beaver hat.

"What the devil are you doing, running around at this hour? You look half frozen."

He drew her aside so that she stood with her back to the many-windowed façade of A. T. Stewart's. "I had to deliver a dress," she told him. "The customer insisted that she must have it for this evening. And then I lost my way coming back, and now—"

"But your letter said you were working as a seamstress," Logan said.

"I run errands too." She was aware, all at once, of how completely exhausted she felt. She had not eaten since morning, for several rush orders had come in and the girls had been forced to remain at their work tables all day, stopping at noon for coffee only.

"What's wrong?" Logan asked. Garnet swayed and then his arm was around her, supporting her. "Are you ill?"

"No, only hungry. And I'm afraid I've missed dinner."

"I'll buy you dinner," he said. "You look as though you need a good meal."

But Garnet hesitated, for Madame Arlette imposed strict rules on her employees: They were not permitted to entertain gentlemen in the dismal back parlor of the shop. They were allowed to attend church services on Sunday morning, and once they had completed their apprenticeship, they might visit their families one Sunday afternoon each month. They slept in a dormitory over the shop, all of them in one room.

Garnet knew she should refuse Logan's invitation, but she could not bring herself to leave him. She felt the hard strength of his arm around her, reviving her, and she realized how much she missed him since that day when they had said good-bye on the South Street dock.

She hesitated. "I'm not properly dressed," she said. Her neat black dress with its white linen collar and cuffs was respectable enough, but scarcely suitable for dining out. She thought longingly of the jade-green velvet gown that had been returned; it stood in the workroom of the shop, and tomorrow she would sew on the elaborate beading.

The snow was falling more heavily now, swirling around them in large, wet flakes. "Give me half an hour to change," she said. "I'll meet you here."

A half hour later Logan was helping her into a hansom cab. She looked at his strong, familiar profile in the light of the lantern that hung beside the cab door, and realized how good it was to see him again. She pushed away all thoughts of the shop and of the risk she was taking. Leaning back against the seat, she gave herself up to the luxury of moving through the snowy night, warm and comfortable, with Logan beside her.

The cab drew up at the corner of Beaver and William streets, and her eyes widened. She had never seen Delmonico's restaurant, although she had heard the girls at the shop speak of it with awe. As Logan helped her down she saw that the place was even more impressive than she had imagined, with its entrance flanked by two Pompeiian columns. Even on such a stormy night a steady procession of cabs were drawing up, and fashionably dressed ladies were hurrying inside on the arms of their escorts.

A few moments later she was seated opposite Logan at a corner table. When he first saw the gown she was wearing under her plain, serviceable cloak, he had raised his dark brows, but he did not remark on it. Still, he must have wondered why she, in her present circumstances, should be able to wear so fine a dress. Smoothing the folds of the handsome, jade-green velvet, she felt a stirring of guilt but she set it aside.

She turned her attention to the first course, a steaming shrimp bisque thickened with cream and fragrant with herbs. Although she was ravenous, she forced herself to eat in a lady-like way. Gradually she relaxed and smiled.

"That's better," Logan said. "Now, shall we sample the wine?"

She nodded, and he went on. "This is a special occasion, and you must help me share it."

"A special occasion?" Then why wasn't his wife with him, to celebrate?

"We'll drink to my new steamer, the *Sea Dragon.*"

"What a curious name," she said, leaning forward and looking at him with the flattering attention she had been taught to show to gentlemen during her growing-up years in Charleston.

"She'll be making the China run," he said. "And when the Chinese see the smoke and sparks shooting from her stacks—"

She nodded with swift understanding and touched her glass to his. The fine Burgundy warmed her and went tingling through her veins. For the moment she felt carefree, light-hearted. Not since those first weeks with Keith Jardine had she felt this way. But she must not allow herself to remember Keith.

"What about the *Ondine*?"

"I'm putting her back on the New York to San Francisco run," Logan told her.

"You will have to hire a captain, then," she said.

"Dermot Rankin's more than capable," he told her,

plainly stimulated by her interest in his business activities.

"And will Mr. Rankin be able to round up a crew for the return voyage—with all those seamen rushing off to the gold fields?"

"If anyone can, I'll put my money on Rankin," Logan said.

"I hope you're right. I mean, I would not like to think of the *Ondine* rotting in San Francisco Bay. She was a—a kind of refuge for me, you see."

Their eyes met, and she wondered if Logan, too, was remembering how he had carried her from that tent on the beach, her bruised body wrapped in his coat, how he had held her against him while Silas had rowed them out to the *Ondine*.

Or was he thinking, as she was, of the night when she had awakened from a nightmare, crying out, and had found him in her cabin leaning over her? She had clung to him like a frightened child, and he had spoken gently, reassuringly; soothing her back to sleep.

"Finish your wine," he was saying now, and when she had obeyed he refilled her glass. "The *Ondine* has served me well," he said. "And with luck I'll be able to get another voyage out of her, maybe two. But a sailing ship, even one as fine as Donald McKay's *Stag Hound*, will be at the mercy of wind and tide." He went on, speaking with boyish enthusiasm. "I've gotten three hundred miles a day out of the clippers I've sailed for Abel Bradford—and I could do it again, with a clipper of my own. But after talking with James Lachlan, who's building my engine, I'm convinced that steamers are what I want for the China run."

"Will you hire another captain for the *Sea Dragon*?"

Logan shook his head. "Not for her maiden voyage," he said. "I'm going to take her out there myself." He grinned.

"But that won't be for a while; we're still going over designs for the engine. I'll be here in New York for several months at least."

"Oh, that's good to hear—I mean—since your wife and son are here, and . . ."

Something in his face silenced her. His fingers tightened on the stem of his wineglass. "My son, Chris, is dead. He died of typhus while I was away at sea."

"Oh, Logan, I'm so sorry," she said. "How terrible for you—and your wife. . . ."

His eyes hardened and there was a frightening remoteness about him, as if he were no longer aware of her presence. She sensed the sorrow in him, and she could understand that. But there was something else: a kind of cold anger. Something was wrong between Logan and his wife—Vanessa—yes, that was her name. Why else would he have taken another woman out to celebrate the building of his new ship?

The waiter came back and served the next course, but Garnet was unable to touch her food. The silence between them was growing more painful by the minute. She pushed back her chair.

"You must not leave," he said. "Not yet."

"Oh, but I—"

"There are several more courses," he told her.

"I shouldn't stay," she told him, her eyes anxious. "Madame Arlette, the woman who owns the shop, locks up at eleven sharp every night. Any girl who isn't inside by that time is dismissed."

"Sounds like a girls' school," he said. He waited for her smile, but her face remained taut with anxiety.

"It's much worse than any school," she said. "I want to make my own way, to work, to be respectable—I really do. But Madame is horrible. She punishes us for breaking any one of her petty rules; she drives us like cattle."

Logan grinned. "When I promote Rankin to captain, maybe I should sign her on as first mate."

"It's not a joke," Garnet said indignantly. "We sleep, six of us, in an unheated room over the shop. Some of the girls are ill; she makes no allowance for that. Why, only the other day, a girl cut a sleeve wrong. She spoiled a piece of lace, but she didn't do it on purpose. And Madame struck her across the knuckles with a pressing iron."

"I'd heard that seamstresses are overworked and underpaid, but I never thought—You can't go back there."

At his words Garnet felt a swift surge of hope.

"What am I to do, then?"

"Another shop, perhaps—" he began, but she interrupted.

"Most of them are the same. Some are far worse. Rebecca Kohler—her bed's next to mine, and sometimes we talk at night. She's worked in several shops and she's told me dreadful things about them. She could open a shop of her own, but on her salary, it will take years."

Logan nodded thoughtfully but said nothing, and Garnet went on, the words tumbling out now. "I have to get back, and before eleven, not only because of the locking up but— Oh, Logan, I've done such a foolish thing."

"Tell me," he said.

"This dress—I borrowed it. Madame doesn't know. A customer sent it back because she said the color was not becoming."

"It is becoming to you." Garnet saw Logan's look, heard the change in his tone, and then he was holding her hand. "That green brings out the color of your eyes." His fingers tightened around hers. "You don't want to go back to the shop, do you?"

"I—"

"Do you?" he repeated.

"No, but—"

"All right, then. Have another glass of wine and finish your dinner. And since you're not going back tonight, we'll have to make other arrangements."

Logan's private office, on the second floor of a three-story building on South Street, still smelled faintly of fresh paint and varnish. "I leased this place only last week," he said. Garnet watched as he quickly built up a fire in the iron stove. "You'll spend the night here," he told her. "Tomorrow you can go back to the shop, get your belongings, and pay the old harpy for the dress."

"Oh, but how can I—"

He closed the door of the stove, then came to her. He was offering her an escape from the shop, from the endless drudgery that had left her friend, Rebecca Kohler, drawn and haggard while still in her twenties.

She knew what he expected in return. She saw the hunger in his eyes. "How can I stay here?" She was not sure if the question was directed to him or to herself. He was married. His wife, Vanessa, lived in a house on Gramercy Park. Before she could still the turmoil of her thoughts, his arms went around her. "How can I—"

"It's only for tonight," he was saying. "That couch over there is quite comfortable. I have blankets in the chest."

He had been sleeping in his office, then. How serious was the rift between him and Vanessa? Even if she could have found the courage to ask him, it was too late, for now his mouth, hot and demanding, found hers. He kissed her gently at first, and then, when she yielded herself, his kisses grew more urgent. His tongue explored her mouth, awakening an answering need inside her.

Then they were together on the couch, and his hands were stripping off the jade-green velvet dress, letting it slide to the floor. He took the pins from her hair slowly, so that it tumbled down over her shoulders in a cascade of pale gold. Now he was drawing off her camisole, and his lips were tracing the curve of her throat, the swell of her breasts, and she was reaching out to him, clinging to him. Her doubts, her misgivings, fell away, and she reached out to him, trembling with her own need. She raised her body, and at the moment of climax, she knew, for the first time, all that passion could be between a man and woman.

Early the next morning they went looking for lodgings and found them in one of the boardinghouses that were springing up on the southern tip of the city. Like so many others, this neat brick building had once been a fine private home.

"When will I see you again?" Garnet asked as Logan prepared to leave.

"In a few days," he assured her. He kissed her, his lips brushing hers, but she sensed that his thoughts had moved on to the business ahead: procuring a cargo for the *Ondine*, perhaps, or meeting with the Scottish engineer to study designs for the *Sea Dragon.*

Seeing her downcast look, he pressed a few bills into her hand. "You can shop at A. T. Stewart's or one of the other stores on Broadway," he said. "Buy a warmer cloak—you'll need it here in New York."

But after he was gone she stood, still clutching the bills. Logan was generous, and she was grateful to him for setting her free from the shop. But now, as she turned away from the window, she began to realize how precarious her position was.

Chapter 16

By early February the snow had melted, and now, when Vanessa took her daily walk in Gramercy Park, she caught the fresh smell of damp earth and saw the outlines of the buds on the elms and maples. But for her it was still winter, for she was numb with unhappiness and dread. Ever since that night when she had locked Logan out of their bedroom, a bleak emptiness had settled over the house. Often he rose and went down to South Street at dawn, and sometimes he stayed out all night.

Even when he joined her for dinner he had little to say to her. When he did speak, it was with an impersonal courtesy that was more chilling than the anger he had shown her immediately after his return from California. His gray eyes were remote, and he ate what was set before him with no more relish than he would have shown for the salt beef and hard biscuits that were his shipboard fare.

Once she had tried to draw him out over the matter of Delia. "A runaway slave, is she?" he had said. Then he added, "I suppose you knew that when you hired her."

"Yes, Felicity told me. She belongs to an organization that helps runaway—"

"So Felicity Bradford's got herself mixed up with the abolitionists. I can't say that I'm surprised."

"You make it sound like . . . It is not a trivial matter, Logan."

"No, it isn't. Right now Congress is debating a new fugitive slave law. Not that debates will settle the question of slavery. And neither will Felicity and her well-meaning friends."

"But, Logan—about Delia—"

"I'm not about to turn her over to the law, if that's what's worrying you," Logan said. He looked past her. "I know what it feels like to be a hunted fugitive."

Vanessa stared at him. She realized how little she knew about him, and all at once she wanted to know, to share his thoughts and feelings. A hunted fugitive? What had he meant? Before she could question him he rose from his chair, leaving his coffee and dessert unfinished.

"As long as Delia does her work she has a home here," he said. "Now, if you'll excuse me, I have work to do."

"But Logan—"

"James Lachlan will be here soon. We have designs to go over."

Vanessa's heart sank, for she had met the lanky, sharp-featured young Scottish engineer before, and she knew that when he and Logan got together on business, they were likely to remain shut in the library half the night.

A chill wind drove the rain against the parlor windows a few nights later when Silas Pringle came to the house unexpectedly. Logan had not returned home for dinner, and Vanessa, who was taking tea and sandwiches from a tray in front of the fire, welcomed the company of the big man, with his weatherbeaten face and pale blue eyes. He had come, he said, to talk to Logan on the matter of insurance coverage for the *Ondine*.

"The appraisers from the insurance company aren't satisfied with the condition of the *Ondine*," Silas said. "They're not going to insure a coffin ship—"

Vanessa caught her breath sharply, and Silas hastened to explain. "She's not that, but she will need some expensive repairs, and if Logan will give me the word, I can go ahead. He left the yard early, and he isn't in his office, so I thought I might find him here."

"He said not to wait dinner for him," Vanessa said, unable to meet Silas's frank gaze. "The truth is . . . I'm not sure when . . . if . . ."

Silas cleared his throat. "I wouldn't have come to the house tonight, except that Logan's in one hell of a hurry—begging your pardon, Vanessa. He wants to get the *Ondine* loaded and out to sea as fast as he can, because those miners in San Francisco'll pay anything they have to for plain tin pans and shovels and flour."

"But how can you be certain that she'll make it around the Horn, even with repairs?" Vanessa felt her body go tight with fear.

Silas shrugged. "There's no certainty when you're at sea. But when I've made the repairs, new copper sheathing for the hull and the rest of it, I figure Dermot Rankin'll stand a better chance than most. He's a hard man, and he knows how to drive a ship and a crew."

"But Logan will be risking his life, too, and I . . ."

Silas stared at her in bewilderment. He had been thoroughly soaked by the rain, and it dripped off his coat and plastered his hair against his forehead. "Logan won't be sailing aboard the *Ondine*, not this voyage. But you must know that already."

Vanessa looked away. She did not know. Logan had not told her. He had scarcely spoken to her since that night when she had locked him out of their bedroom, and when he had, it was with mechanical courtesy. Only in their brief conversation about Delia the other night had she felt a moment of closeness. But she could not share her hurt feelings with Silas.

Instead, she spoke quickly. "Your jacket's wet through,"

she said. "Please, take it off and hang it by the fire to dry. And have a cup of tea." She forced a smile. "Logan keeps a bottle of rum over there in the cabinet. I'll put some in your tea, and that will keep you from getting a chill."

"I don't want to be a bother," Silas began, but Vanessa took his jacket, then served his tea, liberally laced with rum.

Logan would be staying on here in New York, then. Her relief was mingled with her pain, because he had not bothered to tell her. She had to force herself to concentrate on what Silas was saying. "Logan's satisfied to trust the *Ondine* to Rankin—it's the *Sea Dragon* he's thinking about now. He's taking a risk there, but that Scotsman, Lachlan's pretty smart and he—"

"The *Sea Dragon*?"

Silas, who had seated himself in a straight-backed wooden chair, swallowed his tea. "The new steamer," he said, obviously surprised at her lack of comprehension. "The one for the China run."

"Oh, yes—yes, indeed. I'd forgotten the name for a moment." Her hand was unsteady as she raised her own cup to her lips. "Please have one of these sandwiches, or a piece of Mrs. Skene's cake. She—"

But Silas shook his head, and then his pale eyes were fixed on her face. "You didn't know. You didn't know about Rankin's being made master of the *Ondine*. You didn't know the name of Logan's new steamer."

"A woman does not concern herself with such matters. Logan's business affairs have never—"

"It isn't exactly business when a wife doesn't know if her husband is going off to sea in a couple of weeks or in a year." He hitched his chair closer to the small velvet-covered sofa where she sat. When he spoke again, his voice was surprisingly gentle. "You've been through a bad time. And Logan—

he's not easy to deal with sometimes. I know that too. But you're his wife. He needs you."

"I doubt he'd agree with you." Vanessa spoke more sharply than she'd intended because of the pain Silas's words caused her.

"He married you. He got this fine house for you."

"And he was so sure that Chris would be safe here. And now . . ." Vanessa could not keep back the words. "Now he blames me because his son is dead. His son. As if Chris was not . . ." Her voice shook and she felt the tears stinging at her eyelids. She tried to fight them back. Then Silas was beside her, gripping her hands. "Maybe I've got no right to talk to you like this," he said, "but I've known Logan a lot longer than you have. Ever since he was a half-starved little gutter rat—no more than ten."

Vanessa stared in surprise. She wiped away her tears and said, "Tell me about him."

"You care enough to want to know?"

"I love him," she said, and she realized that it was true, and that she felt no embarrassment in speaking so frankly to Silas.

Silas helped himself to a second cup of tea, the delicate china cup looking lost in his huge, weatherbeaten hand. "First time I saw him, he was running from the law," Silas said. "Part of a gang, he was—the youngest of the lot. Skinny enough to boost through windows, quick and clever. Guess he had to be to grow up on his own in the Five Points. But this time his luck nearly ran out. The constables were after him."

"A hunted fugitive," Vanessa said half to herself, remembering their conversation at dinner a few nights before.

"That's what he was, all right. He and the rest of the gang had been bolder than most. Looting ships, they were, up and down the East River. Using a rowboat with greased oarlocks to muffle the oars. From what Logan told me later on, they'd been plundering a brig, and he was stealing stuff out of the captain's cabin on a brig anchored off James Slip. Only this time the constables were waiting for them when they came ashore. A few of them were caught right off, and the rest scattered. It was before daybreak, hardly light out, and Logan went tearing down an alley behind the shipyard where I was working as an apprentice. I was on my way to work, and he came barreling into me. He fought like a cornered wildcat. Skinny as he was, and half my size—but he never stopped fighting until I got him down on his face and near broke his arm."

"And then?"

"He didn't beg or whine like most of his kind. Not Logan. He said if I'd let him go, he'd take me to the fence where he unloaded his loot and split the money with me. Then he showed me what he'd stolen. The captain's own sextant, and as fine a one as I'd ever seen."

Vanessa knew that the sextant was the instrument used for measuring the angle of the sun and other celestial bodies above the horizon, that it was used by the captain to calculate his position each day. "There it was," Silas went on, "wooden case and all." Silas grinned at the memory. "I clouted him over the head and told him I was no thief. I said I had no mind to end my days in a jail cell or at a rope's end."

"You didn't turn him over to the constables."

"No, I didn't. I dragged him into the shipyard and made him scrub himself under the pump. By then it was getting light. He was looking at a schooner that was under construction. He asked if I'd built it. I said I'd had a part in the building of it. There was something in his eyes when he looked at that ship. I told him he could get work in the yard too. Carrying supplies to the men, running errands. And he did. Then a couple of years later he signed on a frigate as a cabin boy—"

Silas broke off abruptly. He and Vanessa had been too intent on their talk to hear Logan coming down the hall. Now he entered the parlor, and after a few moments Vanessa left the two men alone and retired to bed.

But she could not sleep. She was remembering all that Silas had told her. Abruptly she sat up and put on a warm robe, then hurried down the hall to the guest room. It was here that Logan found her when he finally came upstairs.

For a moment she saw his startled look. Then his eyes were mocking, and he spoke lightly. "Have you come to bring me extra blankets? I should have thought that was Alice's work."

"You aren't going to California at all!" She had not meant to start this way, but she was not able to stop herself now. "You're going to be right here all through the summer. Working on the new steamer. The *Sea Dragon.* You didn't even tell me what you were going to call her. Silas told me."

He was beside her now, shaking her lightly. "What's wrong with you tonight? Vanessa! What is it?"

"I thought you'd be sailing aboard the *Ondine.* I thought I'd be here alone again, this time . . . when the baby . . . when I—"

"You're going to have a baby?"

"Sometime in August, Dr. Fairleigh said. So you'll have your own way. As you always do. I wish I could promise you a son. I know you want a son, but I—"

"Be still," he said, holding her against him.

But she could not stem the tide of words even now. "You'll have another ship and maybe another son. You said you expected me to give you more sons. That night . . . you said—"

"I said too damn much that night. I'm sorry for that. And for—for the rest of it."

Vanessa knew that this was as close as Logan would ever come in asking her to forgive him for having taken her in anger that night. He was reaching out to her now, but he had gone as far as he could. Perhaps it was not fair, but she would have to offer the response he needed.

"I want this baby," she said. "I want your child, our child, more than anything."

He lifted her and held her against him, and she raised her mouth for his kiss. A long, slow, searching kiss that deepened until she felt the warm, sweet languour envelop her whole body. A sense of peace, of completion, that grew as he carried her down the hall and back to their own bedroom. And then, when she was beside him in their large, canopied bed, the languor gave way to another, stronger sensation.

She reached up to draw him against her, and she heard him say, "You're sure?"

There was no need for words now. Her hands, her mouth, gave him all the answer he needed.

Garnet Spencer sat at the small desk in her shop on what was beginning to be called the "Ladies' Mile," going over her account book. Only four months in business, her own business, she thought proudly, and she was beginning to make a profit. She had hired Rebecca Kohler away from Madame Arlette, and the young woman had been only too happy to invest her small nest egg in the venture and to contribute her skill and experience. But Garnet knew that without Logan's money the venture would not have been possible; he had looked over property, examining it with the same care he used in determining the soundness of a ship. He had spoken at some length with Rebecca Kohler, satisfying himself that the lean, plain-faced young woman knew her business. He had asked countless questions about the commercial possibilities of this particular location and had gone over the terms of the lease, and only when he had been completely satisfied with the feasibility of the venture had he advanced the money.

His investment was already proving to be a sound one, for this was the start of a splendid new era in the city of New York. The simplicity of past years was quickly vanishing as wealthy men built their magnificent mansions farther uptown. Money was pouring into the city, some of it from the China trade and some from the gold strikes in California. Balls and dinner parties were becoming ever more elaborate as hostesses vied with one another for social prominence.

Dressmakers profited, too, from the changing fashions. The simple gowns of lawn or muslin had given way to bell skirts of ever-increasing width, supported by as many as a half dozen petticoats, and decorated with ribbons, lace, and intricate embroidery.

Only a few weeks ago Garnet's shop, along with all the others on the "Ladies' Mile," had been besieged by frantic customers who ordered the most elegant costumes they could afford to wear to Jenny Lind's concert at Castle Garden. The "Swedish Nightingale" had been brought to New York by Phineas T. Barnum, who had whipped up the public into a frenzy of excitement so great that the chief of police, with sixty of his officers, had been called in to keep order. Six thousand people had crowded into the auditorium at Castle Garden for the great occasion.

Garnet herself had not been able to attend, for she, Rebecca, and the four seamstresses were all exhausted by the rush to provide their customers with flounced, lace-trimmed taffetas and velvets. But no matter how much business came in or how great the demand for her services, Garnet prided herself on providing decent working conditions for her employees, on giving the girls good, nourishing food, a well-lit and properly ventilated sewing room, and clean, comfortable sleeping quarters.

All the same, she found that she was able to make a decent profit, and, she was sure, as she bent over her account book, that her business would grow steadily. She would have security, even success.

She looked up as she felt the crisp autumn breeze sweeping in, and she caught her breath, her lips curving in a smile, for Logan was standing there. It had been so long since she had seen him. Only once during the stifling hot summer had he come to the shop, and then, it was for a brief, friendly call.

During July and early August he sometimes appeared at her boardinghouse late in the evening, and after taking her to dinner in one of the raffish taverns on Bleecker Street, they returned for a few hours of feverish lovemaking. Never once had he stayed until morning.

Toward the end of summer she had not seen him at all, and now, on this late October afternoon, he had reappeared without warning. She told herself that she must be cool and impersonal, but seeing him there, looking into his eyes, feeling the familiar excitement rising in her once more, she did not know how long she could keep up the pose of calm indifference. "Garnet," he said, and held out his hands to her.

She forced herself to remain seated, when all the time she wanted to run into his arms. How dared he! All these weeks and now he came walking into the shop without a word of warning.

He glanced down at her open account book. "Not having business problems, I hope."

She shook her head. "Certainly not. I'll be able to pay

off your loan before long."

He was standing over her now, and at the touch of his hand on her shoulder she went weak inside. "I don't care a damn about the loan, and you know it. I wanted to give you the money outright, remember?"

"Then why have you come?"

"To take you out," he said. "It's late."

"We'll be open another hour," she said. How was it possible to maintain a businesslike façade when even now the pressure of his fingers sent darts of fire through every nerve of her body. "There are always a few customers who come in late."

"Let Rebecca wait on them. Change your dress. Put on something pretty. We're going to the theater and then to the Astor House for dinner."

She wore her usual business costume, a heavy black moiré, well-cut but perfectly plain, with a white silk collar and cuffs. "I don't think I can," she began, but he swept aside her objections.

"There ought to be plenty of fine dresses around here," he said. "Borrow something that you've made for a customer. As you did that night when I took you to Delmonico's."

Now she felt a warm flush rising from the top of the prim white collar to the roots of her hair, for the memory of that night was taking possession of her, overpowering her.

"I have a suitable dress of my own, and a velvet cloak," she told him. "Rebecca made them for me." She still hesitated, unwilling to show how much she wanted to be with him tonight. A moment later he took the account book from her hands, blotted the page, then closed the book and put it aside. "Go and change," he said. "And hurry. We're going to see something called *The New York Fireman and the Heiress of Bond Street* at the National Theater."

This time she could not resist answering his smile. "That does sound like an unlikely couple," she said, rising and hurrying to the rear of the shop.

A half hour later, when they left the shop together, the sun was going down, but Broadway was still noisy and crowded. A steady stream of carriages, wagons, and carts rumbled by, and there were ladies on foot, doing their shopping or staring into the show windows filled with satins, laces, and jewelry. Logan led Garnet to the curb and signaled for a hansom, but it was no easy matter to find one that was unoccupied. Meanwhile, they drew more than a casual glance from the passersby, perhaps because of the striking contrast between the tall, powerfully built, dark-haired man in his fine broadcloth suit and tall hat, and the slight young girl in her fashionable new gown of turquoise taffeta, with its bands of blue velvet, the lavishly embroidered cloak of dark blue satin, her pale-golden hair barely concealed by the small bonnet with its blue and green ostrich plumes.

Even on this thoroughfare, where fashionable women abounded, Garnet's costume was noticed and admired. But one woman, seated in her open carriage, was particularly interested in the sight of Logan and Garnet emerging from the dress shop together. Her coachman had already started for home when she called out, "Wait! Stop here."

And moments after Logan and Garnet had entered their hansom and moved away into the crowd, the lady, her lips compressed, her eyes narrowed, got down and made her way into Garnet's shop.

At the theater Logan kept up a flow of casual conversation during the intermissions. The *Sea Dragon* was nearly finished. He planned to seek backing for a second steamer for the China run. The *Ondine* was now in service hauling lumber from Maine to New York.

Later, over dinner at the Astor House, an uneasy silence fell between them, and Garnet found herself speaking of the weather, of how welcome the coolness of autumn was after the enervating heat of the summer. "I should be used to such heat," she said, "but the pace in Charleston was always so much slower than it is up here. We drew the blinds and napped during the afternoons."

"The heat didn't stop all those people from crowding into Castle Garden," Logan said.

"Did you and . . ." She paused for a moment and then went on carefully. "Were you and your wife at the performance?"

He too, was choosing his words with caution. "I've never cared much for concerts. And my wife was still recovering from . . . She gave birth to a son. The last day of August."

Anger flared up in her. That first night when Logan had taken her to his office on South Street, when he had made love to her—had Vanessa been carrying his child then? Or had she become pregnant afterward? She would never know. She did not want to know.

Vanessa McClintock. Logan's wife. She had been no more than a name to Garnet all these months. Garnet's anger deepened. Those hot summer nights when he had shared her bed at the boardinghouse. His wife must have been far along in her pregnancy then.

He had wanted a woman to satisfy his physical needs, and she had been more desirable than a paid prostitute, for she had been eager, willing. She had loved him. And he had been selfish enough, cruel enough, to take advantage of her love.

For one moment of blind, unreasoning rage she wanted to spring at him, strike at him, claw his tanned, imperturbable face. The room blurred before her eyes and the soft music that was being played for the pleasure of the diners sounded off-key . . . far away. . . .

Then she heard Logan's voice speaking her name quietly. "Garnet," was all he said, but there was affection in his tone, and concern for her.

From somewhere she gathered her strength and fought her way back to sanity. He had never said he loved her, had made no promises for a future together. He had come to her when her world lay in ruins about her, when she cowered, broken and violated, in the tent on the fog-shrouded beach of San Francisco. He had carried her to the sanctuary of the *Ondine*. And that night, in his office on South Street, he had been an ardent yet tender lover, giving pleasure as well as taking it. He had given her security of a sort too. Financial independence was rare for a woman, and she would have it because of her shop.

All this she told herself fighting down the pain that clutched at her throat, that shook her inwardly. Logan's wife had given him a son, and now he would have the *Sea Dragon* too—the flagship of his fleet. But what was left for her?

The answer came to her, and she forced herself to find the strength to accept it. If she made a scene now, showed weakness, wept and pleaded, she would never see him again. Raising her head, she held out her glass, and he filled it. "We must drink a toast," she said. "To your new son. What have you named him?"

She saw the swift flash of admiration in Logan's eyes. "Blake," he said quietly. "My mother's maiden name."

She raised her glass to his. "Blake McClintock," she said. She managed a smile. "It's a fine name," she told him.

And later, when he left her at the door of her boardinghouse, she was able to ask him when he was going to sail.

"In a month, perhaps a little longer," he told her. "If I don't see you again before I sail, I want you to know—"

She raised her lips to his. "For luck," she whispered. "And a swift passage." For a timeless instant her mouth clung to his. Then he was gone, walking back to the waiting hansom with his familiar long stride, and she was alone in the autumn night.

Although Vanessa had obeyed Logan and had never again gone to the shantytown on Dutch Hill or any of the other pockets of disease and misery that were a part of the darker side of New York, she had gained his consent to do charity work of a sort. "You may attend all the teas and musicales you like, to raise money for good causes," he had told her with a smile. "You can invite the ladies here to the house too."

She had started to thank him, but he had gone on quickly. "It might be a good idea for us to start mixing with these people. Not only the ship owners, but bankers too, politicians."

Good for business, that was what he meant, and although she could see the logic to his suggestion, she could not help wishing that he had been moved by more altruistic considerations. "May I invite Felicity?" she asked with a touch of asperity.

"Certainly," he told her. "And Kitty, too, if you want to. I won't be around in the afternoons."

"But suppose we were to give a dinner? We could scarcely invite Felicity and Kitty without asking Abel and Horace, could we?"

He was silent for a moment. "By all means, invite them. Abel will probably refuse, but that weasel, Horace, may come—if Kitty asks him to. Besides, he'll probably want to do a little polite spying, to find out what I'm up to."

"That could be dangerous," Vanessa began. Logan shook his head.

"Not this time. I've found a few powerful backers through the Halliwells. Mill owners who want new markets for their cotton cloth." He gave her a triumphant smile. "The Bradfords don't control all the trading ports of China. No one does, or ever will. I have some connections of my own in Canton and Macao."

Vanessa remembered when she had met Logan immediately after his return from China. She knew that he, like other captains on the China run, engaged in trading of his own. "This house is too small for a really impressive ball," he was saying. "But not for a dinner party. I'll give you a guest list. We'll have Jeremy Halliwell, for one—"

"And Ross."

Logan shrugged. "Why not?" he said. "He's no businessman—never will be—but he did talk his brother into investing in the *Ondine*."

Even in the midst of the preparations for the dinner, Vanessa did not neglect her other social obligations, and on an afternoon early in November she gave a small afternoon musicale to raise money for one of Felicity's new projects: an orphanage to shelter the homeless children one saw on every corner here in the streets of New York. Felicity made a speech explaining the desperate need of these children for shelter and food and for a decent education. "We must prepare them to go out into the world able to earn their keep," she told the ladies assembled in Vanessa's parlor.

She had persuaded Kitty to come along, and now, while the ladies nibbled at Mrs. Skene's excellent fruit cake and sipped Souchong tea, Kitty drew Vanessa aside. "Horace and I are so looking forward to your dinner party," Kitty said. "I've ordered a new gown already."

Logan had been right, then, about Horace accepting the invitation. "I brought a length of blue silk," Vanessa said. "But now I'll have to get something else."

"Whatever for? You've always looked charming in blue," Kitty assured her.

"I've decided to use the silk to make a house flag for the *Sea Dragon.* It's to be a surprise for Logan. Delia will help me."

She stopped, for Kitty was looking at her with a peculiar expression. Vanessa had seen that look before, but she could not remember when. She knew only that it made her oddly uneasy.

"You must come to the shop where I'm having my gown made," Kitty said quickly. "They do beautiful work, and they have all the latest designs from Paris."

"I don't think—" Vanessa began, but Kitty went on.

"You want Logan to be proud of you, surely. You must come with me. I'll call for you tomorrow morning and we'll drive over to Broadway. And after you've ordered your gown, we'll take refreshments at Thompson's ice cream saloon. I do enjoy their ices, don't you?"

"I've never been there," Vanessa admitted.

"Oh, but then you must try it. How pleasant it is to find an establishment where unescorted ladies can take refreshments without damage to their reputations." Kitty put a hand on Vanessa's arm. "You will come tomorrow, won't you?"

Chapter 17

Vanessa followed Kitty into a small but elegant dress shop on Broadway and looked about dubiously.

"It's sure to be expensive," Vanessa said. "Perhaps if I bought another length of silk at A. T. Stewart's I could make a suitable gown. Delia could help with the fittings."

"Nonsense," Kitty said. "If Logan can afford to build a steamer, he can afford to keep you properly outfitted, and besides . . ."

The jade-green velvet draperies that divided the front of the shop from the fitting rooms in back parted, and a thin, round-shouldered woman came hurrying out to serve them. But Kitty insisted that they must be waited on by the manager herself.

"As you wish, ma'am." The woman disappeared, and a few moments later Vanessa heard a soft voice saying, "It's all right, Rebecca."

Then a slender girl came forward to greet them.

"I did not expect to see you this morning, Mrs. Widdicomb," she said politely. "Your dress is not ready for final fitting yet."

"So you told me last time I was here, Miss Spencer," Kitty said. "It is Mrs. McClintock who wants to order a gown." Kitty gave the girl a frosty little smile. "Mrs. Logan McClintock."

Vanessa stared at Kitty. Logan's name was known down on South Street, but he was scarcely in a class with the Bradfords or the Grinnells. And the girl's reaction was equally puzzling, for her green eyes widened and her lips parted on an indrawn breath. How pretty she was, Vanessa thought, with that striking shade of hair, silvery-blond, and a figure whose shapeliness was not concealed even by her prim black silk, with its high white collar and long, white-cuffed sleeves.

"Mrs. McClintock, if you will step this way . . ."

She led Vanessa into one of the small fitting rooms and showed her a selection of sketches. Kitty remained in the front of the shop, looking over a display of fans from Paris.

Vanessa, who had never been in such an elegant dress shop before, noticed that the walls of the fitting room were covered with pale green Chinese silk, that the small gilt chairs were upholstered in velvet of the same shade. Miss Spencer appeared to be ill at ease. Her hands were not quite steady as she passed one of the sketches to Vanessa. She could not be more than twenty, Vanessa thought, young to be managing such a luxurious shop. "We have received a new shipment of Lyons velvets," Miss Spencer was saying. "Lilac would be most becoming, or perhaps a soft shade of blue."

"I was going to make a blue silk dress for myself," Vanessa said. "But then I decided to sew a house flag for my husband's new ship. The *Sea Dragon.*"

How pale the girl was all at once. Naturally fair-skinned, the color had now drained from her lips. Was she faint, perhaps, from overwork? Surely, if she managed the shop, she would not have to toil like an ordinary seamstress.

A seamstress. A half-buried memory stirred in Vanessa's mind. But before she could bring it to the surface, Miss Spencer had recovered herself, and a few minutes later the fitting room was filled with bolts of fabric, with laces and satin ribbons, and the thin round-shouldered woman who had joined them was adding her own suggestions to those of the manager. Kitty, who had selected a fan, came to join them, and she persuaded Vanessa to order a cape and a few afternoon dresses as well as the dinner gown.

"After all," she said when she and Vanessa were seated in Thompson's ice cream saloon a short time later, "I'm sure you're not planning to shut yourself up in your house after Logan sails. You'll be needing all sorts of clothes. And besides shopping is one of the few pleasures we ladies have. What did you think of Miss Spencer's shop, by the way?"

"It's beautiful. But she's young to be the owner of a place like that."

"I doubt she owns it. She's so pretty and has such charming manners. I'm sure she would know how to coax some male into putting up the money, in exchange for her favors."

"Kitty!"

"Oh, for goodness' sake, Vanessa, we're both married now. We don't have to pretend not to know about men and their ways." A look of disgust crossed Kitty's face. "Men are so selfish. Wives have to submit to—to their needs. And go through childbirth to satisfy their ambitions—to give them sons. But they have all the pleasure."

"Not *all* the pleasure, surely," Vanessa said. Since their reconciliation, she and Logan had been closer than ever. A smile curved her lips as she remembered the joy they had shared only last night. Then she saw the expression in Kitty's dark eyes—a look of naked envy. And she could not blame Kitty, married to Horace Widdicomb, a man she had always disliked. "Naturally Logan is proud of Blake," she said quickly. "But so am I."

"And now he's leaving you again, going off to China. Or don't you mind that?"

"Certainly I mind. I wish that he could stay with Blake and me. But he is ambitious. And that is a part of him, his ambition, and I'm learning to accept it."

Kitty spooned her lime sherbet, then said, "Perhaps it is best that Logan's going to be gone for a year or more. It means he'll be leaving her too."

"Her?"

"Miss Spencer. Garnet Spencer," Kitty said. "I didn't want to tell you. But it is better for you to hear it from me now than to find out by accident later on."

Garnet Spencer. Vanessa remembered now. Logan had received a note from Garnet Spencer. A widow he had brought back from San Francisco. But that had been only a year ago. How had Garnet Spencer moved from an apprenticeship in someone else's shop to being manager of a shop of her own? When Logan had mentioned the name, Vanessa had been far too preoccupied with other matters to pay much attention. She had pictured Garnet as a drab woman, middle-aged, perhaps, and then had dismissed all thought of her.

She heard Kitty rattling on. "I saw them together only a few weeks ago, I was getting ready to return home, and there they were, Logan and that girl, coming out of the shop together."

"You must be mistaken," Vanessa said, forcing herself to speak calmly.

"Miss Spencer wore a most sumptuous gown," Kitty went on. "I wasn't the only one who stared at her. And then she and Logan got into a hansom together and went driving off."

But there must be a perfectly innocent explanation, Vanessa told herself. She would speak to Logan tonight, and he would set her mind at rest, and they would share these last few weeks with no shadows between them. Then, as Vanessa realized how little time was left before Logan's sailing, she knew that she could not ask him about Garnet.

She turned her anger on Kitty. "You brought me down to the dress shop today because you wanted to hurt me, because you are jealous. You are not happy in your marriage—you told me so yourself—and so you can't bear the thought that any other woman is happy in hers."

Kitty's eyes slitted like those of an angry cat. Vanessa had hit home. But Kitty rallied. "And are you happy now that you know the truth about Logan? Do you still love him as much as ever?"

The house on Gramercy Park had no ballroom, so Vanessa had decided to limit the evening's festivities to dinner, conversation, and a few musical selections from those ladies who were eager to show off their talents.

Alice had been promoted to the position of parlormaid, and Logan had hired a second maid to help Mrs. Skene in the kitchen. He had bought a carriage, too, and had taken on Mrs. Skene's burly nephew, Ben, to drive it, so that Vanessa would be able to get about more conveniently while he was away at sea.

Then, only a few hours ago, while Vanessa was dressing for the dinner, he had told her that he was buying the house, which he had only leased before. "The deed's safe in Enoch Halliwell's office," he said. Enoch was now Logan's lawyer. Vanessa had been moved, for she understood that Logan was doing everything possible to give her a feeling of security, of stability, during the long months when they would be apart.

Now, as she stood in the parlor, surrounded by her guests, she knew that she had done the right thing in not questioning him about Garnet. These past few weeks, she had felt closer to him than ever, more cherished and protected. She glanced at Kitty, who was standing with Horace at the opposite side of the room. If Kitty had come here tonight to see how her malicious little scheme had worked, she was doomed to disappointment, Vanessa told herself. Or perhaps it was Horace who had insisted that they accept the invitation, for although he and Logan had not settled old scores, Horace was shrewd enough to realize that since Logan was now a part of the tight circle of successful New York ship owners, he was no longer a man to be ignored.

Certainly there were others from that circle here tonight: Aspinwalls, Lows, and Grinnells. Vanessa was still unable to realize how completely her social standing had changed since that day only a little over three years ago when she had hidden herself in the back of Logan's wagon down on South Street.

She came back to the present with a start as Alice, in a trim uniform, with a starched apron of white cambric, stepped out through the dining room doors to announce that dinner was served.

Some of the guests began to move toward the dining room, but Logan was still deep in conversation with Jeremy Halliwell, Moses Grinnell, and James Lachlan, the Scottish engineer who had designed the *Sea Dragon.*

"Take the *Stag Hound*," Grinnell was saying in his deep, booming voice. "There's a clipper for you. Her first voyage to China, she cleared enough to pay for herself, and a profit of eighty thousand dollars for her owners, Sampson and Tappan. And why? Because McKay designed her for speed."

"McKay's a great designer and builder of ships," James Lachlan conceded. "But the *Stag Hound*—all these clippers, their lines are too sharp, and that reduces cargo space."

"And the *Sea Dragon*? Those engines take up space, don't they? Space that could be used for cargo. And they burn up a fortune in coal," Grinnell said.

"If you'd care to come down to my shipyard, I'd be

pleased to have you look over the *Sea Dragon*," Logan said cordially. "You'll find that we've made certain improvements in design to deal with the problems you've mentioned."

Vanessa tried to catch Logan's eye, but instead, it was Ross Halliwell who came to her side. He had been visiting his father here in the city, and now he was thinking of remaining for a time. "May I have the pleasure of taking you in to dinner?" he asked.

She took his arm.

"I've learned all I can in Boston," he told her when he was seated beside her at the table. "Next year I hope to go to Paris to continue my studies."

"But your paintings are of the waterfront and the ships of Salem."

"So far, yes. But there are other subjects, and I believe I'm ready to attempt them now. I want to try my hand at portraits." He looked at her, his eyes warm with admiration. "Perhaps you would be willing to sit for me."

Logan, overhearing Ross's words, said, "That's a fine idea, if my wife's willing. Sitting for a portrait would occupy your time while I'm away, wouldn't it, Vanessa?"

"We'll talk of it before the *Sea Dragon* sails," Vanessa said.

She was pleased that Ross wanted to paint her portrait, but she was also troubled by Logan's words, for she knew that he was reminding her that he expected her to keep busy only with genteel, safe pastimes while he was away. He was warning her that she must never again venture into places like Dutch Hill, and while she could not entirely blame him, she felt a stirring of rebellion.

A man might go off to the other side of the world and take the greatest risks to fulfill his ambitions, and he would be praised for his daring and enterprise. His wife, however, was supposed to remain at home, waiting patiently, drinking tea with friends, playing hostess at musicales, doing handiwork for charity bazaars. She might make the flag for his ship, but he would be the one to sail under that flag, to cross oceans and visit distant lands.

Felicity Bradford had found an outlet for her restlessness in her charity work, and many other women, like Kitty and her friends, filled their days with shopping and gossip and parties, but Vanessa knew that she needed something more. If only she could have persuaded Logan to let her come with him, but this, she knew, was useless.

During the next two months Vanessa saw little of Logan, for he was often busy at the shipyard and he discouraged her from coming down there. Then, too soon, the *Sea Dragon* was ready to leave and she was standing on the deck with Logan. "Look there," he said, and she shaded her eyes and tilted her head back to watch the ball of silk that went soaring up the masthead. She forgot her misgivings, her dread of their parting, for the moment, for there was the new house flag, snapping out in the wind and flaunting its blue and scarlet for the first time.

The McClintock house flag. She felt Logan reach for her hand, and his fingers closed tightly around hers. She was sharing in the realization of his dream: She was seeing the beginning of the McClintock Line.

This was a gala occasion. The crew had cast off the lines and had taken the *Sea Dragon* to a point near Battery Park, at the foot of Manhattan, where she now rode at anchor while visitors brought out by harbor boats milled around on the deck. Jeremy and Ross were here, along with their father, who was holding his tall stovepipe hat steady, to keep it from flying away in the stiff January wind.

Vanessa saw another familiar face: Dermot Rankin,

bearded and flushed with the rum he had been drinking. A man from the crew of the *Ondine* was with him: his short, barrel-chested first mate. "Not much like the *Ondine*, is she?" Rankin said in a booming voice.

"I'll take a sailing ship any day," the mate replied.

But now Vanessa forgot all about them, for she realized that this was the moment of parting. Logan's arms went around her and she clung to him, indifferent to the crowd of onlookers as she responded to his kiss not only with her lips but with her whole being. She was determined not to give way to tears. He was her love, her life, and although he was leaving her, she was a part of him.

Gently he freed himself and moved away as a group of visitors came to say their good-byes. She stood aside so that he might speak with Enoch, then with Ross and Jeremy. Looking up, she took what comfort she could from the sight of the flag that she had made.

"His wife's a beauty," she heard someone saying. She recognized Rankin's voice, better suited to shouting orders from a quarterdeck.

"If I had a wife like that, I'm damned if I'd go off to China without her." That was the barrel-chested mate, who was preparing to climb over the side and down into one of the small dories that circled the *Sea Dragon.*

"McClintock won't lack for women wherever he goes—even to China," Rankin said. "Got a way with 'em, he has."

Vanessa realized that since they had started climbing down the ladder they did not realize how their voices carried. She lost a few words of their conversation, and then she stiffened when she heard Rankin saying, ". . . that girl he brought back to the *Ondine*, the night we left San Francisco, remember?"

". . . carried her aboard, wrapped in his coat and not much

on under that. All that pale yellow hair . . . thought she was a mermaid except for them long legs of hers. . . ." The mate's words came to her, etching a picture in her mind.

Vanessa shared a carriage with the Halliwells on her return trip to Gramercy Park. She sat, tense and silent, in the carriage, trying to maintain her composure until she reached the privacy of her room.

"The *Sea Dragon*'s a fine ship," Ross was saying. "But no steamer will ever have the beauty of line or the grace of movement that a clipper does."

Enoch snorted impatiently. "Grace and beauty! You'll never have any business sense, my lad. But Logan McClintock does." He turned to Vanessa. "That husband of yours'll make his mark in the world. He's already set that Scotsman James Lachlan to work designing a second steamer. And he's made some sound investments in real estate too. Logan's not the kind to put all his eggs in one basket."

Real estate. Logan had said nothing to her about real estate. Was Enoch speaking of the house in Gramercy Park?

She felt a tightness in her chest. What was it Kitty had said after their visit to Garnet Spencer's shop?

I'm sure she would know how to coax some male into putting up the money.

Yellow hair . . . pale golden hair . . . and Logan had carried her aboard, wrapped in his coat. . . .

"Are you feeling ill, Vanessa?" Ross asked anxiously.

She tried to speak, but no sound would come. She turned her face away and stared, unseeing, out the carriage window.

"You mustn't start moping, child," Enoch was saying. "Keep busy and the time will pass quickly enough, and then

Logan will be coming back with a fortune—you think about that. A fortune in the China trade!"

"That's right," Jeremy said. "And in the meantime you can . . ." For a moment he was at a loss, wondering what Vanessa might do to keep occupied now that Logan had hired servants to wait on her and care for her baby.

"You promised Ross you'd sit for your portrait," he said, obviously pleased with himself for remembering. "Ross, when will you start work on her portrait?"

"I will leave that up to Vanessa," Ross said quietly.

"We'll start as soon as you like," Vanessa said.

Ross had rented a studio on the top floor of a four-story house on Great Jones Street in Greenwich Village, a street that was still respectable but not quite as fashionable as it had been only a few years before. During her first sitting, a few days after Logan's departure, Ross made preliminary sketches and tried to keep Vanessa entertained by telling her something about his new lodgings and the woman who owned them.

"Mrs. Crothers, my landlady, would probably not have taken in an artist if she could have avoided it," he said. "No doubt she thinks artists are a dissolute lot. But her late husband was one of my father's clients. Lost most of his money in the Panic of Thirty-seven. Pa told her that unless she wanted to sell her home, she would have to take in a few 'paying guests,' as she likes to call her tenants."

"And how long will you be staying here in New York?"

"I'm not sure. Through the winter and maybe into spring. I hope to get a few more commissions for portraits before I leave for Paris."

"But—forgive me—you must have made a good profit on your shares in the *Ondine*."

"An excellent profit, thanks to Logan's decision to take

the schooner to San Francisco. Please tilt your head a little more to the right. There, that's perfect." He went on sketching, the charcoal moving in his fingers with swift, sure strokes. "But I suppose I'm still trying to convince Pa that I can earn a decent living from my work." He smiled ruefully. "Not that I'm ever likely to make him understand why I've chosen to paint instead of going into law, as he did. He approves of Jeremy's decision to enter politics."

"Is Jeremy giving up his own law practice in Salem?"

"He will if he is elected to Congress," Ross said. "And I believe he will be. He'll certainly get all the financial support he needs from his future father-in-law."

"Is Jeremy engaged? He said nothing about it at our dimmer party."

"The engagement has not been announced yet," Ross said. "Miss Octavia Pollock, his fiancée, relishes the idea of waiting until she can flaunt her alliance to Congressman Jeremy Halliwell."

"Oh, but it sounds so . . . calculating," Vanessa protested.

"I'm sure she's fond of Jeremy, and he's well-suited with her. But it helps that her father owns a controlling interest in half the Lowell textile mills." He looked up at Vanessa and smiled. "Pa's given Jeremy his blessing, on the choice of Miss Pollock—and his new career."

Although Ross spoke lightly, Vanessa sensed how deeply he wanted his father's approval. "Surely, by now, your father has come to accept your determination to be an artist," she said.

"We don't quarrel about it, if that's what you mean," Ross said. "But I doubt Pa'll ever believe that a man should spend his life putting brush strokes on canvas when he could be in Washington, helping to shape the future of the nation. Or off in China, building a shipping empire. You heard the way he spoke about Logan when we were driving back from South Street last week."

Yes, she had heard, and she had not been able to forget Enoch's words any more than she had been able to forget the words of Dermot Rankin and that other seaman; ever since the day that Logan had sailed she had been tormented by her suspicions, afraid to have them confirmed, unable to convince herself that they were groundless.

Now Ross gave her a searching look, making her realize once more how aware he was of her moods even when he did not understand what caused them.

"I'm afraid I've been thoughtless," he said. "Holding a pose can be exhausting, especially when you're not used to it. Why don't we stop for the day?" He helped her down from the dais. "Let me get you a glass of sherry."

When she left Ross's studio Vanessa did not go back to the house on Gramercy Park; instead, she ordered Ben to drive her to Garnet's shop. The early winter dusk had fallen, and when she came inside she saw that Garnet was wearing her bonnet and cape, preparing to leave.

"Why, Mrs. McClintock." Garnet's lips curved in a professional smile of greeting. "Both your afternoon dresses are ready to be fitted. If you had come in last week . . ."

On the drive from Great Jones Street to Broadway, Vanessa had tried to imagine how she would begin this encounter. Even now, she knew she could pretend she had come only for a fitting. But all at once the prospect of being closeted into one of the small fitting rooms with its walls of green Chinese silk, of having Garnet's hands touching her, those delicate fingers adjusting the bodice, pinning the sleeves—it was unthinkable.

"I was busy last week," Vanessa heard herself saying. "My

husband's ship sailed—so much to do."

Garnet remained poised, listening politely, but Vanessa saw the tightness in her face. "It was a most impressive sight, the launching of the *Sea Dragon*," she went on. "There are still those ship owners who think that only a clipper is suitable for the China run, but my husband believes in the future of steamers."

"Indeed," Garnet said, still the courteous saleswoman. "I know so little of these matters."

"You know more than I do"—the words came in a rush, unbidden—"since you sailed back from San Francisco aboard the *Ondine*."

"Logan—Captain McClintock—told you that?"

"He mentioned it when you sent that note to our home."

"But you said nothing about it on your first visit here. I should have thought—"

"My husband carried a great many passengers back from San Francisco."

Garnet made an attempt to recover her poise. "Oh, yes. Naturally he did. You could not be expected to remember."

"But I doubt any of the others came aboard as you did. Carried by Logan, half-naked and wrapped in his coat." Seeing Garnet's shocked expression, she went on. "You made an unforgettable impression on certain members of Logan's crew."

In the silence that followed, Vanessa heard the noises from Broadway: the rumble of carts and carriages, the shouts of drivers, the clopping of horses' hooves.

"Mrs. McClintock, you must understand. San Francisco is not like New York. It's a primitive settlement, dangerous for a woman alone and unprotected."

"And were you alone? Are you really a widow or—"

"I have never been married," Garnet said. "I was living

with a man—a gambler. I thought I was in love with Keith when I ran away from home with him. I thought he would marry me."

"Go on," Vanessa said, determined not to allow herself to feel pity for Garnet.

"Keith was suspected of cheating at cards. The men he'd taken money from followed him to our tent on the beach. I don't know if he was guilty or not, but those men—drunken animals, they were—beat him to death. I saw it. And when they had finished with him, they turned on me. They raped me. All of them. Two held me down while the other—"

"Dear God!" Vanessa had forgotten her resolve not to feel pity for this girl.

"Logan found me—I think I was crying—I'm not sure, you see, because I was so dazed, so . . . He came into the tent with Silas Pringle. I begged Logan to get me out of there. I had no money, no one to help me. I can remember Logan wrapping his coat around me; my clothing was torn and filthy."

She drew a long breath and regained her control.

"Mrs. McClintock, your husband did not try to—to make love to me, not once during the return voyage. A few times he came into my cabin because I had cried out in my sleep. I had terrible nightmares, and he comforted me as if I'd been a child. I don't know what the crew thought, or what sort of gossip . . . But I'm telling you the truth. I swear it."

Vanessa believed her, for she was remembering that first night when she herself had come to Logan's lodgings on Tompkins Street. He had given her his bed and had slept in the outer room until she had been able to offer herself freely.

Was it possible that her suspicions about Garnet and Logan had been completely false? She longed to believe that, but she needed to be sure.

"I believe you found work as a dressmaker's apprentice when you arrived here in New York," Vanessa said. "And now you have this fine shop. I know the sort of wages that a dressmaker's apprentice earns."

Something flickered in the depths of Garnet's green eyes. Vanessa went on quickly. "I'm sure there are many men here in the city who would be pleased to be your—your protector. But Enoch Halliwell, our family lawyer, is also a close friend of mine, and it would be easy for me to find out from him if Logan owns this shop."

"There's no need," Garnet said. "Logan bought the shop for me. I hope to be able to pay him back one day."

"A simple business transaction?" Vanessa could not keep the irony out of her voice.

"Logan and I were lovers," Garnet said.

Vanessa had come here to learn the truth. Now she knew, and she felt the hot anger surging up inside her, a blind, unreasoning fury against this girl, who for all her soft-spoken, dignified ways was no better than those shrill painted drabs who haunted South Street. "You—you are shameless. You knew that Logan and I—that he had a wife. . . ."

"I knew that he was married," Garnet said quietly. "If it makes you feel better, you can call me what you like. But remember, Logan came to me the night he started work on his new ship. He needed a woman to sleep with, but he needed more than that. Why didn't he go home to his wife? No doubt you know the answer, Mrs. McClintock."

Now Vanessa's anger ebbed away, leaving her cold, shaken, stripped of her righteous indignation. Somehow she managed to turn away, her head high, her back straight as she walked to the door.

Only later, after she had seated herself in the carriage and ordered Ben to take her home, was she able to give way to her feelings, to bury her face in her hands, to try to shut out the picture that Garnet had branded into her mind. Logan and Garnet, naked and locked in each other's arms.

Chapter 18

At first, Vanessa told herself that it was good that Logan was away at sea. How could she have faced him across the polished mahogany dinner table, how could she have slept beside him in the large, canopied bed, how could she have allowed him to make love to her, knowing what she knew about Garnet? Alone in the house except for the servants, she could at least have time to try to come to terms with the bitter knowledge that he had taken a mistress.

She tried to be fair and reasonable, reminding herself that she had, for a time, denied him his rights as a husband, and what was more natural than that such a man would have turned to another woman? But this was no casual affair, no visit to a sporting house on Greene Street.

He had sought out Garnet, had told her about the *Sea Dragon*, had shared with her his plans for the future. And later, he had bought the shop for Garnet. He owned it, but she managed it. How practical of Logan, and how characteristic, too, that he had arranged the matter in such a way. Why, even Enoch Halliwell had praised Logan's business acumen, his foresight in buying real estate.

No doubt many married women who were living in comfort would have accepted the situation, would have put it out of their minds. Some, like Kitty, might have welcomed it. Kitty would probably have been relieved if Horace had found a mistress to satisfy his physical needs, for she had certainly made it plain enough that she loathed that part of marriage.

But it isn't—it wasn't—like that with Logan and me,

Vanessa thought miserably.

Even now, sitting in the nursery, rocking her son Blake in her arms, she saw the growing resemblance between Logan and the boy. The first blond fuzz was darkening—one day it would be black, like Logan's, although the eyes were blue, and likely to remain so. Logan's son. She loved the baby so much. But how did she feel now about Logan?

Oh, it wasn't fair. Logan had taken her by force that night, for the first and only time in their marriage. He had begotten a son. But he had also found a mistress. And then, when his ship was ready, he had sailed away once more. He had left Vanessa imprisoned in this house.

She was free to attend suitable social functions, or to give them, to raise money for any one of Felicity's worthwhile causes. She might give teas for other ladies, or attend musicales in their homes—but only in the afternoons. She might make small, frivolous items of beadwork, of shells, of embroidery, to be sold at the bazaar that was soon to be held to raise funds for the Shelter for Homeless Infants, another of Felicity's projects.

Because of her promise to Logan, she would not go out to places like Dutch Hill, and certainly not to the Five Points to deliver baskets, to care for the destitute. Indeed, remembering Chris, she was not sure she would ever want to venture into such places again, even if she had not made that promise. For Blake was far too precious; she could not risk his safety. She pressed her cheek to his soft curls, and her arms tightened about him. He must be sheltered, protected against the danger of infection, of illness, in every way possible.

But Blake could not occupy all her time, and she was growing ever more restless. Tomorrow there would be a tea at the home of Miss Eleanor Griswold, a spinster lady and a friend of Felicity's. The purpose of the tea was to make arrangements for the bazaar, and Vanessa was not looking forward to the occasion. Except for Felicity, she had no real friends among these ladies. Their husbands or fathers were well established in shipping or in other mercantile enterprises. They could speak with pride and at great length about their families, Dutch and English, most of whom had come to New York before the Revolution. Vanessa sometimes wondered what would happen if she were to speak of her origins, or Logan's. True, her uncle Gifford Kenyon had died a hero in the War of 1812, but her mother had run a boardinghouse, and she herself had helped with the scrubbing and cooking.

And as for Logan, she wondered how the ladies would respond if she spoke of his childhood in the Five Points or if she repeated the story Silas Pringle had told her of Logan's exploits as part of a gang of young dockside thieves. At times she had been tempted, for anything would be more interesting than the eternal chatter about the newest fashions from Paris, the number of petticoats to be worn under a bell-shaped skirt, the scandalously low cut of a bodice. She could not join in, either, when they started their complaints about the difficulties of finding a really good servant girl from among the dirty, ragged horde of Irish immigrants who were pouring into the city in ever-increasing numbers. Did they expect an Irish girl to come out of the appalling filth of steerage aboard an immigrant ship looking as if she had stepped from a bandbox?

Even in this matter of the newly established orphanage, some of the ladies had wrangled over what sort of children ought to be accepted. Was it proper to give refuge to the babies abandoned by prostitutes? And what about the older children? "Even at four and five, I am told, some of them are already steeped in the ways of sin," Miss Griswold had said at one of the earlier meetings. "They use dreadful language, and

I'm sure they are completely lacking in the rudiments of religious training."

"Whatever their origins," Felicity had said, "I mean to see to it that when they leave our institution they will be prepared to go out into the world able to support themselves by honest work."

Miss Griswold had backed down temporarily and had even offered her home for the next tea. But it was plain that neither she nor her supporters had been convinced, and Vanessa was not looking forward to spending tomorrow afternoon in Miss Griswold's parlor.

It was late afternoon when Vanessa hurried up the three flights of stairs to Ross's studio on Great Jones Street. The winter sunlight was already fading, and Ross told her that it would be useless to work on the portrait that day. Instead, he offered her sherry and sat down beside her on the rather shabby sofa.

"I'm so sorry," she told him. "The meeting went on for so long."

"Meeting?" His warm brown eyes had a teasing glint. "Surely you have not joined Mrs. Amelia Bloomer and her followers in the campaign for woman's rights and temperance."

"Would it shock you if I said I had?"

Ross shook his head. "Not at all. Although I don't think I'd care to paint you tricked out in one of those knee-length skirts over baggy trousers. And I'm sure that Logan would refuse to pay for such a portrait."

"Why no, I don't suppose he would—"

"Certainly not. He wants you to look dignified, even a little aloof, perhaps. Like those portraits of the Grinnell ladies, and the Aspinwalls and the Bradfords. With the most ornate and expensive frame I can find."

Ross was smiling, but she caught an undertone of irony in his voice.

"He told you that?" she asked.

"Oh, yes. He took me aside at your dinner party to explain exactly what he wanted. And he'll have it—a portrait of a lady, wife of the founder of a great shipping dynasty."

"The *Ondine* and the *Sea Dragon*," Vanessa protested. "That is scarcely—"

"He'll have more." Ross was still smiling, but there was something in his eyes, a kind of baffled anger that disturbed Vanessa.

"Surely you are not jealous," she said. "You told me that you have no business aspirations. You are doing what you want to do. Soon you will be going off to Paris to paint."

"I don't envy Logan his ships," Ross said softly. He gave her a long, direct look, his brown eyes lingering on her face. "And he'll get the portrait he wants. It will hang in the parlor of his house, and he may even look at it occasionally—when he is not occupied with business matters."

"That's not—I mean, Logan's not. . . You don't understand him."

"No, I don't. A man who would leave a woman like you to go off to San Francisco, to China."

There was no mistaking the naked longing in Ross's face now, and Vanessa was aware all at once that she was alone here with this handsome young man, gentle, yes, and a friend since their schooldays together in Salem, but a virile and ardent man, for all his quiet, well-bred ways.

She spoke quickly, feeling a desperate need to distract him, and perhaps herself, from these thoughts.

"Logan must go where his business takes him," she said. Then she went on. "And as for me, I assure you I have not joined the followers of Amelia Bloomer. If I was late today, it was because I was detained at a meeting to discuss plans for an orphanage. The Shelter for Homeless Infants. There are so many here in the city—infants and older children too. Abandoned, starving, living in the streets."

"I know," Ross said. "I haven't forgotten that New Year's Day when we went for our sleigh ride and you pointed out that shantytown. Dutch Hill, wasn't it? I hope you are not still going there."

"No, I'm not. Logan has forbidden it."

"I don't blame him for that," Ross said. "Such places can be dangerous. . . ." He broke off and studied her stricken face. "Vanessa, my dear, what is wrong? What have I said?"

For a moment she could not speak, and then the words came swiftly. "It is—it was dangerous. I caught typhus caring for a mother and her children there. And I gave the disease to Chris. Logan blamed me for that. He said I was reckless and . . ."

Then she felt Ross's arm around her, and his embrace was comforting. "Forgive me," he said softly. "I never meant to hurt you. To stir up such memories."

"You had no way of knowing." For a moment she remained as she was, listening to Ross's soothing voice.

"You were not to blame," he told her, drawing her closer. "You did a brave and generous thing, helping those people. Most ladies are content to help the poor by giving tea parties, charity bazaars, but you—"

"I must be content with teas and bazaars, too, from now on," she told him. She moved away and stood up.

"Where are you going?"

"Perhaps you might still do a little work on the portrait?"

He shook his head. "It's too late," he told her. "Look out there. The light has already begun to fade. The days are so short this time of year."

"I'm sorry," she told him. "Truly I am. I'll try to be more punctual in the future."

"I wouldn't want to take you away from your charitable causes," he said.

"The discussion about the orphanage might have been completed in an hour," she told him. "It was all the rest of it—the chatter about fashions and . . ." Her lips curved in a smile. "The gossip about those ladies who were not present. And complaints about the kind of servant girls who are coming into New York these days. They go on and on. It is foolish and boring and small-minded. Why, only today one of the ladies, who claims to have great concern for abandoned infants, said that she had dismissed an Irish parlormaid because the girl was . . . because she had been meeting secretly with a young man, and he deserted her when he found out that she was—"

"That she was pregnant," Ross finished for her. Such a word was not used in polite society. A lady was said to be "in the family way" or "in an interesting condition." But Ross spoke in such a quiet, impersonal way that Vanessa was not at all offended. Instead, she was indignant over the plight of the unfortunate parlormaid.

"What does that foolish Mrs. Wainwright think will become of the maid and her baby? The girl may be forced to abandon the child when it is born. If it is born." She did not go on. There was no need, for abortionists advertised in New York newspapers, boasting blatantly of "an infallible cure for ladies in trouble" and "relief to married ladies, without injurious results."

"They sound like a small-minded group, Mrs. Wainwright and her kind."

"Felicity Bradford's different," Vanessa said. "And besides, if I am not permitted to go out to do charity work with the people who need it, how am I to spend my days?" Then she added hastily, "I've enjoyed posing for my portrait—"

"You need more than that," Ross told her firmly. "In a city like New York, why, there is so much. Have you been to a Sunday-evening reception at the home of the Cary sisters? The talk there is not boring or trivial, I assure you."

"The Cary sisters? I don't believe I know them."

"No, you probably don't. They are not married to men who own ships or textile mills or department stores. The fact is, they are not married at all, either of them. But you will not be bored by trivial conversation at the Carys' home, I'll bet on that. Will you come with me next Sunday evening?"

"I can't."

"Why not? Do you have another engagement?"

Startled by Ross's question, and even more by the swift urgency in his voice, she said, "Why, no. I don't go out in the evening at all since Logan's left."

"What do you do, then?"

"I read or embroider. I'm going to work on a new tablecloth to sell at the bazaar for the Shelter."

"Not next Sunday, you won't," Ross told her with quiet determination. Then he leaned forward, his eyes holding such urgency that she could not look away. "Say you'll come to the Carys' with me on Sunday, Vanessa."

The Cary sisters were not wealthy, and their wide, low, old-fashioned house on East Twentieth Street near Fourth Avenue was a little shabby, but when Ross and Vanessa arrived, they found the parlor already crowded and the conversation lively. Alice and Phoebe Cary were spinsters, but both men and women thronged their home, drawn by the stimulating talk that went on there.

"They are remarkable ladies," Ross had told Vanessa on their drive across the city. "They came here from a farm in Ohio, and they were without money, formal education, or social connections. They were determined to make their way as writers, and they've succeeded. They're bright and hard-working, and I think you'll like them."

When Ross introduced her to the Cary sisters, Vanessa was somewhat surprised to see that both ladies were not at all unfeminine in spite of their daring way of life, for it was considered daring for women to support themselves except as domestics, seamstresses, or governesses. Alice Cary was slender, with delicate features, while Phoebe was plump, with dark hair and sparkling eyes.

Vanessa also met Kate Field, a blue-eyed, auburn-haired beauty smartly dressed in blue taffeta and looking the picture of a fashionable young lady; she might have married any one of a dozen eligible men, Ross told Vanessa later, but she preferred to pursue her career. "She is writing a book about Charles Dickens, and she contributes to the *Atlantic Monthly* and several other magazines."

Not all of the guests were women, however, and Vanessa was impressed at meeting Phineas T. Barnum, whose museum on Broadway drew thousands of visitors, and who had brought Jenny Lind to New York on her well-publicized tour. The publisher of the *Tribune*, Horace Greeley, a tall, stout, balding man, stood at the center of a group of people who were discussing the question of the abolition of slavery, a cause that was of personal interest to Vanessa ever since Delia had come into her home.

Although the Cary sisters served nothing stronger than tea, Vanessa felt herself stimulated by the brisk and sometimes heated exchange of ideas. Moving from one group to another, she heard talk about vegetarianism, about rights for working women, and about the difficult conditions in the Lowell textile mills. She was particularly impressed because here she found men and women speaking together about the issues of the day, and as equals. One young woman was describing the mob rescue of Shadrach, a fugitive slave who had nearly been recaptured in Boston. Another held forth about the first national convention in Worcester of women who advocated woman suffrage, and of the women's rights convention in Seneca Falls.

Vanessa realized that while women like Felicity believed that there was little to do about deplorable social conditions except to set up shelters for orphans or fallen women and to distribute food and clothing to those in need, others were demanding more drastic solutions, like higher wages, particularly for female workers, utopian colonies far from the large cities, temperance, and even birth control.

At the polite dinner parties held in the Bradford house and at Vanessa's party, too, it was assumed that many matters suitable for masculine conversation must not be discussed before ladies. Here that rule did not apply, and Vanessa, having told Horace Greeley that her husband was a ship owner, was taken aback when he and others spoke of the new law, passed only last year, outlawing flogging in the Navy and on merchant ships as well. She admitted that she had heard nothing about it, nor had she read the novel *Two Years Before the Mast*, by a gentleman named Richard Henry Dana.

"But you should," Mr. Greeley told her. "That book was instrumental in abolishing such brutality on merchant ships, including those owned by your husband."

At first, Vanessa was unable to contribute to these conversations, but when someone mentioned the founding of the Asylum for Friendless Boys, she began, timidly at first, then with growing conviction, to talk about her own part in establishing the Shelter for Homeless Infants.

After that Sunday evening, although she continued to take part in genteel charity gatherings, they were only a small portion of her activities. Ross had opened up a new world to her, right here in New York, and she was grateful. Perhaps under other circumstances she would have hesitated to go about with a handsome young man who was plainly attracted to her, even though he never overstepped the bounds of friendship. But she had not forgotten Garnet Spencer. Once, she might have accepted Logan's infidelity, might have told herself that it was a wife's duty to overlook her husband's adventures with other women.

But now, since she had heard the new and startling ideas discussed so freely at the Carys' receptions, about equality between the sexes, she was changing. Sometimes she felt a stirring of excitement; at other times, she was confused and even frightened, and she longed for the safety of the rules by which her mother and Felicity Bradford had shaped their lives.

Through that winter and more and more as spring came to the city, Vanessa was seized by a growing restlessness, a need she did not want to recognize. Logan was halfway across the world, and how long would it be before he came home? Did she want him to come home quickly, as she had before, when he had taken the *Ondine* to San Francisco? Sometimes, remembering that first voyage and its aftermath, remembering her talk with Garnet, she felt she hated Logan. Hated him . . . wanted him . . . In the softness of the May nights she found herself lying awake, aching for the strength of his arms around her, for his hands and his mouth exploring her body, arousing her. For the sweet, drowsy fulfillment that had come when she had fallen asleep with his head resting on the curve of her breast, his flesh warm against her.

★★★★★

Although Felicity Bradford planned to remain in the city for the summer to carry on her work of establishing the new orphanage, most of the other ladies who had helped with the project were already preparing to leave New York to refresh themselves in the sea air of Newport, or the cool, pine-scented breezes of Saratoga Springs. The Cary sisters were vacationing in Long Branch and would not return to hold their receptions before next autumn.

Except for her visits to Ross's studio, summer would be uneventful for Vanessa. She found herself dreading the day when her portrait would be finished and Ross would go off to Paris.

One afternoon late in May when she was preparing to leave the studio, she brought herself to ask Ross how long it would be before the portrait was completed.

"Only a few more sessions," he told her. "Are you bored with sitting for me?"

"Oh, no!" Vanessa had never been any good at dissembling her feelings.

"Maybe you're eager to get rid of me," he went on.

"You know I'm not," she told him.

"I'm pleased to hear it. Because I'll be here through the summer. Or most of it. I have an important commission, from Mr. Low."

"A portrait?"

Ross nodded. "And Low's paying handsomely." He smiled, his brown eyes sparkling. "Not that money is my main consideration, with such a subject."

"She is pretty, then."

"Oh, she's far more than that."

Vanessa had seen a few of the young ladies in the large and powerful shipping family, and none of them had impressed her as being beautiful. But a man might feel differently—particularly if he had become infatuated.

"A proud young beauty, she is," Ross said. Vanessa told herself sternly that she should not care, had no right to care.

"I congratulate you . . . on your commission." Vanessa was taken aback by the stiff cold sound of her own voice. "And now I'd best be leaving. Ben is waiting to drive me home."

Ross put a restraining hand on her arm. "I've been commissioned to paint the *Sorceress*," he told her. "Low's newest China Clipper." He smiled down at her. "Long and sharp, she is, with a concave bow and a champagne-glass stern. I hope none of the Low girls has a similar shape."

He was laughing, and in spite of herself Vanessa began to laugh too. "It isn't easy to tell, with the new fashions. These crinolines . . ."

"In any case," he said, still smiling, "The *Sorceress* is no rival to you. You've no cause to be jealous of her."

"Or of any young lady you might become attached to," Vanessa said.

"Because you're married? To a man who goes off and leaves you for months—years—at a time."

"Please, you must not—"

"I know," Ross said. "I have no right. It's only that I can't understand how any man can be so driven by ambition that he can turn from you even for all the wealth of the China trade."

"You know nothing about Logan," Vanessa said. "How can you, when you grew up secure, wealthy—"

"Scarcely wealthy," he reminded her.

"You didn't have to survive in the cellars of the Five Points, without parents. You didn't have to steal to keep alive."

"You're right about that," Ross said. "And Logan's to be admired for having come so far from such a beginning. But that sort of beginning, what does it do to a man?" He broke off abruptly. "Forgive me, Vanessa. I have no right to judge Logan McClintock. Perhaps I spoke out of envy . . . not for his business success—I've never wanted that—but because he has a wife like you, a woman I—"

"Ross—no! You must not . . ." She started for the door.

"Vanessa, please don't go, not like this," Ross said.

"My carriage is waiting. Delia will be concerned if I am late for dinner."

"Send Ben home with a message for Delia saying you are going to be out for the evening. I'm hungry, and I'm sure you are too."

"I'm not suitably dressed," she began. Ross had persuaded her to wear a simple white silk afternoon dress with a lilac sash for the portrait.

"That doesn't matter, not at the restaurant where we're going. And I'm sure you won't meet anyone you know. Only bohemians gather at this place."

Polite society still held sway on Washington Square, and some wealthy families had begun building mansions farther uptown, along Fifth Avenue, but artists, poets, actors, and musicians were beginning to take studios on Waverly Place and Bleecker Street. And small restaurants, some of them in cellars, served as meeting places for these "bohemians," as they called themselves.

"Say you'll come with me," he urged. "Look, your portrait's nearly finished. Let's call this a—a celebration if you like."

Ross took Vanessa to a large, shadowy restaurant a few steps down from street level, and although it had no glittering chandeliers or velvet hangings, she found the place, with its small candlelit tables and its slightly raffish customers, exciting.

The food was excellent: oysters and sirloin steak with fresh mushrooms. Ross ordered a bottle of wine, reminding her that they must drink to the completion of her portrait. "The best work I've ever done," he said, "And how could it be otherwise, considering the beauty of my subject?"

The dinner was long and leisurely, and later that evening the diners provided their own entertainment. A stout baritone sang an operatic aria; an actor recited a speech from the melodrama in which he had appeared only a few hours before. And then a girl with short-cropped blond curls sat on one of the tables, lit a cigarette—Vanessa had never seen a woman smoking before, even in private—and began to read from her own verses.

"That's Ada Clare," Ross whispered. "Calls herself the 'Queen of Bohemia.' " He added that Ada Clare was the mistress of the handsome pianist, Louis Moreau Gottschalk, a romantic idol adored by the ladies of Europe.

Vanessa knew she should be scandalized not only by the information Ross had given her but by the verses Ada Clare read aloud in a soft, husky voice—words that spoke frankly, passionately, of love between men and women, words that mocked those sentimental verses printed in ladies' silk-covered albums.

Should she be shocked? Vanessa asked herself. Perhaps, but she wasn't. She had been stirred by the same emotions. The reckless abandon with which she had given herself to Logan that first time. The anger that had gripped her when she had learned about Logan and Garnet . . .

She drew in her breath sharply.

"Vanessa, are you all right?"

She could not answer. Ross gave her a long, searching look in the light of the small candle that flickered between them. Then he led her out of the restaurant.

The warm, sultry May night enveloped them, and she felt the hint of an approaching thunderstorm.

"You are angry with me," Ross said.

"With you? Why should I be?"

"That place. Ada Clare's poetry."

"She is honest," Vanessa said. "But maybe she should leave such feelings unspoken."

"Should she be hypocritical, then?"

"It's what men expect, isn't it?" Was it the heaviness of the spring air that was making it difficult for her to breathe?

"Some men, perhaps—not all." He reached out for her and drew her into the shadows. "I've never wanted one of those proper young ladies I knew back in Salem, one who would entertain my guests, be an ornament in the parlor, and submit herself to me because it was her duty. I want—"

Her face was upturned to his. "What do you want?" she heard herself saying.

He did not answer. His arms were around her, crushing her body against his. Her senses began to waver. Was it only the wine they had shared? The warmth of the May evening, heavy with the promise of rain?

He released her. "My studio—"

"No, you must take me home."

"Not now," he said. "It's too late for that. . . ."

Standing in the studio, he kissed her again, and she felt her senses take fire at the touch of his hard, lean body pressed against hers. He released her long enough to light a single lamp, to loosen his clothing, and then he was drawing her down on the rug. His hands were moving swiftly, stripping off the white silk dress, untying the ribbons of her camisole, baring her breasts. His mouth, seeking her nipples, started a sweet aching in her loins, a heaviness, a warm, spreading hunger.

He was taking off the rest of her clothing, then his own, and now she lay naked in his arms. His strong, sensitive fingers explored the curves and hollows of her body, and she felt the rising heat of his desire, her own mounting response.

From far off she caught the sound of thunder, low and deep. A fresh wind blowing through the half-open window tore away the cloth that Ross had used to cover her almost-finished portrait, and over his shoulder she could catch a glimpse of her own likeness staring down at her. But the figure in the portrait was a lady, calm, controlled, and fashionable, in a gown of white silk, her breasts and thighs concealed by the folds of the garment.

That lady had no relationship to the woman who lay on the hearth rug, her flesh warm and moist, her lips parted to receive the searching tongue, caressing, probing. The woman who gloried in the voluptuous sensation of her lover's flesh moving against her own, the hardness of his chest, the pressure of his thighs.

Her hands moved swiftly, caressing him, his shoulders and back, her fingers curving, drawing him closer, and still closer. She felt him trembling with the urgency of his need, and then he was inside her, and her legs were locked around him, and his breath burned her throat, her shoulder. She cried out, a wordless, primitive cry, asking, pleading for release. A release that came in a torrent of liquid fire carrying her higher and higher, joining her to him in a timeless ecstasy. . . .

Then they lay together, savoring the gradual ebbing of

passion, the lingering, sensuous sweetness.

At last she moved out of his arms, raising herself to her feet in a single fluid motion. She went to the easel and covered the portrait.

"She isn't you," Ross said softly. He held out his arms and she came back to him, dropping to her knees, her desire rising again as he rested his face against her thighs. "This is you, this is my love. Now, always . . ."

But Vanessa knew better. Even as he drew her down again, she knew. The lady in white silk was still a part of her. There was no always, only these stolen hours of summer. After that, Ross would leave for Paris. And she, trying to see into the future, was filled with brooding sadness.

"But why won't you come to Paris with me?" They stood in the parlor, looking out at Gramercy Park. The first of the yellow leaves warned of autumn's approach.

"I can't. There is my son."

Ross hesitated. Now, with the portrait completed and hanging over the parlor mantelpiece, with his other commissions finished, he was impatient to go. But not without Vanessa.

"We—if you want to take the child with us . . . I'll love him because he's yours."

"He is Logan's son too. And Logan will be returning soon."

"Soon? You don't know when he's coming back. It could be winter, or even next spring. He'll stay in China as long as his business holds him there."

"But he will come home. And I must be here. Blake must be here."

Ross's mouth tightened. "If you were another woman—any other woman—I'd believe that you were only amusing yourself with me. Easing your loneliness, perhaps."

"No! It isn't—it has not been like that."

He put his arms around her and tried to draw her close, but she held back. She had to think clearly, to fight her way back to sanity.

"I'm Logan's wife. Whatever he's done, however he has failed me, even hurt me, nothing can change that. You know what sort of man he is. Do you suppose he would give up his son without a fight?"

Ross was silent for a moment. "No," he said slowly. "But we will be together. As long as you love me, I'll fight back. I'll fight Logan, and the whole world if I must."

"He'd never free me." Vanessa struggled to find the words to make Ross understand. "And even if he did, how could I risk losing my child, to be raised by strangers?"

"That's not all you're thinking about," Ross said accusingly. "Look at me, Vanessa. I need you. Logan is selfish, hard. He'll build his shipping empire, and he'll find another woman to share it."

She wanted to deny his words, but how could she, remembering Garnet Spencer? Why, then, was she not free to go with Ross? Convention had nothing to do with it, for, in the circles in which they would move in Paris, she guessed that strait-laced morality would have little meaning.

She took Ross's hand and held it against her cheek for a moment. "When will you sail?" she whispered.

"Next week, but I can wait for another ship if you need more time to—"

She released his hand and steeled herself against the sadness that rose up in her. "There is no reason for you to wait," she told him, and saw him flinch before the determination in her voice. "Good-bye, my love."

She did not go to the window to watch him leave. Instead,

she stood before the mantelpiece, looking up at the figure of the woman in the white silk dress.

Mrs. Logan McClintock. . . .

Chapter 19

The autumn wind blew from the northeast, driving dead leaves across the yellowing grass of the park and heaping them up against the tall iron fence. In the firelit warmth of Vanessa's parlor, Felicity, who had come on an unexpected visit, sat sipping her tea before the fire.

"We've seen so little of each other all summer," Felicity said. "No doubt you were occupied in sitting for your portrait." She glanced upward. "A charming likeness," she said. "Perhaps now Enoch Halliwell has reconciled himself to Ross's pursuing a career as a painter. The young man has talent."

For the first time, Vanessa wished that Felicity had not come to see her. Or, at the least, that she would stop speaking of Ross and the portrait. It was nearly a month now since Ross had left for Paris. At first, Vanessa had felt only sorrow at his departure, regret over hurting him. Then another emotion, stark, mounting fear, had blotted out all other feelings. She had fought against a trap that was closing in on her, and she had found no escape. Had Delia guessed the truth? Delia would not betray her. But it did not matter, for soon there would be no hiding the truth.

". . . and we will have an evening of *tableaux vivants,* and you must take part, my dear." Abruptly Vanessa was aware that Felicity had been speaking and that she, struggling with her private terrors, had lost the thread of the conversation. "Living pictures, Vanessa, they are becoming all the fashion and you must appear in one of them. Scenes from classical mythology would be suitable, I believe. Perhaps you might appear in one of them as a sea nymph. The costumes will be perfectly respectable, naturally. You might wear a robe of pale green or turquoise, and your hair loose about your shoulders. And perhaps Mr. Ross Halliwell would be so kind as to help with the lights and the settings—"

"No! It isn't possible."

"But in a good cause—to raise additional funds for the orphanage. Surely Mr. Halliwell would—"

"Ross left for Paris nearly a month ago," Vanessa said.

"Oh, I see. But even so, you will help, won't you? Mrs. Schermerhorn is offering us the use of her ballroom. And you will have plenty of time to get a suitable costume made. We will hold the entertainment late in November, I think. Before the holiday parties are in full swing, and . . . Vanessa, what is wrong?"

"November will be too late! It's already too late. . . ."

Then Felicity was beside her on the small velvet love seat and Vanessa was speaking quickly, a little incoherently.

"I'm going to have a baby. I'll be in my fourth month in November. Madame Restell told me so after she had examined me."

"Madame Restell." Felicity's body stiffened but she spoke quietly.

"You've heard of her, surely. Madame Killer, that's what some people call her. But she was not unkind to me. She examined me and she said there could be no doubt, and she offered to . . . help me. One hundred dollars, that is her price. But I couldn't do it, I couldn't bring myself to . . ."

Felicity was silent for a few moments. Then she said, "Not Logan. He's been gone since—"

There was no room left for modesty, for shame, not now. "It was Ross Halliwell."

"Does he know?"

Vanessa shook her head. "I did not know myself until after he was gone."

"And then you went to see Madame Restell."

"Yes, in her house on Chambers Street, not far from City Hall. She said she could perform an—an operation."

"An abortion," Felicity said with directness. "A most painful procedure, I've been told. Is that why you—"

"Oh, no. I didn't care about the pain. It was only that . . . Felicity, no matter what you must think of me, now you know, I did not . . . There was more than physical need that made me give myself to Ross. I cared for him. I think I still do."

"Your reasons do not matter," Felicity said sharply. "You are a married woman. Whatever the circumstances of your marriage, you had no right to forget that you are Logan's wife."

Vanessa's heart sank, for she knew that Felicity, for all her kindness, her generosity, lived by a stern code. "I'll be punished for what I did," Vanessa said.

Now Felicity spoke more gently. "You have been punished already, I think. And there is the child to consider. The child you are carrying."

"But what can I do? There is no way out for me."

"Come now," Felicity said, "you surely don't suppose you are the only woman who has ever broken her marriage vows and found herself in your condition. I could name a few who are received in good society. A woman can turn to someone like Madame Restell. Or she can deceive her husband into thinking he is the father of another man's child."

"I'm not sure I would trick Logan into believing such a lie even if he had not been away for so long. It's almost a year since he left. And he won't be back until late spring or early summer. I received a letter only a week ago, carried by a clipper captain." Vanessa's shoulders slumped, and she was filled with a sense of growing helplessness.

"Not until late spring . . . or early summer . . ." Felicity repeated slowly. "That should give us time."

"Time for what?"

Felicity took her hands. "Listen to me," she said. "I cannot condone what you have done. I can't even understand why. But I will help you if I can. Because I believe that you still care for Logan. And because I do not wish to see your children suffer for something that was not their fault. Not only the child you are carrying, but Blake too. He must not grow up shadowed by the scandal of a mother who—"

"I can't destroy this baby," Vanessa said stubbornly.

"And I do not suggest it. You will go on a trip. To visit friends in Boston."

"I have no friends in Boston, and even if I did—"

"Who is to know that? You met a great many people at the Carys' receptions. You've told me so. You were lonely here in New York without Logan, and when a friend asked you to come on an extended visit, you accepted. I'll help to spread the story about. No one will question my word," she added with the calm confidence of a Bradford and of a woman highly respected for her charitable works.

It was Felicity who found the cottage outside the town of Newburgh on the Hudson. "And most convenient to Peekskill, where Edith and Jasper Bradford live. You will stay there, under an assumed name, as a young widow, attended by your maid, and with your little son. You will find a country doctor who will deliver the baby, and afterward, you will get word to me. I'll pay a visit to Abel's brother and his wife, and I'll bring your newborn infant back here to New York."

"And what then?" For the first time, Vanessa realized the

full extent of the deception that would be necessary. "What will become of the infant after that?"

"We have the Shelter for Homeless Infants," Felicity said.

"Oh, but an orphanage—"

"Clean, carefully supervised. Far better than any of those unspeakable baby farms, where infants are drugged or smothered if they become too troublesome. Where the prettiest of the little girls are sold into a life of shame. Where boys, if they are quick and clever, are handed over to thieves or beggars."

"I know, but, to give up my baby—"

"It is the only way, Vanessa," Felicity said firmly.

The only way. Vanessa repeated those words to herself over and over again all through the long, bleak months of winter when the wind wailed around the small cottage near Newburgh; when the country doctor, whose services had been arranged for in advance, had finished delivering the baby on a warm night late in March; when Vanessa first held her small daughter to her breast.

"Yuh still got yo' li'l boy," Delia comforted her. "An' yuh'll be able t' go see yo' girl child at that orphan home."

Vanessa's heart was stirred with pity as she remembered that Delia, too, was a mother, but that she would never see her own children again, would never know of their fate.

"Ah'll fix yuh a medicine that'll dry up yo' milk," Delia was saying. "By the time mastuh come back from over d' sea, you'll be fine. He'll nevah know—nobody will 'cept Miz Felicity."

"But I'll know," Vanessa said softly, half to herself. She would remember, and have to keep her grief hidden always.

Felicity paid a visit to Edith and Jasper Bradford early in April and returned with the baby girl. No one was surprised, least of all Abel, who was long since resigned to his wife's charitable endeavors. He scarcely listened to her sketchy account of the farmer who had found the baby abandoned in his shed and who had no use for a girl, another mouth to feed and no help in the fields, even when she was full-grown.

And so the baby was given a place in the Shelter for Homeless Infants and registered under the name Miranda, parentage unknown.

The *Sea Dragon* came into port late in May, the news of her arrival sent by semaphore from the signal tower on the Navesink Highlands near the entrance to New York harbor. A runner brought word from the offices of the McClintock Line to the house on Gramercy Square, and Vanessa, who had begun to recover from the first searing grief of giving up her daughter, now knew that she faced another challenge. For a few moments after the messenger had departed she stood in the entrance hall of her home. How could she face Logan, how could she go into his arms, with the memory of her deception so raw and painful in her mind?

As if reading her thoughts, Delia shook her arm gently. "Yuh got t' do it, Miz Vanessa. Ain' no other way."

Felicity's words all over again. "I can't go down to the dock. . . ." Vanessa began.

It would be easier, perhaps, to wait here at home, to allow Delia to help her to select a suitable gown, of violet silk, and to arrange her hair becomingly. Meanwhile, Mrs. Skene had set to work preparing an elaborate dinner as Alice bustled about, polishing and dusting the already-spotless parlor and entrance hall.

Blake, under protest, was scrubbed and arrayed in the Highland dress that was now popular with the mothers of small boys. He squirmed indignantly as Delia fastened on the velvet bonnet with its white heron's plume.

And all the while Vanessa was gripped with a mounting uneasiness as the time for Logan's arrival drew closer. How could she face him, speak with him, go into his arms, without betraying her guilt?

But during the first moments of their meeting, Blake eased the tension, for he had no memory of his father, who had left when the boy had been barely six months old. There in the entrance hall Logan picked up his son, swung him up into his arms. The child stared, round-eyed and a little afraid of this tanned giant. Logan grinned at Vanessa. "What is that outfit he's wearing?" he demanded.

"Why, it's a Highland kilt and jacket. It is all the fashion now. Perhaps because of Queen Victoria's fondness for Scotland, or maybe because of the popularity of Sir Walter Scott's novels."

Logan shook his head. "You don't have to wear that bonnet unless you want to, son," he said, holding Blake close for a moment, then setting him down and showing him a pile of boxes. "Delia, take that hat off the boy and help him open his presents."

Blake was fascinated with a brightly painted wooden cricket that made a wonderful clicking noise when he pulled it by a string over the gleaming black and white tiles of the entrance hall. Vanessa found herself smiling while she said, "Couldn't you have brought him something less noisy?"

Logan laughed. "I've brought him a kite and . . ." Then he caught Vanessa in his arms and crushed her against him. She raised her lips for his kiss, and if she could not respond as eagerly as she had on other homecomings, he did not appear to notice, for he was filled with triumph, eager to tell her all about his voyage and the months he had spent in Canton.

"Not inside the city, really," Logan explained. "I've set up our company's 'factory' in Wampoa; that's reserved for foreign traders. I've made a dent in Bradford's trade, and I'll soon beat him at his own game."

"But will people buy tea that's been shipped by steamer? The flavor . . ."

"At one time, tea was a luxury item, and there was a great deal of talk about smoke taint and mildew. But now, with the demand for tea growing all the time, plenty of people will buy what they can afford without fussing about the fine points of flavor. And for every clipper that sets a speed record, there are two that find themselves becalmed, drifting helplessly at the mercy of the weather. The finest clippers are only able to set speed records under almost gale-force winds, and at that, they're good only for a few voyages. Bradford's tying up all his resources in clippers, and he'll be made to pay the price one of these days."

"They are beautiful, though. The *Athena* . . ."

She broke off, not wanting to remind Logan of his defeat at the hands of Abel Bradford and Horace Widdicomb, although she knew that he would never forget. Or forgive. Logan did not have a forgiving nature. The thought sent a small shudder through her and caused a tightness at the pit of her stomach so that she was unable to do more than pick at Mrs. Skene's excellent dinner.

Logan did full justice to the meal, however, and later that evening he took her upstairs to display his gifts for her. She had heard the carters going up and down the backstairs all evening, but he had kept her downstairs until they were finished. Only then did he accompany her to their bedroom and fling open the door. "You've never seen anything quite like this, have you?" he said with a satisfied smile.

Vanessa stared, wide-eyed, at the huge new bed he had carried home from China, at the elaborate carving, the inlaid designs in mother-of-pearl, the red and gold curtains.

"You do like it, don't you?" There was a boyish eagerness in the question, a desire to please her.

"It . . . must have belonged to a prince," was all she could say.

"Hardly, my love. Only a mandarin—a high official. He was forced to sell it along with all his other possessions, including his youngest daughter."

"You can't mean that."

"Oh, but I do. He was caught conniving with opium smugglers—turning a blind eye to their trade, in any case. The penalties are severe. He was lucky to escape with his skin."

"But his daughter—"

"I didn't buy her," Logan said with mock seriousness. "Why would I when I had you to come home to?"

He drew her into his arms, and now his mouth was hot against her cheek, her throat. She could not hold him off, not without arousing his suspicions, but she was unable to relax against him.

"What is it, Vanessa?"

"The bed—it takes up almost the whole room," she said quickly.

"Is that all? Perhaps you're right. But one day we'll have a much larger bedroom—a mansion on Fifth Avenue. My second steamer is finished now, and she'll be putting out to sea."

"You've only come home, and already you're talking of leaving." Even as she spoke Vanessa realized that stronger than guilt and shame, stronger than her anger when she had discovered the truth about Garnet, was her need to have him here, beside her.

"I'm not taking the new steamer to China," Logan said

quietly. "Dermot Rankin will be her master. I can't be at sea, halfway across the world, and run an important shipping line here in New York."

"You'll miss the sea," Vanessa said.

"I will. But a man has to make choices and abide by them."

And Logan had chosen to stay ashore. Was it only because of the shipping line? Was Garnet a force in keeping him here? She did not ask. She had no right to ask, to confront him with her discovery about Garnet, not now.

"I don't want to leave you alone again," he was saying. "I've missed you, my love."

His arms tightened around her as he lifted her and carried her across their bedroom, to the mandarin bed with its curtains of scarlet and gold.

Chapter 20

Logan kept his word to Vanessa, buying a plot of land on Fifth Avenue at Fifty-second Street, but although he had managed to survive the financial panic of 1857, he had not started building the mansion he had spoken of. He was making a fair profit, but with the country gripped by the spreading recession he judged that it would be more prudent to wait. Clipper ship owners were in far worse difficulties, for their insurance rates were much higher and the risk of damage greater. Now it was the steamers that got the pick of the tea crop at Macao and Wampoa, and even the beautiful and prestigious *Flying Cloud*, owned by Grinnell and Minturn, had to remain idle, waiting for cargo.

But Logan had managed to diversify his interests, and the little *Ondine*, along with a second coastal schooner, was kept busy hauling lumber while the *Sea Dragon* and her sister ship the *Sea Sprite* continued to bring back their rich cargoes from China. He had bought shares in a lumber company in Maine, and a textile mill in Massachusetts as well. He rarely made it a point to discuss his business affairs with Vanessa, but he did not stint on money necessary to keep the house on Gramercy Park running smoothly, to outfit his wife in style. While banks were closing their doors and business houses were shutting down, while mills and factories were laying off workers, Logan managed to remain solvent.

In the fall of 1858, however, he had not been able to raise money to add to his fleet, and Vanessa was somewhat surprised when he told her to go out and buy a fashionable new wardrobe. "I've plenty of perfectly good clothes," she began, but he interrupted impatiently.

"Jeremy Halliwell and that wife of his—Octavia, isn't it—they're coming up here from Washington. We will entertain them, and you must be as well turned out as she is."

"Octavia is a congressman's wife," Vanessa said, "and the daughter of a Lowell mill owner."

Logan put an arm around her. "And you are the wife of the owner of the McClintock Line," he said. "And the most beautiful woman in New York. I want you to dress the part, my love."

Vanessa suspected that he also had some practical reason for entertaining the Halliwells, but she flushed at the compliment nevertheless. She went to A. T. Stewart's store, to Arnold Constable, which provided horsehair chairs for lady customers, and porters in blue uniforms with red binding, and to the now-fashionable Lord & Taylor, with its skylighted dome, beneath which ladies in hoop skirts, which were becoming ever wider, promenaded around the great central rotunda.

But although Vanessa was dazzled by the fashionable dresses she saw, she spent cautiously. Times were hard, and Logan still lacked the money to add ships to his fleet. It was not easy to resist the temptation to splurge, however, for in this year of 1858, with the nation moving steadily toward war, feminine fashions had never been more flattering. She looked at gowns of organdy and grenadine, decorated with sprays of velvet flowers; she fingered cloaks of moiré or velvet and permitted herself to sigh over a floor-length opera cloak of sable.

On the autumn evening when she and Logan, together with Jeremy and Octavia Halliwell, attended a performance of the melodrama *Little Katy, the Hot Corn Girl*, she was satisfied with her appearance. Her gown was made of mauve silk, the bodice trimmed with bands of lilac velvet, and, when the play had reached its melancholy end and Logan had helped her on with her purple velvet cloak, she knew that her appearance did him credit. Octavia, a plump, pale young woman with sandy hair and colorless lashes, was amiable but not impressive in spite of her regal costume of deep red brocade, and her sable wrap.

Later, on the way to the dining room of the Fifth Avenue Hotel, Octavia dabbed at her eyes with a lacy handkerchief. "Such a sad play," she said. "But then, it is all made up. . . ."

Vanessa nodded, forbearing to tell her that here on these streets were girls as badly off as Katy, who, after her father had been reduced to penury as a result of drink, had been driven to peddle hot corn on Broadway. Poor Katy had taken a chill and perished of pneumonia. A more merciful ending than some, Vanessa thought, remembering her talks with Felicity and her own visits to Dutch Hill during that summer years before.

Felicity had not been content with a shelter for infants, and now was working to enlarge the orphanage to accommodate older children as well. Vanessa, who was on the board of directors for the shelter, was able to pay frequent visits, and, although she ached with longing each time she saw Miranda, six years old now, she was thankful that her daughter had a safe, decent home. But it could not be called a home in any real sense, for although the attendants were carefully chosen for their competence and their love of children, it was not right that Miranda should be one of fifty little girls dressed exactly alike in dark-brown poplin and white starched aprons, that she should sleep in a narrow cot in a dormitory while on the other side of the city Blake McClintock was growing up, petted and cherished, even somewhat spoiled, by his parents and by Delia and the other servants.

Vanessa was brought back from her private thoughts as the carriage came to a stop in front of the Fifth Avenue Hotel, for she realized that Logan and Jeremy were deep in conversation about business, a conversation that continued after they were seated at one of the tables in the hotel dining room.

"It's the chance you've been waiting for, Logan," Jeremy was saying. "The cancellation of the federal mail subsidies means that those Panama mail ships will be put up for auction. In less than a month—you can take my word for it."

"There'll be others bidding too," Logan said slowly.

"No doubt. But with money as tight as it is, I'd guess you could get them at—maybe twelve thousand each."

Octavia, obviously bored by this discussion of business, concentrated on the huge, ornate menu. Vanessa, however, seeing Logan's growing excitement, asked, "Why have the mail subsidies been cancelled, Jeremy?"

"Old man Vanderbilt's at the bottom of it," Jeremy said with a grin. "He learned all about price wars during his Hudson River days. He and Daniel Drew have been threatening to put their own ships on the Panama run, and he's been forcing the owners of the mail steamers to pay off at ruinous rates. The owners can't show a profit any longer, so they are giving up their subsidies, and no one else wants to lock horns with the Commodore, or 'Uncle' Daniel Drew. Can't say I blame them. But if Logan can get hold of those steamers, he can find other uses for them. Coastwise trading or the Carribean run."

Vanessa saw the rising tension in her husband's face, the hunger in his eyes. Logan was no longer the half-starved boy fighting for survival in the stinking gutters of the Five Points, but although the stakes were higher now, the driving ambition was still there under the surface.

Octavia, who assumed that Vanessa's interest in Jeremy's

proposal was only pretended, out of courtesy turned the conversation to more domestic matters.

"I am told that Ross painted your portrait before he left for Paris," Octavia said as the waiter put down the soup and left. "I would so like to see it."

"And you shall," Logan said. "It's a fine likeness. Can't see why Ross had to go junketing off to Paris. I thought he'd learned his craft well enough, if that portrait's any sample of his work."

"Oh, Ross is not in Paris any longer," Octavia said, obviously relieved that the gentlemen were no longer talking business. "He is over in London now, and he has more commissions than he can handle. And it is said . . ." She paused for effect.

"Now, Octavia, my dear," Jeremy protested.

"But Ross is a friend—surely Captain McClintock and dear Vanessa are interested."

Vanessa heard herself speaking calmly. "Indeed, we are," she said.

Octavia leaned forward. "Ross has been seeing a great deal of a certain young lady, a Camilla Marchant. She was presented at court last year, and Ross painted her portrait. She has an aunt who is married to a viscount, and although her own branch of the family has no title—"

Jeremy laughed. "Miss Marchant's father has not yet announced the engagement, although it is probable that he will shortly. But even so, I'll never be able to understand why American ladies are so dazzled by foreign titles."

He spoke with good-natured affection, and Vanessa guessed that although his marriage had not been a love match, perhaps it had become an amicable relationship on both sides. Then she considered her own feelings. Ross, married to another woman. She tried to call up the emotions that had swept her into her affair with Ross that summer six years ago. All that remained was a certain tenderness, a stirring of the senses, and Miranda, the child born of their passion, the daughter she could never acknowledge before the world. What was to become of Miranda? What sort of future could she hope for?

Then, unexpectedly, she felt Logan's hand close over hers. "Are you all right, Vanessa?" he asked her, and she was surprised by the concern in his voice.

"Why, yes," she said quickly. "I was only thinking about—about the play we saw."

"So tragic," Octavia agreed. "That poor little girl, abandoned by her drunken father, driven out into the snow."

Jeremy shook his head. "Next time we attend the theater, we must be sure to see something less harrowing." He laughed, and Logan joined in.

The ship auction was held a few weeks later at the Merchants' Exchange. The preceding day Logan, accompanied by Silas Pringle, had gone down to the waterfront to inspect the sidewheel steamers and to go over every foot of the hulls, to examine every engine.

On the day of the auction Vanessa insisted on accompanying Logan to the Exchange, although she would not be allowed inside, since these precincts were forbidden to ladies. She would have to wait in the carriage until the auction was over.

Logan was in good spirits until the carriage drew up before the Exchange. Then, all at once, his face hardened.

"What is it—what's wrong?" she asked.

"Over there," he said. "Horace Widdicomb is going in. He's going to put in a bid for the Bradford Line."

Vanessa felt a tightening in the pit of her stomach, for she knew what this auction meant to Logan, but she made herself speak calmly. "We don't know that he is going to bid on the ships," she said. "You had special information about the auction from Jeremy."

"The Bradfords have political connections too."

"No matter," she went on firmly. "You must outbid him, whatever the cost."

"Do you know what you're saying? Bradford took a loss during this recession true enough, but he still has immense resources. He doesn't need these ships, but if he is determined to get them, even if only to damage me financially, he'll do it."

"We have resources too. The profits from the *Sea Dragon* and the *Sea Sprite.* Your warehouses could be mortgaged if necessary. And there's the land on Fifth Avenue."

"That's not for sale! I promised you a mansion on Fifth Avenue."

"The fleet comes first." Vanessa's eyes met his, and she spoke with quiet intensity. "It's what you have always wanted. With these steamers and the ships you already own, you will have the foundations of the shipping empire you told me about—that night—at Kitty's birthday ball. You've got to have it. Nothing else is important."

Logan was looking at her with an expression she had never seen in his eyes before. "Vanessa, I . . ." He drew her against him, holding her so tightly that she could scarcely breathe. His kiss was swift, hard, his mouth bruising hers.

Then he released her, and she watched as he got out of their carriage and went into the Merchants' Exchange. She did not know how long the auction would take, but she was prepared to remain here until it was over.

"Horace didn't want those mail ships," Logan told her

that night in their bedroom. "He kept bidding until he knew I couldn't go any higher. Then he dropped out. The other bidders had dropped out long before that."

"But if he didn't want the ships—"

"He wanted to leave me short of cash, he and Abel both. It won't be easy going for quite a while, Vanessa. I haven't the money to hire more men for my shipyard. Or to cover any future losses."

"And if this recession gets worse," Vanessa said slowly, "what then?"

"I don't know." The corner of his mouth lifted in a mirthless smile. "Maybe it'll be back to Tompkins Street."

They did not have to go back to Tompkins Street, but during the next years they had to make changes in their way of living. The new kitchen maid was dismissed, and then Mrs. Skene and Alice. Only Delia remained, because she loved Blake and refused to leave him, and because a closeness had sprung up between mistress and servant in the time when they had been together in the cottage on the Hudson, awaiting the birth of Miranda.

Logan mortgaged his shipyard to the hilt. He sold the carriage and horses and disposed of his shares in the lumber mill in Maine.

Even so, by the spring of 1861 he admitted to Vanessa that he could no longer pay wages to his crews. It was a time of tension for them. She knew that he hated to see her doing the work that Mrs. Skene and Alice had done, but she had no choice. He spent long hours down at his office on South Street, and even when he came home in the evenings he often shut himself up in the library with Silas Pringle to go over his accounts, to try to find some way to keep the McClintock Line from going under.

Vanessa's heart ached for him, and then, in April, her private fears were swallowed up, lost in the overwhelming catastrophe that gripped New York, and the whole nation. Numb with apprehension, she read about the secession of one southern state after another, of the formation of the Confederate States of America.

Abolition of slavery had to come—she was convinced of that—but she had hoped that it might be brought about by peaceful means, through compromise.

Logan's face was drawn, and he looked haggard as the news from the South grew steadily worse. "This means the end of my coastal trade," he told her. "Those steamers I bought at auction are useless to me now—even if I could pay the crews the vessels would be left to rot in the harbor."

"But the blockade ordered by President Lincoln can't last forever," she said, trying to console him.

"It can last long enough to ruin us," he said, and went stalking out of the house into the gray, rainy April morning.

While he was out a letter arrived, and Vanessa put it aside. It was for Logan, and it bore Jeremy Halliwell's personal seal. She felt a brief stirring of resentment. If only Jeremy had not come to Logan with news about the auction of those mail steamers. If Horace had not been there at the auction to bid against Logan. She thrust these profitless thoughts aside and went down to the kitchen to see what could be done to make a palatable dinner out of the remains of a ham, a little rice, and a few vegetables.

Logan found her standing at the stove, a lock of hair escaping from her neatly braided chignon. He told her that he would not stay for supper, that he was going to pack at once and take a train for Washington. He looked tense and preoccupied. He refused to discuss the contents of Jeremy's letter or to take Vanessa with him to Washington.

"But how long will you be gone?"

"I don't know," he told her.

It was a week before he returned, but from the moment he came through the door Vanessa saw the change in him. She had been scrubbing the kitchen floor, and she had hurried up into the hall, where he caught her in his arms without giving her time to remove her apron.

"Logan, you look . . . different. What's happened?"

He released her and for a moment he was silent.

Then he said slowly, "The blockade, that's what has happened."

"But you already knew about the blockade. It has destroyed your trade with the South."

"That's right. But it will save us from going under. It may even make us a fortune." He paused, his eyes sober. "There are miles of coastline to be guarded, and southerners who know every inlet, every cove, for all those miles. The Navy will need ships to enforce the blockade. I've arranged to charter my mail steamers to the government, with Jeremy's help. The profits will be enormous."

"But to profit from this war . . ." Vanessa began.

"It's not the way I'd have chosen, believe me," Logan said. "But without these leases I'd have lost everything. You know that. And the leasing of the mail steamers will only be the beginning. I'm going to get a new shipyard, up in Connecticut, because prices on those East River yards will go sky-high."

"But surely the war will be over before you can build more ships."

"Jeremy doesn't think so, and neither do I. The South is as certain of the justice of its cause as we are of ours."

"Justice? How can it be justice to keep black people like Delia in slavery, to separate them from their children?"

"Then you approve of the war, but not of my making a profit on it?" he said.

She looked at him, shaken and confused. "I don't know. I'm not sure how I feel."

"One thing I can tell you," he said with conviction. "So far, Lincoln's blockade exists only on paper, and it will take ships, the best and the fastest, to enforce it, to strangle the commerce of the South. And the ships I'm going to build will be the best and the fastest." He put his arm around her. "Let me take care of business. As for you . . ." He gave her a long, critical look. "That dress is terrible—it looks like a sack."

"It's perfectly suitable for wearing to scrub the kitchen floor," she said sharply.

"No doubt. But you won't be doing any more of that. I want you to find a kitchen maid. And hire back Mrs. Skene. If you can find her, that is."

"She's working for a family at Murray Hill."

"Offer her twice what they're paying," Logan said expansively. "And get hold of little what's her name—Alice."

"That won't be difficult. Felicity was kind enough to find work for Alice at the Shelter." Seeing that Logan did not understand, she added, "The Shelter for Homeless Infants. Only now it's being enlarged to make room for older children. The building next door is for sale, and if we can raise the money to buy it—our committee, I mean—it will be a great help."

"If things go according to my plans, I ought to be able to make a substantial contribution to that pet charity of yours. Would that please you, Vanessa?"

"Oh, yes," she said. "Every donation means so much."

"Even profits made from a war can be put to good use, you see," Logan told her. "Try to remember that if it will make you feel better."

* * * * *

In the months that followed, Logan carried out his plans with his characteristic, single-minded drive. He lost no time in going up to Connecticut with Silas Pringle to look for a suitable shipyard, and he found one in the small port of Stonington. After that he was away from home for days at a time.

Vanessa found some consolation for his absences when he gave her an impressive donation for the Shelter. Then, too, while he was away, she was free to visit the Shelter as often as she liked. She was careful never to single out Miranda for any special attention, no matter how much she longed to do so. If only she could hold her daughter, play with her, sing her to sleep at night, but she did not even dare to question Miranda's teachers about the little girl's progress. No one must ever suspect that the child called Miranda Warren, with her deep chestnut hair and hazel eyes, was in any way related to Mrs. Logan McClintock.

"We give all the children here last names," Felicity said. "It's a matter of form."

Miranda Warren. "How is she coming along in her studies?" Vanessa asked Felicity.

"She is bright and studious. Overimaginative, perhaps, but I hope that she will outgrow that trait before she must go into the world to earn her living."

Miranda, nearly eleven now, was an imaginative little girl, perhaps even more imaginative than Felicity Bradford suspected, a quiet, thoughtful child who kept most of her fantasies to herself, for fear of being laughed at.

She often brooded over the future, and what might happen to her when she left the Shelter. What sort of wonderful adventures lay in store? She knew that she would be expected to earn her living, perhaps as a teacher, since she loved her studies and excelled in all of them, except for arithmetic, which was a chore.

The only world she really knew was this narrow, red-brick building here on Houston Street, a world of spotless dormitories with neat rows of cots, a dining hall where the food was plain but nourishing, and classrooms smelling faintly of chalk and serge uniforms.

Sundays were more exciting. Those inmates who were old enough to attend church services marched in rows, escorted by the matrons, and were taken to sit in the special section at the rear, reserved for them. The sound of the organ made Miranda shiver with pleasure, and she stared in wonder at the small, stained-glass window, with its pattern of colors: amethyst and ruby and amber.

Even better was the walk to and from the church: a glimpse of a bonnet trimmed with sprays of lilac in a shop window; a lady in a blue silk gown, stepping into a carriage; a tree, glittering like a rainbow, in the wake of an ice storm.

And the families driving by in their open carriages in spring, the father wearing a tall silk hat and a gleaming watch chain across his vest, the plump mother arrayed in plum-colored taffeta, smiling as she tried vainly to keep order among her chattering, jostling children.

Where were they going? What did their house look like? What did it feel like to gather around a table in one's own dining room for Sunday dinner?

Miranda would never know, because she had no father. Dolly, the girl who slept on the cot next to hers in the dormitory, had explained about families. "I have no father and neither do you. None of us do." Dolly spoke with the superior knowledge of one who had lived outside for the first nine years of her life in a filthy shanty near Paradise Square.

"We're fatherless brats. That's what I heard the cook telling one of the washwomen." Dolly spoke without self-pity. She thought that the Shelter, with its regular meals and clean clothes, was wonderful. "We're lucky to be here," she went on. "Otherwise we'd be out whorin' t' earn our keep. My ma was a whore—"

"What's that?"

"A whore goes with men . . ." Then, seeing that Miranda did not understand, Dolly went on to explain in some detail.

"I don't believe you! You're making it all up!"

"No I ain't," Dolly said indignantly. "I seen it lots of times."

"No lady would let a man do . . . what you said!"

"I ain't talkin' about ladies," Dolly told her with scorn. "I'm talkin' about whores. Ladies are different. They—they're like that Mrs. Bradford and the rest of them on the Board. Don't you know nothin'?"

Miranda was silent, thoughtful. She knew one thing: her mother had not been a whore. She had been a lady. And Miranda was going to be a lady, too, when she went out into the world.

Chapter 21

Vanessa had watched proudly as New York's own Seventh Regiment had marched off to serve the Union cause. Later, holding Blake up to see the pageantry, she had been impressed by Colonel Elmer Ellsworth's brigade of Zoaves, in their dazzling, colorful uniforms, and by the jaunty Fighting Irishmen of the Sixty-ninth, recruited, many of them, from the immigrant population of the Bowery. Although she read of the horrors of battle in Horace Greeley's *Tribune* and in *Harper's Weekly*, the events reported there did not touch her life directly.

Logan was spending more time in his Stonington, Connecticut shipyard, or in trips to Washington, where he met with Jeremy Halliwell and other government officials to discuss naval contracts. But when he was at home he and Vanessa entertained frequently or attended the theater or the opera at the Academy of Music, along with crowds of other affluent New Yorkers for whom war had brought prosperity.

Vanessa, like Felicity, Kitty, and the other ladies of their circle, gave time to service on the Women's Central Association and raised funds for the United States Sanitary Commission, the organization that helped to ease the suffering of the wounded. But at Logan's insistence, she also arrayed herself in the newest fashions. Not that she needed much persuasion, for the new styles were most becoming. She bought tiny new bonnets with sloping crowns, trimmed with roses, passion flowers, or water lilies, as well as ostrich tips.

Logan had purchased a new brougham, and he took Vanessa out riding whenever he came home. She wore a carriage cloak of amber velvet trimmed with sable for these occasions. Ben had been reinstated as coachman, Mrs. Skene was back in the kitchen, and Alice answered the front door in a smart black poplin with a ruffled white apron and a saucy cap. Delia, who had worked without wages during the lean times, now had a salary.

But Vanessa knew that there were hundreds in New York who were still living in terrible poverty. In the Five Points, conditions were scarcely better than they had been when Logan was growing up there. Irish immigrants also lived in the rat-infested, disease-ridden tenements and shanties of the Bowery and Mulberry Bend, while dozens of squatters' shacks had been destroyed to make way for the laying out of Central Park.

A wide social gulf stretched between those shanties and tenements of the Five Points and Mulberry Bend and the McClintocks' house on Gramercy Park, where Logan and Vanessa now entertained businessmen and government officials at elaborate parties catered by Taylor's, whose desserts were likely to include ice cream molds in the fashionable shapes of citadels, forts, or even cannons. Vanessa, in jewel-colored gowns of velvet or moiré, her hair parted in the center and framing her face in the popular waterfall coiffure or gathered into a net that shimmered with crystal beads, had learned to preside over these functions with dignity and charm.

But in the spring of 1863 Vanessa had to curtail these entertainments, for she was pregnant again and beginning to show, and, like all respectable ladies, she would have to confine herself to the house and receive only close women friends until after the birth of the baby. Logan, delighted at the prospect of another child, pampered her and insisted that she looked lovelier than ever in her silk wrappers trimmed with

Alençon and point d'Angleterre lace.

Early in July, Logan left New York to travel up to Connecticut to look in on the work at his Stonington shipyard and to conclude arrangements to buy an iron foundry not far from the yards. "Why should I buy engines and boilers for my new steamers when I can manufacture them in my own works?" he said. Then, looking troubled, he went on. "I don't like to leave you alone, Vanessa."

"Delia's here, and Mrs. Skene and Alice. Besides, Dr. Fairleigh doesn't think the baby will arrive before the end of the month." She was shading the truth slightly, but only because she did not want to burden Logan with unnecessary worries when he was preoccupied with business.

Logan had been gone nearly a week when, on a stifling, humid Sunday evening, Alice came to Vanessa's room with a glass of lemonade and a plate of biscuits. The maid's round face was troubled. Vanessa remembered that Alice had been out walking that afternoon with her "young man," a clerk in the offices of the *Tribune*.

"Is anything wrong between you and Jimmy?" Vanessa asked.

"Oh, no, ma'am, nothin' like that. It's all this talk we've been hearin' about the draft. A lot of folks are against it."

"The draft?" Vanessa remembered having read something about it, but she had been too preoccupied with her own affairs to worry about outside matters.

During the years since Miranda's birth, when she had not conceived another child, she had been troubled by a sense of guilt and had wondered if she was being punished for her affair with Ross. But now that this fear was gone, she felt placid, hoping to bear another son. She knew that Logan was eager for another boy, to carry on the McClintock Line.

But as Alice set down the tray and went on speaking, she recalled several inflammatory editorials she had read during the spring after President Lincoln had issued his proclamation calling for 300,000 men to be drafted into the Union Army.

"Folks are against it, ma'am. Poor folks that can't pay no three hundred dollars to buy their way out of the Army. Jimmy and me, we saw lots of men this afternoon on street corners, and they were in an ugly mood. One of them, over by Union Square, was makin' a speech. About how some rich men whose names've been drawn have bought their way out. An' Jimmy's heard talk that some of them awful gangs—the Dead Rabbits and them others—have been collectin' brickbats an' clubs an' they're sayin' they're goin' t' take the arsenal over on Thirty-fifth Street an' get hold of guns."

"Now, Alice, you must not believe such talk. And please don't repeat it to the others in the house. The Metropolitans are strong and well-armed. They can put down any sort of disturbance."

"Yes, ma'am," Alice said, looking somewhat reassured. "But ma'am, I wouldn't send Delia out on no errands if I was you."

"Delia?" Vanessa stared at her. "Why would Delia be in any danger?"

" 'Cause she's black, ma'am. An' these men who were talkin', they blame the blacks for the trouble. If it wasn't for the blacks, there wouldn't be no war, would there?"

"Abolition is only one of the causes of this war," Vanessa said, speaking more sharply than she had intended. With Logan away, it was up to her to keep the household calm and in order. "We are also fighting to keep the Union together. To keep the southern states from going their own way."

"I guess that's right," Alice said doubtfully. "But there are lots of folks don't see it that way. That man who was makin' the speech, he said he'd like t' string up every black in the city."

Monday morning dawned clear and sunny, with a promise of scorching heat to come by noon. Vanessa sat up in bed gripped by a nameless sense of fear even before she remembered Alice's words of last night. She got up and put on her robe, then went to the window and threw it open. Her eyes widened and her body tensed with foreboding as she saw a line of carriages and wagons piled with trunks, and even household goods, moving slowly down the street and out of the square. She recognized a few of her neighbors and their servants. Were they leaving the city to escape the heat?

Or had they, too, heard the talk of a threatened uprising?

She remembered the rioting here in New York back in 1857, when the municipal police had clashed with the newly formed metropolitan police force. The Metropolitans had emerged victorious, and since then they had managed to keep order, no easy task in this rapidly growing city with its crime-ridden slums and its savage street gangs. Logan had spoken with respect of Superintendent John A. Kennedy, who was now in command of the Metropolitans, saying that he was a tough, courageous man. Surely he and his men would quickly bring this new disturbance under control.

Vanessa, standing at the open window, tried to fight down her fears. But then, as the last of the carriages and wagons left the square, she heard an ominous sound—the tramp of marching feet and a distant roar. The noise of an enraged mob somewhere to the west of Gramercy Park, and on the march.

"Miz Vanessa!" Delia had come into the bedroom unnoticed. "What we goin' t' do, ma'am?"

"Send Ben to the livery stable to get the carriage and team. And tell him to try to hire a wagon."

"Ben ain't come in yet, Miz Vanessa. Mrs. Skene, she's mighty worried 'bout that brother of hers. He's livin' down near the Bowery an'—"

Vanessa spoke with a calmness she did not feel. "Get Blake dressed in the meantime. Tell him . . . say we're going on a picnic. Have Mrs. Skene pack a couple of baskets of food and . . ." She shut her eyes for a moment and put her hand to the small of her back, where a sharp pain had caught her unaware.

"Miz Vanessa, are yuh feelin' poorly?"

"No. I'm perfectly all right," Vanessa said, as much to reassure herself as Delia.

"I'll be helpin' yuh get dressed."

"I can manage. Take care of Blake and give Mrs. Skene my instructions. And tell me the moment Ben gets here."

But as the morning dragged on, the heat enveloped the house. The air grew heavy with the smell of smoke, and still Ben did not come. Doggedly Vanessa went on making preparations. Logan kept most of his ledgers and business papers in his office on South Street, but there were certain documents in the library safe. She went to get them, and bent to pack them in a lacquered Chinese chest. Another pain struck and she cried out for Delia. Even if Ben were to arrive now, it would be too late for her to leave the house.

On the following day, July fourteenth, Logan returned to Stonington from the iron works, five miles away. He had concluded negotiations for the purchase of the iron works. He stopped at a local tavern on the waterfront for a meal and a mug of ale before going on to the shipyard. He felt pleased with himself and with the way business was going here in Connecticut.

Only two weeks before, Dermot Rankin had brought the *Sea Dragon* into Stonington after a successful China run. Now that the tea cargo had been stowed away in the warehouse Logan had purchased in this small, port town, Rankin and his men idled about the waterfront, waiting for repairs to be completed on the steamer, to make her ready for her next voyage. A few of the sailors complained openly, for Stonington lacked the pleasures of New York's Pearl and Water streets, and there was only one small, shabby house on the outskirts of town to cater to the needs of the men seeking female companionship.

Because he was familiar with the complaints, Logan was not surprised when he looked up from his meal to see Rankin approaching with a grim expression on his sunburned face.

"Trouble?" Logan asked.

Rankin remained standing, ignoring the chair opposite Logan's. "A couple of my men went off to New York—figured they'd have time to cut loose down there and get back before we sail again."

"If they don't come back, we'll get a couple more hands up here," Logan began, but Rankin interrupted.

"Oh, they're back—and damn lucky to get back alive. All hell's loose down in New York, Logan. Mobs roaming the streets burning and looting. They broke into the arsenal and armed themselves. The Metropolitans can't bring them under control."

"Superintendent Kennedy—"

"He's in the hospital—a mob beat him half to death, from what my men heard. And they're lynching blacks and wrecking the waterfront. Damn good thing we've got the cargo stowed away safe up here."

He broke off, silenced by the look on Logan's face.

"My wife and son are in the city," Logan said.

"Maybe they got out—a lot of people are getting out."

"My wife is pregnant. She's near her time."

Logan was on his feet. "Get the men together—the crew of the *Sea Dragon*—I want them sober and on board in an hour."

"Pringle's still working on the ship—her engines—"

"Will she make the run back to New York?"

"She might. But once we're ashore, those mobs—"

"Break out every weapon in the arms locker and get hold of as many more as you can. We'll go in through the Sound and make a landing as close to the city as we can." He paused. "Tell them they'll be well paid for this voyage."

"If they live long enough to collect," Dermot Rankin said. He left the tavern with Logan, and then they separated, Logan to go to the shipyard and talk to Silas, and Rankin to gather his crew.

Abel Bradford, his face flushed brick red, his body streaming sweat from the heat of the fires along South Street, was shouting orders to his terrified clerks. They scurried about, clutching ledgers. Then he turned to confront Horace. "Move, you idiot! Get me longshoremen to empty my warehouses. And boats—we need anything that will stay afloat to off-load the goods and get it away from here."

"There are no longshoremen working. Most have joined the mobs." Horace wiped his forehead with his shaking hand. "It was madness to come down here, sir. And in a carriage like that." The mobs were turning the brunt of their senseless rage on blacks and on those who looked wealthy. Abel's carriage sparkled with brass, his coachman was in full uniform, his horses sleek and well fed, their harness fastenings glittering in the sunlight.

"Madness, is it?" Abel's face was turning purplish now, and he was choking, gasping for breath as the smoke thickened along the docks. "Madness to save my goods from those mobs of ruffians? I built the Bradford Line and I'm not going to see it destroyed by these . . ."

He broke off to order the clerks to pile the boxes of paper and the ledgers into the carriage, then wheeled on Horace again. "I want my goods out of those warehouses, I tell you!"

A skinny clerk tugged at Abel's sleeve. "It's too late, sir—look there!"

The roof of the nearest warehouse was on fire. "Get back, sir," the clerk urged, pulling at Abel's arm. "That warehouse has tar and turpentine stored inside."

Abel broke free. "Get men, Horace! Do as I say—and buckets of water and—"

The flames raced across the roof of the warehouse and Abel heard the crash of timbers. He started for the warehouse, his eyes bulging, glassy. "Men and buckets and—" He began to choke as thick black smoke rolled out of the blazing roof. His incoherent commands were drowned out by a deafening explosion, and the windows shattered outward, glass flying in all directions. He stumbled back. That fool Horace—a damn idiot—no use at all, standing there like a frightened sheep. He coughed, drew a breath to shout out orders. But he could not get air into his lungs. He was strangling. Something exploded inside his head. A thick red mist was enveloping him, blotting out the warehouse, Horace's face, everything. . . .

Liam, the burly coachman, helped Horace to get Abel into the carriage, then took his place on the box and brought his whip down on the backs of the sleek team. Horace, surrounded by ledgers and papers, supported Abel as best he could as they started on the nightmare journey through the devastated city, heading west, in the direction of Hudson

Square. Abel was breathing stertorously, and the right side of his face was twisted in an unnatural grimace, the eye and the side of the mouth pulled downward.

It was nearly dark now, Horace thought gratefully. They would be less likely to attract attention from passing bands of hoodlums. Liam had shed his coat and hat and stuffed them under the seat. With his smoke-blackened face and grimy shirt, he might be mistaken for a marauding Irish rioter who was making off with a wealthy citizen's carriage. Better that way.

They moved through familiar streets, changed now by the two days of rioting, and in years to come, Horace would remember that ride only in snatches, nightmarish images of death and destruction.

The body of a black man was hanging from a lamppost on Water Street, his flesh slashed and set afire by a band of creatures whose twisted, hate-filled faces bore little resemblance to the faces of men and women. There were women in the mob, screeching harpies who joined their men in singing obscene songs and capering about the burning body. Horace pressed his hand against his mouth, his stomach lurching.

Broadway now. The window of a jewelry store smashed in and looters battling over their spoils.

Liam swerved the carriage aside to keep from running over a man in the uniform of a Metropolitan. The brawny police officer had been horribly beaten, one side of his head smashed in.

There were fires everywhere, and the sound of gunfire and the shouts of the rioters.

Once they had to halt to allow a platoon of the National Guard to march by. Horace remembered hearing that Mayor Opdyke had sent telegrams to the War Department in Washington the night before, asking that the New York regiments that had seen action at Gettysburg be sent back to the city with all possible speed. Would they arrive in time to save New York from complete devastation? Horace wondered.

Liam cut into a side street, where the inmates of a brothel, half-naked, their hair tangled about their faces, leaned out a window to cheer on a gang of men chasing a terrified black woman. He heard Liam calling, "Mr. Widdicomb, do ye think we might try to help that poor creature?"

"We'd be killed by the mob," Horace shouted back. "Keep driving. Go on, hurry!"

At dawn on Tuesday, Vanessa was still in labor, aided only by Delia and Mrs. Skene, for she had refused to allow any of the servants to risk the danger of a trip to Murray Hill, where Dr. Fairleigh lived. Delia's hands were gentle and her voice reassuring; Mrs. Skene, calm and efficient, carried in fresh linen and prepared the cradle.

But the labor was difficult, and made worse by Vanessa's fears. Blake was in the basement with Alice, and she could only hope he would be safe there, but Miranda was all the way across the city in the Shelter on Houston Street. Vanessa tossed fretfully between the pains. "So many children—how can the matrons protect them all?"

Delia, who understood, could only wipe Vanessa's forehead with a damp cloth and make comforting sounds.

Several hours earlier Mrs. Skene had barred the front door, and in spite of the heat she had closed and locked the shutters. As the day went on, Vanessa grew oblivious to the noise from the streets; she was only aware of her pains, which were coming closer together now, tearing at her. There was a moment of rending agony when she felt that her body was being torn apart. And then Delia's voice, saying that she had given birth to a son.

It was early evening when Vanessa awoke from a long, exhausted sleep and took the baby from Delia. How beautiful he was, a little smaller than Blake had been at birth, but perfect. She touched her lips to the small head, with its fuzz of reddish hair, then, as he wailed loudly, she held him to her breast, smiling as she felt his hungry mouth drawing nourishment from her body.

Because of the stifling heat, Delia had opened the shutters and pushed up the windows a few inches. When Vanessa had finished nursing her baby, she gave him back to Delia, who placed him carefully in his cradle beside the bed. Only now did Vanessa begin to remember that there was a world outside, and to realize the dangers that still surrounded everyone in the house. Gramercy Park was unnaturally quiet, and Vanessa found the silence frightening. Most of her neighbors, perhaps all of them, had fled. She strained to hear the familiar sounds of horses and carriages, delivery wagons, the laughter of a servant girl. The square was deserted.

But farther off, fires blazed and were reflected on the windowpanes. From south of the square she heard the roar of mobs, the crashing of timbers, now and then a woman's shrill scream. Sounds of a city under attack, not by foreign invaders, but by its own citizens.

"The riots," she began.

Delia turned her face away.

"Tell me what you know," Vanessa insisted.

Delia spoke with forced cheerfulness. "Now, don' yuh go worryin' yuhself, Miz Vanessa. It's goin' be over real soon."

"Don't lie to me, please."

"Ain' lyin', ma'am. That Jimmy Callum, Alice's young man, he been here. He was worried 'bout Alice and he made it 'cross the city from City Hall Park an' he say some big man in Washington—Mistuh Stanton—that was it—"

"The Secretary of War," Vanessa said automatically.

"Yessum, that's the one. He sent a telegram t' Mayor Opdyke an' he say five regi'ments are on the way. They goin' to stop all this riotin'."

"Where is Jimmy now?"

"He's downstairs with Alice an' Miz Skene an' Mastuh Blake in duh kitchen. He say ain' no use goin' back t' duh newspaper office 'cause that mob—dey smashed duh presses an' set duh place on fire—"

"Did Mr. Greeley escape?"

"Jimmy, he think so. But all duh business places is shut down or burned out—ain' no street cars runnin' . . . an' duh orphan home . . ." Delia's eyes filled with tears. "Dey went an' burned the orphan home and—"

Vanessa's body stiffened and she cried out in horror.

"Oh, no ma'am, not duh white chillun' shelter. Duh Colored Orphan home on Forty-third Street."

Delia had not been talking about the Shelter on Houston Street, Vanessa thought with relief. Miranda was still safe so far as she knew. Miranda had to be safe. Then, moments later, Vanessa was moved by pity and revulsion as she thought of the plight of those black orphans. "Dear God! What kind of men would turn their hatred on children, on babies?"

"They crazy, Miz Vanessa. Crazy an' mean, like a pack of wolves."

Delia stopped speaking, her dark eyes wide with fear, and Vanessa cried out, for they both heard the sound of tramping feet. There were men coming into the square, breaking the unnatural silence that had hung over the park all that day. Vanessa stared in terror at the glow of torchlight moving across the bedroom windows. She tried to get to her feet, but she dropped back against the pillows, exhausted by her long, difficult labor.

"Duh front door's barred," Delia said, trying to reassure her. "An' Jimmy's still downstairs."

Jimmy, one boy against a mob of savage men. "Take the baby, Delia. Get him down to the cellar. Tell the others to keep perfectly still."

"Ah ain' leavin' yuh alone, Miz Vanessa."

But even now they heard pounding against the front door. Rifle butts, Vanessa thought, or clubs. Was the door strong enough to withstand the assault of the mob? Delia, moving quickly, seized a poker from the fireplace.

"Delia, no! Take the baby—run and hide."

Then Vanessa heard Mrs. Skene crying out. "Captain McClintock!"

And Logan shouting orders: "You men, surround the house. Dermot, take those others to patrol the square."

Through her tears Vanessa saw Logan at last, and she held out her arms to him. His face was haggard and grimed with smoke, and there was a cut on his forehead and a livid bruise on his cheek. He gathered her to him. "That's the crew of the *Sea Dragon* down there," he said. "They won't let anyone get through. No one's going to hurt you—no one. Vanessa . . ." She could not see his face any longer, for it was pressed against her breasts, but she felt the convulsive shaking of his shoulders. "I was so afraid of what I'd find."

Logan, afraid. His fears had been for her. She had needed him and he had come to her through a city that had turned to a battlefield. She stroked his hair, saying, "It's all right. Everything is all right now that you're here."

He only released her when he heard the shrill, indignant wailing from the cradle. "A boy, suh, a fine, strong boy."

He went to the cradle and stood looking down with an expression of mingled relief and pride in his face. He drew back the blanket as if to reassure himself that the baby, born in the midst of this hell, was, indeed, strong and perfect.

Then he came back and sat down at the foot of the bed. "No, not there," Vanessa said. "Come to me. Hold me." His arms were around her, and she could find no words to express her feelings, for she knew the depth of Logan's love for her now, and she was sure that nothing could ever harm her or frighten her again.

Although the rioting went on through the night, the seasoned troops were starting to move into the city: cavalry, infantry, and artillery regiments came to put an end to it. On Thursday the Irish of New York's Sixty-ninth marched into the worst sections of the city and the tide began to turn against the mob. Nevertheless, Logan's men remained stationed around the square until Friday, when Mayor Opdyke declared that the insurrection was at an end.

"The crew wanted shore leave in New York," Rankin told Logan with a grim smile. "I guess they've earned it now."

On Sunday afternoon a messenger brought a letter to the house on Gramercy Park, and when Delia handed it to Vanessa, she recognized Felicity's handwriting. Logan, who was standing at the window, looked at Vanessa inquiringly.

"Felicity wanted me to know that the Shelter was unharmed," she said. "The children were taken out of the city right after the rioting broke out."

"They were lucky," Logan said.

Vanessa was weak with relief, knowing that Miranda was safe. Then, as she went on reading, her lips parted and she drew a quick breath. "There is more," she said. "Abel has had a stroke."

"When did that happen?"

"A few days ago. Abel went down to South Street to try to save the contents of his warehouses, but he was too late. He collapsed right there, and Horace got home."

"How is he now?" Logan asked quietly.

"He's still alive, but Dr. Fairleigh is not hopeful about his condition," Vanessa said.

Chapter 22

By the end of the week the riots were over, and the people of New York set about assessing the extent of the destruction. Although no one could be sure of the number of casualties after four days of savage fighting, one newspaper estimated that as many had been killed or wounded in the city as at Shiloh or Bull Run. Nearly every man of the Metropolitans had been injured, so regular Army troops had to be divided into detachments and sent to patrol the streets. Eighteen blacks had been killed by the rioters, and many more were reported missing. More than a hundred buildings had gone up in flames, including the Colored Orphan Asylum, three police stations, an armory, and countless factories and stores.

Late on Saturday afternoon Garnet, who had been in her boardinghouse throughout the rioting, had ventured to come down to look over her dress shop. It had escaped the flames, but the show windows had been smashed and the stock looted or scattered about. She stared helplessly at the fine silks and brocades, the elegant parasols and fans left torn and filthy on the floor, trampled by the mobs. She stooped and picked up the remains of a lace shawl, then let it fall. Slowly she walked back to the fitting rooms. Mirrors had been shattered and velvet chairs broken.

She started, hearing the sound of footsteps in the front of the shop, a man's steps crushing shards of broken glass under heavy shoes. Moving cautiously, she went to the remains of the velvet draperies that divided the back of the shop from the front, then gave a cry of relief and ran forward to fling herself against Logan.

"You're safe," she said. "I was so afraid that you . . . I'd heard that the rioters had attacked South Street and I thought . . ." She touched the bruise on his cheek. Aside from that, he looked uninjured. Indeed, he was composed, clean-shaven, his shirt freshly starched.

"I haven't been down to the offices yet," he said. "Probably they are a shambles; that wouldn't surprise me. I was lucky I set up my shipyard and warehouses in Stonington. That's where I was when the rioting broke out. Buying an iron works to make engines for my steamers. No damages up there. But your shop here . . ." He shook his head. "I'll have it fixed up. Don't you worry." He patted her shoulder, but he did not put his arms around her. She moved closer, pressing against him, feeling the warmth of his powerful body, inhaling the familiar odors of shaving soap and starched linen. "It doesn't matter about the shop. You're all right; you're here with me. That's all that matters."

Why didn't he put his arms around her? "Garnet," he said, and she heard the strain in his voice. She looked up at him and saw that his gray eyes were remote, his dark brows drawn together.

She was being foolish, expecting him to embrace her here, where anyone might walk in and see them. "We'll go back to my boardinghouse," she said quickly. "We'll celebrate, because you're back."

But he was moving away, freeing himself from her clinging arms. "Garnet, I can't come home with you," he said.

"Because you've promised you would be at home tonight? But tomorrow night, you'll come to see me tomorrow night?"

Logan did not answer; he looked past her at the ruined shop. "I'll hire workmen as soon as I can, carpenters and glaziers. You'll need new mirrors and counters, and you'll have to replace your stock. Rankin brought back a cargo of fine silks. You can choose what you want."

"The *Sea Dragon*'s come back?"

"Rankin brought her into Stonington a few weeks ago for repairs. But she still needs more work, because we sailed her back to New York on Tuesday. We came down through Long Island Sound and the Hell Gate passage, and we anchored off the Battery." He was talking quickly, as if he were using words to keep her at arm's length.

"I suppose, with the rioting, you could not come ashore before today," she interrupted.

"We came ashore at once and managed to get through to Gramercy Park. The crew had their weapons and I ordered them to guard my home until the rioting was over."

"You've been back all this time, and you've only now come to see me." Her voice was tense and accusing. "Why did you come here today, Logan? Was it to see what had happened to your . . . investment? Was that the only reason?" She knew that she had no right to question him this way, but she could not control herself.

"I've been concerned about you," he said quietly.

"And yet you waited all this time—"

"My wife and my son were in the house, unprotected. And she was—"

"What about me?"

He looked down at her for a moment, and then he said, "Vanessa gave birth to a second son during the riots."

In spite of the matter-of-fact way he said it, she saw the pride in his face, and the devotion to his wife. He had always loved Vanessa, and he always would. She could no longer deceive herself about that.

"Now, about the shop," he was saying briskly, "I can have it fixed up in no time, and I'm willing to bet that your business will be better than before. This war's bringing more money into New York all the time. You can—"

"I don't want the shop." She was surprised at the steadiness of her voice. "Have it fixed up if you want to, and let Rebecca manage it. Or you might consider selling it to her."

"But what about you? What will you do?"

"I've been offered a position in Chicago, a good one, managing the ladies' dress department of Gibson and White."

"You never mentioned it to me."

"I haven't seen you often since you've been going back and forth between New York and Stonington," she reminded him.

"How can you be sure the offer's still open?"

"It is. I saw Mr. White only a few weeks ago when he was here on a buying trip. That's the third time he's offered me the position. One of my window displays caught his eye when he came to New York about a year ago. He's a most determined man, and he's willing to pay me an excellent salary."

"I know of the company," Logan said. "It has a sound reputation, and Chicago's becoming quite a city, I'm told."

She tried to fight down the pain that grew and spread inside her. "Yes, it's a great opportunity for me." She gave him a long, direct look. "And I have nothing to keep me here, really."

He did not answer.

"Have I, Logan?"

If only he would deny it, if only he would ask her to stay on, if he would offer the slightest hope that one day they would be close again, she would remain here. She would manage the shop and live for the brief hours when he would come to her, make love to her as he had on that first night in his office on South Street.

When she could bear his silence no longer, she said, "I will write to Mr. White and tell him that I'm ready to accept his offer. I'll do it tonight." She had to do it as quickly as possible, before she wavered and let herself be lured by impossible hopes of a future with Logan.

She looked at him in silence, and then he was taking her face between his hands and kissing her lips. It was a kiss of farewell, and, knowing this, she did not let herself cling to him. Then he turned and left the shop, the broken glass splintering under his feet. Only when he was out of sight did she give way to tears. Standing there in the ruins of the shop, the ruins of all she created for herself, she leaned against a scarred wall, her body shaken with wracking sobs.

By autumn the city was moving back to its bustling tempo, although here and there smoke-blackened buildings still stood as grim reminders of the summer's rioting. The Metropolitans, sometimes with military escorts, invaded the cellars and garrets of the Five Points and the Bowery in search of stolen property, and for months they kept coming upon all sorts of loot: mahogany and rosewood chairs, expensive paintings and Oriental rugs, as well as barrels of sugar and chests of tea from the warehouses along the waterfront.

But New Yorkers were an energetic, forward-looking lot not given to brooding over past disasters too long, and now, in September, they found something new to talk about, something far more pleasant than the events of summer. The *Osliaba*, a warship bearing the ensign of the czar of Russia, dropped anchor off Manhattan. She was quickly joined by the steam frigates *Alexander Nevsky* and *Peresviet.* Other Russian vessels of the czar's Atlantic fleet continued to arrive throughout the month, and the citizens of New York gave the Russian officers a royal welcome.

Because England and France had until now shown

marked sympathy for the Confederate cause, New Yorkers spoke hopefully of a possible alliance between the United States and Russia. In any case, their presence in New York harbor during this crucial year of the war would impress the governments of England and France, whose ships were also anchored in the harbor. As for the people of New York, they hastened to fete the Russian visitors, first with a splendid parade along Broadway and a few weeks later with a dazzling ball at the Academy of Music, followed by a *soirée russe,* an imposing banquet catered by Delmonico's.

Vanessa attended with Logan, who had remained in the city since the birth of their son, Darren. She was becoming increasingly aware of Logan's importance in the ship-owning society of New York, and she saw the way older men—Aspinwalls, Grinnells, Schermerhorns—listened to his opinions and accepted him into their ranks as an equal. She was filled with pride, remembering how he had fought his way up from the Five Points to make a place for himself in this closely knit group.

A few weeks later, Logan and Vanessa attended another ball, given by the Russian visitors aboard the *Alexander Nevsky.* Vanessa, in a magnificent gown of honey-colored satin with an enormous, bell-shaped skirt, was whirled about in the arms of the czar's officers; although conversation was difficult, there was no mistaking the admiration in their eyes.

"I feel like a young belle again," Vanessa told Logan. He laughed.

"You are more beautiful than any female here," he told her, pressing her hand.

"You are prejudiced," Vanessa said. Then, looking about at the dancers, she added, "I'd have thought Kitty would be here tonight. She loves parties, and I do believe there's never been another quite like this one here in New York."

★ ★ ★ ★ ★

The society editor of the *Herald* agreed, and the following day the newspaper was filled with rapturous copy describing the ball aboard the *Alexander Nevsky*. Vanessa sat reading the paper in bed while Logan, who had already gotten up, was finishing dressing.

She turned the pages, and then she gave a wordless cry.

He turned, still holding his cravat. "What's wrong?"

"It's Abel Bradford. He died yesterday afternoon. A second stroke . . ."

Late in November, Vanessa received an unexpected caller. Alice announced Mrs. Horace Widdicomb, then went off, at Vanessa's order, to bring refreshments. But when the tea and cakes had been set down on the small table in front of the parlor sofa, Kitty showed no interest. She paced up and down, and Vanessa saw that her face was white and drawn, her eyes swollen. The heavy black taffeta of her skirt crackled as she moved about. "Please sit down," Vanessa urged, indicating a place beside her on the sofa. "The tea will warm you."

Kitty obeyed, but when she tried to raise her cup to her lips, her hand shook so that a little of the liquid spilled over. She set down the cup. "Vanessa, it is all so terrible, and you're the only one who can help us. If you refuse—but you won't refuse—you can't. . . ."

Vanessa, thoroughly bewildered, waited for Kitty to go on.

"Horace doesn't know I've come. I didn't dare mention it to him. He's half out of his mind with worry. You must speak to Logan."

Vanessa stared at Kitty. "I don't see what Logan has to do with—"

"Logan is determined to ruin my husband."

Vanessa remembered a brief conversation she had had with Logan after the funeral.

"Horace has what he's wanted for so long," she had said. "The Bradford fortune."

"Has he?" There had been a curious, tight smile on Logan's face, a thoughtful expression in his eyes.

"How could Logan harm Horace now?" Vanessa asked.

"According to the terms of Papa's will, Horace has control of the business. Mama is to be paid a generous allowance from the profits each year. But there are no profits."

Kitty fumbled for her small, black-bordered handkerchief. "Papa's company has been in trouble for some time now. Horace knew it, but he thought he would be able to make changes now, to recoup the losses. But he won't have that chance—not with Logan driving him to the wall."

Vanessa felt a stir of sympathy, but she fought it down. Why should she or Logan care what happened to Horace? Her mind flew back over the years. She remembered Horace, driving her from the door of the Bradford offices without giving her a chance to explain what she was doing there. Horace, joining with Abel to take away Logan's unfinished clipper ship, the *Athena.*

"I'm not asking for Horace's sake," Kitty said quickly. "I've never loved him. You know that. But he is my husband, and if he goes under, so do the rest of us. I've seen it happen to other families. They have to move to some wretched little crackerbox of a house, and no one comes to call, and after a while no one even speaks of them. It's as if they no longer exist. I couldn't bear that—I couldn't."

"You're exaggerating," Vanessa said. "I know the Bradford warehouses were burned during the riots, and a number of cargoes destroyed. But surely the company has other assets."

Kitty was twisting her handkerchief in her small hands.

"It was partly Papa's fault," Kitty went on. "He kept building clipper ships long after so many others had turned to steam. He'd made his fortune with clippers, and Horace could not make him understand that they were no longer profitable. And Horace doesn't have the money to start building them now. With Logan hounding him, he—"

"Logan has made his own fortune, building and leasing ships for the Navy," Vanessa said. "Why should he care about destroying a competitor? Indeed, if what you say is true, Horace is in no position to compete."

But she felt an inward uneasiness, for she knew Logan too well to believe that he bore Horace no malice over all that had happened down through the yearns. Horace had tried to break him, and Logan had not forgotten.

"Logan's been pressuring banks to call in our loans. He's been buying up mortgages on whatever business property we have left and using his influence to get our creditors to demand full payment. At once. But it isn't too late, not if you talk to Logan right away. Oh, Vanessa, please. We've been friends for so long—almost like sisters."

Was it possible that Kitty had made herself forget that incident with Garnet Spencer? Or had she managed to convince herself that she had been acting for Vanessa's own good by informing her that Logan had a mistress? Even now Vanessa did not know for certain whether or not Garnet was still a part of Logan's life. She doubted it. But the uncertainty was still there, and the pain.

"Vanessa, even if you don't care what happens to me," Kitty was saying, "you do care about Mama. She's always been kind to you."

Far kinder than Kitty could imagine. Without Felicity's help, what would have become of Miranda?

Vanessa was silent, unable to deny what Kitty was saying. Encouraged, perhaps, Kitty went on, her dark eyes frantic. "You want what is best for Blake and—and Darren. I feel the same about my children. It would be bad enough for Thomas, if we lost our money. But for Roxanne, what is there for a girl but a suitable marriage? And without money, that is impossible."

A suitable marriage, Vanessa thought. Once, Kitty had been eager to run away with Logan aboard the *Athena.* Instead, she had been forced into marriage with Horace.

"Roxanne is ten years old," Vanessa said quietly. "Aren't you thinking too far ahead?"

"No, I'm not! Little girls go to dancing classes with little boys from the right families. And in a few years they're attending cotillions with those same boys. You don't have a daughter, so maybe you've never thought about how important it is for a girl to have a home at a fashionable address. And a wealthy father who can give her a substantial dowry."

Kitty was still speaking, but Vanessa was no longer listening closely. *You don't have a daughter.* Kitty's words had struck Vanessa like a blow. What would become of Miranda when she had grown to womanhood? Kitty knew nothing about Miranda's existence, because Felicity had kept the secret all these years. Loyal, generous Felicity had done that, and so much more for Vanessa. . . .

If the Bradford family went under, Felicity, too, would suffer. That must not happen.

"I can't promise anything," Vanessa said, her quiet words cutting across Kitty's desperate pleading. "If Logan's made up his mind to destroy Horace's business, he may not listen to me."

"Oh, but he will, he must. He loves you so."

"Does he?"

"I've seen the way he looks at you," Kitty said.

"And Garnet Spencer? Perhaps he looked at her in the same way."

"I doubt it," Kitty said. "Anyway, she's gone. She went off to Chicago, and Logan's sold the shop to another woman. I found out when I went in to buy this bonnet. I asked about Miss Spencer, and this woman—the new owner—she told me."

"She told you?"

A faint smile touched the corners of Kitty's lips.

"I did ask a few discreet questions. I pretended to be disappointed that the charming Miss Spencer was not there to wait on me. And the new owner said that she had gone to manage the ladies' department of a store in Chicago and would not be coming back. So you see, Logan could not have really cared about her."

"Maybe Garnet left New York because she felt that she would find a better business opportunity in Chicago."

"If Logan had wanted to keep her here, she would have stayed," Kitty said. Her dark eyes softened. Was she remembering herself, at her own birthday ball, kissing Logan in the conservatory?

"Oh, Kitty."

"You're a lucky woman, Vanessa." Then the tension came back to her face. "You will try to help me, won't you?"

Vanessa sighed. Whether she liked it or not, her life had somehow become bound up with Kitty's. From that first day when she had arrived at the mansion on Hudson Square, Kitty had taken a hand in her destiny by suggesting that Vanessa should be hired to care for Aunt Prudence.

"I'll speak to Logan," Vanessa said. "Now, let me ring for Alice and have her bring a fresh pot of tea. And we'll have a little rum in it. The way Aunt Prudence liked it."

Chapter 23

On the day after Kitty's visit, Logan and Vanessa drove out together, north along Fifth Avenue, to see the building lot on which their new house was under construction. Standing some distance from the workmen, who were swarming over the foundations, Vanessa confronted Logan, who made no attempt to deny the truth of Kitty's words.

"But why? Logan, why must you do this? Surely, if the Bradford Line is already on the verge of bankruptcy, there is no reason for you to try to do Horace further harm."

"There's every reason. Old Abel still had a few valuable assets when he died. Not many, but a few. I'm going to take them over. The shipyard on the East River. The clipper that's due back from China within a month or so. I'm going to buy that clipper and her cargo dirt cheap."

"You don't want more clippers," Vanessa began.

"I'm not about to build more," Logan said. "But they still have their uses. The *Ondine*'s nearly ready to be broken up for scrap. This China clipper of Horace's can take her place, running lumber from Maine to Stonington."

"Surely you can buy another clipper if you want one for carrying lumber. You have no need to—"

"I know what I need. This is business, Vanessa, and no concern of yours. Now, let's go over there and have a closer look at the house. I want you to see the blueprints. The ballroom will take up the entire third floor—"

"We've got to settle the matter of Horace first," Vanessa said stubbornly.

"Your concern for Horace is touching, considering what he did to you. Getting you thrown out of the Bradford house—"

"I don't like Horace Widdicomb any more than you do. But I'm thinking of Kitty and her children, and Felicity."

Logan's eyes were angry. "Horace didn't concern himself with what would become of you when he cut off my trade with Cuba. He didn't care that we had a child."

Chris.

Vanessa shut her eyes and heard Logan saying, "Forgive me. I didn't mean to remind you . . ."

For a moment there was a gentleness in him, and she put aside her own painful memories to resume their talk of Horace. "Logan, please try to understand. I know what it took for you to build the McClintock Line. I know better than anyone. You've always been ambitious, and maybe sometimes you've driven a hard bargain. But I've never been ashamed of you, ashamed to be your wife. I've been proud to share your name and to bear your children. Until now."

His gray eyes darkened. "You've said enough, Vanessa."

"No, I have not. I've more to say, and you are going to listen."

Never in the years of their marriage had she spoken to him this way. She saw the flush rising under his deeply tanned skin, saw his mouth harden.

"You've always been hot-tempered and stubborn. And you've never been able to forget those early years. Oh, yes, Silas has told me all about them. You had to be hard and ruthless then, or go under. But now you have everything a man could want."

"Except for the loyalty of his wife."

He spoke harshly, and she took a step back, as if he had struck her. Her fingers closed on the handle of her parasol, so tightly that the carved wood bit into her palm.

"If you destroy another man—a whole family—out of spite . . . a need for revenge . . . then I cannot—"

"Go on."

"Oh, Logan, please try to understand. I—I am afraid for you."

"You're not making sense. It's Horace who has cause to be afraid. Before I'm finished with him he'll consider himself lucky to get a position as a clerk in some other shipping house."

"I don't care about that! It's you I'm thinking of. Because if you go through with your plan, if you hurt Kitty and her children, and Felicity, then I'll never be able to feel the same about you again. You won't be the man I've loved all these years."

He stood frozen for a moment, and she felt his anger, a tangible force, beating against her own will. She stood firm, her eyes fixed on his face. Even when he reached out and his hand closed on her arm, she kept on looking at him.

"Come on," he said. He jerked at her arm so that she was forced to go along with him back to the carriage. He called up to Ben, who was seated on the box. "Take Mrs. McClintock home," he ordered.

Ben leaped down to help her into the carriage.

"Logan—wait! Aren't you coming with me?"

He did not reply. Instead, he turned on his heel and strode off, up Fifth Avenue.

It was nearly midnight of the same day when Horace, sallow and tired, came into Kitty's bedroom in the house on Hudson Square. "I saw your light under the door," he said.

She had been riffling through the pages of *Harper's Weekly*, unable to concentrate on it. Now she let it slide to the floor.

Horace came and dropped into a chair beside the bed.

"Where have you been?" she demanded.

"Surely you have not been concerned for me," he said.

"The way you've been going on these past few weeks, I thought you might have . . . done something foolish."

"And that would have broken your heart, wouldn't it, my dear?"

"It would have created a scandal," Kitty told him, not bothering to hide her feelings. "God knows, it would be dreadful enough for your children, growing up with a bankrupt for a father—"

"That isn't going to happen," Horace told her. "I have been with Logan McClintock. He came to see me down on South Street late this afternoon. I still don't understand why, but he is going to lend me money to rebuild the warehouses. And to set up a coastwise trade with the ports of New England and to keep the Caribbean trade, Cuba and Jamaica."

"He means it? You're sure?"

"Logan McClintock is always serious about business. He's having Enoch Halliwell draw up the papers. I'll have to make concessions. McClintock's asking for a seat on the board of directors, and he's to be the majority stock holder. And he—"

Kitty made an impatient gesture. She cared nothing about the details. "We are not ruined, then? We will be able to go on living as we have? Roxanne will be able to go to Miss Haines' Academy and Thomas will—"

"Yes, Kitty. And you will be able to go on shopping in the 'Ladies' Mile' and filling your closets with the latest fashions in gowns and bonnets." Horace paused and shook his head in bewilderment. "I was certain that Logan McClintock was out to ruin me. But I must have been wrong."

"No, you weren't. And if he has changed his mind, you can be grateful to me."

"You went to him for help? And he gave in because he—because the two of you—"

"Don't be an idiot, Horace. I went to Vanessa for help. And she came through."

"Vanessa? What reason would she have to try to help me after I—"

"You don't know Vanessa," Kitty said slowly. "I think perhaps I did not really know her until now."

By early summer of the following year the McClintocks had moved into their brownstone mansion on Fifth Avenue. Only now, on this warm June evening, had all the furniture been moved from the house on Gramercy Park, and tonight Vanessa and Logan would spend their first night there. The children had long since gone to sleep, and the new gaslights had been turned low. But Vanessa lingered in the drawing room.

She picked up a small porcelain figurine and set it down again. Then she looked up at her portrait, which Logan had insisted should be hung over the mantelpiece. She had hoped that it might be hung in some less conspicuous part of the house, where she would not have to see it so often. This was a new house. She and Logan should make a new beginning here.

She smiled ruefully. No one could start over simply by moving to a new house. The past would be with her always. Memories of that long-ago summer with Ross.

And even if the painting had been packed away in some corner of the attic, she would not forget Ross Halliwell, not ever. For there was Miranda. She had seen the little girl only a few days before on one of her frequent visits to the Shelter.

Miranda had grown taller, slender, and leggy, and so pretty, with her soft, gold-flecked hazel eyes and her thick chestnut hair. Felicity, who now spent much of her time at the Shelter, had made an excuse to call Miranda to her office there. "Mrs. McClintock was admiring the sampler you embroidered so neatly," Felicity told Miranda.

The child curtsied and smiled up at Vanessa. The small oval face flushed slightly with pleasure.

"Would you like to have it, ma'am?" Miranda asked.

"Why, I . . . Yes, indeed, I would."

After Miranda had left them, Vanessa stood looking down at the words carefully cross-stitched on the square of linen.

Who can find a virtuous woman?
For her price is far above rubies.

Vanessa sighed and turned to Felicity. "Is it necessary for the girls to dress so severely?" she asked. Miranda's pliant young body had been clothed in a shapeless uniform of dull brown poplin, and her hair, which had a tendency to wave at the temples, had been pulled back and plaited into two tight braids.

"We have our rules," Felicity said gently. "We emphasize neatness and simplicity. Even if we could afford to dress the little girls more smartly, we would not be doing them a kindness. When Miranda leaves here, she will get work as a seamstress, perhaps—or even a governess. But she cannot hope for anything more than that."

Felicity had been right, but her words had hurt Vanessa all the same, for Miranda was precious to her. Now, as she lingered in the drawing room of this imposing new brownstone, she felt her heart contract with pain. Ross was married, Jeremy had told her. He had made a name for himself as a portrait painter and had settled down in a fashionable section of London with a wife who was wealthy in her own right. He had three daughters born in wedlock, Vanessa remembered. Those little girls would not have to wear shapeless brown poplin. None of them would have to look forward to a life of drudgery as a seamstress or a governess.

But what lay ahead for Miranda, if not a dull, respectable occupation?

Vanessa turned away from her portrait and left the drawing room. She climbed the long flight of stairs and went down the hall to the master bedroom, where Delia was waiting to help her disrobe and put on her nightdress, to take down her hair and brush it into a mass of red-gold waves about her shoulders.

Logan had suggested that now Vanessa ought to have a personal maid, but she had refused. He knew nothing of the bond that had been forged between her and Delia during those long, bleak months when she had been awaiting Miranda's birth.

Vanessa had compromised by hiring a sturdy, hard-working Irish girl as nursery maid so that Delia, although still in charge of the nursery, would not have any heavy chores to do in caring for Darren. As for Blake, he was nearly as tall as Vanessa and was being tutored each day in Latin, Greek, and mathematics by a student from nearby Columbia College. He was working harder than he ever had before so that at the beginning of the new year he would be ready to go off to the expensive preparatory school that she and Logan had chosen.

Now Delia, having completed her nightly ritual, left the bedroom. Vanessa remained seated before her dressing table until, a half hour later, Logan, who had been arranging papers in his new desk in the library downstairs, came to join her.

She rose, the folds of her lace-trimmed pale lilac gown falling about her. "You see," Logan was saying. "The mandarin bed looks fine now that we have it in a room that's big enough." Vanessa had added other treasures, brought by Logan's captains on the China run: a thick, intricately designed rug, a tall, black-lacquered chest, a fireplace screen painted with willows and curving bridges.

Logan put his arms around her, holding her close.

"You've had to wait a long time for all this," he said softly, "but it's yours now. All of it. You are pleased with the house, aren't you?"

"It's so large, I feel lost. . . ."

"You're not lost, though. You're here with me. And now that we've given the bed its proper setting, why don't we . . ." He did not finish the sentence, for there was no need. He bent and kissed her hair, the curve of her throat, and pushed aside the bodice of her nightdress to savor the softness of her breasts. Then he led her to the bed, and the red and gold hangings enclosed them, shutting out everything else.

In the autumn of 1866 the house had become home, although Vanessa was still sometimes overwhelmed by the size and magnificence of the rooms, which, more and more often, were filled with guests. She presided over formal dinners in the spacious dining room, and over balls that were described the following day in the *Herald* and the *World.* But on this October evening she knew a special kind of happiness as she welcomed visitors to celebrate the christening of Alison, the small, delicate girl who had been born a few weeks before.

Alison had been premature, and young Dr. Fairleigh, who had taken over his father's practice, had been able to give no reason for the infant's early arrival. "She is a bit frail," he had reassured Vanessa, "but she's perfectly healthy."

Logan was delighted, if a little awe-struck, to find himself the father of this dainty little creature. Even now, at the christening party, he stood beaming with pleasure as he and Vanessa welcomed their guests.

Because it was a party for family and friends rather than one of the larger, more formal gatherings, Blake and Darren had been permitted to attend. Three-year-old Darren, in Delia's charge, stared round-eyed at the guests while Blake, fifteen now, tried to look dignified in his new suit, with its fawn-colored trousers and black coat.

But when the Widdicombs arrived with Thomas and Roxanne, Blake led Thomas off to see his new model of the *Great Eastern*, the steamship that had completed the laying of the Atlantic cable back in July. "May I see it too?" Roxanne asked, casting an admiring glance at Blake. Roxanne had Kitty's dark hair and eyes, and her coquettish mannerisms as well. The pretty twelve-year-old took a few quick, light steps in Blake's direction, so that her white silk skirt belled out around her.

"Girls don't know anything about ships," Thomas said, but she ignored her brother and gazed hopefully at Blake.

"Oh, do let me come along," she urged. Blake shrugged.

"Come on if you want to," he said. He and Thomas sauntered off with Roxanne close behind them.

"That's quite a concession," Vanessa told Kitty with a smile. "Blake has shown no interest in little girls so far."

"Roxanne is hard to resist when she wants something," Kitty said. "She usually gets her own way."

"You are spoiling her," Felicity said, coming over from the buffet table to join them. "Silk gowns from Paris for a child that age!"

"Oh, Mama, how can you blame me?" Kitty said. "Roxanne is so pretty."

"No reason to turn her head, certainly not now, when she is only twelve. Oh, yes, I know that these days young girls are being presented to society at sixteen and seventeen, but not in families like ours."

"Mama, you do have such old-fashioned notions. Why Vanessa is going to spoil Alison too—see if she doesn't. That cradle she's in right now—rosewood with silk and lace pillows—and her christening dress! I've never seen a prettier one." Kitty put a hand on Vanessa's arm. "And who can blame you? Your first daughter. Oh, Vanessa, I'm so happy for you."

She spoke with sincerity, for she had not been able to forget how Vanessa had saved the Bradford shipping empire from ruin. But Vanessa flinched and went white. *Your first daughter.*

She tried to make a suitable reply, but no words would come. Her eyes met Felicity's, and the older woman came to her rescue. "Vanessa, I would like to sample a bit of Mrs. Skene's pineapple cake. And perhaps a cup of punch."

Putting her arm about Vanessa's waist, she led her off in the direction of the buffet table. Logan was standing near the punchbowl, his eyes warm with pride and satisfaction. "My daughter's a real beauty, isn't she, Mrs. Bradford?"

"Yes, indeed," Felicity agreed. Vanessa did not speak, but through the confusion of her thoughts one thing was plain: she must do nothing, say nothing, not ever, that would betray the truth. She must carry the weight of her secret, alone, for Logan's sake.

Chapter 24

"Vanessa, you are making a mistake," Felicity said. "You must consider the consequences."

On this early spring afternoon Vanessa had come to Felicity's small office at the Shelter. Over the years Felicity was spending more and more time at the Shelter, and she had found it convenient to set aside this room for herself.

"I have thought about the matter," Vanessa said, "and I know it would be a great opportunity for Miranda. And as for Alison, she needs a special kind of governess."

At seven, Alison McClintock was a shy, delicate little thing. Vanessa knew that it was time the girl started receiving lessons, but Delia could not teach her. Delia's only duties for the past year had been those of personal maid to Vanessa. The stern, middle-aged Englishwoman Miss Simmons, although she had come with the highest recommendations, had proved entirely unsuitable, and her rigid notions of discipline had caused Alison to draw into a shell. When Vanessa realized that Alison was having nightmares and sleepwalking along the hallway outside the nursery, she knew that Miss Simmons would have to go.

Logan had been in complete agreement, and he had given Miss Simmons three months' salary, an unheard-of concession. Vanessa had added a letter of recommendation praising the governess for her many accomplishments: a knowledge of French and German, of needlework and sketching, but had said nothing about lack of skill in dealing with a particularly sensitive little girl like Alison.

"Miranda is so gentle," Vanessa said to Felicity. "And she would have patience with Alison's flights of fancy. I'm sure of it."

"No doubt you're right," Felicity agreed. "Miranda herself was a fanciful child. But Vanessa, my dear, think what it would mean, taking Miranda into your home. Surely there are other, equally suitable young women who would jump at the chance to—"

"Perhaps there are," Vanessa said, "but I want Miranda!"

Felicity gave her a long, level look. Although now in her sixties, her brown hair graying, her face lined with deepening furrows, Felicity's eyes were as keen as ever. Through the years of dealing with people in trouble, of going into the homes of the poor and desperate, she had seen far more of life than many women of her class. "You've been talking about what Alison needs, but have you thought of Miranda?"

"Certainly I have. It would be a wonderful opportunity for Miranda, living in our home. Oh, I'm not criticizing the Shelter. Surely you know that. It is clean and well run, and the children receive a good education. But there are so many rules."

"An institution cannot be run without rules."

"I know that," Vanessa said impatiently. "But when I think of Miranda, all these years, rising at the sound of a bell, eating in a dining hall, never even having a room of her own where she can be alone, never knowing what it is to go out and shop for a pretty dress, to attend a matinee at a theater, to go riding in Central Park with a friend and linger for an hour over tea and cakes. To go directly from being a pupil here to being a teacher."

"She became a teacher by choice," Felicity reminded Vanessa. "For goodness' sake, Miranda is twenty-one now.

Free to do as she wishes. We're not holding her here against her will."

"I didn't mean—"

"If you feel that it is so important for her to leave the Shelter, I'm sure we could arrange for a position with a good household. I happen to know of a family up in Boston where—"

"No! Oh, Felicity, no! This is the only home she's ever known. She can't go to live with strangers. You know what conditions are in many so-called good homes. A governess has to put up with all sorts of petty humiliations. She has to cater to spoiled children who refuse to obey her because they know that their parents will always side with them. And if the master of the house makes advances, she must either submit or seek a new position without references."

"I know all about these things, but if we are careful, if we select the right sort of family—"

"In our home, Miranda would be treated as one of us. She would have a comfortable room of her own, attractive clothes. I could give her—"

"You could give her special treatment, completely unsuitable to her station in life, and you would do so. And would that be kind in the long run? Think of it, Vanessa. If you cosset the girl, what will become of her when you no longer need a governess for Alison? When it becomes necessary for Miranda to move on to another position?"

"I don't want her to have to spend her whole life as a governess, caring for other people's children. She is a beautiful young woman. In my home she would have a chance to meet young men—"

"And do you think that the Lows or the Grinnells would approve a marriage between any of their sons and a governess without a family—without any name except the one we gave her when we took her in here? Miranda Warren. Who is Miranda Warren? Who were her parents? Those are questions that would be asked, and how could Miranda answer?"

Pain clawed at Vanessa, but she went on, determined to convince Felicity. "Logan brings home young officers from his ships. Clerks from South Street. They come to talk business, but they stay for dinner. Such young men would not expect to find a wife with—with lofty social connections. And as for a dowry, I would see that she had one, at the proper time. If she should meet a suitable young man, I would make some sort of arrangement."

"Perhaps she's already met a suitable man. Not young, perhaps, but a good man."

Vanessa stared for a moment, then her lips parted with surprise. "Dr. Thorne? Clive Thorne? Oh, but he is so much older—a widower."

"He is thirty-five, fourteen years older than she is. His wife died of fever out in China, and he nearly died too. But that was years ago, and surely there is no reason he should not remarry. A difference of fourteen years is not unthinkable."

"Not if the young woman is mature, with some experience of the world perhaps. But Miranda's never known any young men close to her own age. She may be fond of Dr. Thorne—"

"She is. I assure you. And I have reason to believe that he cares for her, although he has never spoken of his feelings as far as I know. I have seen the way he looks at her, the tone of voice with which he speaks her name."

"You think . . . And you never told me?" Vanessa had always loved and respected Felicity, but now her maternal feelings, frustrated all these years when it came to Miranda, surged up inside her. "I had a right to know."

"No, my dear, you have no rights, not where Miranda Warren is concerned."

"She is my daughter, the same as Alison."

"Not quite the same," Felicity reminded her. "Alison is Logan's daughter too. She is legitimate."

"And is Miranda to be punished because Ross and I—"

"It is unfair, I know," Felicity said with deep compassion. "But we must be realistic."

"All right, then," Vanessa said, her eyes darkening to violet, spots of color burning on her high cheekbones. "Let's be fair. Miranda is no more worldly than a young novice straight out of a convent. She is in no position to make a choice before she knows something of the world. Suppose she were to fall in love with Clive Thorne, and he with her, and suppose they married. He's made no secret about wanting to return to China. To work in a hospital for the natives there."

"And that makes him ineligible?"

Vanessa knew the futility of trying to deceive Felicity. "Miranda is as dear to me as Kitty is to you. But I never had the chance to watch her grow up, to get to know her. A few weeks after she was born I gave her up."

"What other choice did you have?"

"None. I know that. But Felicity, think of it. Suppose you had been forced to give Kitty into the keeping of others when she was a baby."

Felicity was silent. The warm spring breeze blowing in through the half-open window tugged at the plain white curtains. The walls were clean, freshly painted, and bare, except for a few institutional paintings: portraits of Washington, of Lincoln, of the new President, Ulysses S. Grant.

Vanessa rose and leaned across the desk, her eyes fixed on Felicity's face. The older woman sighed. "My dear, I think I know what you are feeling. But you have always been impulsive, swayed by your emotions. Think of the risk you would be taking. You've built a good marriage, a home. You have other children, Logan's children. If he were to suspect the truth about Miranda, would he be able to understand, to forgive?"

"He'll never suspect. Why should he? What is more natural than that I should find a suitable governess here at the Shelter? My pet charity, that's what he's always called it. There'll be no risk, and Miranda will have a chance to enjoy a small measure of all that my other children have taken for granted."

"I can see that nothing I say will stop you," Felicity said. "All right, I'll call Miranda and we will allow her to decide. If she accepts your offer, I won't try to change her mind."

Miranda had finished packing her small trunk early that morning. Now she stood in the downstairs hallway of the Shelter, her hazel eyes sparkling with small gold flecks, her cheeks flushed with excitement.

"You can't wait to leave us," Dr. Thorne said. He was a tall, spare man with blunt features and dark hair, and his clean but rumpled suit showed that he had nothing of the dandy about him. The children here at the Shelter loved and trusted him. Miranda was not sure of her own feelings for Clive Thorne.

"I'll stay here with you and help you with your trunk when the carriage comes," he told her.

"I wish you would," she said. "I want to go, but I'm a little nervous too. That great house on Fifth Avenue. What will they think of me there?"

"You have nothing to fear," he told her. "If you are sure this is what you want."

"Oh, I am. I've seen pictures of the McClintock house in the newspapers. It's like a palace. And I read about a ball they held there, last Christmas—"

"You are not going there to attend balls," he reminded her.

"I know that," she said impatiently. "But I'll be able to watch, won't I? To see all those fine ladies in their ball gowns. And I'll have a room of my own, and fifteen dollars a month."

"That much?" He looked at her in surprise, and for a moment she thought he was teasing her.

"I know it is not a fortune," she began.

"It is more than most governesses receive, even if they care for three or four children, and you will only have charge of one little girl. Are you sure about the salary?"

"Oh, yes. Mrs. McClintock is most generous." He was watching her, and she grew uneasy under his steady look. "It is a wonderful opportunity for me."

"I hope it may prove to be," he said. He hesitated, then added quietly, "If you should change your mind, if the world out there does not live up to your expectations, you can always come back here."

"Here? Oh, no! I mean, I'll be coming back for visits, but not to stay—not ever."

"Have you been so unhappy here, then?"

"No, but there is so much more to life. I—I know it may sound foolish to a man. You can go where you wish. You've already been halfway around the world, but I have known nothing except the Shelter. I want . . ."

He moved closer, his eyes searching her face. "What do you want, Miranda?"

"I don't know, but whatever it is, I will have to go out and find it for myself. I—"

She was interrupted by a knocking at the front door, and a moment later a big, heavyset man in the livery of a coachman, the McClintock livery, blue with scarlet facings, stood in the doorway.

She felt a flurry of excitement. She held out her hand to Clive Thorne, who took it. "Remember what I said, Miranda, if you decide to return . . ."

She shook her head. The sight of the carriage, brightly painted, glittering with brass in the spring sunlight, dazzled her. Clive stooped to pick up her small trunk, but the coachman had already lifted it and was carrying it out to the carriage, and she hastened to follow.

During her first days in the McClintock house Miranda found herself thinking less and less often of the Shelter, for, from the moment she arrived at the impressive brownstone mansion a few blocks below the newly completed St. Patrick's Cathedral and the stately buildings that housed Columbia College, she was caught up in a new way of life totally foreign to her. No newspaper sketches, no descriptions, could have prepared her for such splendor.

All her life she had been starved for beauty, for color, and now she lived in a house where the windows were set off with velvet draperies of deep red and forest green and purple, fringed in gold. She marveled at the heavy Chinese rugs, with their intricate patterns, the glittering chandeliers, the gold-framed paintings.

Captain McClintock, discovering Miranda's interest in the treasures his ships had brought back from China, took the time to tell her about them. Her first shyness in the presence of the tall, handsome master of the house soon faded as he showed her some of the exotic wares of the Orient: a large porcelain vase with a green and gold dragon painted on it; an exquisitely carved replica of a flower boat, made of ivory; a splendid silver bowl with a frieze of Chinese figures, warriors, and mandarins.

She met the rest of the family on her first evening in her

new home: Alison, a small, light-footed little girl with honey-gold hair and wide, violet eyes; Darren, home from school for the spring holiday, a sturdy, amiable boy of ten; and Blake.

Seeing Blake McClintock for the first time, she had all she could do to keep from staring at him, for he was so handsome: nearly as tall as his father, slender, with dark-blue eyes and black hair and an air of careless assurance that she found completely intriguing. That night, when she went to bed in the room that had been prepared for her, she found herself thinking, over and over again: It's too good to be true . . . too good to be true.

Surely she would awaken to find herself back in the drab little room she had shared these past three years with Lena Currie, the stout, heavy-breathing teacher who snored loudly for a good part of every night. But no, when she awoke, she was still there, in the room she had all to herself, a room with ruffled white curtains and a lamp painted with flowers. On the marble-topped chest of drawers Mrs. McClintock had provided not only a set of new toilet articles, a comb and brush and a small hand mirror, but also a vase filled with lilacs, and a music box. No doubt one of the maids had placed them there, but she was sure that it was Mrs. McClintock who had thought of giving such luxuries to the new governess.

Miranda swung her long, shapely legs over the side of the bed and hurried to look at herself in the mirror, to inhale the rich scent of the lilacs. Then she opened the box and shivered with pleasure at the tinkling notes of the waltz. Barefoot, she whirled around in her plain skimpy, cotton nightdress. *You are not going there to attend balls.* Clive Thorne's sensible words came to her briefly, but she pushed them to the back of her mind. He was right, of course, but maybe . . . maybe . . .

* * * * *

It did not take long for Miranda to slip into the routine of the household or to win Alison's trust and affection. Miranda was a conscientious teacher, but she did not force Alison to sit for long hours over her lessons. She read her stories from books with brightly colored illustrations and gently pointed out that soon Alison would be able to read them for herself. At her suggestion, Captain McClintock provided an abacus with large wooden beads, to encourage the child with her arithmetic. "This came all the way from China on one of your papa's own ships," she said, and went on to explain how Chinese boys and girls used this method of doing sums.

Because Alison had a small appetite, she did not force her to finish the food on her plate as Miss Simmons had done, sometimes with disastrous results. And she saw to it that the two of them spent plenty of time outdoors, driving through Central Park in one of the open carriages.

During July and August Mrs. McClintock and the two younger children went to their summer home in Newport, and Miranda accompanied them. Miranda was awed by her first glimpse of the ocean. She stared with parted lips, her hazel eyes glowing, and then she noticed that Mrs. McClintock was watching her with a curious expression. She had seen Mrs. McClintock looking at her that way before.

Feeling self-conscious, she said, "It is so new to me."

"I know," Mrs. McClintock said softly. But why did she sound so—so sad. Miranda told herself sternly that she must be imagining the sadness, for how could a woman like Mrs. McClintock have any cause for sorrow? She had a husband who loved her; she was wealthy and still beautiful.

Miranda had often admired the portrait that hung over the mantelpiece in the drawing room of the house on Fifth Avenue. Once, shortly after she had come to work as Alison's governess, Captain McClintock, pleased by her interest, had spoken with pride of the portrait.

"Ross Halliwell had no great reputation when he painted this, back in Fifty-one, but since then he's become famous. I think this is one of his best works, though." McClintock had smiled at her. "I'm prejudiced. What do you think of it?"

Miranda had been moved by the light in his eyes as he looked up at the painting of his wife, but she had to agree that by any standards, the portrait was a good one, for it had captured the glowing beauty of its subject: the violet eyes, the red-gold hair and the full, soft lips, slightly parted; Vanessa's strength and her warm, lush femininity were reflected there.

"Halliwell's painted members of the British royal family and a lot of London society women," McClintock went on. "But I don't believe any of his other portraits can hold a candle to this one."

"Is Mr. Halliwell English?"

"No," McClintock said, "although he and his family have made their home there. Ross was born and raised in Salem as my wife was."

Yes, Mrs. McClintock had been lovely as a young woman, Miranda thought, and now her beauty had even greater depth, for although she moved with the grace of a young girl, there was a strength and dignity about her that few young girls could achieve, a dignity tempered with generosity, as Miranda had cause to know. Vanessa McClintock treated Miranda with unusual informality. During the long, lazy summer afternoons at Newport she told Miranda about her own early years, about how she had grown up in Salem, about her mother, who had been the widow of a sea captain. Miranda was surprised to discover that Mrs. McClintock had once worked in the Bradford home as a companion to an old lady called Aunt Prudence Campbell, one of Felicity's relatives.

Perhaps that was why Vanessa McClintock was so kind to her, Miranda thought. She had known what it was to be a dependent in a wealthy household. But that did not explain the wistful expression in her eyes when she looked at Miranda.

When they were back in New York she had Miranda fitted for a new wardrobe and not in the drab browns and grays that were considered suitable for other governesses.

"Jade green, I think. It will go well with your coloring. And russet and deep burgundy."

Miranda reveled in her new wardrobe, in the well-cut gowns that emphasized her rounded breasts and small waist. Modest, perfectly respectable, but flattering too. And nightgowns of soft sheer linen, and a robe of burgundy silk, with slippers to match.

Too good to be true.

During that summer Alison had only the briefest lessons. Mrs. McClintock said that it would be better for the child to run free on the beach, to drink in the salt air and the warm sunshine, and Miranda was in complete agreement. By the time they had settled back in the house on Fifth Avenue, Alison was stronger, she chattered more freely, and was gaining a little weight.

But she had not completely gotten over her fears. One night early in September, when Captain and Mrs. McClintock had gone off to a costume ball and a thunderstorm swept over the city, Miranda was awakened by Alison's scream of terror. She threw on her robe over her nightdress, thrust her feet into her slippers, and ran across the darkened hall to the nursery.

"A dragon!" Alison sobbed. "A big one—like on the vase downstairs."

Miranda took the child in her arms and rocked her,

stroking her curls. Alison gradually grew quieter. "Miss Simmons used to say there wasn't any dragons. Heathenish nonsense—that's what she said." Alison pressed her face against Miranda's shoulder. "But there are dragons. I know!"

"How do you know?" Miranda asked gently.

" 'Cause how could people make pictures of them if they aren't real?" she demanded with childish logic.

Miranda smiled. "Perhaps there were dragons once, millions of years ago. But maybe, as time went on, they became smaller and smaller and finally disappeared. That vase downstairs in the entrance hall is old, you know."

"Millions of years old?" Alison murmured, relaxed and drowsy now.

"Millions of years," Miranda conceded. This was not the time for telling the exact truth. "In China, the dragon is considered a noble creature. He guards the people in the house where his picture is kept, and he brings rain to make the crops grow." She spoke in a soft monotone now. "Your papa told me about it, and he knows all about China. He named one of his ships the *Sea Dragon.*"

Alison's eyelids closed, and her breathing was even. Miranda sat holding her for a few moments. Only when Alison was sleeping soundly did Miranda put her back into her bed and tuck the blanket around her. Then she started back to her own room and almost collided with a dark shape in the dimly lit hallway. Blake McClintock, returning home after an evening out on the town. He was standing so close to her that she caught the scent of brandy. In the soft glow of the gaslight she saw that his eyes were brighter than usual. But his voice was steady enough.

"What's wrong, Miss Warren? What are you doing out here at this hour?"

"Alison had a nightmare. About a dragon."

"Is she all right now? Shall I go in and talk to her?"

Miranda was touched by Blake's obvious concern for his small sister. "She is asleep," Miranda said. She did not move, and neither did Blake. How handsome he was, his face wet with the rain that still fell outside, his curling black hair plastered against his forehead.

"She does not have nightmares nearly as often as she used to," Miranda assured him.

"And that sleepwalking, that's stopped altogether, hasn't it? Thanks to you, Miranda. May I call you Miranda?"

She nodded. All at once she was aware of her own costume, the burgundy robe tied carelessly over her nightdress, her hair loose about her shoulders. Blake's eyes moved over her, and she knew that he, too, was conscious of her not as his sister's governess but as a woman. She felt a soft stirring that started deep inside her and spread, like ripples of fire, out along the nerves of her body. Under the burgundy silk of her robe her breasts rose and fell with her quickened breathing.

When Blake took her hands in his, the touch sent a shock of response through her. "I'm glad you've come to the house," he said, looking down at her, his eyes holding hers. "Not only for Alison's sake. Miranda, I—"

It was a startling effort for her to look away, to free her hands from his light grasp. "Good night, Mr. McClintock," she said.

"Blake," she heard him correct her as she hurried back into her room and closed the door behind her. She got into bed, but the sound of the rain on the windows, usually so soothing, did not serve to lull her to sleep.

She tossed restlessly, wondering where Blake had been tonight. He was not engaged, but she knew that he was seeing a great deal of Miss Roxanne Widdicomb, a flirtatious, dark-haired girl whose family owned a shipping line, Bradford-

Widdicomb. Roxanne was the granddaughter of Felicity Bradford. But there was no formal engagement, not yet.

And what difference could that possibly make to her? She had come here to work as governess. If the family treated her with informal friendliness, if Blake had called her by her first name and had taken her hands in his, it was no cause for her to forget her place. When the glow of brandy had worn off, he would probably not even remember their encounter under the gaslight globe in the hallway.

You are not going there to attend balls. Who had said that to her? Oh, yes, Dr. Thorne. She tried to see his face in her mind, to remember the sound of his crisp, matter-of-fact voice. But both were dim and faraway. Instead, when she closed her eyes, it was Blake's face she saw, his voice she heard. *Miranda, I—* What had he been about to say when she had freed herself and returned to her room?

She thought that she had outgrown her imaginative flights years ago. Back at the Shelter there was no place for romantic fantasies, for daydreams. But here it was different. She had seen the third-floor ballroom, with its gleaming polished floor, its glittering chandeliers that made rainbows. Suppose that one night she and Blake should dance there. She would wear flowers in her hair and a taffeta skirt that rustled, and his arms would hold her and she would feel the warmth of his tall, slender body. . . .

Chapter 25

Alison had not forgotten Miranda's comforting words, on the night of the rainstorm, and a few weeks later, when the *Sea Dragon* was to set sail for China, the little girl had asked to be taken down to South Street to see the vessel with this fascinating name. "I'm not afraid of dragons, not anymore," Alison had confided to her mother. "They're lucky. Miss Warren says so." Vanessa, grateful to Miranda for helping the child to overcome her fears, readily granted permission.

But as she stood on the bottom step in front of the house, Vanessa had cause to wonder if she had done the right thing. She had expected that Miranda and Alison would drive down to South Street in the landau; now she watched them getting into Blake's smart, expensive new four-in-hand, a vehicle only Blake drove. He had stayed behind, lingering over coffee until Alison and Miranda were ready to leave, and then had casually announced his intention of accompanying his sister and her governess.

Vanessa tried to dismiss her uneasiness, telling herself that since Blake, like many wealthy young New Yorkers, had taken up the sport of coaching, it was natural that he should want to try out the elegant new four-in-hand and team, and what better occasion than this beautiful cloudless day in late September, a perfect Indian-summer morning.

But why had he not asked Roxanne Widdicomb to go driving with him? Although he and Roxanne were not formally engaged, he had been paying marked attention to the pretty, flirtatious young girl for some time now. He had escorted her to several balls, had taken her driving in Central Park and to the opera at the Academy of Music. And Roxanne had made no secret of her attraction to Blake.

Now Vanessa stiffened slightly as she watched Blake, who, having lifted Alison up onto the high seat of the four-in-hand, should have put a hand under Miranda's elbow to assist her. Instead, he picked her up as he had his little sister and lifted her from the pavement, but he held her for a moment, her body against his. And Miranda, resting her small, gloved hands on Blake's shoulders, was looking at him with an expression that caused Vanessa to catch her breath in dismay. Miranda's lips were parted slightly, and her lovely hazel eyes were glowing. She wore her best dress, a handsome, jade-green broadcloth trimmed with velvet. The fitted jacket accented the high, rounded curves of her breasts and her slender waistline. The morning sunlight struck glints of auburn fire in her lustrous brown hair.

Blake set her down on the seat, then went around and got up into the four-in-hand. He leaned across Alison and said something to Miranda, and Vanessa heard Miranda's soft laughter. Then Blake cracked his whip, and the horses trotted forward, the four-in-hand rolling off down Fifth Avenue.

Even when it was out of sight Vanessa remained standing on the step. She drew her shawl more closely around her, and realized that in spite of the warmth of the day she felt a chill deep inside. She turned and climbed the remaining steps to the front door, her movements slow and uncharacteristically stiff.

She went to the morning room and rang for one of the maids, who brought her a fresh pot of coffee, but even as she sipped the steaming brew the coldness within her would not go away. She told herself that everyone in the family was fond of Miranda. Alison adored the beautiful new governess.

Logan had taken a liking to Miranda, who had done so much for Alison. "I didn't want to say it before," Logan had said only a few nights ago, "but I was starting to worry about the little one. She was so jumpy, and that sleepwalking really had me concerned. Miss Warren's done wonders for her." Even Darren, when he was home for the summer vacation, had approved of Miranda, who had shown a flattering interest in "the menagerie": his two dogs; a battle-scarred, ragged-eared tomcat; a brilliantly colored parrot, and a large lizard. Darren, a sturdy, amiable ten-year-old, had given Miranda the unusual privilege of holding the lizard, and if she was squeamish about it, she made no sign.

"She's kind of nice—for a girl," Darren told his father, who had repeated the remark to Vanessa.

"From a boy of ten that's a high compliment," Logan added.

Now, as she poured a second cup of coffee, Vanessa told herself that things were going as she had hoped they would when she had taken Miranda from the Shelter. The girl had blossomed as she had learned to accept the new, luxurious surroundings, the comforts she had never known before. And why shouldn't Blake drive Miranda—and Alison—down to South Street? It was no more than a small courtesy on his part.

And if Miranda had been pleased by the attention of a handsome young man, already experienced with girls, easy and charming in manner, what was so wrong? . . .

Vanessa's hand shook, so she set down her cup hastily. A handsome young man. That was what Miranda saw when she was with Blake. That was all she saw—and how else could it be? Blake had a way with women, like his father before him. But Blake and Miranda . . . No, it could not, must not, be!

Vanessa began to plan quickly. Kitty was more than

willing for Roxanne to marry Blake; she had made no secret of that. And although Horace would never like Logan or Vanessa, he had cause to be grateful to both of them. Besides, he was practical enough to realize the advantages of a match between his daughter and the heir to the McClintock fortune.

The holiday season would soon be here, the perfect time to make sure that Blake and Roxanne would see a good deal of each other. There would be the usual round of parties, dinners, sleigh riding, ice skating on the lake in Central Park, visits to the theater and the opera.

But in the meantime there was the danger that Blake and Miranda might become too closely involved. She would take steps to prevent that from happening.

The opportunity for separating Blake from Alison's governess came unexpectedly, and Vanessa, tense with apprehension, used all her influence to make sure that it did not slip by. Logan had already made a trip to Washington a few months before to confer with Jeremy Halliwell and several other politicians about the possibility of revolution in Cuba. Logan was still concerned about the effect such a political upheaval would have on the sugar trade down there. Although Logan had admitted to Vanessa that his personal sympathies lay with the revolutionaries, he knew what problems a change in government could present to a ship owner.

Early in October, Logan prepared to make another visit to Washington, where he would be able to get certain information on conditions in Cuba through his strong political connections. But Vanessa suggested that he should send Blake to Washington in his place.

"Blake! What the devil does Blake know about dealing with those politicians? He's smart about business, damn smart for his age, but he doesn't have the experience to deal with—"

"Then isn't it time he learned?" Vanessa interrupted, driven by a fear she scarcely wanted to explore fully, even in her own mind. Blake and Miranda. Blake and his half-sister. "Let him go to Washington," she persisted with an urgency that startled Logan. "He's going to have to get to know those politicians sooner or later. He gets along well with people. And Jeremy would smooth his way, make the introductions."

"Blake's so young," Logan said.

"He is no younger than you were when Abel Bradford first made you master of one of his clipper ships. You had responsibility for the ship, the cargo, and you had authority over the life of every man on board. Surely this trip to Washington is not so great a challenge."

"Look here," he began impatiently, but she cut off his protest.

"Now that you have the shipping empire you've always wanted, your interests are far too wide for you to manage everything. If Blake's to be of help, let him start now."

"After all these years," he said slowly, his eyes revealing his puzzlement, "I still don't understand you, Vanessa. Don't you want to keep Blake here?"

She smiled at him. "Blake's not going to China, only to Washington." She held out her arms to him. "It's you I want here, my love," she told him, grateful that in this, at least, she could speak the truth. She did want Logan beside her.

He smiled. "If you put it that way, how can I refuse?" He drew her into his arms, and his lips brushed hers, then lingered in a kiss that deepened, ardent and demanding.

She clung to him. There was nothing she would not do to hold her family together, to keep the love, the trust, of her husband. As he held her, his strong hands caressing her body, she felt the same sweet passion, the blending of tenderness and excitement that she had felt for him on that first night together.

Blake, obviously proud of his father's confidence in him, departed for Washington within a few days. Now Vanessa felt the tension leave her. She went about making elaborate plans for the holiday season.

If only Blake and Roxanne would agree to announce their engagement during the Christmas holidays, she thought. Since the family had moved to this house here on Fifth Avenue, the Christmas cotillion had become a tradition, and what better time to make the announcement?

Somewhat to Vanessa's surprise, it was Kitty who expressed reservations. "I hope that Blake and Roxanne will marry one day," she said. "But it must be their decision. Remember, they've known each other since they were children. Perhaps it will take time for Blake to see Roxanne as something other than a childhood friend."

Was Kitty thinking of her own forced marriage to Horace? Surely she must know that this was completely different, that Roxanne was in love with Blake. She hinted at this, but Kitty said, "It's Blake I'm concerned about. I know he's fond of Roxanne, but does he love her?"

"I'm sure he does, it's only that he doesn't realize it yet."

Early in December, Blake returned from Washington and Logan expressed his satisfaction with his son's efforts. While Blake and Logan spent hours in the library discussing the best way to proceed with the Cuban sugar trade, or, if it should become necessary, to establish connections with coffee exporters in Haiti and Venezuela, Vanessa went on with her own arrangements.

She encouraged Kitty to hold a masquerade ball, although

Kitty was a bit doubtful, since there were still those who considered such entertainments improper. Roxanne sided with Vanessa, and Kitty gave in. Vanessa was pleased to see how charming Roxanne looked, with her dark hair and eyes. She wore the costume of a Spanish lady, complete with a fine mantilla of silver lace, held in place with a jeweled silver comb. Blake singled her out for several dances, and at midnight, he took her in to supper.

A week later Vanessa invited Kitty and Horace, along with Roxanne and Blake, to a play at Booth's Theater, a splendid new renaissance structure at Sixth Avenue and Twenty-third Street. Since Mr. Booth himself was to appear on stage, tickets were much in demand, and while Logan and Horace spent the intermission discussing business matters, Blake was attentive to Roxanne.

On the morning of the day before the McClintocks' Christmas cotillion, Fifth Avenue lay white and sparkling under a blanket of snow, and soon the clear, crisp air rang with the sound of sleighbells, the laughter of passengers in big, brightly painted sleighs.

Vanessa was busy in the drawing room, overseeing the maids who were arranging spicy-smelling pine boughs, when she heard Blake's voice from the entrance hall.

"Come along, Miranda. You've told me that you've never been out for a sleigh ride, and I know of an inn in Westchester that serves the best oyster stew and beef pie you've ever tasted."

"I ought to stay here with Alison," Miranda protested. "She has a slight cold, and I was going to amuse her by sewing a new dress for one of her dolls."

"Delia can do that," Blake assured her. "Here, fasten your cloak. It's cold out there."

"I should ask your mother."

"She's so busy preparing for tomorrow night's cotillion she won't even know we're gone. And we'll be back by dinnertime." Blake's voice held a persuasive note. "Mother won't mind. She wants you to have some time off to enjoy yourself, and besides, I haven't seen nearly enough of you since I came home from Washington."

Vanessa hesitated, trying to formulate a reason why Miranda should not go with Blake. By the time she came into the hall, she felt a blast of icy air and knew that Blake and Miranda had already left.

She could scarcely go chasing out after them, and if she did and then refused Miranda permission to go with Blake on a sleigh ride, it would appear peculiar, since she had made such a point of treating the girl like one of the family. She turned away from the door and saw Mrs. Skene bustling down the hall. The cook had come to consult with Vanessa about the details of tomorrow night's splendid dinner.

Vanessa had hired a fashionable caterer to provide the special touches—the towering pagoda carved in ice, the elaborate ice cream molds, and fanciful sugar confections, including a ship in full sail—but Mrs. Skene would give her talents to the preparation of more substantial dishes: baked hams, roast suckling pig, venison, and beef. Logan had invited a few of his captains and several young officers, and, as he had warned Vanessa, those men would want hearty foods, "not a lot of cakes and fripperies."

Toward the middle of the afternoon Vanessa could no longer stay in the confines of the house. She went out to visit the caterer on Broadway and made sure that everything would be ready for the ball. She knew that there was no real need to do this, but she was too tense to remain indoors. She lingered, driving from one shop to the next, stopping at a toy shop to buy a miniature circus chariot complete with lions and tigers for Darren and a doll's tea set for Alison.

On the way home she saw that it had started to snow again, and by the time the carriage reached the house, the thick, soft flakes were shutting out her view of Fifth Avenue, turning the other brownstone mansions to vague shapes, with only a gleam from a lighted window here and there. She hurried inside and went upstairs to the nursery, where Alison, nearly over her cold, showed her the dress that Delia had made for one of her many dolls.

"Miranda isn't home yet," Alison announced. Her eyes were round as she looked out the window. "It's snowing awful hard. Do you think she and Blake got lost, Mama?"

Vanessa reassured Alison, fighting down her own panic. If Blake and Miranda "got lost" it would not be in the way Alison meant.

Returning downstairs, Vanessa saw Logan in the hall, handing his wet coat to one of the maids. "We're going to have a blizzard by nightfall," he predicted cheerfully. "Come on, let's go into the library. I want some brandy, and you look as if you could stand some too. You look pale, my love." He took her arm and led the way into the library, with its heavy brown velvet drapes and its rows of books bound in leather and gold. A fire was burning in the ornate marble fireplace, and his favorite brandy had been set out on a tray.

"All right, what will it be, brandy, or would you prefer sherry?"

"Miranda's not back yet," she said, unable to restrain her anxiety even long enough to answer his question. "She and Blake went sleigh riding this morning. I heard him say something about an inn in Westchester."

Logan looked at her in surprise as he handed her a glass of brandy, then took one for himself. "This'll warm you," he said. "I don't want you wearing yourself out arranging for the cotillion. If Mrs. Skene doesn't have time to take care of things like that, I'll hire a housekeeper."

Vanessa heard his words, but they scarcely registered. She sipped the brandy and felt it burning down into her chest, but it did not melt the icy tightness in the pit of her stomach. "They should have been home by now."

Logan drew her down beside him on the sofa close to the fire. "Blake knows how to handle a team," he said with a smile. "And he'll take good care of Miranda. Don't you worry."

"But what if they can't get back tonight?" Vanessa's voice shook with agitation. "What if they're stranded?"

"They can stay overnight at the inn, can't they? Or, if they've already left, they'll find someplace else to stay. There are several inns out along the Bloomingdale Road, and Blake certainly has enough cash with him to pay for a good dinner and a night's lodging." He paused, his eyes searching Vanessa's face. "Good Lord, Vanessa, what is it? You're as jumpy as a scalded cat." Then, slowly, comprehension dawned. "Are you thinking that if those two spend the night at an inn, they might share the same room? What if they do?"

"You don't know what you're saying!"

"Oh, yes I do. Look, Vanessa, Blake's a hot-blooded young man." He grinned. "Comes by it honestly, I'd say. But he's decent enough not to force Miranda."

"I know that. I didn't mean—"

"All right, then. They're attracted to each other. I've noticed it too. And if he takes her to bed, it'll be with her consent. I'm sure of it. Blake's got a way with girls."

Vanessa flinched at Logan's words, at his easy acceptance of this terrible possibility. But how could she blame him? He had no way of knowing—he must never know—the truth.

"But he can't . . . they mustn't—" she began incoherently.

"I don't see what we can do to stop them," Logan said. "We don't even know where they are, and if we did, I wouldn't be about to saddle a horse and go tearing off into a blizzard to go after them. Come to that, I can't understand why you think it would be so wrong."

"Miranda's a governess, a servant," Vanessa said, hating herself for having to make such a distinction but knowing no other excuse to give. "Blake's the heir to a shipping fortune."

Logan stood up and finished his brandy, then poured another glass. "I never thought I'd hear you talking such claptrap," he said, his face hardening. "Kitty might, but not you."

"Such distinctions are important."

"The hell they are. Miranda's a governess. What of it? What were you when you worked in the Bradford house? A companion to Aunt Prudence. Have you made it a point to forget that?"

"You know I haven't."

"I'm beginning to think that there's a lot of things I don't know about you anymore." His voice was tight with anger. "I never thought you'd become a snob."

Surely it was better for Logan to put down her behavior to snobbery than to even guess at the truth. All the same, it hurt her that he should believe she was like those foolish women who, because their husbands had risen to sudden wealth and power during the Civil War, now chose to forget their humble origins.

"Miranda has been brought up a lot more strictly than some of those young ladies I've seen flaunting themselves at parties, looking for a good catch, wiggling their tails around like a lot of trollops looking for a sailor on shore leave. Miranda's not like that. She's bright and she's good-looking. And if she and Blake want each other, there's no reason why they shouldn't marry."

"Blake's going to marry Roxanne. You know that."

"The hell I do! Maybe you and Kitty have cooked something up between you, but my sons will choose their own wives. Oh, I'm not blind, Vanessa. I've seen you pushing Blake and Roxanne together, especially these past few months. And I guess I don't have any objections to Roxanne for a daughter-in-law." He shook his head. "Although I'm damned if I ever thought that weasel Horace would be a part of my family, even by marriage."

"Roxanne's a lovely girl."

"Maybe so, but if Blake prefers Miranda, he can have her with my blessings. I'm not going to object, and neither are you."

Vanessa recognized the seriousness in Logan's voice and knew that he was warning her not to interfere. She fought against the rising hysteria that threatened to engulf her. Logan had never had any patience with tears or emotional outbursts from women. He would listen to reason, though.

"Suppose Miranda did marry Blake," she said carefully, feeling sick at the thought. "How could she be happy if she were not accepted into society, if other ladies snubbed her?"

"She'd have the McClintock money behind her," Logan said with assurance. "Maybe back in the forties and fifties that wouldn't have been enough, but these days it's all changing. Look at us. What did we have when we married? Not even the *Ondine*; that came later. I've never taken the trouble to hide my beginnings from you or anyone else. I never will. And that cellar in the Five Points was a lot worse than the Shelter where Miranda grew up."

"You don't understand."

"Any institution run by ladies like Felicity Bradford and you, my dear, is a decent place. Haven't you been telling me for years that the children at the Shelter get a good, sound education?"

"Yes, but—"

"And I've talked to Miranda. She's got intelligence and taste. And think what she's done for Alison. She'll make a good mother; you can't deny that."

"Logan, you don't—"

"Didn't you bring her here to care for Alison? And treat her like . . . almost like one of the family? I can't understand you. I know you're fond of her."

Fond of her? She loved Miranda as she loved Alison and the boys.

"We don't know. I mean, she is a foundling, a—"

"A bastard, is that what you're trying to say? It's certainly possible, even likely. Is that her fault?"

"No, of course not, but—" He stopped his pacing before the fireplace, put down his brandy glass, and came to stand over Vanessa. "I thought I knew you almost as well as I know myself," he said slowly. "You've always had a warm, generous nature. That's part of the reason I love you."

At any other time his words would have sent joy coursing through her, for Logan did not speak of love easily. Tears filled her eyes, and she turned away but not quickly enough. He sat down beside her again and put his arm around her. "You've got yourself all worked up over this," he said. "I suspect it's because all this socializing has tired you. And you've been running around, preparing for the party tomorrow night." He drew her head down on his shoulder. "As soon as the season's over, why don't we get away together, the two of us. A tour of Europe or a voyage to the West Indies. If the revolution's cooled down, we'll go to Cuba. Otherwise there are so many islands for us to explore. Jamaica, Haiti, Martinique. It's always warm and sunny down there, and we'll bathe in the ocean and make love on the beach."

"It sounds wonderful," she said. But even as she felt his hand stroking her hair, she was looking past him, her eyes on the windows, staring at the heavy flakes that swirled and danced before her blurred gaze.

And she knew with terrible certainty that she would have to take charge of separating Blake and Miranda without any help from Logan. Without his knowledge.

If it was not already too late.

Using her preparations for tomorrow night's cotillion as an excuse, she left Logan's side and for the rest of the afternoon, and later, after dinner, she kept away from him, fearing that she might betray herself. Red and silver ribbons must be looped across the high ceiling of the ballroom; more pine boughs must be put into vases. The elaborate ornaments of glass must be put up carefully. A red carpet must be stretched across the pavement in front of the house tomorrow evening, and would that be possible with all this snow?

Even when Logan, still putting her nervousness down to exhaustion, ordered her to come upstairs to bed, she could not sleep. She lay still, trying to breathe deeply and evenly, to deceive Logan, but long after he had fallen asleep she was still wide awake, the muscles of her body rigid as she stared into the darkness. Only toward morning, when she was finally overcome by exhaustion, did she drop off for a few hours of fitful sleep.

It was nearly noon before Blake and Miranda returned. Vanessa, hearing the sounds of their arrival, hurried to the drawing room door, but they were not aware of her standing there. Miranda had never looked more beautiful, for her cheeks were flushed a rosy pink from the cold and her hazel eyes glowed with golden lights as she stood looking up at Blake. When he helped her off with her cloak his hands lingered on her shoulders.

Vanessa retreated back into the drawing room. She could not yet bring herself to question them, for she was too afraid of what she might discover. Instead, she waited until Miranda went upstairs and Blake joined his father in the library. Then Vanessa went downstairs into the big kitchen, where Mrs. Skene and her helpers were hurrying about, preparing food for the party.

Mrs. Skene looked surprised, and no wonder, since Vanessa did not come down here often. The room was filled with the appetizing smells of roasting meats and tempting pastries. "You hardly touched a thing at breakfast, ma'am," the cook said, her forehead wrinkling in a troubled frown. "And it'll be hours until the party. I hope you'll do justice to lunch. There's soup and nice cold ham and some fresh-baked rolls."

"I'm not hungry," Vanessa began, but Mrs. Skene had been with the family too long to stand on ceremony.

"You sit yourself right down," she ordered. "And have a nice hot cup of tea and a sandwich."

Vanessa obeyed to please her, but although the golden-brown roll was warm and the ham sliced thinly, the way she liked it, she had to force the food down.

And all the time she was remembering Felicity's warning on the day when she had come to hire Miranda.

You are making a mistake. . . . You must consider the consequences. . . .

Chapter 26

In her bedroom Roxanne Widdicomb took a long, admiring look at her reflection in the mirror and smiled with pleasure. Such a lovely new gown to wear to the McClintocks' Christmas ball. She took a few waltz steps and smiled as she saw the shimmer of the white satin skirt, the elaborate train fastened with silver roses. The bodice was edged in silver lace and cut daringly low, to reveal the swell of her rounded breasts. Her hair had been carefully arranged, piled high on her head, and more silver roses glittered among the dark curls.

Papa had grumbled about the expense of the new gown, but, as usual, Mama had won out. Mama always got her own way, Roxanne thought. Hadn't Mama talked Papa into building this fine new house on Madison Avenue?

"We'll have to move somewhere else," Mama had said. And she had been right, for in 1866 Commodore Vanderbilt had announced that he was purchasing the park and all of Hudson Square so that he could put up his huge new Hudson Terminal on the site. Immediately Mama had gone looking for a suitable location for a new home, and had found it here on Madison Avenue, where they had been living for seven years now. The house, though not as large as the McClintocks' mansion, was impressive.

Grandmother Felicity had her own suite of rooms, and she was reasonably well satisfied here, although sometimes she spoke with sadness of the changes she saw around Hudson Square. "It used to be so pretty, with all those trees and shrubs in the park. And now there's nothing but cheap boardinghouses and even a few factories." But she had little time to brood over the past, for she was always busy working for her charities, raising money for the care of homeless children, impoverished wives of seamen, and now she was involved in establishing a home for fallen women.

How, exactly, did one become a fallen woman, Roxanne wondered. Once, when she had ventured to ask, Papa had glared at her, and Mama told her that unmarried girls should not concern themselves with such questions.

Roxanne smiled and pirouetted before her mirror. She would not always be an unmarried girl. If only Blake would hurry and propose to her. She knew that both Mama and Mrs. McClintock were in favor of the match, that they had been arranging occasions at which she and Blake would be together. But for the past few months, since his return from Washington, Blake had been maddeningly remote.

He had danced with her several times at the masquerade ball and complimented her on her costume; he had been attentive and polite when they were together at the opera and the theater. But he had made no attempt to speak with her alone. Roxanne felt a small stirring of doubt. Had Blake met a girl down in Washington, the daughter of a senator or of a congressman?

It didn't matter, she told herself. Tonight, in this beautiful gown, she would make him forget every other girl he had ever met. Her dark eyes grew thoughtful. Suppose the gown were not enough? What more could she do to draw him to her, to get him to propose?

Until now she had remembered the shy, modest manners that she had been taught at school, and by Mama at home. Maybe tonight she would take steps to show him that she had strong feelings, that she was capable of loving him with all her heart. If she could draw him away from the others, if she could get him to kiss her, perhaps that might lead to a proposal.

She whirled about, and the glow of the gaslight on her dark curls and on the silver roses caused her spirits to lift.

In a small, bare room off the infirmary at the Shelter, Dr. Clive Thorne sank wearily into a worn leather chair. He took a sip of coffee left there for him by one of the matrons. It tasted bitter and it was already lukewarm, but at least it might serve to keep him awake for a few more hours. He had not had an unbroken night's sleep for nearly a week now.

The bitter cold and the recent blizzard had caused an increase in the number of patients in the infirmary, and there were always more children who were brought in abandoned, starved, half-frozen.

Only last night a police officer in the neighborhood had carried in a boy and a girl, probably brother and sister, thin, dirty, their clothes and hair infested with lice, and both running high fevers. It was pneumonia, complicated by a condition of semi-starvation. The girl had improved slightly, but the boy was still delirious and fighting for every breath. Another child, a recent arrival, had come down with diphtheria. Thorne had isolated him at once in the hope that the disease would not spread. And there were the usual cases of croup and intestinal infections.

Thorne swallowed his coffee and rubbed the back of his neck, which was tense and aching with fatigue.

He found himself thinking of Miranda Warren. If she were here she would be working beside him, for although she had been hired as a teacher, she had skill at nursing too. She could soothe a frightened or fretful child with a few words and a touch of her hand.

Miranda. Thorne leaned back in his chair, his eyes half-closed. Should he have tried to persuade her to stay on here at the Shelter? Perhaps if he had told her how he felt about her, it might have made a difference.

But it would have been unfair to the girl, who had lived her whole life here, who knew nothing of the world, or of men. If he had reached out to her, had told her how much he had come to care for her, would she have responded? And if she had, would he have taken advantage of her hunger for love?

He stood up and told himself to stop dreaming. The girl was beautiful, and she was fifteen years younger than he was. And those years in China had aged him, as had the attack of cholera, the disease that had nearly killed him. It had claimed Lucy, his young wife, and their unborn child, and had left him dazed and numb with despair.

On the boat coming back to New York he had asked himself why he was still alive and had not cared one way or the other. But later, working here at the Shelter, he realized that he had a purpose to keep him going. He was still a doctor, and there were children who needed him.

He had not thought that he would ever fall in love again, for he did not want that kind of closeness to another person, not after losing his wife. But slowly, gradually, he had been drawn to Miranda, to her gentleness and strength.

He put the thought of Miranda from him with an effort of will and went back to the infirmary to sit with the small boy who was fighting for his life.

"Oh, how charming," Kitty said, seating herself in the bower of potted palms and oleanders arranged at one end of the ballroom. The cotillion was a dance for the young unmarried guests, and the married ladies and their husbands gathered together to watch the festivities. The orchestra began tuning up, and Jeremy Halliwell, who was visiting the city with his wife over the holidays, had volunteered to act as cotillion leader, a role in which he was thoroughly experienced.

On the other three sides of the ballroom, pretty young ladies and well-dressed young men took their places. The air was heavy with the scent of expensive perfumes: heliotrope, Jockey Club, Orange Flowers, and Wood Violet. These mingled with the scent of the pine boughs and the masses of flowers banked against the walls.

Kitty leaned over and tapped Horace on the arm with her ostrich-feather fan. "Horace, we must have a proper ballroom like this one, and soon."

Horace looked glum, but he did not venture to contradict his wife, for, since that time when he had been faced with bankruptcy and had only been saved through Kitty's intervention, the balance of power in the Widdicomb marriage had shifted. Now it was Kitty who gave the orders and Horace who, after a few complaints, allowed her to have her own way.

Felicity, who did not stand in awe of Kitty as Horace did, spoke up. "A larger ballroom? Whatever for?"

"To entertain our guests, Mama."

"Not at another masquerade, I hope," Felicity said. "With a lot of stout, middle-aged females who should have known better, prancing about dressed as Madame Pompadour and Cleopatra. And Horace in that silly powdered wig and those ridiculous leggings—"

Logan stifled a grin.

"Hose, Mama," Kitty corrected her. "Horace wore a doublet and hose."

"Foolishness," Felicity said firmly.

"But you must admit that Blake looked handsome as— What was he, Vanessa dear? Was he Sir Walter Raleigh or Sir Francis Drake?"

"I believe he was—" Vanessa began, but Kitty chattered

on. "At any rate, I'm not thinking about a masquerade, Mama. There are other occasions, far more important, when a family—two families—have reason to celebrate."

"An engagement party?" Felicity demanded. "You'd best wait until Blake and Roxanne make up their minds about that. Roxanne's only a child."

"I agree with you, ma'am," Logan said. "There's plenty of time."

But was there? Vanessa tried to control her agitation. If only Blake and Roxanne would become engaged quickly. After that there would be plenty of time for Miranda to meet a suitable young man, one of the officers who had been hired only a few months before to work on Logan's newest China steamer.

Her thoughts were interrupted when Jeremy, at the opposite end of the room, blew his whistle for the first figure of the cotillion. She looked about for Blake, but he was not seated with the others; instead, he stood in the doorway, which was framed in holly, talking with Dermot Rankin and Silas Pringle.

Jeremy chose eight young people to be the lead couples. He paired off Roxanne with a tall blond young officer from Logan's *Star of the Indies.* The orchestra struck up a waltz, and Roxanne and her partner and six of the others who had been chosen rose and went out onto the floor.

Vanessa cast a hopeful glance at Blake, but he was deep in conversation with his companions and he scarcely glanced at the dance floor. She waited impatiently as the couples whirled and dipped and swayed. At last Jeremy blew his whistle again, and the dancers went to the favor table. Here they picked up the small glittering favors: miniature bells and stars and tiny glass balls. Those on the sidelines waited eagerly to be chosen for the next dance.

Roxanne, with a purposeful look and holding a silver trifle, started for the doorway, and Vanessa sighed with relief. Kitty's daughter had more determination than Vanessa had given her credit for.

But before Roxanne could reach Blake he had turned and was looking down at the wide stairway. A moment later Miranda stood on the threshold of the ballroom. "Who is that?" Vanessa heard a lady whisper from one of the seats in the bower.

"Isn't she . . . the governess? That Miss Warren?" The second speaker sounded affronted, as if a governess had no right to wear such a dazzling gown or to look so striking.

The heavy silk, brought on one of Logan's China steamers, was of a new kind that changed from pale apple green to deepest jade with every movement of Miranda's slender body. It had been made for her by Vanessa's dressmaker a few months before. The design was simple, without any of the crystal or amber beads, the ruffles and panniers, flutings and flouncings, that ornamented the gowns worn by the other young girls tonight. The simplicity of the gown, the modest cut of the bodice, the absence of ornaments, made the other gowns look a little garish by contrast.

Blake hesitated for a moment. It was against the rules of the cotillion for him to choose a partner at this point, and he did not even have a favor in his hand. But he moved quickly, broke off a small sprig of holly from one of the branches around the doorway, and handed it to Miranda. Then, as the orchestra struck up another waltz, he led her out onto the floor with a self-assurance that reminded Vanessa of Logan.

"Shocking," someone said from one of the chairs behind Vanessa's. Now there was an exchange of outraged conversation.

". . . in my day, a governess was happy enough to sit and

watch the dancing. . . ."

". . . the girl should know her place. . . ."

". . . far too indulgent with the hired help. . . ."

To Vanessa, who sat motionless, this waltz went on and on endlessly. Miranda looked up into Blake's face, and they might have been the only two people on the dance floor. When Jeremy blew his whistle again, Blake and Miranda were approaching the bower. And then, somehow, Vanessa was on her feet. "Miss Warren!" Her voice was louder, sharper than she had intended, and all at once the other matrons and their husbands were silent.

Miranda was looking at Blake with a dazed expression, her face glowing with happiness, her hazel eyes soft.

"Miss Warren, I have something to say to you."

Miranda blinked like someone waking from a blissful dream. "Yes, Mrs. McClintock?"

"You are to go to the nursery and remain there with Alison."

"She is sound asleep," Miranda began.

"She was overexcited," Vanessa said coldly. "She should not have been permitted to watch the guests arriving."

"Oh, but surely one of the servants can stay with her," Blake began.

Now the guests were staring avidly, eager to hear Mrs. McClintock put this pretty little upstart in her place.

"Miss Warren is paid to look after Alison," Vanessa heard herself saying. It was cruel, reprimanding Miranda before all these people, shaming her, and, worse yet, destroying her evening of happiness. Cruel, but necessary. "You have your duties here, Miss Warren. Go and attend to them."

Miranda went white, and Vanessa feared that the girl might faint. But then, somehow, Miranda managed to recover herself. She curtsied to Vanessa. "I'm sorry, Mrs.

McClintock. I . . ." She turned away and walked quickly to the stairway, her head high, her shoulders squared.

"Mother, you should not have—" Blake began.

Vanessa cut him off. "Miss Warren may be excused for not knowing the rules of the cotillion," she said. "You have no such excuse."

"The rules of the cotillion! Oh, for . . ." Blake restrained himself with an effort. The orchestra broke into a polka, and this time Roxanne made her opportunity. She stood before Blake and pressed a tiny glittering favor into his hand. For a moment Vanessa thought he might refuse to dance with her, but she had already put a small, gloved hand on his arm, and his training took over as he bowed and led her out onto the floor.

Only then did Vanessa turn to Logan, and she caught her breath, seeing the anger in his face. He spoke softly, but his voice slashed out at her like the crack of a whip.

"You had no right to do that, Vanessa," he said. His gray eyes were cold. "You will go to Miranda and tell her that you are sorry."

Vanessa stood, unable to move from the spot. "Logan, you don't understand—" she began.

"Shall I go with you?" He spoke with outward courtesy but she feared that if she did not obey, he would be fully capable of dragging her out of the ballroom before all these people.

Excusing herself, she fled from the room with the strains of the polka echoing down the stairs behind her.

She had meant no harm when she had brought Miranda into this house; she had only wanted to have her daughter near her, to make up for all the years of separation and perhaps to arrange a suitable marriage. And now she had hurt Miranda deeply and had caused Logan to turn against her in anger.

She found Miranda outside the door of the nursery and she realized that the girl had paused here to regain her self-control before going to Alison.

"Wait a moment," Vanessa said. "Please come with me. We must talk."

She led the way into her small boudoir off the master bedroom. Seating herself on a bamboo sofa, she motioned to Miranda to take a seat nearby.

The silence between them grew until Vanessa began to find it unbearable. How could she explain the reason for her outburst in the ballroom?

"Mrs. McClintock, I don't understand. You said that I might attend the cotillion, you had this dress made for me and then you . . . you shamed me in front of Mrs. Bradford, in front of all your guests. And Blake."

The words came swiftly. "You are not to have anything more to do with Blake. You must keep away from him for your own sake, and for his."

"Because I'm a servant, because you don't think I'm good enough."

"Your feelings for Blake, whatever you believe them to be, can bring you nothing but pain. Believe me, Miranda. Blake is going to marry Roxanne Widdicomb."

"There is no engagement," Miranda said. "Blake told me so."

"But there will be, and soon. Probably before the holidays are over. It is a suitable match."

"Even if he doesn't love her?"

"He is fond of her. They've known each other for years. Our two families . . . Miranda, I know this isn't easy for you. But you must accept the fact that you have no future with my son. You must forget your feelings for him, now—before it's too late."

"It is already too late," Miranda said.

Chapter 27

"Too late?" Vanessa stared at the slender young girl in her green silk gown. "That night when you and Blake were stranded by the blizzard, did you—" She did not want to know the truth, but she could avoid it no longer.

Miranda's hazel eyes were steady. "If you want to find out if Blake and I spent the night together, no, we did not."

"But you were at the inn, the two of you, all that night."

"We weren't the only two people stranded there, and the inn has only a few rooms for rent. The ladies shared the bedrooms, three or four of us in each one. The gentlemen were bedded down in the dining room on cots and blankets."

"But Miranda, you said it was already too late."

"I am still a virgin, if that's what you mean," Miranda said with dignity. "But it is too late for me to forget about Blake, because we love each other."

Vanessa felt a measure of relief. "Oh, my dear, you are so inexperienced. I know that you believe you love my son, but that is only because you've had no chance to meet other men." She forced herself to speak lightly. "Why, there are a half dozen young girls who have been attracted to Blake, infatuated with him."

"I am not infatuated," Miranda said. "I love him, and I always will. I did not plan for it to happen, but now that it has, can't you try to accept me not as a governess but as a future daughter-in-law?"

"I can't. Miranda, it is impossible. Even if Blake shares your feelings—"

"He does. I'm sure of it. He has not said that he loves me, but when we danced together tonight, when he looked at me, I knew."

"Even so, you must give your word—you must swear to me—that you will do everything possible to convince Blake you don't love him."

"I can't! You've been good to me, and I am grateful. But surely you don't expect me to agree to your demands, not in something that . . . Blake is my whole life! He always will be."

She's so young, Vanessa thought sadly and so hungry for love, for belonging. Oh, Miranda . . .

"You are my employer. I've done my best to please you, to care for Alison as you would want me to. But you must understand, you have no right to control the rest of my life, to order me to stop loving the only man I can ever care for."

"If you are to remain in this house—"

"Then I'll leave now, tonight. I'll find another position here in the city. I'll go back to teach in the Shelter if I must. But I will go on seeing Blake."

"Even if I forbid it?"

Miranda's voice was unsteady now. "Am I so unworthy that you can't accept me into your family? Is it because I have no family of my own, no background, no money? I've no way of knowing who my parents were, but isn't it possible that they were married? Most of the children at the Shelter are illegitimate—I know that but surely not all. Won't you even give me the chance to prove to you that I can be a good wife to Blake?"

Because she still hesitated to tell the truth, knowing that it would shatter Miranda, she forced herself to keep up the pretense that she had decided upon. "You will ruin Blake; you will make him an outcast. And he will come to hate you for it."

"I don't believe you. Blake could never—"

"He is my son. I know him. He is ambitious, like his father, and if you destroy his chances for advancement, if you shut him off from his friends, you'll be asking him to make more of a sacrifice than he's capable of. If you love him as you say you do, surely you would not make him risk his whole future."

Miranda was silent, and Vanessa knew that her words, cruel as they had been, had made an impression. "I would never hurt Blake in any way," she said at last.

"Then you'll agree to—"

"I can't. I want to be his wife. I want that more than anything. But if I have no other choice, I'll do what I must, so long as we can be together. You can't stop me from being his mistress once I'm no longer living in this house. No one condemns a man for keeping a mistress, and as for my reputation, what does that matter? As you've said, I have no family, no social standing, in any case."

Miranda was headstrong and passionate as she herself had been at that age. As Ross Halliwell had been when he had defied his father's wishes and had become an artist. And Vanessa realized with mounting fear that there really was no way that she could prevent Miranda from becoming Blake's mistress once the girl was out of this house. No way but the one she had tried so hard to avoid. Until this moment she had deluded herself into believing that she could keep the whole truth from Miranda and still manage to break up the relationship between her daughter and Blake. Now she knew that she must use her only remaining weapon, and she shrank from the thought of how it could change not only Miranda's life but her own, how it could destroy the whole family.

"I don't care what other people think of me. Their rules don't matter."

"There are other rules," Vanessa said. Oh, if only Ross could be here now to help her, to make Miranda understand. No, this was something only she could do, and she must do it quickly, before she lost her courage. "You think I can't understand what you are feeling," she said. "But I can. I do. Only now I have to ask for your understanding, Miranda. Years ago, when Logan was away on a voyage to China—he was master of the *Sea Dragon* then, and he was setting up his trade in Canton—I was left alone here in the city. For nearly two years. And I . . . There was another man. Someone I had known even before I met Logan—Captain McClintock. A fine, sensitive man who cared for me deeply. That man was your father, my dear."

It took a moment for the full implication of her words to sink in, and then Miranda cried out, half rose, and then sank back into her chair. "My father—"

"He doesn't know about you. He went away before I learned that I was pregnant."

"Even when you knew, you kept the truth from him?"

"He would have wanted me to leave my husband, and I could not do that. Because there was Blake, and because . . . I still loved Logan. We'd had our differences, and he'd done things to hurt me, but it didn't matter. By the time Logan had returned from China, you had been born, and I had placed you in the Shelter."

"You abandoned me. . . ."

"There was no other way," Vanessa said. "I've told you how it was."

"You've told me that you loved Captain McClintock and yet you gave yourself to another man, like any common slut. I don't believe you. If you had really loved your husband, you would never have turned to another man, never."

"You are too inexperienced to understand that there is

more than one kind of love for a woman. You know so little of the world, growing up as you did in the Shelter."

"You should have left me there! Why didn't you leave me alone?"

"I had reasons. Believe me. I was concerned about your future, and I wanted you to have an opportunity to make a suitable marriage. And you still can. I know it will take time for you to get over your feelings for Blake, but when you do—"

"I'll never marry anyone."

Vanessa would have protested, but she realized the futility of trying to convince Miranda that there was a future for her, with marriage and children. Later, perhaps, when Miranda had adjusted to the shock she had received, that would be time enough.

"I had another reason for bringing you here," Vanessa said. "I wanted you with me, if only for a little while, because you are my daughter. You are as dear to me as Alison. I wanted you to share the comfort, the luxury of this house, to wear pretty clothes and have a room of your own and . . . Felicity Bradford tried to caution me, but even she could not have foreseen that you and Blake—"

"Mrs. Bradford knows?"

"She does. And Delia too. They are the only two who do know, because I needed their help when I was pregnant with you, and when you were born."

"You've kept this a secret from everyone else, even Captain McClintock?"

In spite of the warmth of the small room, the glowing fire close by, Vanessa felt an icy touch that started in the pit of her stomach and spread through her.

"He must never know. Oh, Miranda, no matter how you feel about me, you must promise me, I beg you—"

"Do you think I would ever tell him, or anyone? He's been kind to me since the day I came into this house. Why should I want to hurt him? He won't find out the truth from me. I promise you. No one ever will."

"Miranda—"

The girl's voice shook with anger and revulsion.

"It's bad enough that I know you for what you really are." Vanessa caught the rising note of hysteria, saw the fixed stare in her daughter's eyes, and she was frightened for Miranda. "You know," Miranda was saying in a strange, tight voice, "a long time ago, back in the shelter, Dolly—she was a girl who had the cot next to mine—she told me that her mother was a whore. I . . . didn't know what that meant, so Dolly explained to me. And even then I didn't believe her. I thought that it might be true about her mother, but not about mine. I made myself believe that my mother was different, a lady who had been forced to give me up because . . . Oh, I invented all kinds of fairy tales. But now I know the truth."

"What do you know? Miranda, after the guests have gone home, after you've had a chance to rest, we'll talk again quietly, the two of us. I must make you understand."

"I understand," Miranda said in that same strange voice. "I understand that my mother is no better than Dolly's, worse maybe. Because Dolly's mother did what she had to do to survive, down there in the Five Points, in Paradise Square. But you! You had Captain McClintock and a house on Gramercy Park. I don't know the word for a woman like you. I don't know any word bad enough to call you. I only know I'd rather have anyone for a mother but you."

Miranda stood up, her slender body shaking under the folds of green silk. Vanessa held out a hand to her, but she pushed it away, and, lifting her skirt, she ran out of the room.

It was no use to go after her now, Vanessa realized.

Miranda needed time to be alone, to take the full impact of their talk, to try to come to terms with the truth.

Later, when the cotillion was over, when the last guests were gone, or perhaps tomorrow morning, she would go to her daughter, and make her understand about that long-ago summer.

Miranda went straight to her room, moving like an automaton, stunned and sickened. She walked to the window, and her numbed mind took in the fact that it had stopped snowing. She stared down at the circle of light made by the streetlamp on the surface of the snow-covered sidewalk. White and silver, it was, like Roxanne's ball gown. Roxanne was pretty. Roxanne would make a suitable wife for Blake.

Miranda went to the closet and took out a cloak, the first that came to hand. It was heavy and made of dark-green wool. Carrying it over her arm, she left the room, taking nothing else with her, not the small trunk that she had brought when she had come to the McClintock home, not the carpetbag that Mrs. McClintock had bought for her when they had gone to Newport, not even the money she had saved from her salary and had tucked away in one of the bureau drawers.

On her way downstairs she passed two of the maids, and one of them started to speak to her, but she did not listen or even pause. She had to get out of this house at once.

She crossed the entrance hall, with its holiday decorations: loops of silver ribbon, glittering Christmas bells, vases filled with evergreen branches, with holly, with masses of hothouse flowers. She tugged at the handle of the front door, and then she felt the icy chill of the December night enveloping her. She welcomed the clean, cold air as she descended the front steps.

Once on the pavement below, she caught her breath, feeling the cold through the soles of her green leather dancing slippers. The wind tugged at her hair and she put up her hood with a mechanical gesture.

She moved like a sleepwalker, going down Fifth Avenue without the slightest idea of her destination. The sidewalks in front of these huge mansions had been cleared of snow, but her slippers were not meant for walking outdoors, and soon her feet and ankles were numb with cold. She kept going, her eyes blank, her thoughts turned inward.

Bits of her conversation with Mrs. McClintock—how could she think of the woman as her mother—kept coming back to her.

There is more than one kind of love for a woman.

That had been nothing more than a feeble excuse to explain away a wrong for which there could never be an explanation.

Miranda remembered all those visits that Mrs. McClintock had made to the Shelter over the years. Had the woman ever given her the slightest sign that there might be any connection between them? Never, Miranda thought bitterly, except perhaps that time when Mrs. Bradford had sent for her to come to the office, the day when Miranda, pleased by the attention and praise from the beautiful, smartly dressed Mrs. McClintock, had offered her the sampler. What was the verse that had been embroidered on the square of linen? Something out of the Bible, Miranda thought.

What were the words, though?

Who can find a virtuous woman?
For her price is far above rubies.

A virtuous woman. How proud Miranda had been that

day when Mrs. McClintock had praised her on the neatness of her stitching and had accepted the sampler as a gift.

Now Miranda had reached a stretch of the avenue where the snow had not been cleared away, and she sank into the frigid white blanket up to her ankles. She kept on going, only pausing every few blocks to empty the snow from her slippers. Once when she stopped she found herself looking up at the looming walls of the Fifth Avenue reservoir, a massive structure of granite that covered four acres of ground between Fortieth and Forty-second streets. She paused and thought of how it would feel to climb up to the top of the wall and to drop down into the icy water. No, there were guards on duty even at this hour, and she might be seen and stopped, perhaps sent back to the McClintock house, to the woman who called herself her mother.

She moved on again, heading south along the avenue, her mind confused. Had Mrs. McClintock ever felt any love for her?

You are as dear to me as Alison.

Another lie, Miranda thought bitterly. But then, why had Mrs. McClintock allowed her to be born? Even during the months that Miranda had lived in the McClintocks' home she had learned something about the outside world; she had overheard gossip and had even seen the house of Madame Restell, who called herself a "female physician" but whose fortune had come from her services as an abortionist. Many of her clients, it was whispered, were well-known society ladies. And there were countless other abortionists who also did a flourishing business in the city, who advertised their trade openly in the newspapers.

Why had Mrs. McClintock chosen to give birth to a child conceived out of wedlock? Why? Was it possible that she had really felt some fondness for Miranda's father?

No, she could not allow herself to weaken, to forgive. She might have accepted the knowledge that Alison was her sister, Darren her younger brother. But Blake was her brother too. She shuddered, remembering how she had allowed him to kiss her for the first time, during the drive back from the inn, after the blizzard.

She would never see Blake again, she thought, stumbling on through the icy night. Few people were abroad at this hour, and those who were did not linger to look at her or question her. Most of the houses were dark now, and silent, but not all of them, for there were a number of holiday parties in full swing, with candles glowing in curtained windows, and here and there a bit of music, a waltz, a polka, or reel came floating out when a door was opened briefly.

Washington Square stood quiet and aloof, still surrounded with the handsome, dignified houses of those well-to-do New Yorkers who had refused to follow the march of the city up along Fifth Avenue. Miranda saw a couple leaving one of these houses, and she heard the light, carefree laughter of a girl whose escort was holding her arm, helping her down the steep front steps. The door closed behind them, and Miranda caught a glimpse of a holly wreath fastened to the outside.

Blake had given her a sprig of holly for a cotillion favor. How long ago had it been? She turned away from the square, and gradually she found herself in a maze of noisy, shabby streets lined with barrooms and concert saloons and sporting houses. Miranda was indifferent to the few painted women who still trailed their bedraggled finery along the pavement, to the men who stumbled past, reeking of alcohol. She did not notice the sign that marked the corner of Mulberry Street. Even if she had, she would not have felt uneasy. She was unaware of her surroundings, moving without plan or destination. She turned the corner of Mulberry Street and now she was on Houston Street, a few feet from Harry Hill's Concert Saloon, one of the most notorious dance houses in New York. She stared at the huge, red and blue glass lantern that identified the place, and she heard the shrill laughter of the "pretty waiter girls" who were the great attraction here. From the dance hall on the second floor came the blare of loud, raucous music.

She leaned against the wall, near the door, and realized dimly that she would not be able to go on much longer, for she had lost one of her slippers somewhere in the snowy street, and her body was beginning to ache with cold and exhaustion.

She stumbled forward and collided with two well-dressed young men who had come out of the saloon, talking and laughing. "Look here, Fred," said the shorter of the two who was stocky and fair-haired. "What's your hurry sweetheart?"

The other young man, tall and rangy, sounded impatient with his companion. "Haven't you had enough for one night, Jerry? We're going to be in the city for a week. Let's get back to the hotel now."

The fair-haired young man called Jerry laughed. "She's different—take a look at her." He caught hold of Miranda's arm, and she made no move to resist, even when he said, "I'll bet she's got a good shape under that cloak," and pulled the garment open. "What did I tell you? A little beauty. Come on, sweetheart. You don't have to stay out here in the cold. We'll take you up to our hotel and send out for a bottle of wine to warm you up."

"Stop it!" Fred ordered sharply. He peered into Miranda's face. "She's no streetwalker. She looks sick, or maybe drugged. But she isn't wearing paint on her face, and she's not dressed like—"

"What other kind of girl would be loitering down here at this hour of the night?" Jerry said, but he sounded uncertain.

Fred ignored him. "What's wrong, miss?"

She swayed, and Fred put his arm around her to support her. "Are you ill?"

"I . . ." Miranda's voice sounded weak and faraway.

"Where do you live? We'll get you home if you'll tell us where you want to go."

"I don't know," Miranda whispered.

"You must have a home. How can we help you if you won't give us the address?"

Some instinct told her that this man was trying to be kind. She searched her mind. "My address," she repeated.

A hansom cab was moving slowly along the street, the driver looking for fares from Harry Hill's and the other concert saloons nearby. "Get that cab," Fred ordered his friend. "Now, miss, please, where do you live?"

From somewhere in her mind she remembered a man's voice, kind and concerned, like Fred's. "You can always come back to the Shelter, Miranda."

The cab pulled up to the curb. "The Shelter," she said faintly. "The Shelter for Homeless Infants. On Houston Street on the corner of Wooster."

"You don't look like any infant to me, sweetheart," Jerry said.

"Shut up, you idiot," Fred told him. "Help me get her into the cab."

The warmth inside the cab made her feel even more lightheaded than before. She slumped against Fred's shoulder as he gave the driver the address, and then the cab was moving along Houston Street, block after block, the sound of the wheels muffled by the snow. She had no idea how long it was before they pulled up in front of the tall, narrow brick building. "We'll be in plenty of trouble if she's given us the wrong address," Jerry said. Then Fred was helping her up the steps, half carrying her. "Waking up the house at this hour," Jerry went on.

The sound of the knocker, a silence, and then the knocker again. The door was swinging open now and she squinted, temporarily blinded by the gaslight in the hallway.

"Good Lord! Miranda!"

"You know this girl?"

"Certainly I know her. What happened to her?"

"We don't know. Found her out in front of Harry Hill's place. She didn't say where she lived at first and then she gave us this address."

Somehow Miranda stumbled forward a few steps before her legs gave way. A moment later Clive Thorne caught her in his arms and carried her inside.

Chapter 28

After her talk with Miranda, Vanessa had longed to shut herself up in her bedroom, to see no one, to try to come to terms with her daughter's anger and her own guilt but she knew that she could not follow her impulse to withdraw in silence. She had other duties, other responsibilities. She stood up, took a long, steadying breath, and returned to the ballroom.

She felt as if days had gone by since she had left the crowded, brightly lit room, but it must have been less than an hour, for the cotillion was only now coming to a close. She looked about for Logan, but she could see him nowhere. If only all these people would go home, if only the house could be left in stillness; instead, as the orchestra finished playing the last notes of a polka, enhanced for the holiday season with the merry jingling of sleigh bells, Vanessa remembered that it was now time for supper. She looked about in desperation. Surely Logan, no matter how angry he had been a short while ago, would not forget his duty to his guests. Surely he would not shame her by leaving her to lead them into dinner alone.

No, there he was now, coming toward her, taking her arm. She looked at him hopefully, but he did not return her forced smile. "Forgive me," he said, his voice cold and distant. "I've been down in the library with Silas and Blake. And Dermot Rankin. Silas had a few ideas about improvements to be made on the new steamer."

The orchestra was playing softly now, and the guests began to pair off to go into the section of the ballroom that had been set aside for supper. The caterer and his assistants had outdone themselves, Vanessa thought. The pagoda carved in ice stood five feet high, glittering under the light from the chandeliers. Guests were murmuring with pleasure as they saw the confectionery pieces spread before them: the clipper ship in full sail, the steamer with real smoke coming out of the stacks, through some complicated means that Vanessa did not understand. The rich fragrances of baked ham, of turkey, of venison, made her feel slightly sick.

The effect on the people around her was quite different, however, and she saw Silas Pringle a few minutes later holding a generously laden plate. He came over, a wide grin on his weatherbeaten face. "Sorry I kept this husband of yours downstairs talking business, ma'am," he said. "We were discussing changes to be made in the design of the *Gazelle.* A fine ship, she'll be, and the fastest McClintock steamer so far. And there'll be elegant cabins for the passengers too. A lot better than the ones on the *Ondine*, right, Logan?"

"Passengers expect a lot more comfort these days," Logan said. "And we'll give it to them."

Silas nodded and applied himself to his food with enthusiasm. "Quite a spread," he said, watching the guests crowding around the long buffet table. "But I can't say the confectioner knew much about clippers when he made that thing. It certainly looks handsome, though," he added quickly. But Logan made no reply and instead turned to Vanessa.

"Is Miranda going to come down here for supper?"

"No, I don't think so."

"I'm not surprised," Logan said. "You've spoken to her?"

"Yes, Logan. I—"

He nodded briefly, then turned away and went to speak with a group of male guests at the far end of the room.

"Talking about the Panic, I'll wager," Silas said. "All this speculation these past few years. Couldn't last. You can be thankful Logan was one of those who saw this blowup coming. He had better sense than to go into debt, to overextend his business like a lot of the others did."

Silas went on and Vanessa nodded or made a brief remark from time to time, although her thoughts were elsewhere. Logan had told her back in September of the closing of Jay Cooke's powerful banking house, the result of unwise speculation in the Northern Pacific Railroad. Because of Logan's astute and conservative handling of his shipping business, he had not been damaged, and since he also controlled the Bradford-Widdicomb line, keeping a tight rein on Horace's activities, the Widdicombs, too, had escaped disaster. They were fortunate, for by now at least five thousand businesses had been wiped out.

"You and Logan are lucky," Silas was saying. "Plenty of people are having a rough time of it and will be even worse off during these next few years."

Later, after Silas had moved on, Felicity came over to Vanessa. She looked closely at Vanessa and sighed.

"You've told Miranda?"

Vanessa nodded, unable to speak. She was seeing Miranda's white, stricken face, the disillusionment in her eyes.

"Perhaps it is for the best, my dear," Felicity began.

"She will never forgive me—never!"

"She is young. In time, she will come to understand."

"And Logan—"

"He loves you," Felicity assured her. "He can't see why you acted as you did tonight, and he must never know the real reason, but he—"

Felicity was forced to stop short as Kitty and Horace came over to join them. Kitty had put on weight during these last few years, and she looked plump and matronly in her elaborate gown of dark-blue taffeta.

"Vanessa, you're so pale," Kitty said. "Horace, do bring a glass of champagne for her."

Horace obeyed. Vanessa sipped at the champagne, hoping that it would dull the edge of pain inside. Instead, everything looked somehow sharper, the colors unnaturally vivid; the chatter of the guests sounded too loud.

"You certainly put that young woman, that Miss Warren, in her place," Kitty was saying. "And about time, if you'll forgive me for saying it. You pampered her outrageously, and I suppose that it was only natural that she should get above herself. That gown! Really, she did not buy that out of her salary."

"My dressmaker made it for her," Vanessa said.

"Oh, but my dear, what were you thinking of? If you treat your staff that way, even with the kindest of intentions, you'll only fill them with a lot of notions that will make them unhappy. And you really must have a talk with Blake. It was thoughtless of him to encourage the girl."

"Kitty, be quiet." Felicity spoke sharply, and Kitty stared at her mother, blinked, opened her mouth, and closed it again. Never had her mother used that tone with her before.

"Miss Warren's a good-looking little creature," Horace remarked. "She has a fine shape, and she carries herself like a lady."

If only she could tell the truth to everyone here, Vanessa thought miserably. If only she could claim Miranda as her daughter. She had to silence Horace, to change the topic of conversation.

"What a becoming gown Roxanne is wearing tonight," she said.

Horace glanced down the length of the table to the alcove where Roxanne was having her supper, with Blake beside her.

"Becoming?" Horace said. "Should think it would be. All the way from Worth's in Paris. Why she could not have found a suitable dress at A. T. Stewart's, I don't know."

"Naturally you don't," Kitty said calmly. "Men can't be expected to understand such matters." She smiled at Vanessa. "Don't you agree?" she asked.

"What? . . . Oh, yes, indeed."

Kitty sent Horace back to the table to bring her another helping of lobster salad, and Vanessa found herself thinking that in a few years Kitty would be really stout. Sadly she remembered how light-footed and dainty Kitty had been all those years ago at the birthday ball in the house on Hudson Square. She thought of Kitty in Logan's arms among the flowering plants and shrubs of the conservatory.

She looked over at Roxanne and Blake. Perhaps they would marry in time. But what about Miranda?

After supper the orchestra played for the dancers again. Vanessa danced with Dermot Rankin, with Jeremy Halliwell, and at last with Logan. But Logan held her stiffly and scarcely spoke to her at all.

And when, at last, the guests began to take their leave, there was still no immediate respite for Vanessa, who had to stand with Blake and Logan on one side of the ballroom, to say good night, and to acknowledge gracefully the endless stream of compliments on the decor, on her gown, on the originality of the ice pagoda on the buffet table. If only Logan would turn to look at her, really look at her, or if he would press her hand as he usually did on such occasions, as if to remind her that her duties as hostess were nearly over for the evening, that soon they would be together in the huge mandarin bed.

Instead, during a lull in the procession of departing guests, he spoke to Blake. "I want to get down to the shipyard at a reasonable hour. Why don't we skip breakfast and have something to eat down on South Street?"

"It's nearly morning now," Vanessa protested.

"So it is," Logan said. "No matter—there's no need for you to rise early."

Then it was over, the last of the guests had gone, and Vanessa lay in the darkness beside her husband. But he made no move to touch her, to draw her into his arms. Had he decided to leave early to avoid having breakfast with her?

Even after his breathing told her that he was asleep, she remained wide awake, waiting for morning. Should she go to Miranda as soon as it was light? No, better to allow the girl to rest, to have time to herself.

It was nearly noon when Vanessa, unable to restrain herself any longer, went to the nursery to find Miranda and saw Delia there instead. "Miz Miranda ain' been in here yet," Delia said. "Guess she tired out fum all duh dancin'."

Vanessa hurried across the hall and knocked softly. Then, when she received no answer, she knocked harder. She hesitated, then turned the knob. The bed had not been slept in. She hurried to the closet. The door was open, and Miranda's dresses were all there. Even so, she knew what had happened, for Miranda's heavy woolen winter cloak was gone.

Vanessa questioned the servants, and Bridget, one of the new maids, remembered having seen Miranda going downstairs late last night. "I started to ask her where she was goin' at that hour in her cloak an' all, but she didn't say a word. She looked strange."

"Strange?" Vanessa repeated.

"Like she didn't really see me."

By late afternoon Vanessa was close to desperation. Should she notify the Metropolitans? Or should she wait for Logan to return? Let him be angry with her—let him say whatever he wanted to—so long as he was beside her to advise her as to what she should do. She thought about taking the carriage down to South Street and was preparing to have it sent around when the messenger came with a note from Felicity, saying that Miranda was at the Shelter.

Weak with relief, Vanessa sank down on the chair in the reception hall and carefully reread the letter. Miranda had arrived chilled and exhausted but not ill, according to Dr. Thorne. She had been brought to the Shelter in a cab by two young men, visitors to the city who had found her wandering about in a state of shock in front of Harry Hill's Concert Saloon.

Vanessa felt her stomach lurch, for she knew the name of the place and its reputation. Even respectable ladies gossiped about Harry Hill's place, and preachers delivered sermons against this "den of iniquity" at West Houston Street.

Miranda had not been molested, Felicity went on to say, but she added that the girl was still dazed, unable to take care of herself, unwilling to speak to anyone. It would be better, Felicity said, if Vanessa made no attempt to see Miranda for the time being, and if she did what she could to keep Blake away too.

On the day after Christmas, Vanessa went to visit Felicity, and the two women sat in the parlor of the third-floor suite, which had been set aside by Kitty for her mother's use. Felicity poured the tea and offered Vanessa a plate of small sandwiches.

"I wanted to come sooner, but I had to go through the motions of celebrating, if only for Alison's sake. She's so upset. She keeps asking me over and over why Miranda left. She scarcely looked at her presents."

"And the others?" Felicity asked.

"Logan and Blake both believe that Miranda left because of the way I spoke to her in the ballroom on the night of the cotillion."

"Better that way," Felicity said. "Do drink your tea while it is hot. And try one of the sandwiches. I don't suppose you've eaten properly since Miranda disappeared."

"Don't fuss," Vanessa said impatiently. "I'm perfectly all right."

"You don't look it. Remember, you have Logan to think about, and your family."

"Miranda is—"

"She is being looked after. Dr. Thorne is taking excellent care of her."

"But you said—in your note—that she was not ill. You told me—"

"She is not ill, in the usual sense. But she has remained in bed in a kind of apathy. She scarcely speaks, and only Dr. Thorne can get her to eat. The only time she has shown the slightest emotion has been when I tried to persuade her to allow you to come and visit her. And then she . . ."

"Go on," Vanessa said. She had gone to the Shelter immediately after she had received Felicity's note, and had been turned away by one of the matrons. Blake, too, had tried to see Miranda, on Christmas afternoon, and had also been unsuccessful.

"She does not want to see any member of your family, and

she becomes quite irrational when anyone tries to persuade her. I know it's difficult for you to accept, my dear, but Dr. Thorne has had considerable experience, not only with illnesses of the body but also—"

"Oh, God! You can't mean that Miranda—that her mind has been afflicted."

"She's suffered a terrible shock. Try to understand. Her upbringing has been strict, perhaps overstrict. She might have been able to accept the fact that you are her mother, that she was born out of wedlock. But her feelings for Blake, those she cannot accept, and so she has withdrawn. She has detached herself from all that happened to her while she was in your home, and has returned to the one place where she feels safe."

"But what if she goes on this way? What if she remains withdrawn, if she—"

"We must give her time," Felicity said. "We must hope that she will find the strength to sustain her, to bring her back."

Felicity smiled and took Vanessa's hand in hers.

"Surely you don't expect me to stand by while my daughter withdraws into a world of her own, away from reality, from . . ."

She could not bring herself to go on, to speak her deepest fear aloud.

To her surprise, Felicity's lips curved in the trace of a smile. "I do not believe that Dr. Thorne will allow that to happen," she said.

Miranda lay on her cot in her room at the Shelter. Sometimes, when she turned her head she saw the empty cot beside her own. Where had the other teacher gone? What was her name? It was as if Miranda's mind were wrapped in a kind of protective darkness.

Lena. Lena Currie. A stout young woman who had also taught here at the Shelter. Had Lena gone out into the city to find other employment? Miranda withdrew from any thought of the city outside. Beyond the four walls of this room lay something ugly, frightening. Here she was safe.

She looked up as the door opened. It was Clive Thorne. He would urge her to eat and she would try, to please him. Raising herself from her pillow, she saw that he was not carrying a tray this time. And his face was somehow different; his mouth looked stern. "I want you to get up and get dressed, Miranda. At once."

"No! I won't see that woman, I won't."

"If you mean Mrs. McClintock, she is not here."

"Blake, then?" She shrank back against the pillow, as if faced with a physical threat. Clive Thorne did not miss her movement or her expression.

"He is not here either. And I have given orders that they are not to try to see you unless you ask them to visit you. I don't know what happened to you in their home, and I don't wish to know. But they will not trouble you, so you need not worry about that. I do want you up and dressed, however. I need your help in the infirmary at once."

"No, I can't."

"You can and you will. Miranda, you are not ill."

"You don't understand."

"I know that you have no fever, that you have not been physically injured. There's work for you to do and you will do it, or you will leave the Shelter. Today."

She was shaken by the abrupt change in his manner. He might have been a hospital resident giving orders to a student nurse. "There are other teachers who can help—and the matrons."

"Several of them are away for the holidays, and the rest are already badly overworked."

"Holidays?"

"The day before yesterday was Christmas Day."

Christmas. She closed her eyes as if to shut out the vivid images that were crowding into her mind: pine boughs in tall vases, a ballroom filled with guests and decorated with holly and silver ribbon, a pretty girl in a white dress ornamented with silver roses.

Now Clive Thorne was beside her, his hand closing on her shoulder, his strong fingers biting into her flesh.

"I have an infirmary full of sick children downstairs. I need more help. I need you down there, Miranda."

She tried to bury her face in the pillow, but she heard him say, "Sit up, damn it!"

And somehow she obeyed. Never had he spoken to her that way before. For the first time, she became aware of him as a man. How tired he looked, with dark smudges under his eyes and deep lines around his mouth.

"You're good with children. Especially those who are sick and frightened."

"I can't—"

"Listen to me," he told her, his eyes hard. "If you have come back here to work, you will start now. If not, there's no place for you here. This is not the Astor House, Miranda. We have an epidemic here. One child came down with diphtheria, and because of the overcrowding in the dormitories and classrooms, the disease has spread. I've had to turn the storeroom next to the infirmary into a contagion ward, to keep those children away from the rest, the ones with the usual winter croup and bronchitis and that sort of thing. You can bathe the children and change the linen at least."

She tried to draw away from Clive Thorne and the force of

his words, from his hard eyes. Even to venture out of this room was to become a part of the world again, to remember, and to have to live with her memories.

"You'll find an old dress of Miss Currie's in the closet there," he was saying. "And you left a pair of your own shoes behind when you went to work for the McClintocks. And do something about your hair."

Shakily she put her legs over the side of the cot and got to her feet. She swayed, seized by a spell of weakness, but although he was beside her, he made no move to steady her. Instead, he turned and left the room, saying over his shoulder, "Half an hour, no more."

Miranda had assisted in the infirmary before, but she had never seen it so crowded. In the small, improvised contagion ward, children cried in pain or lay sunk in apathy, unable to swallow even the soft foods that were offered to them. Clive was working in the larger infirmary, where the less serious cases were kept. He glanced up briefly at Miranda when she appeared, her hair braided and twisted into a plain chignon at the back of her head. He showed her where to find a clean, starched apron to put on over Lena Currie's old cotton dress, which was several sizes too large for her. "Start in here," he ordered. "Those two were brought in only an hour ago. Malnutrition and severe colds. They need to be fed. Then I want you to change the linen on these beds near the window and empty and scrub the bedpans."

Because of the urgency of her work she did not have a chance to think about anything else. From time to time she felt an overwhelming weakness, the result of having remained in bed for the past few days. She leaned against the nearest wall and waited for the weakness to pass, then kept moving quickly, efficiently, taking up her routine.

She stopped at noon to swallow a cup of strong coffee and a stale roll, and then Clive called her into the contagion ward, where he was preparing to remove the membrane that would otherwise strangle a four-year-old boy. The child was sitting upright, throwing his head back from time to time in an instinctive effort to get more air, and his pale face was covered with sweat. He whimpered with fear at the sight of the doctor with his shiny metal instruments spread on a tray.

"Don't be frightened, love," Miranda said, the words coming unplanned. "The doctor will help you. He'll take the sickness away. There, now."

The child clutched at her in mindless terror.

"Hold his head steady," Clive ordered. Then he set to work, his hand moving quickly, deftly, as he stripped away the deadly grayish membrane from inside the child's throat. Then she held the basin to catch the blood and mucous. Not until the child's breathing was easier did she place his head back on the pillow. "Empty the basin and scrub it with disinfectant, then change the boy's linen and his nightshirt," Clive said.

She worked through the day and into the evening taking orders from Clive and from the matrons. Her back and legs began to ache, but she was scarcely aware of the discomfort. By the time evening came she was exhausted, but she was recovering from the state of shock in which she had existed since she had left the McClintock house.

Even when Clive ordered her, at last, to go to her room and get a few hours' sleep so that she would be rested and ready to help him early tomorrow morning, she obeyed, only because she knew how much work still lay ahead.

Back in her room she hung the worn cotton dress away. Sometime during the afternoon one of the matrons had explained Lena Currie's absence, saying, "She's got herself a good-paying job, teaching in one of those fancy finishing schools for young ladies up in Boston."

No doubt Lena had considered the dress too old and shabby for her to take along. Now, as Miranda stood in her underthings, she realized for the first time that they were the ones she had worn to the Christmas cotillion. She glanced down at the delicate cambric petticoats with their trimmings of lace and ribbons. And there, on a hanger in the closet, she caught a glimpse of the jade green silk gown. Who had cleaned and pressed it so carefully? It looked as good as new except for the water stains on the hemline. She had dragged her skirts through the snow on her flight from the McClintock house. Memory stirred inside her, and she shrank from the awakening of pain. She had danced with Blake that night, and she had been so proud of the way she had looked in that dress.

Then physical exhaustion overtook her, and she stripped and put on her flannel nightgown. Her fingers felt raw and stiff, she thought with surprise. Oh, yes, that was because of the harsh soap and disinfectant she had been scrubbing with all that day. The condition of her hands was not important; nothing was important but her overpowering need for sleep. She climbed into bed and then she was conscious of nothing until dawn, the next morning, when it was time for her to report to the infirmary again.

For the next five days she went on working beside Clive. Now and then he nodded approvingly. She was pleased that he found her work satisfactory, but beyond that she felt no emotion at all until late one evening when Clive asked her to come into his office.

She took a seat beside him on the battered old horsehair sofa and wondered if she had done something to displease him. Then she saw on a low, wooden table a coffeepot, two cups, and two neatly folded cloth napkins along with a few slices of raisin cake. "It's New Year's Eve," he said. "I thought you might take a few moments to join me in a celebration."

She looked at him in surprise. One day had flowed into another since she had been working in the infirmary. Now she realized that out there in the city people were dressing to go to balls, to dinner at Delmonico's, the Fifth Avenue Hotel or the Astor House. Even in the taverns on South Street sailors and their women would be crowding around tables to drink in the new year. And tomorrow morning the streets would be filled with sleighs and carriages carrying well-dressed gentlemen on New Year's calls.

"We don't have much to celebrate here," she began.

"I think we do," he told her, pouring coffee for her. "The epidemic has passed its peak. We'll have other sick children to care for, but only those with the usual winter ailments." He gave her a smile. "Maybe you have had enough of nursing, though. I've spoken to Mrs. Bradford, and she said that if you wish to return to your teaching duties, you can take over a class of eight-year-old girls."

She hesitated. "I think I would rather stay on in the infirmary."

"The work's a lot harder," he reminded her.

"I prefer it." How could she explain to him that so long as she worked with him, following his orders, she felt safe and free from the need to think, to plan on her own?

"As you wish," he said. Then, watching her closely, he went on. "Oh, by the way, I have to make a New Year's call tomorrow. I wonder if I might ask you to go with me."

"Thank you, but I'd rather not." She was not ready to go out, to face a festive gathering.

"I have to go to Bellevue Hospital," he told her. "A friend of mine has been caring for a child who was brought in a few weeks ago. She is well enough to leave now, but she has no place to go, no family."

"What sort of illness did she have? Was it diphtheria?" Miranda asked, feeling a stab of pity.

Clive shook his head. "She'd been badly abused," he said.

Miranda flinched. "Beaten—so that she had to be sent to a hospital?"

"Yes, she'd been beaten. But that wasn't all. She was found in a cellar on Mulberry Street with several other children who were being kept there by an old harridan who was selling their services to men."

Miranda's eyes widened in disbelief. "The little girl, how old is she?"

"She isn't sure. My friend, Dr. Fleming, believes she is about ten."

"But that's not . . . How could any man . . ."

"Such things are quite common over in China," Clive told her. "And they are not unknown here in New York either. Forgive me if I've shocked you, Miranda, but I want you to understand why it would help if you came along to get the child. She has little reason to trust any man, and I thought that if you were with me, she would not be so afraid."

Miranda looked at him in surprise, for although she already respected him for his dedication and skill, she had not realized until now that he was such a sensitive and caring man. He not only was concerned for the child's physical well-being but was eager to spare her from further emotional shock if he could.

"If you'd rather not come along, perhaps one of the matrons would—"

"Oh, no! I want to go."

Although she did not fully realize it, and would not for some time to come, Miranda had begun to feel again; a part of her that had been numbed began to awaken at that moment.

Chapter 29

Even with Miranda along, the cab ride back from Belleview Hospital was not an easy one, for Sophy, the unhappy ten-year-old, was tense with fear. She would have been a pretty child, with her mop of dark curly hair and her brown eyes. But Miranda could feel the tension in the small body. Clive, who was seated on the other side of the child, made quiet conversation, pointing out a sleigh in the shape of a swan filled with merrymakers on New Year's Day calls, or a group of boys and girls, pelting each other with snowballs. Sophy scarcely looked at these sights.

When the hired hansom drew up in front of the Shelter, Sophy went rigid, and for a moment Miranda thought that she would have to carry the child inside. "This is a good place," she said soothingly. "You will be safe here. No one will hurt you again."

Clive got down and was paying the driver. Miranda went on talking gently. "You know, Sophy, I was far younger than you are when I came here. I was only a few weeks old. I grew up here."

The child stared at Miranda, round-eyed and doubtful, but at least she was listening. Miranda went on. "You will have a cot in the dormitory with other little girls your age, and plenty of food."

"What'll I have to do?" Sophy asked timidly.

"You will have to be a good girl and study your lessons."

"What's lessons?"

"Why, reading, writing, geography, arithmetic."

"An' that's all?"

Miranda understood, and she fought down the overpowering tide of pity, for she must not give way to her emotions yet. "You will be safe here," she said, taking the little girl's hand. "I promise, you'll be safe."

Although still doubtful, Sophy asked no more questions but closed her fingers around Miranda's and allowed herself to be helped from the cab and up the steps to the Shelter.

After Sophy had been assigned a cot next to a girl of fourteen who was given the responsibility of looking after her, Miranda went out into the second-floor hallway, where Clive was waiting. She did not want to give way to tears in front of him, but she was powerless to control herself any longer. "She's only a baby. How could anyone ever have forced her to . . ." Clive put an arm around Miranda's shoulders and passed her his handkerchief.

"I saw many such cases in China," he said quietly. "Girls are considered a burden over there, and farmers often sell their daughters to pay the taxes. Or to buy opium if they are addicted to that habit. Some are sent to teahouses, and others are shipped across the Pacific to the brothels of the Barbary Coast in San Francisco."

"But that is terrible."

"More terrible than you can imagine. Although even those Chinese girls who escape such a fate are not free, and many suffer cruelly. I have seen farmers' wives working with crippled, deformed little feet, and some have told me that they suffer pain all their lives. It is the custom, and no foreigner, not even a doctor, can do much about it."

"I don't wonder you've never thought of returning to China."

"Oh, but I have. Because there is still a great deal that I could do there. In fact, I have been corresponding with an elderly doctor, a Scotsman, who is thinking of returning to his home. He wants a younger man to take over his work, though."

Miranda felt a swift, sinking sensation at the thought of Clive's possible departure, but she concealed her feelings and accompanied him down the hall to his office. Before they could reach it, they were stopped by a fourteen-year-old monitor.

"If you please, Dr. Thorne, there's a gentleman here to see Miss Warren. His name's Mr. McClintock."

"Blake?" Miranda asked.

"That's right, and he's dressed ever so fine." The girl's eyes were round, and it was evident that she had been impressed by Blake's appearance.

"I left orders," Clive began.

"It's all right," Miranda said. "I'll see him."

She was surprised when Clive took her arm and accompanied her into the shabbily furnished office. She was grateful for his presence, but she knew that sooner or later she would have to see Blake alone.

He looked as handsome as ever in his fine new broadcloth suit cut in the latest fashion and his striped satin vest. Miranda felt Clive's arm go hard as iron under her fingers, and she sensed the anger in him. "Miranda . . ." Blake began. Then, turning to the doctor, he said, "You must forgive this intrusion, but I really could not allow you to keep me from Miranda any longer. She looks perfectly healthy, and I don't understand why I haven't been permitted to see her before now."

"If she is, it's no thanks to you and your family," Clive said, and there was no mistaking the belligerence in his voice.

"Now, see here . . ." Blake began. But something in Clive's tone and in his face shook Blake's poise. "I would like to speak to Miranda," he said more quietly.

"Go ahead," Clive said.

Blake flushed. "Alone, if you please."

Miranda realized that there would be no possibility of saying the things that must be said with Clive beside her, glaring at Blake. "It is all right," she told Clive. "I will see Mr. McClintock alone."

"As you wish," Clive said. "If you need me, I'll be right across the hall in the infirmary."

Then he strode out, leaving the door ajar. Blake recovered his self-possession somewhat. "Shall we sit down?" he said, and Miranda took a seat beside him on the horsehair sofa. "Now that your watchdog's gone, perhaps we can—"

"Dr. Thorne is my friend," Miranda told him.

She saw that he was staring at her, his eyes moving over her, and she realized for the first time that she was still wearing Lena Currie's old cotton dress. She had altered it to fit but it was undeniably shabby and most unbecoming. A few weeks ago she would have flinched at the thought of allowing Blake to see her in such a dress, but now it was no longer important.

"I've brought your trunk," he began. "And your wages."

He held out a small leather purse, the one she had left in one of the drawers of the chest back in her room at the McClintock house. "I don't want the clothes or . . . anything."

"Don't be foolish," he said impatiently. "You earned this money, and the clothes are yours. And if you'll forgive me for saying so, I can see that you need clothes. That dress you are wearing is not suitable."

"It is perfectly suitable for the work I have been doing. We've had an epidemic, and I've been helping Dr. Thorne in the infirmary."

"What sort of a life is that for a girl as pretty as you? Miranda, I don't understand any of this. You ran off without even saying good-bye, and now you've shut yourself up in this place." He glanced around the office with a look of obvious distaste.

"This is my home," she said. "I grew up here. And I'm perfectly content to remain here."

"I don't believe that. Not after you've seen what the world has to offer. I'm not saying you should come back to our home, not after my mother spoke to you so harshly, and in front of all those people. That's another thing I don't understand. She's never treated anyone that way before so far as I know. I'm sure she is sorry."

"I don't want to talk about that night," Miranda said. Somehow, she had to get through this meeting without giving way, without betraying her real reason for leaving the McClintock home, but she must manage in such a way that Blake would make no more attempts to see her.

"You can find another position as a governess for the time being," Blake went on. "And we can go on seeing each other, and I know that my mother will come around. I'll start making inquiries and I'll find the right sort of home for you to work in."

"Please, don't. I've told you, I want to stay on here. I don't want any help from you or any of your family."

"But why?" Blake's handsome face darkened. "Surely I have a right to know. What have I done? Dr. Thorne looked at me as if he wanted to break my neck. What did you tell him about me?"

"Nothing at all," Miranda answered truthfully.

"I find that hard to believe. Twice I've been turned away by that—that matron downstairs, and this time I had to force my way in."

"I'm sorry for that," Miranda said slowly, choosing her words carefully. "But it is better that we don't see each other again. And believe me, I am perfectly happy here. I'm needed, you see."

"Needed? I need you, Miranda. I thought that you cared for me. Have you forgotten that kiss on the sleigh ride, coming home from the inn? Or the way we danced together at the cotillion? I wanted you, Miranda, and you wanted me."

"No! You must not say such a thing, or even think it!"

He reached out for her, but she was on her feet and backing away. "Don't come any closer," she said. Maybe she should have accepted Clive's offer to remain in the room, she thought desperately. His presence would surely have served as a buffer. Blake would not have said these things in front of Clive.

"I'd never harm you, Miranda. You ought to know—"

"Then you must not touch me again, ever."

She stood behind Clive's large wooden desk. "When we danced together at the cotillion," she went on, "I was carried away by my feelings for a little while. Try to understand. I was not used to such surroundings, such festivities. I'm not like those girls you grew up with. Roxanne Widdicomb and the rest. I suppose I was carried away by the music and the flowers and that beautiful dress. All that luxury and color, like something out of a—a storybook. And so I allowed myself to forget why I was there in your home, to forget my place."

"Your place is wherever you want it to be."

"We both know better," Miranda said, "and your mother was right to remind me that I was hired help, the governess, not a social equal. Believe me, Blake. She was right."

"Don't say that, Miranda! I know there are obstacles, but they can be overcome. Are you so afraid of gossip that you are willing to throw your whole future away? I want you."

Hearing his words, she saw him for what he was—a handsome, rather arrogant young man who was not used to being refused by any girl who took his fancy.

"If I loved you, I would be willing to risk a scandal," she said. "But I don't, and I never have."

She saw that she had shaken him badly. "I'm sorry," she went on, "but you might as well accept the truth."

"It's that—that doctor, isn't it?"

For a moment she did not understand.

"Oh, it's plain enough how he feels about you. And I think that you feel the same about him. That's why you came back here that night without even saying good-bye. And why you refused to see me all these weeks."

Although she had had little experience with men, she realized that Blake had offered her the means of driving him away.

"You might have told me before you let me make a fool of myself," Blake said angrily. "No wonder you're content to remain here working beside him. Though what the devil you see in him, I don't understand. He's older than you."

"He is about thirty-five," Miranda said. "And he—he is good and unselfish and . . . What do you know about him? I've watched him fighting to save the lives of these children here, and when he lost one of them, it hurt him so terribly. And only this morning he took me with him to Bellevue Hospital to bring back a little girl who had been cruelly abused. He wanted me with him because he thought the child might be less afraid. He cares about such things, you see."

"All right, perhaps he is a dedicated doctor and a kind man, but is that enough? What sort of a life can he offer you?"

There was still time to speak the truth, to deny that Clive Thorne had offered her anything at all, to tell Blake about her talk with Vanessa. She had it in her power to speak the words that would tear his family apart forever.

Instead, she spoke coldly, willing herself to finish the charade while she was still able to. "And what have you to give me?"

Blake stared at her, bewildered, for never before had any girl confronted him with such a question. Indeed, he had never suffered a rebuff from any girl, and his easy confidence was shaken.

"There is the McClintock fortune," Miranda went on. "Perhaps you think I am so calculating, so shallow, that I would be willing to sell myself, even to someone I don't love."

She saw the hurt in his eyes, the baffled anger.

"I . . . you'll find your trunk downstairs in the parlor." He pushed the purse into her hand. "And this—you earned it—you were kind to Alison and she misses you."

She longed to ask him to take a message to the little girl, explaining why she had gone off so suddenly, but she could not find the words, and, more important, she did not want Blake to remain here any longer now that she had accomplished what she had wanted to do.

As if sensing her feelings, he said stiffly, "I won't trouble you again, Miranda." He left the office and she heard him going down the long flight of uncarpeted stairs. Slowly she moved to the window that overlooked Houston Street. She stood there, staring down, until a few moments later she saw Blake coming out and getting into his brightly painted four-in-hand. She thought with faint surprise that he might have been any well-dressed, handsome young man. She watched as he cracked his whip above the sleek, shining backs of his team and the horses started forward. But even before he had disappeared from sight, her thoughts returned to Clive.

What were her feelings for Clive Thorne? She was grateful to him, for she realized that he had saved her from the shadowy half-world she had slipped into after the night she had fled from the McClintock house. He had forced her out of her apathy and had set her to work, often treating her in a brusque, high-handed way and giving her the most distasteful tasks; but the work in the infirmary had healed her.

Clive did not have any of Blake's careless charm or dazzling good looks, but he had strength and determination, and so often, when she had looked at his face, with its lines of fatigue about the eyes and mouth, she had felt a surge of tenderness.

Now she remembered Blake's question, spoken in anger. *It's that doctor, isn't it?* And she remembered, too, the sinking sensation she had felt when Clive had spoken, only a little while ago, of returning to China. She tried to imagine what it would be like here at the Shelter without him and felt only a sense of loss and emptiness.

On a sunny afternoon late in March, Blake came home early. He had been spending most of his time since the beginning of the year at the McClintock offices on South Street, or at his father's new shipyard on the East River. He had found solace in studying the workings at the shipyard and even welcomed the heat from the furnaces and the noise of hammers and steam derricks. Some of the workmen had been wary at first, but they soon realized that Logan McClintock's son had a driving interest in every phase of the building of the *Gazelle.* When he was in the yard he wore the same rough clothing that they did, and he asked sensible questions and listened respectfully to the answers. He went over every part of the new vessel and studied the plans of the engine.

This afternoon, however, he had left the yard early, remembering that he and his parents were to attend a dinner party at the Widdicombs' house. He would need a thorough scrubbing to remove the grime of the yard. Although he was not particularly enthused about the dinner party, which would probably be a dull affair, with Horace Widdicomb saying little while his wife chattered to fill in the silences, he had not been able to refuse his mother's request that he come along. She had looked so troubled lately, not at all like herself, her face tense with some inner stress.

He went upstairs and was passing the open door of Alison's nursery when the child called to him. His mother was inside with Alison and the new governess, a short, stout young woman who had been working here for nearly a week now. In his preoccupation with business matters, Blake had never been able to recall her name, although he did know that she was the daughter of a Dutch minister and had come from Kinderhook, up the Hudson.

At his entrance Alison ran to greet him and stretched out her arms so that he might pick her up.

"I'll get you all dirty, little one," he said with a smile.

"I don't care," she insisted. "Miss Vanderplanck says I've got to have a bath before bedtime anyway." He laughed and swung the little girl up in his arms and kissed her soft curls.

"Darren's cat had kittens," Alison informed Blake as he set her down. "And Miss Vanderplanck's going to help me pick one out for my own. And she's going to show me how to take care of it too."

"That's kind of her," Blake said.

"Oh, she's nice," Alison said, taking the hand of the amiable, round-faced governess. "Only I do wish Miranda would come back to see me."

"Perhaps she will one day," said Miss Vanderplanck cheerfully. "She has a great many little girls to care for now, you know."

After Alison and her governess had left the nursery, there

was an uneasy silence between Blake and his mother. At last he said, "Miranda won't be coming back at all. She was quite definite about that."

His mother looked at him, her eyes widening. "You've been to see her, then."

"Back on New Year's Day," Blake said.

"You never said a word to me."

"I did not realize you might be interested," Blake said. "At any rate, she's content to remain at the Shelter, so she said. It was all I could do to get her to accept her trunk with those clothes you gave her, or even her wages."

"Felicity said that Miranda was busy, working in the infirmary. She is so devoted to the children there."

"And not only to the children," Blake said.

"Whatever are you talking about?"

"Dr. Thorne. She's in love with him."

"And is he—"

"I'm sure of it. Thorne struck me as a surly sort of man, and too old for her," Blake said. It had not been easy for him to come to terms with Miranda's choice of Clive Thorne, for ever since he had reached sixteen, he'd had a way with women. A group of his older friends had taken him to Josie Wood's elegant parlor house, where the girls had been eager to initiate him into the mysteries of sex. Then, while he had been in Washington on business for his father, he had had a brief but memorable fling with the beautiful wife of a member of the French diplomatic service and had been flattered by her undisguised pleasure in his lovemaking, for she was obviously a lady of considerable experience.

Naturally he was far more circumspect with unmarried girls of his own class, but they had hinted that a kiss, or even a few other liberties, would not be unwelcome. With the prettier ones he had taken the hints.

And then Miranda Warren, a girl without friends or family, had made it plain that she was not at all interested in carrying on their friendship; she had put him aside for another man. It had been a bitter blow to his vanity.

"Dr. Thorne is older than Miranda," his mother was saying slowly. "But Felicity Bradford thinks highly of him. Are you quite sure that he and Miranda—"

"She told me so. And if you could have seen the way he glared at me after I finally forced my way in to see her, you'd have no doubt of his feelings either."

"If only I could be sure that she would be happy with him," Vanessa said.

"I didn't realize that you were so deeply concerned with Miranda's happiness or her plans for the future," Blake began. Then something in his mother's face silenced him. Really, women were impossible to understand, he thought.

First his mother had befriended Miranda, had gone to great lengths to make her comfortable and had bought her fine clothes. Then, at the cotillion, she had turned on the girl and had reminded her that she was only a servant. Now she was behaving as if Miranda's happiness was of the greatest importance.

And Miranda's behavior was scarcely less confusing and contradictory. She had responded to him with unmistakable warmth, had been soft and pliant in his arms when they had danced together at the cotillion, had looked up at him with eyes that had promised everything. Then, on that same night, she had run off without leaving any message, and when he had finally come to see her, she had asked him never to come again. It made no sense, any of it.

He thought of Roxanne Widdicomb, who would be at the dinner tonight, and found that he was looking forward to seeing her. Pretty and flirtatious, she would be a soothing companion. Maybe tonight would be pleasant after all; indeed, as he left the nursery, he decided that the dinner party would be a welcome break from the demanding schedule of the past few months.

Because Logan had warned her that he would be coming home a little late this evening, Vanessa had sent Blake on ahead in his four-in-hand. Now, with Logan beside her in the handsome brougham, lined and cushioned in gray velvet and drawn by a new team of sleek gray horses, they moved down Fifth Avenue in the direction of the Widdicomb house. They turned onto Madison Avenue, and Logan was saying, "Do you remember when this was nothing but mudholes, with goats and pigs running free?"

"And now Kitty's after Horace to build a new wing onto their house."

"What does she want with . . . Oh, I see. You are both determined to arrange this match between Blake and Roxanne."

Stung by his words, Vanessa said, "Blake is too much like you to be pushed into any marriage against his will." She broke off abruptly, for she remembered now the circumstances of her marriage to Logan. For a moment they rode along in silence. Then, to her surprise, she felt his hand close around hers.

"You're right about me," he said.

Her voice was unsteady. "Am I? Wasn't it Felicity who . . ."

Now his eyes were glinting with amusement. "Felicity was most persuasive, but I married you because I wanted to."

It was not a passionate declaration of love, but after the coolness between them these past few months, Logan's words moved Vanessa deeply. She looked up at him, and all at once the years fell away and she saw him again, young and hot-tempered, driven by ambition, sure of his future.

Her eyes misted with tears, and then his arm was around her. "What is it?" he asked gently.

"You told Felicity that I would not be needing charity. That you would provide for your wife and child. Only . . ." She laughed a little shakily. "I never imagined that you would do so on such a grand scale. The house, this carriage."

He smiled and his arm tightened across her shoulders.

"I'll grant you, this isn't quite like our first drive together. When I found you hiding in the back of that freight wagon, you looked scared out of your wits."

"Who wouldn't have been, with you shouting as if you were standing on the deck of a clipper?"

"But I did take you to Hudson Square, didn't I?"

And the memories came flooding back, engulfing her. Aunt Prudence Campbell, sharp-tongued but generous and wise; Abel, with his cold, probing eyes and iron-gray hair, dignified and secure in his power. Now there were other, far wealthier men who had risen to power here in the city: Commodore Vanderbilt, whose imposing Hudson Terminal had swept away all those dignified old houses on Hudson Square; Belmonts and Goulds and Astors who had built other, greater mansions far from the southern tip of the city.

"You were always one for taking risks," Logan was saying. "Remember the night you came to my lodgings down on Tompkins Street in the middle of the night. Tell me, Vanessa. Why did you come?"

"Because I'd promised to deliver Kitty's note."

"And was that the only reason?"

Before she had time to answer, Ben had pulled up in front of the Widdicombs' house. Perhaps, after all the years of their marriage, there was no need for an answer, Vanessa thought.

Chapter 30

On a warm afternoon early in May, Miranda and Clive took a hansom to Central Park and then got down to go walking on the heights to the north of the lake. Clive led the way along a wooded path in the new section called the Ramble. Although many pleasure-seekers were here in the park today, they tended to congregate at the Casino or on the Mall, so Clive and Miranda soon found themselves alone. He took her hand as they crossed a small bridge over a brook, and then he found a sun-warmed outcropping of flat rock, where he spread his coat for her to sit on.

She had dressed with unusual care, for although she had not been able to bring herself to wear any of the fashionable and expensive dresses given to her by Vanessa, she had used some of her savings to buy a becoming new walking costume. It was all right to spend the money she had earned while working as Alison's governess, she had decided. Now, as she saw Clive's eyes on her, she was glad that she had worn the becoming dark-green poplin walking dress, with its close-fitting basque and full skirt. The costume emphasized the roundness of her breasts and the graceful lines of her trim waist; her small straw hat with its green ribbons was tilted at a fashionable angle, completing the picture. Clive gave her an appreciative smile and she felt warm inside.

At the Shelter they were seldom alone, and she leaned back, luxuriating in the quiet surroundings. "It is hard to believe we're still in the city," she said.

"You've been to the park before, haven't you?"

"Not this part," Miranda said. "I used to take Alison skating on the lake last winter." She stopped abruptly and looked away, fixing her eyes on the stone tower called the Belvedere, which served as an observatory. She did not want to think about that day, last winter, when she and Alison had glided around the lake, and had been joined by Blake, who had said he had happened to be passing by.

"Miranda, I've never asked you about your reasons for leaving the McClintock house," Clive began.

"You've every right to ask," she said, "but I can't talk about it."

"Sometimes it helps to talk," Clive said. "That young man, Blake McClintock . . ." His mouth tightened. "I suppose I can understand how an inexperienced girl might have been attracted, and I know that there are plenty of men who believe that the family governess is fair game."

"No! It wasn't like that! Blake and I were friends, nothing more."

"And yet you ran from his house at night and came back to the Shelter in a state of shock."

"That wasn't Blake's fault. Please believe me."

"And Captain McClintock?"

Miranda stared at him, stunned by the suggestion.

"Clive, no! He was kind to me always." She half rose, fearing that somehow Clive might get her to tell him her reason for leaving the mansion on Fifth Avenue. But he put out a hand and drew her down again.

"Forgive me," he said. "I only wish I'd tried to stop you before you went to that house. Whatever happened there, it nearly destroyed you." She was startled by the violence with which he spoke.

"Why didn't you try to stop me?" she asked.

"I wanted to, but you were so eager to go; and I felt it

would have been unfair—and my own plans were so uncertain."

Since her talk with Blake on New Year's Day, Miranda had struggled against her feelings for Clive. It had been necessary for her to let Blake believe that she and Clive were in love, but in the months that followed, Clive had not given her the slightest reason to think that he loved her. Indeed, after Blake's visit Clive had drawn away and had suggested that since the epidemic was over, she ought to return to her teaching duties, that she was no longer needed in the infirmary.

She had been surprised when he had suggested this outing to the park and had told herself that she was foolish to take such care with her appearance.

"I've had a letter from MacDade, that doctor I was telling you about over in China. He's eager to return to his home in Scotland, you see. He's getting on in years, and his work's taken its toll on his health."

"And you—you've decided to take over his practice?"

Miranda felt a sense of desolation, and if she had had any doubts about her feelings for Clive, they were swept away now.

"I'll be sailing for Foochow within a month or so," Clive said. He hesitated, then took her hand. "Miranda, will you come with me?"

"I haven't had any formal training as a nurse," she began shakily, "but you did say I had a certain aptitude for the work. And I could learn from you."

"I'm asking you to be my wife, Miranda."

She stared at him, her lips parted. Often, during her growing-up years, she had imagined a proposal of marriage: the man would be kneeling in a moonlit garden, and there would be the strains of music from a nearby ballroom.

"Maybe I've taken too much for granted," he was saying. "I thought perhaps you might love me enough to share the kind of life I've planned. It is asking a great deal. You're so young and so beautiful. And you've a right to much more. The hospital I'll be taking over is scarcely worthy of the name, not by our standards, and I suspect that Dr. MacDade's house is far from suitable for a married couple. There would be loneliness, too, and hard work and even danger, perhaps."

Afterward, she never remembered if he had reached out to her or if she had thrown herself into his arms eagerly, shamelessly. All at once they were locked in an embrace, and her head was pressed against his shoulder and she was saying, "Take me with you. I want to go with you always."

His arms tightened around her then, and she felt the hard driving hunger in him, and her own swift response. She had not thought that he was capable of such passion, or that her need was so great, so powerful and primitive. She felt the singing in her blood and saw the trees overhead spinning in a blur of green and gold. Her vague, foolish daydreams were swept away, and she knew with a certainty that went bone-deep that this was love between a man and a woman as it should be. She welcomed the flood of sensations and gloried in the touch of his hard, commanding hands, the force of his lean, strong body. Later, she thought that it was only the lack of privacy that had kept him from taking her then and there.

Driving back to Houston Street through the twilight, Clive sat close to Miranda, with his arm around her. He talked of his plans for the future, for adding space to the hospital and introducing new methods of caring for his Chinese patients. "Many of them are suspicious of Westerners even now," he told her. "Some will be afraid of us, and others will oppose our work. If you want more time to consider, I'll understand."

"There is nothing to consider," she told him with quiet assurance. "Wherever you go I want to be with you."

A few weeks later Logan went to a meeting in the offices of the Bradford-Widdicomb Shipping Company. The depression that had started with the collapse of Jay Cooke's banking house had shown little sign of lifting. Logan, who was not content to leave any of the important decisions to Horace, now carefully considered every new step in their joint ventures, and with his controlling interest in Bradford-Widdicomb, he was able to steer the company through this difficult period.

Conditions would improve in time, Logan knew, but for the present there must be no rash investments, no unwise speculation. The McClintock Line and Bradford-Widdicomb would weather the storm and even expand, but slowly and cautiously.

Other businessmen had not been so fortunate, and now there were hundreds of men and women out of work, walking the streets of New York. With the end of winter there was some slight improvement in conditions, but Logan, driving about the city, had seen the placards that spoke of discontent, signs demanding DEATH FOR MONOPOLIES and WORKMEN'S RIGHTS. Silk workers in Paterson, New Jersey, were holding mass meetings and demanding an immediate tariff reduction of twenty percent. Miners in Ohio and in Pennsylvania were calling on their fellow workers to organize for a living wage. Back in January marchers had converged on Union Square and Tompkins Square, and the Metropolitans had been called out in full strength to prevent rioting.

Logan was thinking of this as he emerged from Horace's office and crossed the reception room. There he saw Kitty in a smart, dove-gray dress, waiting impatiently, tapping a small, slippered foot and playing with the ivory handle of her parasol.

"I do hope Horace won't be much longer," she said as Logan took her hand in greeting. "I shall want him to come with me, for I hate shopping alone."

"Perhaps Vanessa could go with you," Logan suggested.

"She isn't free this afternoon," Kitty said. "She's gone off to a meeting of the Sorosis Club."

This was an organization for women, one of Vanessa's many outside interests, and its purpose was the discussion of the important issues of the day, from women's suffrage to the welfare of working girls.

"I must finish selecting the furnishings for the new wing of the house," Kitty went on. "I've got my heart set on a Turkish cozy corner."

Logan gave her a blank stare. "A what?"

"Why, the Turkish cozy corner is all the fashion now. I read about it in *The Gentlewoman at Home*, and I must have one for myself. It has red plush drapes and couches decorated with real leopard skins, and others strewn with silk cushions. And shelves with copper plates from Kashmir. And brasswork from Cairo. So exotic and elegant."

Logan's mouth twitched at the corners as he repressed a smile. Once, as a young ship's officer on shore leave in North Africa, he had visited a brothel decorated in that way. "Horace may be delayed a little longer," he said. "He's going over the books with his chief clerk."

"Oh, how provoking!" Kitty tossed her head. "And Mama's busy this afternoon too."

"Has she also joined the Sorosis Club?" Logan asked. Many irate husbands complained when their wives, who had been excluded from such male sanctuaries as the Century Club, the Union League, and the Manhattan, had struck back by forming the Sorosis, for ladies only. Logan had no objection to Vanessa's joining the club, for he knew that she was far too energetic and intelligent to spend her time in pursuing the frivolous activities that occupied Kitty. And, mercifully, she had no plans for adding a wing to the house, or even creating a Turkish cozy corner, he thought with relief.

"No, Mama is not at the meeting of the Sorosis today, although she is a member," Kitty informed him. "She is at home getting ready to attend the wedding of that—what is her name? Your former governess, that pushy little creature who made such a shocking spectacle of herself at the cotillion."

"Miranda Warren."

"Yes, that's right. Miss Warren is getting married this afternoon to Dr. Clive Thorne, who works at the Shelter." Kitty sighed "I really don't see the need for Mama to attend at all. But she said that since Miss Warren is without any family, some friends should be there with her today. Mama has always had the oddest ideas about—"

"Where is the wedding to be?" Logan interrupted.

"At that little Methodist church a block from the Shelter at three o'clock. If you should ask me, Miss Warren is most fortunate to find a gentleman who is willing to marry her."

"I think that Dr. Thorne is the fortunate one," Logan said.

He glanced at his pocket watch. "You must excuse me now, Kitty," he said, leaving the office.

Vanessa, who had listened with interest to a talk by Maria Mitchell, the Quaker astronomer from Nantucket, dealing with the future of higher education for women, returned home a little after five o'clock and went directly upstairs to the nursery. She liked spending the hour before dinner reading to Alison or talking with her. Perhaps one day Alison would attend a college for women or even a coeducational institution, although the latter notion was still considered quite daring.

Gertrude Vanderplanck, the stout governess, was seated at the nursery window, working on a piece of embroidery, but Alison was nowhere in sight. "Her papa came home early this afternoon," the governess told Vanessa placidly. "He asked me to dress Miss Alison in her prettiest frock. I chose the new pink one with the Brussels lace trimming. And then off they went in the carriage."

Vanessa was surprised and baffled, for when Logan took Alison on an outing it was usually to South Street, where she explored the shipyard with him and watched the progress on the new steamer. Surely he would not have wanted her to wear a dainty new party dress for such an excursion.

Vanessa went downstairs again and lingered in the entrance hall. She did not have long to wait, for shortly before six, Logan and Alison returned. The little girl's face glowed with excitement as she ran to fling herself into Vanessa's arms. Then she drew back and held out a small bouquet tied with white satin ribbons.

"Look, Mama," she said proudly. "Miranda gave it to me. And she kissed me, and now I know about why she went away. Not 'cause she likes those other little girls at the Shelter better than me."

Logan put a hand on Alison's shoulder. "Why don't you go upstairs now and ask Miss Vanderplanck to put those flowers in water?" he suggested.

"All right, Papa." She went racing upstairs.

"It looked like a—a wedding bouquet," Vanessa said. She felt a trembling start inside her, and she tried to steady herself.

"Miranda and Dr. Thorne were married this afternoon.

Alison has never been able to understand why Miranda went off without a word. I think she'll feel better about Miranda's leaving now."

Vanessa put out a hand to steady herself against the carved newel post at the foot of the stairs. "You said nothing to me at breakfast this morning."

"I didn't know until I met Kitty at Horace's office. She was going on about how Miranda has no family of her own, and when she said that Felicity would be going, I thought I'd go, too, and take Alison with me. As a matter of fact, I had the honor of giving the bride away."

Vanessa tried to make some casual remark, but all at once her throat ached with unshed tears. *Miranda has no family of her own.*

"I'm sorry if you're displeased," Logan said, misinterpreting her silence. "I should have thought that after all this time you'd have gotten over your anger at Miranda."

"I have," Vanessa managed to say. "I'm glad you went and Alison too."

"I doubt the man has much money," Logan went on. "So I'm giving them a practical sort of wedding gift. Free passage aboard the *Gazelle*, in one of the best cabins."

"The *Gazelle*—but she's sailing for China."

"That's where they're going. He worked in China for several years and now he's decided to go back, and Miranda will be of help. He says she has a real talent for nursing, especially with children. And they'll travel to China in style, aboard the *Gazelle.*"

Logan looked pleased with himself, and Vanessa knew that she must not betray her feelings, the pain that was surging up in her. "It was most generous of you, my dear," she managed to say.

"I wanted to do something to show Miranda how grateful

we both are for her kindness to Alison. She did wonders for the little one. And I hoped that it might make up to Miranda for what happened that night."

Then, feeling that he had perhaps been tactless in reminding Vanessa of her outburst at the cotillion, he went on quickly to describe the amenities of the cabin in which Miranda and Clive would be traveling. "It has a curtained bed and a plush sofa, no less, and a writing desk. And a washstand with running water. And I don't know what conditions Miranda will have to cope with once she's settled in that village near Foochow, but at least she'll have a good honeymoon trip to remember."

"How long will Miranda and her husband be over in China?" Surely Logan would see how she was trembling, would hear the shakiness in her voice. But no, he was turning away. "It's a permanent move, from what Thorne said. He has plans for enlarging the hospital there." Then, dismissing the matter, he said, "I'm going upstairs to change for dinner. Are you coming?"

"In a few minutes. You go along, Logan."

He went upstairs, and now she could take the forced smile from her face. She hurried into the drawing room like an animal seeking shelter, and she closed the door behind her. Waves of burning heat moved through her body, and for a moment she feared that she might faint. She went to the fireplace and rested her forehead against the cool, smooth marble of the mantelpiece.

The *Gazelle* was to sail in June. She tried to still her whirling thoughts and to come to terms with what had happened. But it was all a senseless jumble. She thought of Ross Halliwell, living with his wife and daughters in England, unaware of Miranda's existence. And Logan had been the one to give Miranda away in marriage. She tried to picture Logan, standing tall and dignified, with Miranda on his arm. For a moment she felt an insane desire to laugh, and then she realized that she was weeping. In a few weeks Miranda would sail to China aboard Logan's new steamer.

She raised her head and looked up at the portrait over the mantelpiece and remembered the first time she had given herself to Ross, there in his studio on Great Jones Street, how she had lain in his arms with the nearly finished portrait looking down on them. How young she had been then, not much older than Miranda was now. She had been restless and lonely, unable to look ahead and see the possible consequences of her brief passion.

Then, on the night of the cotillion, when Miranda had turned on her in hurt and anger, Vanessa had thought that had been punishment enough, if indeed she deserved punishment. But now she knew that even worse suffering lay in store for her. Miranda must still hate her bitterly, not to have informed her about the marriage. Logan had been welcome at the ceremony, and Alison had carried home the wedding bouquet. Miranda did not blame them—only Vanessa. Felicity had kept silent out of kindness, trying to spare Vanessa's feelings.

And even now, if Miranda and her husband had been planning to remain here in New York, Vanessa thought distractedly, there might still be some hope of a reconciliation. Not for months, or perhaps years, she thought, but someday it was possible that Miranda would come to understand and forgive. Now even that hope was lost, for Miranda was sailing off to the other side of the world, and how many years might pass before she returned, if she ever did?

Vanessa heard the doorknob turn, and she touched a handkerchief to her face. "Yes, Bridget, what is it?"

"If you please, ma'am, dinner's all ready, and the master's

waiting in the dining room."

"Tell him I'll be there in a moment," Vanessa said.

At the end of May the American Jockey Club held the opening races of the season, and those New Yorkers who were not going to attend gathered along Fifth Avenue to watch the fine carriages starting out for the track. Even now, with thousands out of work, facing eviction from their flats on Mulberry Street or the Bowery, there were those who took vicarious pleasure in watching the activities of the wealthy.

The American Jockey Club had been founded by the millionaire, Leonard Jerome, along with William R. Travers, Jerome's partner, and August Belmont, who shared their passion for horses. The races were held at Jerome's track in Westchester, which had opened back in 1866. Each year since then, eight thousand well-dressed racing enthusiasts had crowded into the grandstand.

Logan was too busy at the shipyard to take time off, for he wanted to oversee every detail of the steamer's progress, but Blake had invited Roxanne to drive out with him. Now, standing on the steps of their house, Logan and Vanessa stood watching as their son helped the pretty, smiling girl into the four-in-hand. Logan, who had little interest in horses except as a means to get him where he wanted to go, shook his head. "This whole cult of driving and racing—I suppose they think because we've copied it from the English, that makes it fashionable."

"Blake's been working hard all these months," Vanessa reminded him. "He deserves a day's recreation."

"I've no objection to his taking the day off," Logan said. "And at least he's taking only Roxanne with him, not a whole wagonload of girls, like Jerome's harem."

"I do hope he'll drive carefully," Vanessa said.

Logan smiled down at her. "Don't worry about that," he told her with reluctant pride. "Blake knows how to handle a team with the best of them. It's the little filly sitting up there beside him. I wonder how safe he'll be with her."

"Logan! What a way to talk about Roxanne."

"She's tricked out like a circus pony today."

"Logan, really!"

He gave in. "She's a pretty little thing. I'll admit that. I only hope she doesn't take after Kitty. She's driving poor Horace out of his mind, dragging him around to look at furniture for that new wing of theirs. One thing I will say, if she's planning on setting aside the new wing for Blake and Roxanne, she won't get her way. I'll see to it."

"Blake and Roxanne are not even engaged," Vanessa interrupted.

"Not yet," Logan said, watching Blake crack his whip and wave a white-gloved hand at them as he moved skillfully into the procession of carriages that was streaming northward. "We had a talk down at the shipyard the other day, and I have an idea Blake's planning to ask Roxanne to marry him soon, maybe this afternoon."

"He told you that he was going to ask her?"

"Not in so many words, but we McClintock men understand each other."

Vanessa could not begrudge Logan his closeness with his son; that was good and as it should be. If only she and Miranda . . . She tried to put the thought from her mind and fixed her eyes on the stylish open carriage that was passing now, on the cluster of gaily dressed girls, the driver in his tall white hat, the liveried grooms, but they were all a meaningless blur before her eyes. She was relieved when Logan suggested that they go back into the house to have coffee together before he would leave for South Street.

Chapter 31

Because there were no suitable facilities for married couples at the Shelter, Clive had found a comfortable boardinghouse only a few blocks away. They had come here directly from the church, and when they were alone in the bedroom Miranda felt nervous all at once. She took off her bonnet and wondered if she was supposed to remove her simple white wedding dress, a gift from Felicity, in her husband's presence.

She began to chatter quickly, uneasily. "It was such a surprise to me, seeing Captain McClintock and Alison there at the wedding. But I'm pleased that they came."

"I could see that. His little girl's devoted to you."

"Alison is a darling. And so much less shy than she used to be. And wasn't it kind of Captain McClintock to provide us with passage on his newest steamer? I never imagined we would have such fine accommodations. Think of it."

"Later," Clive said, smiling. "At the moment I can think only of you, Miranda. My wife, here with me."

He came to her then and put his hands lightly on her shoulders. She went rigid at his touch and he looked down at her in surprise. "What's wrong?" he asked. "That day in the park you were not like this."

"We weren't married then," she said.

He laughed, but there was no mockery in the sound, only tenderness. "It's too late for you to become my mistress," he said. "Although, if you like, we can pretend that you are."

"I'm afraid," she said.

"Afraid? Not of me surely."

"I don't know. I want to please you, Clive, only I don't know what . . ."

He drew her close, and then slowly began to undo the buttons of her basque. "We are supposed to please each other," he told her, his voice soft. He bent his head and kissed her, pushing the folds of silk from her shoulders, baring the soft roundness of her breasts. The sensation made her dizzy and she clung to him. Then he was lifting her and carrying her to the bed.

His hands moved slowly, skillfully, stripping away her dress, her undergarments. Then he drew away from her, but only long enough to remove his own clothes. Now she caught her breath as she felt the length of his body pressed against hers. His hands explored the curves and hollows of her flesh, and she felt the awakening of the passion she had known the first time he had kissed her; only now, there was no need to hold back.

Shyly at first, then with growing boldness, she reached out to caress him, letting her instincts guide her in her quest. Her fears fell away, and she drew him to her, and then they were joined together, and even the swift, sharp pain of his entry did not cause her to draw back. He lay still for a moment to allow her to become accustomed to this new sensation, and then he was moving slowly at first, then more and more quickly, and she was moving in response to his need, for it was her need too. Now she understood what he had meant, understood not with her mind but with her whole being; she knew what it was to give and to receive in one soaring moment that went on and on into a timeless, endless fulfillment.

Later, he slept beside her while she looked down at him with brooding tenderness. Then, with a sigh, she settled her body against his and slept.

Miranda and Clive had agreed that until it was time for

them to sail, both wanted to continue to visit the Shelter. Clive would have to explain the duties there to the new doctor, who had recently completed his internship at Bellevue Hospital. As for Miranda, although she no longer taught her class of eight-year-olds, she never failed to find extra tasks to do, for the Shelter was still receiving homeless children, many of whom were victims of the depression that showed no signs of lifting.

Businesses short of money and unable to get credit were closing in ever-greater numbers. Fathers of families dispossessed because they had lost their positions and could not pay their rent were driven to desperation, and many deserted their families to move west. Shopgirls and factory hands who were no longer able to make a living by respectable means turned to prostitution, and those who found themselves encumbered with unwanted infants brought them to the Shelter or abandoned them to be brought there by concerned citizens or by the police.

On an afternoon a week after her wedding, Miranda sat with Felicity in the small parlor on the first floor of the Shelter. She had been questioning Felicity about little Sophy. "I wonder if she will ever be able to forget the terrible things that were done to her in that—that cellar on Mulberry Street," Miranda said.

"Not completely, perhaps. But she has a chance to have a better life," Felicity said. "I have been corresponding with a Quaker couple who own a farm in Pennsylvania. They had a child of their own, but she died, and the wife is unable to have any more children. They are eager to adopt Sophy."

"That would be wonderful for her," Miranda said. Then her spirits sank. "You will have to tell them about her past, I suppose."

"I've already told them," Felicity said. "They don't believe that a child is responsible for her circumstances. They know that she is not to blame for what was done to her."

"Clive says that children like Sophy are often sold to the keepers of such establishments by their own mothers."

"That is true enough, but even if it happened in Sophy's case, perhaps her mother was driven by desperation, perhaps . . ."

"There can be no excuse for a woman who would sell her own child to such a place."

Felicity gave Miranda a long, searching look.

"Are we still speaking of Sophy?" she asked. When Miranda did not reply, she went on. "You were not sold or abandoned."

"I suppose you think I should be grateful for that," Miranda said coldly. "Yes, I know that you and Mrs. McClintock are friends and have been for many years. But I don't understand how you can possibly condone what she did. How could you have taken part in her deception of Captain McClintock? He is a fine, respectable man."

To Miranda's surprise, Felicity smiled. "Perhaps he is now. He was not always respectable, and whatever he has made of himself, Vanessa had a part in it. I've never condoned the fact that she turned to another man, but I am not sorry that I helped her to conceal what she did. Do you suppose that Captain McClintock would have forgiven her, had he known?"

"No, certainly not."

"Miranda, listen to me. Your husband is taking you with him to China. You'll be together."

"What has that to do with Mrs. McClintock?"

"With your mother," Felicity said. "No, don't look at me that way. She is your mother, and it is only fair that you should understand."

"She tried to explain it all to me on the night I left her home."

"I doubt you were in any condition to understand that night. Vanessa was separated from Logan time and again during the early years of their marriage. He was on his way around the Horn to San Francisco when she lost her first child. A boy, it was."

Miranda half rose but Felicity spoke sharply.

"Sit down," she said, "and hear me out. You were born when Logan was away again, on a two-year voyage to China. And Vanessa was lonely. She had not been accepted into New York society then, she had few friends."

"And so she turned to the first man who caught her fancy."

"That's not true." Felicity's eyes were hot with indignation. "The man she turned to, your father, was someone she had known back in Salem when she was growing up. I think perhaps he had always loved her, and when she gave herself to him, I'm sure she felt affection, tenderness and . . . I do not pretend to understand about the rest of it. My own marriage was arranged by my parents, and I obeyed their wishes and fulfilled my duty to my husband as best I could. But I think that Vanessa is different."

For a moment Miranda thought of the passion she had shared with Clive since their wedding night. She pushed the thought aside. Clive was her husband.

Felicity went on, speaking quickly, urgently. "One thing you must believe. Your father is a good man, gentle and gifted."

In spite of herself, Miranda could no longer restrain her interest. "Gifted?"

"A most talented artist." Felicity broke off abruptly, and a moment later Clive was coming into the parlor. Miranda rose to leave with him, then hesitated for a moment. Bending, she kissed Felicity's cheek. "Thank you," she said softly.

Because their boardinghouse was not far from the Shelter, Miranda and Clive walked back through the warm spring twilight. He was talking about the new doctor who was to take over his duties, and Miranda made appropriate answers, but her mind was occupied with Felicity's words. She refused to allow herself to think about Vanessa, even now, but her father, a man she had never seen, was another matter. Even if Clive had not walked into the parlor, Felicity would never have revealed the man's name. Of that much Miranda was certain. *Your father is a good man. . . .*

He was still living, then, and he knew nothing of Miranda's existence. It was better that way, Miranda told herself. She and Clive would be leaving for China in a few weeks to start a new life for themselves. What difference could it possibly make that she had a father somewhere, a stranger, perhaps with a family of his own?

But all that evening her thoughts kept returning to her talk with Felicity.

Something was stirring in the depths of her memory, something half-forgotten yet important. Later, after Clive had fallen asleep beside her with one arm around her, Miranda felt herself drifting off, her body relaxed and contented with their lovemaking. Her eyelids closed and then it came to her—the talk she had had with Logan McClintock soon after her arrival in his home.

He had been showing her some of the treasures that his ships had brought back from the Orient over the years, and then, in the drawing room, he had spoken of the portrait of his wife.

Ross Halliwell . . . back in fifty-one, that was . . . I was off in China. . . .

And when she had asked if Halliwell was an Englishman, Captain McClintock had said that the artist had been born and raised in Salem. That Vanessa, too, had grown up in that New England seaport.

Ross Halliwell. Back in fifty-one, and Miranda had been born in 1852.

Her body went taut, and although Clive did not awaken, he must have sensed the tension in her, for he murmured her name and drew her closer.

She felt comforted by his embrace, but she could not relax, could not sleep now. In a few weeks she and Clive would sail to China. She would never see her father, even at a distance. He would not know of her existence, she thought with pain. It must be that way, for like her mother, he, too, had a family of his own, a place in society. She had no feelings of resentment against him, no desire to disrupt his life, for he had never harmed her. Her only bitterness was directed against Vanessa.

When she and Clive left for China they would make a new start; they would have children of their own and love them and care for them. They would be all the family she would ever need, she told herself.

The engagement of Roxanne Widdicomb and Blake McClintock gave the New York newspapers a respite from their dreary accounts of the depression. "The union of two great shipping families," was one of the phrases used to announce the coming marriage. A society wedding was an elaborate affair these days. Blake and Roxanne were to be married in Grace Church, the most fashionable in the city.

Kitty quickly ordered a gown of heavy white satin for her daughter from Worth, in Paris. "And a veil of rose-point lace, looped up with orange blossoms," Kitty insisted. "And a pearl necklace from Tiffany."

Kitty did not have her own way in everything, however; for, to her surprise, Blake firmly refused to take Roxanne on a long wedding tour of Europe. "There are a number of improvements to be made in the shipyard, and we're going to build a new wharf on the North River. My father needs me right here," he told Roxanne. "Later on, after we're married and settled down, maybe we'll visit Scotland, because I want to learn all I can about the designs for those Clyde steamers. I want to study the newest engines."

When Roxanne told her mother of Blake's plans, Kitty was shocked. "There is no need for Blake to take an active part in his father's shipbuilding work. My goodness, Logan McClintock can hire engineers."

"It is what Blake wants," Roxanne said.

Kitty laughed. "You can talk him out of it, my dear. He's in love with you. It will be easy to get around him."

"No, Mama," Roxanne said with a quiet firmness that reminded Kitty of her own mother. "I don't wish to keep Blake from doing whatever he wants to do."

Kitty did not have her own way about the living arrangements for the young couple either, for Logan announced that he was giving Blake and Roxanne a house of their own as a wedding gift. "On Fifth Avenue, across from the park. I bought a building lot there years ago. That's where I'm going to have their house put up, in the sixties."

"But that's so far out," Kitty protested when Logan told her about it.

"Once, it was," Logan said. "But look around. The city's still growing, moving north."

"But this depression has slowed building down," Horace said.

"It'll pick up again in a few years," Logan said.

"I don't see why Blake and Roxanne can't occupy the new wing," Kitty protested.

"Because," Logan told her, "I want them to have a home of their own right from the start." He turned to Vanessa with a smile. "That's how it was with us, remember? Even when our home was a couple of rooms in a sailors' lodging house on Tompkins Street."

As the flurry of wedding preparations grew more hectic, Logan took refuge in his shipyard, where the *Gazelle* was being readied for her maiden voyage. "At least I can have peace and quiet here," he told Silas Pringle.

"Don't know that a shipyard's much of a place for that," Silas said, a smile splitting his weatherbeaten face.

"That's because you're a bachelor. It's a lot easier to launch a ship than to get a son married; I can tell you that."

He looked up at the *Gazelle* with satisfaction. Here was a vessel to be proud of, for although she might lack the matchless grace of the old clippers, she would provide far more safety and comfort for the passengers. Unlike his other steamers, with their narrow deckhouses and high bulwarks, the *Gazelle* was equipped with a completely new deck, which was covered over, so that the covering deck itself would serve as another deck level, surrounded by railings. The sea might wash over the deck, but thanks to this new design, the water would not be retained.

Logan was pleased, too, with the dining saloon, which extended the full width of the vessel, and with the first-class staterooms, which were much larger and more convenient than those of any of his other steamers. Miranda and her husband, like all the first-class passengers, would have the convenience of an electric bell with which to summon the steward, and they would enjoy gas lighting instead of candles, since the *Gazelle* carried a complete gas-lighting system fed from a gas plant alongside the engine room.

"Not much like the *Ondine*, is she?" Silas said. "That first trip around the Horn to San Francisco, those passengers were a tough breed—they had to be."

Logan nodded. "San Francisco's changed, too, from what I hear. It's not a collection of tents and shacks, not now. They've got mansions as fine as any on Fifth Avenue."

The two men stood in silence, watching as the long shadows of the spring twilight began to stretch across the shipyard and the fog moved in from the East River.

It had been years, Logan thought, since he had stood at the wheel of a ship in such a fog, since he had taken her down the river, past the Battery, through the Narrows and out into the open sea. In those days a clipper captain faced a tremendous challenge for the months of the voyage. He had no engines to help him, but a kind of kinship with the vessel, so each creak of her mast butts, each subtle change in the rhythm of her timbers, the feeling of the wind on his face, kept him in control of her.

All at once he felt a longing to be a part of that once more, but he knew that it was not possible. He could not even remain down here in the yard or join Silas for dinner in one of the small taverns on Water Street, not tonight, for Vanessa had reminded him only this morning that she was giving a small dinner party in Roxanne's honor.

Then, in a few weeks, on the evening of the day when the *Gazelle* was to set sail, he and Vanessa were to attend an elaborate dinner at Delmonico's given by Horace and Kitty. It was all part of the round of activities preceding the wedding, he thought with resignation.

Since he had taken over the controlling interest in the

Bradford-Widdicomb line, he had accepted the necessity of seeing Horace on business, but social contacts were a different matter. At least, he told himself, he had made certain that there would be a minimum of visiting with Horace and Kitty after the wedding, for Blake and Roxanne would not be living with her parents. Logan had seen to that.

Now he said good night to Silas and walked to the gates of the shipyard. Maybe this summer he and Vanessa could go away on the trip to Europe he had once promised her. They had never had a proper honeymoon. Even as he smiled at the notion, he knew that it was not foolish, for his wife still had the power to arouse him and to satisfy him more completely than any woman he had ever known. All that he had learned of warmth and tenderness, she had taught him.

Chapter 32

On the morning of the day on which the *Gazelle* was to sail, Vanessa told Logan that she would not be able to accompany him down to the wharf. "I'm sorry," she said, "but there's so much to be done here."

He was plainly disappointed. "Surely it won't take you all afternoon to get ready for that party at Delmonico's," he said.

She could not tell him that it would be too painful to watch Miranda's departure, knowing that her daughter would not even want her there. "The party's going to be quite elaborate," she said.

"I hope that Kitty's not planning to try to outdo Edward Luckemeyer," he said. Only last year, with the city in the grip of financial panic, Luckemeyer, a wealthy importer, had entertained his guests at Delmonico's with a "swan banquet," as society reporters had called it. Even now Logan had not forgotten his first glimpse of the enormous oval table, with a thirty-foot lake in the center, or of the four live swans that had been brought from Prospect Park to add a touch of splendor to the elaborate setting. Lorenzo Delmonico, in a burst of inspiration, had ordered a table-to-ceiling cage from Tiffanys, to keep the large birds from escaping. But he had not been able to prevent them from hissing and trumpeting so loudly that it had been nearly impossible for the guests to hold any kind of conversation.

"Although I think I might prefer the noise of those swans to Kitty's chatter," Logan said as he prepared to leave for South Street. "I wish you were going to be there for the sailing this afternoon," he added. "You know that this is the last time a McClintock ship will leave from the wharf there."

Logan, like so many ship owners, was building a new wharf on the North River, where it was easier for larger steamers to maneuver in wider channels and to take advantage of the slower tides. The Bradford-Widdicomb sailing ships would continue leaving from South Street, carrying grain to Australia or coal to Boston and other New England ports. Vanessa knew that Logan wanted her with him, but she could not bring herself to face the ordeal.

"Alison's being fitted for her flower girl's costume for the wedding," she said, and looked away.

During the weeks since she had learned of Miranda's wedding, Vanessa had tried not to think about how soon her daughter would be leaving. Several times she had come close to going to Miranda, to try to speak to her, but each time she had been held back by the fear that her daughter might refuse to see her.

Alison, at least, was in high spirits that afternoon, moving about so that it was difficult for the dressmaker, a thin, patient woman in black poplin, to complete the fitting.

"I've already been to one wedding, and now I'm going to be flower girl at another," Alison said blissfully, stroking the pale yellow silk of her dress. "I'd have been Miranda's flower girl, only she didn't have one. But she was glad to have me there all the same. Oh, but Blake's wedding's going to be so fancy." Her small face went serious. "Suppose I do something awful, Mama! Suppose I drop my basket of flowers or trip over one of my ruffles."

"If you will stand still, dear, I'll pin up the hem so that the ruffles will fall well above your shoe tops," the dressmaker said. "Only a few minutes more."

"Why didn't Miranda have a big wedding at Grace Church, Mama?" Alison went on. "I'm sure Papa would have given her one if she'd asked him, because . . ."

Vanessa, who had been seated on a small velvet chair, was on her feet now. "What's wrong, Mama?" Alison said.

"I—there's something I must do. Miss Vanderplanck can keep you company until your fitting's done."

"Oh, but there is your own fitting, Mrs. McClintock," the startled dressmaker reminded her.

"It will have to wait," Vanessa said. "Later this week, perhaps."

"As you wish, madam," the dressmaker said, for she was accustomed to the vagaries of the wealthy, and Mrs. McClintock was more courteous than most of her customers.

There was a crowd on the wharf, when Vanessa's landau pulled up an hour later. Porters were shouting and struggling with luggage; families were exchanging farewells; vendors were selling hot pork pies, corn, and candy. Pennants fluttered along the wharf, and a band was playing a sprightly march. The departure of a new McClintock ship was an occasion, and even those who had no real business here had gathered to enjoy the spectacle.

"This is as close as I can get, ma'am," the coachman told Vanessa.

"Then help me down, please," she said. Her legs felt unsteady, but she pushed forward, the breeze tugging at the ribbons on her small, forward-tilted hat. Then she gave a cry of dismay, for she had caught sight of Miranda, already going aboard, with Clive beside her. Logan would probably be on board, having a glass of wine with Dermot Rankin, and giving him last-minute instructions, as was customary.

Vanessa could not bring herself to return to the landau.

She stood still while the crowd swirled around her and the band launched into another lively tune. I can't let her go, not like this! Vanessa thought, pain clutching at her throat.

For a few moments Miranda was lost in the crowd up there at the railing. Vanessa shielded her eyes against the glare of the June sunlight. Then, moved by an instinct too strong to resist, she forced her way forward, pushing through the closely packed bodies.

At last she caught sight of Miranda again, and she called out her daughter's name and waved. The sailors were getting ready to pull away the gangplank. It was too late.

But a moment later she saw Miranda leaning forward, and she knew that her cry had not gone unheard. She waved again, and now Miranda was raising her arm and waving back. A portly gentleman pushed a pair of field glasses into Vanessa's hand. "Here, ma'am, these will give you a better view," she heard him say.

Her hand was shaking as she raised the glasses and Miranda's face sprang into focus: her hazel eyes and flushed cheeks, and her lips curved into a smile. Vanessa ached to embrace her daughter, but this would have to be enough; it was more than she had dared to hope for.

Then she heard Logan's voice calling to her over the noise of the crowd. "Vanessa! You did come after all!"

Quickly she handed the glasses back to the portly gentleman and murmured her thanks. A moment later Logan had reached her side. He put an arm around her, drawing her close. "It's a fine sight, isn't it?" he said with a smile that was almost boyish.

"Oh, yes, a fine sight," she managed to say.

"There goes the gangplank," Logan said. "And look up there. Rankin'll be giving the order to weigh anchor now."

As the anchor was raised from the depths of the river and

Vanessa watched the strip of water widening more and more between the *Gazelle* and the wharf, she was grateful for Logan's arm, for its hard strength supporting her. Would she see Miranda again?

Logan was speaking and pointing, and she followed the direction of his free arm. She saw the ball of silk move swiftly up the mast, saw it unfurl to catch the breeze, flaunting its blue and scarlet against the sky.

She turned to look not at the McClintock house flag but at Logan's face, at his gray eyes warm with love. "I remember that first house flag you made, for the *Sea Dragon*," he said. "That was the start of it all."

No, she thought, it had started long before that, when a frightened but determined girl had hidden herself in the back of a freight wagon on South Street, a wagon driven by a reckless young clipper captain. The dream had grown from there, and she had shared it, had helped to make it a reality.

"Blake's over there in the carriage with Roxanne," Logan was saying. "Shall we join them?"

"Not yet. Not until the *Gazelle* is out of sight."

He nodded, and they stood side by side in the sunlight, watching the *Gazelle*, with her escort of tugs, move out into the river and then down toward the Narrows, heading for the open sea. Only when the steamer was lost to view did she take Logan's arm and turn away, looking toward South Street and the carriage where Blake and Roxanne were waiting.